OATH BLOOD

Volume Two of *The Fallen* Series

K.N. Nguyen

www.dragonscript.net

Cover design and layouts by Francis Nguyen.

Map of Corinth by J.T. Renehan.

ISBN-13 978-1-949322-02-6

To F.N. And L.N.

You're my whole world,

and now I give you one of mine.

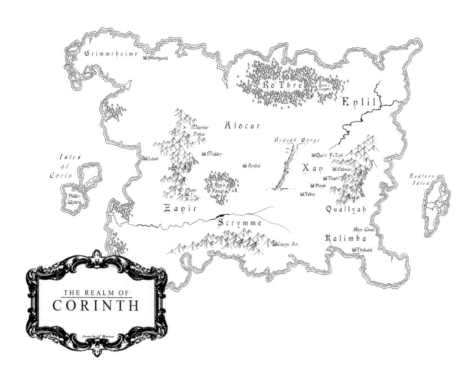

THE REALM OF
CORINTH

OATH BLOOD

I

Finches chirped merrily in the warm afternoon. Golden birds flitted around the tall grasses, darting between the lavender, their melodic song contrasting against the heavy silence that surrounded the haggard group of soldiers as they trudged along. Despite the sweet scent of the flowers, the stench of death overwhelmed the tired contingent.

Shirtless men, the brown blood of their wounds crusted on their sweaty bodies, rubbed at the bandages wrapped around them. Their cuirasses and other pieces of armor lay strewn in a wain amongst the slowly rotting corpses and discarded weapons. Brothers in arms mourned the loss of their friends and family at the hands of the god of fyre, Vahnyre, earlier that morning.

Brody walked through the meadow in a daze. Horses plodded along at a leisurely pace while the ragged army dragged their feet through the grass. Light chatter could be heard interspersed throughout the group, but it was forced and didn't last very long. Just a few short phrases exchanged between comrades. The silence would not be broken easily.

Brody struggled to grasp all that had happened. Only a few days ago he had to step out of his role as a bodyguard to comfort his charge as she contemplated a marriage proposal from the son of her father's best friend. The unity of Zanir and Alocar would have created a formidable alliance amongst the other nations of Corinth. Now, the king of Zanir, as well as the king and queen of Alocar, were dead. Not only did both kingdoms lose their figureheads, but the royal forces of Zanir's capital, Pharn, fell onto Brody. The weight of everything falling onto him, along with the loss of his brother, Bannen, and comrade, Alverick, left him feeling surprisingly hollow.

Damn Dez for getting Alverick trapped in the abyss. First, I lose Bannen, and now Al...

Images of a massive black claw and ruby eyes flashed in his mind. Alverick's battered form swallowed up as the mighty wyrm, Ein, pulled him and Vahnyre into another dimension. Squeezing his eyes shut, Brody tried to push the memory out.

This must be what Al felt like. Bannen did say that war changes you.

As Brody trudged along, he barely noticed Cienna and Caitlyn slogging on nearby.

The two women walked together in silence, matching his stride. He noticed that tears continued to roll down Caitlyn's cheeks, creating small rivers against her dust-stained cheeks, an occasional sniffle was all that could be heard from her. Caitlyn massaged her shoulder as she walked, trying to soothe sore muscles from her earlier exertions. The archer led a beautiful onyx warhorse back to the capital, her bow and quiver strapped to the beast, the horse walking quietly next to the red-headed woman, as though he understood her pain.

Cienna placed a tattooed hand on Caitlyn's shoulder and gave her a gentle squeeze. Caitlyn shot the princess a wan smile before covering her face with her gloved hand and dissolving into quiet sobs. Brody looked over at the girls. He could not believe how strong his little Waterdrop had become over the last few days.

Styx nickered softly and nuzzled Caitlyn.

"It's going to be alright, Cait," he tried to reassure the distraught woman. He struggled to keep his voice from cracking. "Alverick knew the risks. He wouldn't have wanted to go any other way."

Except, it didn't need to end like that.

Caitlyn removed her hand from her face. She walked forward a little way in front of the two, sniffling once more. The warhorse continued to nuzzle her side until Caitlyn pat him on the face.

"Do you really believe that?" Cienna asked Brody.

No.

"Of course, Waterdrop," he replied. "Al worked so hard to protect us all, he'd sacrifice his life to save us. Bannen once told me how upset Al would get when they lost someone, he would rather be the shield than lose someone."

A solitary tear rolled down his cheek as he thought of his friend. *Damn you, Al! How could you trust that Dez woman? If it weren't for her, you'd still be here with us. With me.*

Brody's breath caught in his chest as he thought of Alverick's final moments before being pulled into the abyss by the wyrm once more. Bloodied and barely able to stand, Alverick defied Vahnyre, aethren of Fyre. Bannen, would have done the same thing if he had not been killed a few days earlier.

I can't keep us together like you could. Brother, I need strength...

"Brody," Cienna spoke up tentatively, "I need to tell you something."

Brody looked over at her.

The princess, exhausted from the day's fight, looked down at her hands. She fidgeted with her fingers slightly as she tried to find the right words. "After these last couple of days, I've come to realized that our lives can change quickly. I want to let you know something that I should have told you years ago." Looking up at Brody with her soft, blue eyes, Cienna took a deep breath and said, "I love you."

Brody stopped in his tracks as the words hit him. *No, not now. Not like this.*

The princess' feelings for him never had been voiced before. Sure, she would let her eyes linger on him for a moment or two longer than she should have, or a shy smile would escape her as she saw him enter a room, but she always tried to maintain an appropriate level of decorum as befitting one of her station.

Looking up at the princess, Brody no longer saw the little girl he knew crying in the garden in the rain. Before him stood a young woman.

"Waterdrop, I can't," Brody struggled to find what he wanted to say.

"Please, Brody," she begged. "You are the best person I know. You've always been there for me." Her eyes pleaded with him.

"You have always been special to me, but..."

Before he could finish his sentence, Cienna stepped up and kissed him softly. All of his emotions from the last few days came rushing to the surface. Cupping her cheek and wrapping his other arm around her waist, Brody pulled her in and kissed her with a passion that he attempted to suppress. He felt Cienna melt into his embrace. After the two broke apart, Cienna stared at him with flushed cheeks.

"Perhaps we can explore this possibility," he finished lamely. His eyes found a hint of their boyish spark once more.

With her, maybe I can find peace.

Cienna reached tentatively out and brushed her hand against his. Suddenly aware of their surroundings once more, Brody motioned that they should continue moving towards Pharn.

"We can discuss this when we get home. We should reach the Caer in a few days, but now is not the time."

Somewhere to their right a man cried out, warning them of a stranger drawing near. Brody called for the group to stop. Looking at the back of the retreating army, he saw a lone figure approaching quickly atop a horse.

"Halt!" a cry rang out from the crowd, challenging the newcomer.

Brody recognized the voice as Ronan's. The figure slowed down slightly, but did not stop. As they got closer, Brody noticed that it was an olive-skinned woman with chocolate hair and a voluptuous figure. Her eyes sparkled silver in the sun.

Dez rode through the ranks of Pharn's soldiers and up to Brody and the princess. Eyes stared at her warily as she neared the center of the retreating army. Once she got close enough to the young commander, she stopped her mount and jumped off. Caitlyn walked over towards Brody as Dez approached him. In the afternoon sun Brody noticed that she looked weary. However, he was too angry to feel sympathetic towards her.

"What in the hells are you doing here?" he spat. "I thought I told you to leave us be."

"I've come to speak with the queen," Dez replied. Her normally aloof demeanor was replaced by exhaustion. "And to speak with young Vashe when we reach Pharn."

"You will not be speaking with Her Highness," Brody told her flatly. Ronan and Thol made their way to the group and stood tensely beside him, ready to strike should the order be given. "I thought I told you after you killed Alverick that you are no longer a friend of ours."

Thin silver lines glowed on Dez's body, paralyzing Brody and those within ten feet of her. Thol grunted in surprise as Ronan cried out, "Not this unholy magic!" Confused shouts rang out from those around them as a number of men found that they could no longer move. Cienna and Caitlyn, however, did not appear to be affected by the paralysis.

"You will take me to the queen," she repeated simply. Dez's usually sweet voice carried a sharpness that they'd never heard before. "If you will not take me, I will go by myself. The only reason I ask you to take me is because what I have to say may be of interest to you as well."

The troops around the group stood in tense silence, their weapons raised, ready to strike as Brody, Thol and Ronan struggled to break free of her paralysis.

"Why would we take a person like you to her majesty?" Ronan spat. "How do we know you won't try and kill her?"

A tired chuckle escaped the dark-skinned woman. "I understand you do not trust me. However, please understand that I do not wish you harm. Losing Alverick to the abyss was something that I did not anticipate." Taking a deep breath, she continued. "Ein can be quite the handful when he is in one of his moods." Suddenly, her tattoos stopped glowing and the three found that they could move once more. Scattered chatter broke out as those who were previously frozen were able to move once more. "If you take me to your queen, I will tell you what you want to know on the way over."

"Like hell we will," Ronan snarled. "Why would we trust a conjurer like you?"

"Peace," Thol intoned, raising a hand to quiet the agitated man. "This is Brody's decision to make.

Ronan glared at Thol, but he held in his rage as both he and Brody fumed.

Brody turned to Caitlyn and mumbled as he walked past. "Watch her. My gut is telling me that she's probably not a threat to Queen Hera, but I don't trust her like Al did." Looking around as though he expected to find an answer hiding in the nearby shrubbery, Brody furrowed his brow as he scowled. "I need a moment." Without another word, he walked off.

"Like I would be of any challenge to her should she force the matter," the princess mumbled.

Brody walked a couple hundred yards towards the wain at the back of the retinue. *How can I trust this woman? She shows up and suddenly Pharn is in chaos. Al is dead, and she wants us to just ignore that.* Pacing around the wagon, Brody tried to find a suitable weapon to bring back. *Sure, she helped us banish that demon, but she keeps herself shrouded in mystery. Ghan's mercy, this woman is a nightmare.*

Letting out a growl of frustration, Brody picked up a war axe and dropped it back into the wain after quickly weighing the weapon.

"Brody?" a voice tentatively called out, pulling him from his thoughts.

Brody turned to find Cienna standing behind him. She fidgeted with her hands in front of her. "What is it, Waterdrop?" he asked, trying to keep the strain out of his voice.

"I think we should take her to talk to Mom."

Brody opened his mouth to object, but Cienna held up her hand to continue.

"Think about it. Mistress Vashe personally knows her. Not to mention that she came because she knew we were in danger, and instead of killing us or letting that demon kill us, she fought *with* us. This is our chance to find out what she knows and find out what she is trying to accomplish. Maybe there is more going on that she can tell us."

Brody stood for a moment and weighed his options. His brow furrowed as he ran his hand through his short chestnut hair.

Ghan's mercy, this woman has turned into a problem. Waterdrop's right, this may be our only chance. Al trusted her well enough, but I'm pretty sure he Snapped. She kept him level somehow when he was struggling. Not to mention, Vashe knows her personally. If they can trust her, I think I can too. I hope. For the sake of my men I'll have to.

"I agree, Waterdrop. We'll give her this one chance to prove herself." Resting his hand on her head, he kissed her on the forehead before returning to his officers.

Cienna stood by the wain blushing profusely. Taking a moment to compose herself, she smiled and ran her hands through her curly hair before scampering after Brody. She caught up to him as he began addressing the entire group.

"All right everyone," he began, "let's pick up the pace. It's getting dark and we need to cover a lot of ground." Waiting for the soldiers to disperse, Brody stood with his fellow officers.

Ronan gaped at Brody. "Are you serious?" he hissed. "This woman is a conjurer *and* killed Al. Why would you trust her?"

Dez stood bemused as the men passed them, watching Ronan and Brody's conversation. The soldiers were no longer as somber as before, but the chatter remained subdued throughout the ranks.

"Brody, if I may," Thol broke in. "Conjurer or not, this woman may hold the secret to bringing Alverick back. He may not be alive, but at least she should be able to bring us some closure. For Ghan's sake, we can at least see him off with some dignity. Alverick deserves at least that much."

Brody noticed the pain in Caitlyn's eyes they mentioned Alverick. He marveled at her strength to accept the fact that her former betrothed may be beyond her and already resting in the Halls of the Fallen.

"How can you endanger our people like this?" Ronan asked in disbelief.

"Ro," Brody replied, "This woman, despite what's happened, earned Al's trust. Even at the end when his Spark magics most likely caused him to Snap, Al did not feel any reason to question her motives. Not to mention, Headmistress Vashe of the Mageri can personally vouch for her. I hold both of these people in high regard. I've known Al since we were boys. Vashe, though I barely know her, strikes me as a very discerning person whose trust is not earned easily. Jaste trusted Vashe, and I trust my king."

Ronan did not look satisfied, but he did not press the matter further. His eyes glanced furtively over to the mysterious woman frequently.

Noting the doubt in his expression, Cienna stepped in. "Sir Ronan, I think you should also give Dez a chance to explain herself. I don't know if you remember since you were struggling against her magic, but she did tell us that she would answer our questions. We should give her a chance."

"Yes, Your Majesty," came his stiff reply.

"Let's move out," Brody said, dispersing the group. As Ronan walked by, Brody fell in line with him. "Thank you, Ro. I understand your feelings, and personally I can't stand her, but there's something about her that I can't put my finger on. I want to find out what it is."

"I know, Brody," Ronan conceded. "It's just that I've grown up my whole life hearing that conjurers are not to be trusted. That they practice dark magics given only to those chosen by Aphomet, the chaos bringer. I always thought they were just stories created to scare little kids, but then she shows up and we fight a demon. Not to mention Al..." His voice trailed off as he mentioned his fallen comrade. "The signs are flashing in front of me and I just can't silence them. But if you think we should trust her, I'll follow you. You've never steered me wrong before."

Brody was touched by the faith that Ronan placed in him. "Come, brother, let's see what she knows."

Ronan clapped Brody on the back and the two jogged to catch up with the rest of the group. Cienna and Caitlyn were discussing the basics of archery as they walked, Dez seemed to be speaking softly to herself, while Thol complimented Cody on his improvements with the spear. As the two approached the group, Thol dismissed Cody so that there could be some privacy amongst them.

"Tell me," Brody said to Dez as he neared, "What is your story?"

Dez's eyes focused on those around her and stopped speaking to herself. "My name is Dzeara Wyndbeorn, but I prefer to go by Dez. I was born in Scrymme. I don't remember too much of my past. Comes with being a Tempest, I suppose," she said with a shrug. "I was raised by a kindly old woman when my mother and father were killed. You see, my father was a man from Scrymme and decided to take a foreigner as his wife and, as we all know, that is quite the taboo. They are rather elitist, which goes against all of Her Holiness' teachings, I might add. Growing up, I developed Ghost and Shadow skills."

"Ghost skills?" Caitlyn interjected.

Dez stopped at the interruption and stared at her quizzically. "Yes. I believe it's helped keep me from Snapping, along with being able to Anchor myself."

"But aren't Ghosts limited to the royal family?" Caitlyn's question was met with puzzled expressions from Brody and the other officers. Her eyes gaze dropped briefly as her discomfort increased due to the sudden shift of attention. "I remember Alverick mentioning that at one point when he draughted his first Spark and was struggling with the Snap."

"You're right," Dez replied. "I think my father was a cousin to the king. I know I would never have survived if I was in direct line to the throne."

"So, you're distant royalty to the Scrymmen throne?" Brody asked incredulously. "Are you related to Vashe?"

"I probably am, but I couldn't tell you how close."

As the group marched on, Brody noted the lengthening of the shadows. The weary men started to speak a little more animatedly at the prospect of a warm meal and a refreshing nap after setting up camp.

"Tell me," he said to Dez, "can we continue this discussion later? I have a few more questions I'd like to ask you."

"Of course," Dez said with a smile. "I'm exceptionally famished after summoning Ein and a hot meal will do wonders. One doesn't prevent the Snap by simply ignoring their body's cries for attention."

Waiting until Ronan and Thol broke away from their group, Dez walked a little closer to Brody and said softly, "Please, meet with me later tonight. The winds whisper of an approaching conflict, but I cannot tell what. The words are muddled, but the air is heavy."

"But we just finished with something huge," Brody stuttered. It took a considerable deal of self-control to keep his voice from rising in shock. "What could possibly be coming now? Are you sure it's not just you needing to rest?"

"I can't say," she replied with the shake of her head. "But I would keep a close eye on your princess." Without another word, she broke off from Brody and headed towards the heart of the marching men. "I'll see you tonight, let's say shortly after dusk by that tree," she said as she pointed to a maple tree a few feet away.

Brody thought about it for a moment before calling out in agreement. "I expect you to answer all of my questions, you know. Until tonight then."

Men slowed down and started to set up camp. On the outskirts of the site, the wain carrying the corpses stood watch. A silent vigil kept by the fallen. Cody walked over to the cart and sprinkled a thin circle of pink salt around it.

"What are you doing, boy?" one of the men called out. "You can't be wasting precious salt like that."

The man reached for the small pouch that the youth had. Cody jerked away and put a little distance between himself and the soldier.

"We can't just let the spirits wander freely. The salt will keep them confined to their bodies and allow us to take their souls home to their families," Cody replied.

"That's what you use fire for," the man said. He wore the blue livery of the soldiers of Alocar. "A ring of fire surrounding the bodies to keep the wraiths from inhabiting their bodies."

"Do we really want to use fire after what we've just been through?" one of the cooks called out. "Let the boy use his salt. I'd rather not have a ring of fire around our dead if it's all the same with you. I'm not one for tempting the flames after seeing a demon walking on our plane."

Cody smiled at the man, grateful for the support.

"Go on now," the blue-clad man said with a wave of his hand. "Just don't use too much. I want to be able to enjoy the flavor of my food. Gods know a man needs a few comforts after a day like today."

Brody watched the whole interaction from a distance, an amused smile playing on his face for the first time that day. He felt something soft brush against his hand and looked over to see Cienna smiling sheepishly as she took his hand in hers.

Why does everything have to happen all at once?

He stared into her blue eyes. How he loved how they contrasted against her dark skin. Her cheeks flushed slightly as he looked at her. Taking a quick breath, he placed his hand against her cheek before running off into the camp.

We'll have to talk eventually.

II

HERA GREY SAT on the edge of her bed staring out of the window of her bedroom holding a small effigy. The doll wore the form of a small child with periwinkle hair and obsidian eyes. Looking out the window, Hera stared unseeingly into the distance, running her fingers through the figure's hair. "Bring my little Cienna back to me," she murmured as she stroked the doll's head. "Czand took my love, but please don't take my baby."

A knock on the oaken door pulled her from her reverie. "Your Grace," a call came from the hall, "The headmistress would like to have a word with you. It appears to be urgent."

With a sigh, Hera put down her effigy and stood up. She smoothed her dress momentarily and fluffed her hair before signaling to the servant to bring Vashe into the Great Hall. The man turned sharply and made his way into the hallway.

"Thank you," she told the doll before exiting her room.

Moving slowly, Hera walked out into the hall and headed towards the Great Hall. Tracing her fingers along the woven tapestries in the hall. The texture of the woven fabric was surprisingly soothing against her frayed nerves. A gentle breeze came in through a small window in the hallway. Three periwinkle flower petals fluttered into the hallway and landed at her feet.

Smiling at the petals, the queen bent down and picked them up. Rubbing them in between her fingers, she stuffed the holy flowers into her bodice before continuing her way down the hall. A warmth spread throughout her entire body.

"Mighty Freyna, daughter of Ayr, grant me the strength to lead my people with a just hand like Jaste did. I ask for guidance in this period of transition as the reign of Jaste Grey passes and Hera Allianna Grey's begins. I also ask that you please deliver my little Cienna safely home to me. May I always follow the way of the Ayr," she murmured.

Once her prayer was completed, a surreal feeling of calmness filled her, just as the warmth had a moment earlier.

The chirping of birds seemed muted as she made her way down the hall. She felt a small bump against her leg as she walked. Looking around, she couldn't see anything, but she thought she could hear the sound of a child laughing behind her at the end of the hallway.

With a smile, Hera began humming to herself, satisfied that she'd received an answer to her prayer. After a few more minutes, she found herself in the empty Great Hall. Sunlight streamed through the stained-glass windows, filling the Hall with a pleasant warmth. Walking around the room, she ran her hands over her late husband's chair. She sighed while tracing the intricately carved designs in the chair as she thought about him.

It's hard to believe that just a few days ago we were eating breakfast together. Now you're gone forever.

Despite the ache in her heart, she felt lighter than she had in days.

A muted *thump thump* on the heavy oak door of the Great Hall announced the arrival of Pharn's headmistress of the Mageri.

"Enter," Hera intoned. Running her hands over her husband's chair once more, she gingerly sat in the chair and adjusted her dress.

Dutifully, the door opened and the soldier returned with the lithe headmistress. Waving the man away, Hera motioned for Vashe to sit next to her.

The headmistress looked haggard, as though she hadn't gotten much sleep. Her normally sleek hair was tied in a messy tail. The blouse under her bodice was rumpled. Her disheveled appearance provided a stark contrast against her normally immaculate façade.

Dipping her head in respect to the queen, Vashe sat down and addressed Hera. "Your Majesty, I know that the appropriate grieving period has not passed, however, I have urgent matters to discuss."

"Go on."

"I will be leaving Pharn for a while to attend to a personal matter."

"But why? I need you here to help me with transitioning my rule."

"I'm sorry, Your Majesty, but I need to leave in four days' time, once the new moon arrives and Toron's moon is at its fullest." Seeing the queen's displeasure, Vashe quickly continued. "I promise that I will not leave you helpless."

Leaning in towards the queen and lowering her voice, despite the fact that no one else was in the room, Vashe said, "I have been watching the events of the last few days and this morning I saw something that should please you. Princess Cienna and your forces have been victorious in their battle with Alazi. But at a heavy cost. They should be back before I leave. I will speak with them before I go."

Tears welled in the corner of Hera's eyes at the news that her daughter was alive and on her way home. "Cienna is coming back." She choked out the words through her tears of joy. "She will be the strength that Pharn needs. She's so much like her father."

Vashe placed her hand on the queen's and squeezed it gently. "Your Majesty, you are stronger than you believe. Please do not doubt yourself. You've done much for your people in the few short days since Jaste's death."

Hera smiled and squeezed Vashe's hand in return. Wiping the tears from her eyes, Hera replied, "Vashe, thank you so much for your loyalty to our family. I don't know what we would do without you. If you could speak to my daughter before you leave, I would really appreciate it."

"I will do my best to wait until she returns. I will not make any guarantees though. Until then, if you have any questions please come to me. I will help you as best I can."

"Thank you," Hera said with a smile.

"If you don't mind, I need to go prepare for my journey."

"I understand. I will send Aeliana if I need anything."

Vashe dipped her head once more and slipped out of the chair. With graceful strides, she quickly exited the Great Hall. The heavy oaken doors closed behind her with a dull thud, leaving Hera alone in the room by herself.

Leaning back in the king's throne, Hera closed her eyes and heaved a sigh. The warmth she felt from earlier was gone, but she still felt an unmistakable calmness flowing through her body. Reaching into her bodice, she pulled out the flower petals and rubbed them between her fingers once more. The silky petals warmed her fingertips and filled her with hope. She closed her eyes once more and slowly caressed the petals.

A gentle breeze ruffled her hair as she leaned back in the throne. Opening her eyes, Hera looked around. She scanned the room to find the source of the draft, but no windows were open.

Where did that breeze come from?

The air felt heavy around her. A strong lavender perfume seemed to fill the room, relaxing Hera once more. Closing her eyes, the queen enjoyed the peaceful sensation.

In what felt like seconds, Hera was startled awake when a hand dropped onto her shoulder. Looking around, she saw a small child standing next to her. The child had pale skin with dark eyes. A bonnet covered her periwinkle hair and she wore a simple, cream-colored dress. She smiled at the dozing queen in the reassuring way that only a child could.

"What are you doing in here, young one?" Hera asked. "Where is your mother?"

The little girl shook her head.

"Do you have a daddy?"

Another shake of the head, less emphatic.

Confused, Hera asked, "Can you speak, sweet one?"

The girl shook her head no again.

Hera sat for a moment, trying to figure out what the child wanted. The little girl no longer smiled at the queen but stood staring at her with a strange expression, almost a motherly one.

Reaching out with her pale hand, the girl caressed Hera's face and an overwhelming sense of calmness enveloped her once more. An image popped into the queen's head.

Burning buildings and scorched earth spanned in front of her. Corpses littered the ground and the stench of death filled the air. Blue livery from Alocar, the green livery of Zanir, Xan's orange and several other colors spotted the battlefield. Standing in the distance, a blue-haired figure looked out at the carnage. Her cream-colored dress and long hair rustled in the wind.

Tentatively, Hera made her way towards the lone figure. As she neared the tense form, the girl turned slightly until Hera could see her features. Pain etched the face of the young child standing before the queen. Her dark eyes filled with sorrow. Raising a finger to her lips, the child motioned for Hera to be quiet. Quietly approaching the girl, Hera looked down on the scene below.

A dark-haired man lurched towards a figure swathed in orange. The ground trembled and Hera dropped to her knees. Away from the two, a dark-skinned figure turned and made eye contact with Hera. His deep brown eyes pierced her to the soul and her breath caught in her chest. Tears streamed down her face as the queen struggled to breathe.

The young child placed a hand on Hera's back and her body instantly relaxed as the vision disappeared.

The scent of lavender filled the room as Hera started awake. Looking around, Hera couldn't find the little girl anywhere. The sun streamed into the Great Hall, casting long shadows into the room.

A gentle knock on the door caught her attention.

"Milady, are you all right? The afternoon is almost gone and we still have much to do."

"What? Oh, yes. I'll be right there," Hera replied.

"Shall I wait for you outside the door?"

"Yes please."

The man turned and left, leaving Hera trying to gather her thoughts. Rubbing her head, Hera struggled to piece together what she'd seen.

They are coming, the wind seemed to say.

Hera stood up quickly, causing the flower petals to fall to the ground. With a rustle of her silks, she bent down and scooped them up. A measure of calmness slowly returned to her. Taking a deep breath, the queen tucked the petals into her bodice once more and exited the Great Hall.

III

CRICKETS SANG in the waning sunlight as the sky darkened. A warm breeze rustled the cat lilies, as firelight could be seen popping up in the city windows. Several young children ran through the street, giggling as they chased a dog, their mothers' yelling for them to come in for the evening lest the Faceless grab them in the night.

Len walked his mount leisurely through the quiet capital, Fa'Tinh. Dust caked his shoes as well as his sweat and blood-stained tunic, making him quite the sight as he wandered through the practically empty streets. Behind him, Pram and their remaining forces followed slowly along. Occasionally, a man or two would break off and make his way home, salivating as the hearty scent of delicately seasoned meat wafted through the windows.

"If I may," Pram addressed his leader, "I would like to have a meeting with you tomorrow, Evenhand."

"Of course we do," Len replied tersely. "We have a lot to do if we are going to turn this alliance into our advantage. We'll need to move quickly. Tomorrow will also be the remembrance for our fallen brothers and I want to have our next move ready before it starts."

"Shall I keep it to only the two of us?"

Len thought for a moment. "Perhaps we should bring that Flame to our meeting as well. He appears to be quite loyal to you. It's a shame we didn't find him sooner. He would've been a wonderful addition to my regime before the takeover."

"I agree. Despite being part of the Myrani, he seems to be built for the military life," Pram said.

"Weren't the mercenaries a martial regime?" Len asked.

"Oh no, Evenhand. Though the Myrani are soldiers for hire, due to the fact that they're all magi, they don't actually have any military training. They're accustomed to using brute force to achieve their means."

"I see," Len said slowly. "Then Liir greatly exaggerated his position."

Len stood in silence as the darkness grew. The remaining warriors had vanished into their homes, ready for a warm meal and proper night's sleep. The flickering of the hearth flames lit up the nearby houses in the growing darkness. The shadows they cast on his face created an ominous mood between the two.

Speaking softly, Len clenched his mount's reigns, twisting them between his fingers. "I will not allow for his betrayal to be overlooked."

"But, Evenhand," Pram broached gently. "His death will look like you've already exacted retribution. It's going to be difficult for you to justify anything."

Crumpling the reigns in his hand in frustration, he pulled on his horse and headed back out towards his home. Calling over his shoulder, he replied, "Pram, we will discuss this tomorrow. I need to think."

"Of course, Evenhand. Tell Zaa'ni that I hope Graak has kept her in his favors. Good night, Len."

Len glanced over his shoulder and watched as his general went off to towards his home. "I hope that he has blessed Altansari as well," he replied.

Pram called out his thanks and continued on in silence.

Len listened to the sounds of hooves striking against an occasional stone in the dirt road before making his way home once more. As he passed by the houses of Fa'Tinh, he heard mothers telling their children stories about how the three siblings of Ayr defeated the Faceless. Listening to the women describe the lithe, shadow creatures and their toothy grins reminded him of his mother. His mother, Intan, always found a way to integrate young Len into the stories, telling him that if he followed the tenets of Ayr he would be blessed with Freyna's favor. And, if he was lucky, he may even move one of her brothers, Thuul or Graak, to endow him with their strength.

After what I've been through, I think I would have preferred the Faceless to Alazi and the aethren.

Standing outside of his door, Len led his mount to the side of his home and tied the beast to a post. Checking to make sure that it had grass and water, he patted the horse on the flank and made his way inside.

The smell of fresh bread and curry greeted his nostrils, causing the mighty general's mouth to water. His stomach growled, surprising him.

I haven't eaten since last night. I wouldn't be surprised if I lost a lot of weight during this campaign.

He noted how his pants hung a little loosely around his waist. A mighty rumble from his belly brought his thoughts back to dinner.

Peering around the corner, he saw the lovely silhouette of his wife, Zaa'ni. Dressed in lavender silks, she busied herself at a basin as she washed the dishes. Her long hair was braided and tied in a ponytail, banded in three different spots. Fresh flowers were woven into the braid. She stood in the kitchen, barefoot as she cleaned up. Occasionally, she would grab a pomegranate from the counter next to her and take a bite.

Len cleared his throat.

Zaa'ni spun around, reaching for a knife on the counter. When she saw her husband, a smile broke out on her face.

"Welcome home, my love," she purred.

Her girlishly husky voice brought gooseflesh to his arms. Zaa'ni crossed the distance to Len quickly, despite being close to bearing the child within her belly. The silks around her delicately framed her swollen stomach.

"I've missed you," she whispered into his ear.

Cupping her head in his hand and pulling her into him, he closed his eyes and enjoyed the warmth of her body. Zaa'ni buried her head into his chest and let out a small sigh of happiness.

"I didn't realize how much I would miss you while I was gone," Len said. "It's good to be home, Zaa'ni."

Looking up at her husband, Zaa'ni smiled, her eyes tearing slightly. Her hands moved over his chest and onto his biceps. Feeling a bandage on his arm, she looked down and noticed the brown stain on his side.

Pushing away from him slightly, she asked, "Len, what is this? How bad is it?"

"It's nothing, Zaa'ni, just a small wound." Noticing that she looked skeptical, he quickly added, "I had it treated by a shaman shortly after the injury occurred. It's four days old, at least. Nothing to worry about, my sweet."

Zaa'ni still did not look convinced but did not press the matter. Tracing the line of his jaw, she pulled away and said, "You must be starving. Come, I can warm dinner for you."

"I am." Looking around the kitchen, Len asked his wife, "Where's Bermet? Surely she isn't sleeping right now."

Placing a bowl of stew and a loaf of bread on the table, she replied, "Bermet's been helping me a lot as I come closer to delivery. She wears herself out every day."

"Surely my mother comes and helps."

"Mother Intan has been helping and trying to keep Bermet from working too hard, but Bermet seems to take after her father and pushes herself to her limits."

Shooting her husband a knowing smile, Zaa'ni motioned for Len to sit. Conceding, he sat down and attacked his dinner with vigor. Zaa'ni sat down at the table and watched him. As Len's spoon started scraping the bottom of the bowl, Zaa'ni got up and poured him a glass of wine. Len took a long draught of the rose-colored liquid.

Once he finished his drink, she quietly said, "You've returned early, my love. Tell me, what happened?"

Wiping his mouth with the back of his hand, Len replied, "We caught them off-guard and our initial strike against Zanir was successful. The king and a good number of their men were defeated in that battle. However, we did not anticipate an Avalanche and a Tempest joining the fight. Before our strike, we lost a number of our magi in a scouting mission on the northern border, so all we had was the Shadow and a couple of Flames to aid us in our strike against the capital. Once the Avalanche and Tempest showed up, the tides turned on us and we had to retreat right as victory was in our grasp."

Zaa'ni stared at her husband with wide eyes. "I would have never expected you to encounter so many magi. The Myrani are rare enough, but to have two more, especially combat ready ones, join in is unbelievable."

"We were not ready for them," he agreed. "As we made our way back to the gorge, I decided to summon the fire demon, Alazi, after weighing the benefits given by Liir and Wyr-raji."

Zaa'ni's expression darkened at the mention of Liir. "Liir is a spineless man who surrounds himself with more powerful people. I'm surprised that he would want to take such a gamble."

"Well, lucky for him, he wasn't around to greet Alazi. He was found dead the next morning."

Zaa'ni couldn't hide her smile at the news.

"I see this pleases you, my sweet," Len said sardonically.

"He's gotten no more than he deserves. It's a shame that he couldn't meet Alazi. I would've loved to see him try and talk his way out of the demon's wrath."

Len smiled at his wife. *It's a good thing that I pushed us to arrive tonight. I needed Zaa'ni's council.*

"His silver tongue wouldn't have gotten him very far," Len agreed. Rising out of his chair, Len placed his dishes in the copper basin by the window and headed out to his bedroom.

"I'll see you in a bit. I just need to do something before I wash up," Len said.

Zaa'ni walked to her room and disappeared into the darkness. Len walked down the hallway and stopped outside of a small room. He walked into the doorway and looked at the small form sleeping on a mat. Walking into the room, he knelt down and stroked his daughter's head.

A small sigh escaped her tiny lips as Bermet rolled over. "Papa?" she murmured.

"Yes, my pearl. I just wanted to say good night."

"Are you back forever?"

"We'll see, little pearl. Good night, Bermet."

"Night Papa."

Len quietly rose up and walked out of the room. Making his way to his bedroom, Len took off his clothes and went to the wash basin in the corner. Scrubbing his body, Len tried to remove the blood and grime of the last week. Gritting his teeth as he went over his wound, Len struggled to ignore the pain.

I need to reapply some salve to this. I've let it sit for too long. Hopefully it doesn't get infected.

Once he'd cleaned himself, Len made his way to his mat and crawled under the blanket next to his wife. Placing his hand on her belly, he smiled as he felt the kick of his child. Pulling Zaa'ni closer to him, Len savored the warmth of her body and closed his eyes.

IV

OLDAR GNAWED on a piece of dried meat as the sun slowly rose in the morning sky. His eyes stared off into the distance, replaying the events of the past two days. The thought of being rejected by Cienna, the woman he felt would be the perfect match for him, as well as second best to that young captain caused his blood to boil.

"Choose him over me, will she? She's just like everyone else. I'll show her why she should've chosen me." He mumbled over and over. "I'm king now. I'll not be disrespected."

Looking over at his camp, he growled to the nearest soldier, "Bring me something to drink."

"W-water, Milord?"

"Do I look like I need water? Bring me something to *drink*," Oldar commanded, placing special emphasis on the last word.

The soldier scrambled to find some ale for his king. After finally finding some, he rushed it over to his leader before scurrying away.

Oldar hesitantly brought the tankard to his lips. With a shuddering breath, he brought the amber liquid to his lips and took a drink. Once the ale hit his mouth, he drank it greedily, as though it would be his last. Before he knew it, the flagon was empty. A warmth spread through his body. However, even though he felt good inside, his emotions were roiling about him.

Staring at the empty tankard, he lamented his rashness. *I said I would not touch another drop just a week ago. Can I not keep my word?*

Taking another bite of the meat, Oldar struggled to not think of Cienna and tried to focus on what he would say to his people instead.

Father is dead. Mother too. If I am to rule as Iron Fist, I need to be a man of my word. My word is my strength.

An image of Cienna flashed in his mind. Her curly blonde hair rustled softly in the wind as she smiled. Her freckles disappeared into her bronzed skin.

Oldar's breath caught in his throat and his heart ached for just a brief instant.

Why does she do this to me? We barely even know each other.

Oldar shook his head and stuffed the remaining bit of meat into his mouth.

"Iron Fist," a voice called out.

Oldar looked up and saw Ingmar making his way towards the young king.

"Iron Fist, the camp has been torn down. Are you ready to continue? If we push ourselves today and eat a cold afternoon meal, we should reach Ånchal by dusk."

"Do we have an outpost in Ånchal?" Oldar asked.

"Yes. It's small, but it should house our forces and give us some shelter for the night," Ingmar explained. "Not to mention, the tunnels that serve as a shortcut to Madden can be found below her walls."

"Then let's move out. I want to reach Madden before dusk tomorrow," Oldar said.

All of the men snapped to attention, groans of displeasure barely audible as they began their march. Ingmar brought Oldar his mount. Putting his mug into the saddlebag, the young king swung himself up onto his horse and kicked his heels into horseflesh. The other horses followed suit. Soon, the remnants of the camp disappeared in a cloud of dust.

V

WARM RAYS CREPT through the window and fell upon Len's face. Throwing his arm over his face to block the light, he grunted and tried to roll over. A high-pitched squeal caused him to open his eyes. Next to him lay his four-year-old daughter, smiling at him from under the quilt. Her eyes sparkled with mischief as she stared up at her father. Bermet giggled under the blanket and kicked her little feet.

"What are you doing here, Bermet?" he asked as he ran his hands through her hair. "What have you done to your mother?"

"I made her disappear," she said breathily.

"Disappear, huh? Well I guess I have a little shamanka to add to my army. One as powerful as you, imagine all of the great things we will accomplish together."

"I'm not shamanka," Bermet giggled. "I'm a water faerie."

"An undine? Are you going to take on the Faceless, my pearl?" Len asked. His daughter's imagination surprised him.

"Yeah!" she said emphatically, with a nod of her head.

"Well, then, I shall leave you to your duties, with Freyna's blessing."

"Hey now," Zaa'ni's husky voice interrupted the two. "I can't let you fight creatures from the abyss without making sure that you're at full strength. Come, my loves. Breakfast is ready."

Turning around, Zaa'ni made her way back to the kitchen. The gentle scent of rose lingered where she had been a moment before. Len breathed deeply, taking in his wife's aroma in the early morning light.

"Papa! Let's go," Bermet cried, scrambling out from under the quilt and chasing after her mother.

Thank Freyna that I returned home to these two, Len found himself expressing his gratitude to the gods. With a sigh, he slowly pushed himself out of bed and followed his wife and daughter. *I knew this wouldn't last very long. Time to re-establish my reign as the Great Heart. Freyna, give me guidance for the trials that are up ahead.*

Len entered the kitchen, shirtless and looking around for new bandages or some spare bit of cloth to wrap up his wound. Bermet sat at the table, wolfing down a pile of eggs that would make one of his soldiers envious.

"Chew, Bermet," Zaa'ni chided. "You can't just inhale your food like a gulper fish."

"Eth Omom," Bermet said, her cheeks bulging as she spoke. She reached out for the pewter mug in front of her and took a long drink of goat milk.

Zaa'ni placed a plate on the table for her husband. "I woke up early today and went to the shaman to get something for you. Djie said this should do nicely."

"Thank you, my sweet," Len said as he sat down to his meal.

A pile of eggs, rivalling that of his little girl's waited for him. A small loaf of bread, freshly baked, accompanied them. On a small plate, a mound of butter and some blackberry peach jam. Len grabbed his fork and speared some egg on it. Such a simple breakfast brought him so much pleasure. His mouth watered slightly before he hurriedly jammed the egg-laden utensil into his mouth.

Zaa'ni grabbed a piece of bread with jam and began munching on it absentmindedly. Upon noticing that Bermet finished her small mountain of food, Zaa'ni shooed the girl away.

"How long do you plan on staying?" she asked once their daughter was out of earshot. "I assume that still have work that needs to be finished."

"I have a meeting with Pram this morning. I'm going to speak with him once I'm finished."

Zaa'ni looked at Len with her head tilted and disappointed eyes as she took another bite of bread. "This soon? I thought you would have at least the morning to stay home with us. Bermet missed you so much. Surely you can spare a little time to be with your daughter while you regroup?"

"I'm sorry, but we're walking a thin line. The Pshwani are threatening a revolt thanks to Liir's death. I also need to figure out what to do with Zanir. When we fought Alazi I told their young general that I would become their ally. I'll not bow to some kingless nation. I need to turn this back into my favor."

"Len, everyone knows that everything you do is to better our people. Now that they've all had a good night's sleep and a couple warm meals, they will see that," Zaa'ni tried to soothe.

"I do this because I am destined for greatness," Len replied, his tone irritated. "The gods have chosen me. I cannot fail."

A knock on the door ended their conversation abruptly. Moving towards the door with his wife following behind, Len found Pram waiting outside.

"Come in."

"Thank you, Evenhand," Pram said, bowing his head slightly. Making eye contact with Zaa'ni, Pram dipped his head once more. "Freyna's favor be upon you, Zaa'ni."

"May her winds envelope and protect you," Zaa'ni replied, placing her hand on her belly.

"I'm sorry to disturb you so early in the morning, Evenhand. I had hoped to allow for you to spend more time with your family, but things are worse than we thought. The Pshwani are talking of rebellion with the other clans."

"Surely they can't be thinking that they would be better off without you?" Zaa'ni asked. "You've taken Xan from a volatile and strained peace and showed us that you have a vision."

"I'm afraid that they are. I've spoken to Hroth and he said that he's been monitoring the various clans since the demon was summoned. He said that the flames show him that several people are standing up and rallying them. I don't know how to say this, Evenhand, but it's Wyr-raji."

"What about Wyr-raji?" Len asked slowly. "He's returning to his old self, right?" The general placed heavy emphasis on the second question.

"Oh, yes, he's healing just fine. Too fine, honestly," Pram replied.

"What are you talking about, Pram?" Zaa'ni asked.

"He's encouraging the Pshwani to question our Great Heart's rule. He's claiming that he's been chosen by the gods and went out last night to spread his word. It's causing a little bit of a problem on the outer villages."

Len's mouth hardened as he listened to Pram. His mind raced as he tried to come up with a way to take care of the situation before it got out of hand.

"Let's go, Pram," Len said, striding out of the kitchen and into his room to grab a clean shirt.

⚘

The sun shone brightly on Len and Pram as they walked briskly through the market square. Children ran through the streets, laughing as they chased a small flock of chickens. Women strolled around leisurely in their flowy silk dresses, their hair cascading down their backs. As Len and Pram made their way through the village, people called out to them in greeting.

Len felt a sense of pride as those in his home town showered their Great Heart with adulation. Several women stopped him in the streets and handed him a pouch of spice or a baked treat, giving him their thanks for bringing their loved one home to them. Seeing the reverence and unity that he provided his people brought him great satisfaction.

Ahead, Hroth leaned against the side of a well, digging at the dirt in his fingernails with a dagger. The dark-haired man looked at the pair out of the side of his eyes and put the dagger into the sheath strapped on his leg.

"General, Swordbane, I hate to interrupt your walk, but I have some interesting news for you," Hroth said, his gravelly voice sounding especially harsh in the beautiful morning light.

Len noticed a group of men standing in an alley shooting furtive glances at the three. Their baggy pants and brightly colored vests distinguished them as members of the Pshwani clan.

"What have you heard?" Len asked.

"The flames let me listen to several conversations last night. One that caught my attention is one between Wyrd and a man named Viir."

"Liir's brother?" Pram broke in.

"I guess. I've never met the man," Hroth replied. "Well, Wyrd was telling this Viir that you, Swordbane, allowed for Liir to be killed and turned the rest of the Clans against the Pshwani. He said that you spoke with Alazi and told him that he may use the Pshwani as food sources so that he can harvest their energy."

"Graak's fury," Len swore.

Pram looked at the young general, a look of resignation in his eyes. "Evenhand, I hope you can put aside your childhood bond with Wyr-raji and see things for what they are at this moment. Right now, we are on the brink of a civil war and he is pushing one of our larger factions against us."

Shaking his head, Len struggled to accept the news. "I can't believe that he would betray our people like this."

"I know it is hard, Evenhand, but Wyr-raji is now touched by an aethren. Anything he says now cannot be trusted."

"He's not been trustworthy since I've known him," Hroth said.

The two looked at Hroth. He watched the battle in Len's eyes as the man struggled to accept the fact that his childhood friend was gone. Next to him, Pram stood silently, glancing over at his leader. Taking a moment to collect his thoughts, Hroth continued.

"When I first met Wyrd, there was a... something about him that made me wary. Like the way a deer or rabbit can sense when danger is around and are always on guard, that's how I feel about Wyrd. Before we first attacked Pharn he killed El'zar in cold blood. Wyrd is not one that you can let your guard down around. Now that he's tasted Fyre, he's even more dangerous."

The men in the alley looked at the three before walking off. Grumbling amongst each other, they eyed their leader with distrust as they passed by. Len maintained eye contact with the group as they passed, unflinching. The men broke their gaze after a few seconds, but their grousing did not stop. Mutterings of "traitor" and "betrayal" could be heard as the men made their way into the local apothecary.

"Evenhand," Pram said quietly. "I believe that we must make a proclamation quickly. Hroth, gather our brothers, we will need to address Liir's death before the day is done."

"Meet me at my home by mid-day," Len instructed. Turning to the Flame, he asked, "Hroth, do you have a problem with my rule?"

"Not at all," Hroth replied. "I'll see you at mid-day. May Freyna bless your travels."

Len smiled as the Flame stood in front of him, waiting take his leave. "May Graak's protection envelop you," he intoned.

Hroth turned sharply and sauntered off into the streets. His muted clothes allowed for the man to blend into the crowd almost instantly.

Once the Flame was out of earshot, Len turned to his general.

"Can we trust him?"

Pram looked at his leader. The young man stared at the throng of people, women in silk dresses while the men walked about, patrolling the worn dirt

streets. Women chatted happily amongst each other, giving their praise to
Freyna that their loved ones returned home. Pram tried to read Len's face,
searching for what his commander was looking for.

"I trust him," Pram said slowly.

Len smiled. "Good. It'd be a shame to have him killed. He's a good informant."

Turning around, Len began to head back to his home. The young general
walked with a relaxed step, belying the stress of the new turn of events. Men,
women and children alike parted ways for their leader, bowing their heads
in deference at his passing.

If Viir wants a war, by the gods I'll give him one.

VI

ZAA'NI HUMMED SOFTLY to herself as she cleaned her house. Warm light shone through the open window as she scrubbed the kitchen counters with a worn rag. On the hearth, a large pot of curry cooked, filling the house with a tantalizing aroma. Fresh pastries sat on the kitchen table, their buttery fragrance making her mouth water. Next to the pastries were strawberries and a small bowl of cream that she'd just picked up from the market.

"If Len doesn't get home soon, I may just have to start eating without him," Zaa'ni mused to herself.

She smiled as the child that was growing within her kicked. They were getting more frequent. A good sign according to the shamanka, as that meant that she carried a little warrior.

Like those old wives' tales are ever accurate, she mused. *Bermet was supposed to be boy too. At least the elders would have another daughter to dote on.*

With a sigh, Zaa'ni put down her rag and sat down at the table. Pulling over a pastry, she dipped a few strawberries in the cream and then placed them on top of the snack before taking a large bite. A groan of delight escaped her lips as she devoured the sweet treat. She forced herself to chew slowly so that she didn't eat the plate of pastries in one sitting.

Closing her eyes, Zaa'ni leaned back in her chair and enjoyed the light breeze that played with her hair in the warm morning. Her concerns from earlier in the morning gradually melted away. Len's unexpected arrival, shirt blood-stained and his party ragtag, left her feeling uncertain. With Pram's sudden appearance this morning, surely that meant that something big was happening.

When Uncle was overthrown there was a heaviness in the air. I don't feel that weight.

Zaa'ni didn't want to admit that she felt uneasy, though. A rock seemed to have settled into her stomach, making her uncomfortable. All of her senses were on high alert, her fight or flight response activated and ready to react. At the same time, she couldn't shake the feeling that something momentous was about to happen.

However, she found herself relaxing in the lovely morning. The legs of her chair lifted off of the ground slightly as she pushed against the ground. A gentle scent of lavender tickled her nose. Cracking her eyes open, she saw the silhouette of a small child. Zaa'ni almost thought that it was Bermet, except for the shock of periwinkle hair that flowed behind her. Her eyes flew open and she placed the legs of her chair back on the ground. She stood up slowly and looked for the figure.

Outside the open window, Zaa'ni heard giggling. Making her way to the kitchen, she looked out the window and saw Bermet dancing in the yard with a branch in her hand. The little girl twirled and spun about, her dark hair flying behind her as she moved.

Dancing alongside her, Zaa'ni saw a blue-haired girl copying Bermet's movements, her daughter not acknowledging her companion. The blue-haired girl turned in a slow, graceful motion. Mid-spin, the blue-haired girl caught Zaa'ni's eye. Zaa'ni gasped as she looked into the obsidian eyes twinkling back at her. The blue-haired girl gave Zaa'ni a wink before fading away, replaced by a few swirling leaves that circled Bermet.

Zaa'ni smiled as she watched her little girl twirl about.

We are lucky indeed if we've been chosen by the gods to be worthy of their protection.

"Mommy," Bermet's sweet voice cut through her thoughts. "Are you watching me dance?"

"Yes, I am, my pearl," Zaa'ni cooed. "You're very good."

Bermet beamed at her mother.

"I thought you were an undine though," Zaa'ni continued. "I didn't expect you to be a dancing earth sprite."

"I wanted to get my powers charged up before I fight the dragons of Enlil," Bermet explained. Her eyes sparkled as she spun around, waving her branch in the air. "Lady Aria promised me great power if I open myself to her presence."

"Aria?"

"Yes, Mommy. She's coming. I heard it whispered to me as I was charging my powers," Bermet replied matter-of-factly. "I wanted to be ready for her arrival."

Zaa'ni watched her daughter dancing for a moment, a slight frown creasing her face. Bermet executed a graceful pirouette, her eyes closed and her expression serene. A gust of wind blew around her, rustling her hair and whipping up leaves. The serenity from earlier that morning returned to Zaa'ni. She could almost swear that she'd heard her mother's voice soothing her as she stood watching her daughter.

"I'll leave you to your ceremony then," Zaa'ni said. "Just let me know before you head off to battle the dragons. I want to make sure that your energies are high to ensure your victory." Lowering her voice, Zaa'ni whispered, "I've heard that a full belly helps the undine unleash their true potential. I might have a little something that could help you."

Zaa'ni shot Bermet a conspiratorial smile and brought her finger to her lips, motioning for the girl to keep the information quiet. Bermet's eyes sparkled and she vigorously nodded her head. Swirling her branch in a mesmerizing arc, Bermet resumed her intricate dance.

The sound of the front door opening caused Zaa'ni to return inside. Len walked through the house and sat at the table, grabbing a pastry and shoving it into his mouth. He leaned back into his chair and stared up at the ceiling with his arms crossed against his chest.

"Love?" Zaa'ni asked softly.

Len's eyes broke away from the spot that he was watching. "All is well, my sweet," he said. His tone did not provide her with any comfort despite his reassuring words. "I just need to clear my head before mid-day."

"What's going on?" Zaa'ni asked, unconsciously placing her hand on her swollen belly. "Something has happened, hasn't it?"

"I just need to make an announcement to the village. Take Bermet to my mother. I don't want her to be out on her own after I address our brothers and sisters." Len stared at his wife, his face difficult to read.

"It's bad then?"

"Wyr-raji has betrayed us."

Zaa'ni gaped at the news.

Len raised his hand, asking for silence. "Pram's Flame overheard Wyr-raji talking to Viir. He's been stirring up the Pshwani, pushing them towards rebellion."

"Graak's mercy!" Zaa'ni swore. "After all that you've done for him. Why would he do this?"

Len's controlled expression fell and Zaa'ni saw his stress. His usually alert eyes suddenly looked exhausted; his relaxed mouth was taut, accentuating the sharpness of his cheeks. Zaa'ni moved over to her husband and placed her arm on his shoulder. She rubbed his back gently, trying to ease the tension.

"Everything will be fine, Zaa'ni. I am the Great Heart. I will keep our people together; it is my duty."

What can I do to make this easier? I've placed the burden entirely on him.

Len reached up and took Zaa'ni's hand into his. "I have everything under control, don't worry. Pram has been ever the loyal soldier, thinking of different angles to attack the problem. There's a reason why he's been so invaluable to both myself and Ras."

Despite her husband's reassuring words, Zaa'ni wasn't convinced.

"He's seen so much during his service," Len said, giving his wife's hand a squeeze. "Besides, he's managed to earn the respect of our only remaining mercenary. That's how we found out about Wyr-raji's betrayal."

"Uncle always said that Pram was a good man," Zaa'ni said. "If he's ingratiated himself to one of the Myrani, there must be something that I'm not seeing."

Grabbing second pastry and smearing a bit of cream and strawberries on it, Len took another big bite. He smiled at his wife, a gentleness pushing through his eyes' usual hardness. Zaa'ni wiped at a tear with the back of her hand.

"My love, I have some real food for you before you address our people. Let me get you some."

Zaa'ni busied herself with ladling a bowl of curry for her husband. Chunks of lamb bobbed in the stew amongst sweet potatoes, onions and lentils. The combination of spices and vegetables mixed in with the sweetness of coconut. The fruit was a delicacy, imported from the Eastern shores, making the meal a special treat served primarily at important functions. Zaa'ni's mouth watered as she carried the warm bowl to Len.

Bermet waltzed into the house, the branch no longer in her hand. She spun around and waved her hands around Len. Her parents watched her with a bemused expression.

She spoke in a sing-songy voice. "Welcome home, Papa. I'm here to get more energy before I fight the dragons."

Her hands flowed around her father. Zaa'ni watched as Len appeared to perk up a bit. She watched as Bermet's movements ruffled Len's shirt, as though a gentle breeze just passed by in the still afternoon air. His hair rustled almost imperceptibly as the young girl moved around him.

Scooping up his daughter onto his lap, Len handed her the spoon. "If you're going to battle dragons, you'll need something hearty. Eat up, Bermet."

Bermet greedily took mouthful after mouthful of the curry. In between her bites, Len dipped a piece of bread into the bowl, scooping up bits of meat along with the sweet potatoes. Zaa'ni sat down at the table with her own bowl. The three ate in comfortable silence, enjoying a simple meal with each other.

It's been too long since we've all been together. If only we could keep this going forever.

Zaa'ni smiled into her bowl as she watched the two. A gentle breeze played with their hair and clothes again. It brought with it the scent of lavender once more.

Freyna protect my family in the coming days.

VII

Vashe stood in her now empty lecture hall at the Mageri. She pulled down the parchment diagrams of the human body, energy points marked out on the figures, and smoothed them out on her front desk. Moving to the sheets pertaining to the three Fallen siblings, Vashe proceeded to take those down as well. Slowly but surely, the Scrymmen woman cleared out her classroom of all of her personal affects.

A knock on the oaken door caused her the briefest pause. Without stopping what she was doing, Vashe called for the person to enter. The door opened a crack, the faces of two of her fellow instructors peaking around the door.

"Headmistress," a soft, balding man broached. His timid voice reminded her of the eunichs her father used to keep. "Do you have a moment? Yellena and I would like a word with you."

"Come in, Urthro."

Urthro and Yellena walked into the room and stood in front of her desk, waiting for Vashe to pause. As the Master of Magical History, Urthro smoothed the green sash over his black robes. His pudgy, beringed hand subconsciously flattened the imaginary pleat on his clothes. Yellena, as one of the younger mistresses of the school, stood with an air of disinterest. Her heavy-lidded eyes scanned the increasingly deconstructed room. As Mistress of Botany, she worked closely with Vashe in the Magicerium as a healer.

"What do you need, Urthro?" Vashe asked as she smoothed the remaining pieces of parchment that she'd pulled down from the walls. "I am in a hurry."

"Word has it that you're leaving Pharn for a while," Yellena said. "The queen seems to be all in a panic about finding someone to replace you."

Yellena made her way down to one of the stone benches and sat down, smoothing her red robe. The young woman stared at Vashe and her affects, with her slight, ever-present sneer playing on her red lips. A petite woman, Yellena did not carry the same grace or respect as Vashe from her fellow peers. Her disdain at the perceived disrespect was barely hidden underneath the surface of her personality.

"I will be leaving in two or three days, that is correct," Vashe said absent-mindedly. She carefully folded the pieces of parchment into quarters before placing them inside a large leather-bound tome.

"Headmistress, we are in dire need of your expertise right now," Urthro said. "There are too many men who were injured in the battle at our gate not five days ago. Their wounds are more than my team can handle, and we're running low on your healing salve."

"Urthro, you know how to make a perfectly functional salve on your own. Mine is no better than anyone else's," Vashe replied as she put pressure on the leather cover, trying to flatten the loose parchment further.

"But Headmistress, yours has some sort of fast acting property that allows for the injured to recover at an accelerated pace. I can't figure out what herb you use."

"Please, Urthro," Vashe replied, tying the leather strands of the tome around it several times before making a knot. "You are more than capable of dealing with the infirmary while I am gone for a few days. It should be no more than a span."

"Two weeks?" Yellena broke in. "Vashe — Headmistress," she corrected at a withering glare from Urthro. "Surely there can't be anything more important than keeping Pharn in order after such a tragedy. Who will provide our people council?"

"Hera Grey is stepping up to the task nicely."

"Headmistress, Queen Hera does not fully understand the gravity of the situation. Sure, she is making an effort. I mean, the burning ceremony showed that she can make an appearance and act as more than just a visual figurehead, but she is no King Jaste."

"I must say, Headmistress, that I do agree with Yellena," Urthro cut in. "Our dear departed king, may he rest in the Halls of the Fallen, was a strong man by himself, but with you by his side, Pharn was a formidable force against almost every nation. We kept the barbarians at bay, and you know how much they've wanted to take our borders."

Vashe rubbed her temples. Urthro did make a good point. Before the attack on Pharn, their combined strength of Jaste's muscle and Vashe's vast knowledge was enough to keep most enemies away. When the young Xanan general attacked the spice mines, then the capital itself, he did considerable damage to the nation. Despite not involving herself in combat, the bulk of their forces were gone or incapacitated. As the only mage with any fighting experience, if she did leave, Zanir would be open to an attack. Hera was not equipped to handle any sort of military campaign.

"Urthro, Yellena, while I appreciate your concern, this is something that I must do. By the time I leave, our forces should be home again. We will be more than adequately protected from any threat."

Let us hope that they do not find out about the loss of Alverick. That's the last thing our people need.

Yellena did not look convinced. Her haughty stare told Vashe as much.

"Perhaps I could lead the healer's ward in your stead?" she asked. "As the only other person who is a teacher of botany, I believe I am qualified to cover in your absence."

Of course, you are.

"I will leave instructions with Her Highness before I leave," Vashe replied.

Yellena opened her mouth to argue, but Urthro cut her off.

"That sounds most agreeable," he said.

With a wave of his hand, he motioned for Yellena to follow him out of the room. Yellena gave Vashe one last look before straightening up and following Urthro; her heavy-lidded eyes locked onto Vashe's silver ones.

Once the door closed, Vashe returned to clearing out her room. She picked up the stack of books on her desk and headed out of the room towards her chambers. The stone hallways contained several students milling about. They all greeted the headmistress with respect as she strode past, while she nodded in kind.

At the end of the main corridor she turned right and started heading up the stairs towards the faculty living quarters. She made it to the top of the staircase and continued down towards her room. The worn stone floor was lined with silk carpets and the walls were covered with richly woven tapestries. Images of the great battle between the three Fallen Siblings and their fellow aethren, Vahnyre, were depicted down the hall.

Vashe stopped at one tapestry halfway down the hall. The silver-haired form of Aria lay draped across her brother's arms, a slight trickle of blood coming from the corner of her mouth. Her eyes were closed and her limp form dangled from Ghan's arms. Lines of golden thread emanated from her body, symbolizing the goddess' spirit leaving her body.

The next tapestry showed the middle Fallen, Ghan, presenting the people of Corinth with Aria's blood. Five crystal vials of the crimson liquid were held in his arms. His dark hair contained silver streaks and his eyes were a deep chestnut. Ghan's appearance, even in the image, looked exhausted around the eyes.

Vashe traced his jawline with her fingers, the stack of tomes clutched tightly against her chest with her other arm.

"Second brother, the world will never know your pain. Your sacrifice will never be forgotten."

At the end of the hall, Vashe found her room. To her relief, no one stood outside her door waiting for her to return. Next to her door, the final tapestry on the right side of the hallway hung. The youngest brother, raven-haired with silver streaks and clear blue eyes, stood engulfed in flames. Even in the image, his transformation could be seen laying just under the surface. A slight orange tinge flecked the outside of his eyes and his cheeks were slightly more angled than his siblings'. There was a pain in his eyes, separate from his brother's.

Vashe glanced at the tapestry before shifting the contents in her arms to unlock the door. Pushing it open with her foot, she staggered in and deposited the books onto a chair. In several strides, she made her way over to a bookshelf that was laden with several thick tomes, a smaller one, and various trinkets. In the corner, an elegant dress lay draped over the back of a chair. In the opposite corner, a small stone pool with runes carved into the rim sat by the window.

The Scrymmen woman walked over to the pool and looked within. A deep crimson liquid filled the stone basin. Placing her hands on the rim, Vashe closed her eyes and felt deep within herself, searching for her latent energy. Touching upon her reserves, Vashe opened her eyes and blew gently into the pool, causing a gentle rippling effect. The runes on the side of the basin glowed a soft blue as Vashe stared into its depths.

The landscape of Corinth blurred past in her mind's eye. Through the flashes of green and brown, she spotted the forces of Pharn returning. The haggard group emanated despair, even through the scrying pool. On the outskirts of the group, a figure that glowed silver circled the forces. Vashe pushed herself to look past the silver figure and continue her search.

Trees and homes dotted the horizon. Past the Rydash Gorge, she pushed her way to the realm of Xan. In the capital of Fa'Tinh, a large gathering had formed. Amongst the group, a figure with an orange glow stood in their ranks. Again, forcing herself to ignore this piece of information, Vashe turned her attentions to the far eastern lands of Corinth.

Enlil, the abandoned lands. A realm of past glories long since lost.

"Enlil, show me your secrets," she murmured.

As Vashe tried to focus on the land, she was met with a magical resistance. Pursing her lips, Vashe reached deep within her and tried to push her way through the wall. Again, she was met with something blocking her access.

"Interesting."

Before giving up, Vashe turned her gaze to the southern lands, her home. Scrymme's lands were rich and fertile. Exotic trees grew on Scrymme's soil and sheep grazed on the meadows. A large stone castle lay on the coast near the southeastern border, perched atop an outcropping of rocks.

Cursing quietly, Vashe struggled to view the populace moving around in their underground tunnels.

"Father's magi are doing a good job at keeping prying eyes out of Scrymme. Never mind I'll just make a side trip."

Waving her hands over the blood in the pool, the image disappeared and the runes stopped glowing. Vashe stepped away from the scrying pool and sank into her chair. Leaning her head back, she closed her eyes and took a deep breath.

Scrymme, Enlil... There are too many questions that I need answers to. I'll leave at first light in two days. Calli should be circling Toron; fortune will be in my favor.

VIII

L EN RELAXED on a chaise, dozing in the warmth of the early afternoon. His mind darted about, just in between the dream and conscious stages of sleep. His thoughts raced, trying to figure out where he lost control of his people and how he could regain it.

My magi are gone. Liir is gone. A number of my brothers are gone. Wyr-raji has betrayed me. Even if I can turn Viir and his people against Wyr-raji, I still have to deal with the Myrani. They're not going to be happy when we let them know five of their magi are dead and one's defected. Might try to kill Hroth in the process. I can't allow that. He's become much too valuable. He knows too much.

The Myrani were a mercenary band of magi who lived in the Woods of Lingora. Apart from Scrymme, they were the largest group with magical capabilities. They charged a hefty price for their service. His mind replayed his last conversation with their leader for what felt like the hundredth time since his failed campaign.

"You're asking for quite a bit, young son of Xan," Ka'lev remarked. "A group of that size will cost you more than just a thousand gold. You'd owe us a boon, to be called upon at any time that I want."

The curly-haired woman stared deep into Len's eyes as he stood in front of her. Her expression was almost hungry, as though she wanted to reach deep within him and devour his very essence.

Refusing to flinch, Len met her gaze. "I am not beholden to any ruler. I seek to bring my people more stability. All we have is our wood-carving, spices, and silks.

Though our lands are fertile, we have nothing that the other nations desire. With this campaign, I will bring the brothers of Xan into the forefront of Corinth and make us a force to be reckoned with."

Ka'lev's eyes darkened. Her smile disappeared and she barred her teeth slightly, like a dog. "You do not know what you ask, son of Xan. My resources are precious. What do you bring me that even compares to what you want?"

Liir stood next to Len, sweating slightly. When he spoke, his voice was steady and smooth. "Ka'lev, my dear, you know not who you are speaking to. By adding your men to our forces, you are almost guaranteeing that the nobility will come to you seeking hired protection. Think of all of the caravans you'll have your people guarding, all of the secret soldiers amongst the rich. You will be in such high demand people will pay anything you ask. Our Great Heart is already doing you a great service, yet you insult him by asking for a boon. His patronage is your boon."

Ka'lev kept her face blank as she weighed what Liir said. Len watched as her mind quickly processed Liir's information and calculated her potential earnings. The young general smiled to himself as he saw her reach her decision.

"I'll grant your request, young son of Xan," she replied, her hungry smile back. "On one condition. Your plans are ambitious, and I like that. I have been wanting to send more resources into Zanir for a few years now. If you take them first, instead of Alocar, the rest of the land will fall. Make it so I can plant a spy or two in the midst of Zanir and I will give you two of my best along with the others."

Ka'lev motioned to a man with hazy tattoos that covered part of his arm, and a dark-haired Flame who leaned casually against a tree.

"Done," Len replied.

His mind kept replaying his deal with the leader of the mercenary band. Everything about her radiated a deadly energy, from the way that she watched him to her body language. An accomplished Spark, her whole right arm and the right side of her stomach were covered in jagged tattoos. They intersected so beautifully with the thin scars on her body that it looked as though she had been struck by lightning. A beautiful woman, but deadly.

I'll need to follow up with Ka'lev soon. She'll want an update.

A knock on the door pulled Len from his thoughts. As he opened his eyes, he heard Zaa'ni open the door and greet Pram. Opening his eyes, Len pushed himself onto his elbow with a grunt. His wounded side ached with the movement.

Damn, I need more healing salve and maybe an herb to dull the pain.

"Are you ready, Evenhand?" Pram asked as he and Zaa'ni entered the room.

"Give me a moment," Len replied.

Seeing her husband in pain as he tried to get up, Zaa'ni rushed over and attempted to help him. Len brushed her away with a wave of the hand, pushing himself off of the chaise. His abdomen's silhouette was visible underneath the light blanket he had been sleeping under. Len grabbed his tunic off of the back of the chaise and threw it on.

"I'm sorry, Evenhand," Pram said touching his index and middle fingers to his lips and then forehead in apology. "I should have waited outside until you were ready."

"No, no, it's fine. I was just thinking."

Smoothing his hair, Len gingerly rotated his right arm in slow circles, testing to see if his side still bothered him. When it didn't, he grabbed his short sword and fastened it to his hip.

"Zaa'ni, take Bermet to my mother's. If Viir and his followers don't settle down right away, I don't want her in harm's way. Mother is both well respected and far enough out of the village that she won't be bothered if fighting breaks out."

"Yes, but I'll be joining you once she's safe," Zaa'ni replied. Before her husband could protest, she said, "I don't care what you say. I'm not leaving you out there alone when a rebellion could break out."

"Zaa'ni," Pram said gently, "it doesn't seem prudent for you to be out in the town, especially in your delicate condition. If something were to happen, you would be at a disadvantage."

"Do you really expect something big to come of this?" Zaa'ni asked incredulously. "Viir may be angry, but he's a practical man."

"Wyr-raji's agitating has been making things more difficult than we first expected," Pram said. "He's more unstable than usual."

"Pram is right," Len said. "You will listen to him and stay at my mother's."

Zaa'ni opened her mouth but closed it again as her husband's gaze stared straight through her. It wasn't the cold look that he reserved for those who upset him, rather it was one that touched her soul. Returning his stare, she took a deep breath and said with a cool, steady voice, "Len, while I understand your reasonings, I will make this decision for myself. I will weigh the risks and judge the mood of the crowd when I see them." Seeing her husband's brow furrow, she continued, "If things look bad, I'll go back to your mother's."

Len's eyes hardened, but he did not reply with more than a shake of his head. "If you must, but know that you could be killed," Len replied. Turning around, he said to his general, "Let's go, Pram. There's much to discuss before we address our brothers."

Len made his way out of his home, Pram following behind him.

⋘∽⋙

"Evenhand, how do you plan on handing this?" Pram asked.

The two walked through the village, making their way to the large fountain in the center of town. Both men walked with quick strides, passing their neighbors quickly. Though it was the height of the afternoon, there seemed to be fewer people walking around at that hour. The air was quiet and tense. Perhaps it was because the sounds of children shouting and laughing couldn't be heard anymore, or maybe it was because the women did not seem to be chatting amongst themselves. Whatever the reason, the lack of daily noises put the two on edge.

Len watched the people in the streets out of the side of his eyes. He thought he recognized the group of men from the morning, but he couldn't be sure.

A number of merchants appeared to have closed their shops and stood idly outside their businesses. They spoke quietly to each other as they watched their Great Heart and his general walk by. Several of the men called out to Len, a hesitant greeting to their leader, while others dropped their heads in respect as he passed.

"I think it'll be best to confront Viir without Wyr-raji. He will see reason as long as he's not being poisoned when I speak with him," Len replied. He continued to scan the streets as they walked, his hand ready to move to his weapons at a moment's notice.

Up ahead, Hroth was lounging at a food cart eating a meat bun. When he noticed the two approaching, he popped the remaining bit of the morsel into his mouth and headed over to them.

"Everyone should be here once you start speaking," Hroth said. "They're all waiting to see what your message is."

"Thank you, Hroth," Len said. "Why don't you stand off to the side? I may need your assistance later, and if people are focused on me, whatever you do will catch them off-guard. I've found the effect to be quite helpful."

Hroth slunk back to the food cart and bought another bun. Len and Pram stood at the fountain for a few minutes in silence. The two watched a small group form in their general area, but few ventured closer. Those that did were members of the Pshwani Clan. Once the sun reached its zenith, a large, soft man dressed in the traditional mourning attire walked up to the front of the group.

"Shall I stand next to you or off to the side?" Pram asked quietly.

"Off to the side. I can handle myself," Len replied.

"Len!" Viir called out. Noting Len's expression, he quickly corrected himself, but did not change the tone of his voice, "Great Heart! I come bearing a grievance against you and yours."

Len's eyes narrowed, but he remained quiet. He would let the man speak fully.

"In your grand desire for even greater glory for all of Xan, you committed the crime of treason and murdered my brother, Liir," Viir called out. His eyes shone with a fire as he spoke. "You have also broken your promise to the Pshwani and declared war against our brothers."

Murmurs broke out amongst the crowd. More people had gathered now that Viir began speaking. Men and women looked to each other, confused, before turning to their leader to see what his reaction would be. Len remained impassive as Viir threw his accusations, his posture straight and proud. Viir, by contrast, looked less impressive. His shoulders were slouched and his voice quivered with rage.

When Len spoke, his voice carried strong and clear. "Brother, I don't know where you heard these rumors, but I can assure you that they are not true."

"Don't deceive me, Great Heart," Viir called back.

Holding up his hand for quiet, Len replied, "Brother, I speak the truth. I promised you all that I would bring our people the admiration of all of Corinth, did I not?"

Quiet murmurs could be heard from the crowd as many bobbed their heads in agreement.

"And how would I be able to bring our brothers glory? Conquest requires sacrifice. I put my life on the line to bring our people notoriety, as did many of our brothers. As did Liir," Len nodded to Viir in a sign of respect for his fallen kin. "A number of our brothers paid the ultimate price and have ridden out on Graak's winds. Unfortunately, Liir met the same fate as our fallen brothers. However, I did not order his death, nor did I order an attack on the Pshwani."

Soft chattering broke out in pockets amongst the group. Looking around, Len spotted Zaa'ni standing by Hroth underneath the buttress of a florist's shop. His stomach clenched slightly at the sight of her. A number of Pshwani men pushed their way to the front of the crowd to stand next to Viir, muttering angrily as they shoved the others out of their way.

"How can you deny that our people are being attacked by our supposed brothers?" an older man asked. His thick beard went down to his chest, just above his pudgy stomach. "No one is supposed to act unless it is on your command."

"You will not accuse our Great Heart of deception," Pram cut in, his tone dangerous. "Evenhand is not so short-sighted to betray the Pshwani."

"And yet, he didn't bother to tell them when he made an alliance with Pharn in the midst of battle," a strong voice challenged.

IX

HEADS TURNED, looking to see who spoke. Standing at the back of the crowd, Hroth watched as Wyrd smirked at the two. The left half of Wyrd's body, face included, was covered in clothes that were soaked in a potent salve to treat the burns that lay underneath. His sandy hair was not burned off by Vahnyre. The biggest change could be found in his eyes. Flecked with bits of orange, the hazel eye that was not covered with cloth bore onto his former childhood friend.

A number of people shouted out in the crowd demanding to know about the alliance and the betrayal to Pshwan. The group of Pshwani men from earlier in the morning, led by the thick, bearded man cried out the loudest.

Zaa'ni made a sudden movement to move forward towards her husband, but Hroth placed his hand on her arm to hold her back in the shadow of the building.

"Quiet," he said softly. "Let me handle this."

Biting back a retort, she took a step back and did not draw attention to herself. She pulled her silk shawl over her shoulders nervously and folded her arms over her chest.

"Wyr-raji," Len addressed the man from the front of the crowd. His voice was soft but carried over the calls of the crowd and caused them to quiet to better hear him. "How dare you make such a statement, especially when you betrayed our brothers to summon a demon and put them in jeopardy."

"I tried to help you succeed," Wyrd hissed. "You were not, are not, a strong enough leader to conquer all of the realms. Alazi has shown that."

"Wyr-raji," Len raised his voice, "you have betrayed us all. You are the reason that the Myrani are missing both a Shadow, and I believe a Flame, if what I've heard is correct."

Hroth smirked a little at the mention of the Flame and rubbed his arm. "I'm not complaining that El'zar is gone," he muttered to Zaa'ni. "His death may prove more beneficial than we may know."

"What are you talking about?" she whispered.

Hroth put his tattooed finger to his lips and kept his eyes on the former friends. The loose sleeve of his shirt fell down by his elbow, revealing the intricate tattoos covering the majority of his forearm. They wound around him, almost weaving themselves in a delicate dance on his body.

"Your actions have shamed Xan," Len continued. "Betrayal will not be tolerated. As the leader of Xan, I will show you the only mercy that I can and exile you from our lands. You are no longer welcome in Xan."

The crowd fell silent.

"By the gods," Hroth swore.

Rage burned in Wyrd's eye. Hroth noted that the orange actually seemed to move like fire, crackling behind his anger. Wyrd took a step towards Len. Both Hroth and Pram moved forward, Pram reaching for his sword as Hroth reached within himself, stoking his flames.

Wyrd stared down his former childhood friend. His clenched fist suddenly erupted in fire, startling those around him.

Hroth stopped in his tracks, as did Pram. A raspy hiss filled Hroth's head.

MY SON, WHAT ARE YOU DOING?

Hroth stood, frozen. All time seemed to stop.

I CAN OFFER YOU THE WORLD, IF YOU WOULD JOIN ME. WITH WYRD AS YOUR LEADER, YOU COULD ACHIEVE GREATNESS. WHAT DO YOU SAY?

Wyrd has proven himself untrustworthy. He is only after his own gains and would kill me without hesitation.

Images flashed in Hroth's mind, passing in quick succession, one after the other. Wyrd, cloaked in fire, standing on a hill on the outskirts of Fa'Tinh. The prostrated forms of thousands lay at his feet, heads bowed in worship. He stared wickedly at those who revered his power. Behind him, a shadowed group of men stood, spears raised, chanting. At the end of every sentence, the shrouded force pounded their weapons on the ground in emphasis. Smoke blew past, the soft dark tendrils making their way towards Wyrd and enveloping him.

Below, the corpses of thousands lay rotting on the charred ground. The green livery of Zanir and blue of Alocar dotted the ground. Even the red tunics bearing Xan's eight stars of the brotherhood lay amongst the others. Len's lifeless body lay at Wyrd's feet, a gaping hole in his chest exposing burnt flesh.

Hroth looked up at Wyrd, the Qu-ari man's hands stained a dark brown from the blood that had dried on them, and noticed a dark figure standing behind Wyrd. The form took the shape of a lean man with a smooth head. His blood ran cold as Vahnyre's orange eyes stared at him. A sneer slowly spread on the aethren's face.

YOU WERE ABLE TO GET AWAY FROM ME IN THE GORGE, BUT I WON'T LET YOU GET AWAY FROM ME A SECOND TIME.

Hroth's eyes bulged as he felt Fyre pull at the energies inside of him. His right arm suddenly felt frigid, all heat drained from the limb.

JOIN ME, AND I CAN GIVE YOU THE WORLD, Vahnyre repeated. **REJECT ME, AND I WILL HAVE YOUR SOUL.**

Zaa'ni's warm hand grabbed Hroth's right one, bringing him back to the events unfolding and returning the warmth to his limb.

"Are you okay?" she asked. Her husky voice filled with concern. "You look like you've seen the Faceless."

Hroth didn't respond. He stared at the scene that was unfolding before him. The young general gaped at Wyrd, his eyes wide in surprise. Pram stood next to his leader, hand on his chest pushing the young general behind him, and his axe handle clenched in his hand.

"Wyr-raji, threatening Evenhand is punishable by death. I suggest that you leave quietly," Pram growled with a steely tone.

Wyrd laughed. "What are you going to do, Pram?" He held up his flame-engulfed hand, smiling as the tendrils licked his fingers without blistering the skin. "I have seen the power of the gods. In fact, I have been chosen by them. You can do nothing."

Taking a deep breath, Hroth steeled himself and forced his body to move forward. As he strode through the stunned crowd, Hroth used his energy to envelop his entire arm in fire. His face hardened as he reached the young general before turning to face Wyrd.

"Wyrd, both your leader and your superior have given you orders. If you're are any sort of honorable man, you will heed this decision," Hroth warned.

Wyrd narrowed his eyes at the Flame. Bringing his fire-wrapped hand up to his face, Wyrd flexed his fingers twice before creating a ball of pale blue fire. With a flick of the wrist, he sent the ball speeding towards Hroth.

Hroth raised his own flaming arm up and conjured up a shield made of fire. Bracing himself for the impact, he widened his stance and bent his knees slightly. The blue ball of flame slammed into his shield, causing him to stagger back a step. Heat from the two different flames caused Hroth's face to prickle. The people closest to him fell backwards in their haste to get away from the unbearable heat. The scent of singed hair filled the air.

Sweat dripped off of Hroth's brow. With a groan, he struggled to absorb the other-worldly fire. As he took in the flames, he felt his insides burn. He screamed in agony as his body struggled to keep the blue flames from destroying him from within.

He heard laughter in his mind as his vision swam. Wyrd stood a few feet away from him, smiling at the fallen Flame.

"I believe that it is now you who are banished, Len," Wyrd said. His voice sounded faint to Hroth's ears, as though he was speaking from inside of a bubble.

Dropping to his knees, Hroth clutched his chest before falling to the ground unconscious.

X

OLDAR SAT upon his horse, watching the sky go from oranges to purples. Finches and spotted warblers called out to each other in an evening symphony, the sharp chirps of the finches contrasting against the melodic trills of the warblers. Crickets and cicadas joined in the birds' songs, adding a steady, low buzzing undertone to the evening. Tired from the day's long ride, Oldar felt his mind wander.

What can I do to reclaim my dignity? Father told me that we would be perfect for each other, yet she chose that soldier.

Forcing himself to calm down once more, Oldar actively listened to the sounds around him. The buzzing helped him keep his mind on less stressful thoughts.

I'll need to draft a proclamation to my people, let them know what to expect now that our alliance is all but dead. Oldar's mind raced, looking to find an excuse for his smoldering anger. *The princess betrayed our people, that's what she did. Alocar will not stand for that.*

Unable to keep his thoughts positive, the young king succumbed to his anger once more.

"Bring me a drink," he barked at the man riding nearest to him.

The soldier looked at his king in mild surprise before riding off in search of something that would please his master.

Running his fingers through his hair, Oldar let out a sigh. *What am I doing? I thought I said that my word would be my bond. That is the only way that I will be able to gain the respect of my people.*

"Milord," a voice broached the young king. "I've returned with something that I think you will find most refreshing."

Holding out a tankard of amber liquid, he proffered it to his lord. The ale sloshed in the mug as the two rode their mounts at a leisurely pace.

Oldar stared at the drink. For a moment, he considered rejecting it and asking for water or an herbal drink.

Why should I sacrifice my desires in order to garner respect from my people? As their king, I damn well deserve it.

Reaching out for the cup, Oldar took it from the soldier's hands and quickly downed the ale. The cool liquid went down smoothly, warming him from within. He wiped the droplets that lingered on his upper lip and in the stubble on his face with the back of his hand. Shoving the mug back at the soldier, he dismissed the man with a wave.

A familiar feeling of relaxation and warmth began to wash over him.

Should've eaten something before doing that. We haven't eaten since we rode out at dawn.

Finally able to push his frustrations towards the back of his mind, Oldar continued on in the waning light. The sky was a beautiful shade of deep purple mixed with a hint of magenta and just a splash of gold. In his altered state, he closed his eyes and recalled a similar sunset that he watched with his father when he was younger.

❧

Young Oldar Storm stood with Loran on the balcony tower of Oldar's room. The young prince sniffled as he stared into the heavens. King Loran placed a hand on his son's shoulder, trying to comfort the child. The sleeves of his flowing maroon robes draped over Oldar's slight frame.

"Oldar," Loran said softly. "Your mother did not mean to strike you like she did. She is just going through a difficult time right now."

The prince looked up at his father with puffy eyes. Wiping the tears from his face, Oldar replied, "Father, why would she do that though? She said she would kill me."

Loran stared out into the sunset. Everything about him radiated exhaustion and defeat. Dark circles rimmed his eyes, which, coupled with hollowed cheeks, made him look skeletal in the darkening light. Heaving a sigh, the king struggled to meet his son's gaze.

"Son, you know that your mother is special, right?"

Oldar nodded his head. "She was chosen by the gods to continue their duties and protect our people."

"And how does she do that?" Loran asked gently.

Oldar thought for a moment before replying. "She acts in the best interests of the people. She solves problems, makes sure that we have food, and makes sure that our soldiers are able to protect our borders."

King Storm tousled his son's hair with his beringed hand. "That she does, my son," he said heavily. "But there is one more thing that she uses to protect our people, and that is the Gift of the gods."

"Her markings?" Oldar asked.

"Yes. Your mother carries a heavy burden, Oldar. Because of the Gift she received, she must also pay a heavy price. Sometimes this causes her to act in ways that she normally wouldn't. She just can't control herself when the power of the gods becomes too strong."

Oldar rubbed his cheek. It was slightly swollen from where his mother struck him, but only just barely. "Mom still loves me, right?" he asked tentatively. His voice trembled as his mind flashed back to the rage in her eyes. It was almost as though she didn't remember him.

"Of course she does, son. Like this sunset, there's a beauty in the darkness that comes. Your mother is lucky though and gets to enjoy the vibrant colors and warmth of dusk as well as the cold darkness that comes with the night. Most people with her gift don't get that luxury. The majority of people who share her gift are doomed to wander the darkness forever. It is up to us to be your mother's sunlight. Can you help me?"

Oldar managed a watery-eyed smile and nodded his head. The two turned back to look at the last remnants of orange in the evening sky.

"Will Mom ever lose to the darkness?" Oldar asked.

"Only right before the sun sets," Loran answered honestly.

⌘

The darkness finally caught up with Mother, Oldar thought. *I won't let it catch me.*

His mount's rhythmic gait made the young king a bit drowsy. Darkness lay behind the retreating forces. The faint pinpricks of stars shining in the night sky welcomed the men who marched farther back in the line. The retinue continued on in relative silence. After the long day of travel, exhaustion was a prominent feeling amongst the traveling army. Heads began drooping as the men trudged along. More than one mounted soldier's head popped up suddenly before slowly lolling down towards their chin once more.

A loud shout broke the silence, startling the dozing men. Light chattering broke out amongst the ranks as they tried to figure out what was going on.

"Dead ahead!" the voice cried out.

"Czand's damnation," Oldar mumbled. His pleasant feeling of relaxation was still present, but no longer clouded and weighed down his mind. Sifting through the mental fog, he struggled to compose himself. "What was the first part of his message?"

Squinting his eyes, he noticed a small outcropping in the distance. Bright orange spots dotted the side of the ridge in the darkness. Looking to his left, Oldar saw Ingmar riding next to him. Forcing the last bits of the haze from his mind, he addressed his captain.

"Ingmar, what is going on?"

"Iron Fist, we've arrived at Ånchal."

Oldar watched as the flickering lights got closer. He smiled as he neared the outpost on the outskirts of Alocar. It had been a long time since he'd visited Ånchal. The modest fortress appeared to be abandoned thanks to the overgrowth of ivy covering its stone walls. The archers' kill slots and windows were practically invisible thanks to the blanket of green that consumed the building.

"Let's stop here for the night," Oldar told Ingmar. "We can eat and then use the tunnels to sleep. They should allow for us to spread out nicely."

"The men will like that plan," Ingmar replied. His usually controlled demeanor was undermined by his haggard appearance. Even a man of Ingmar's caliber couldn't hide the stress of the last week's events.

"I, however, will be continuing on home. The tunnels will allow for me to travel, both at my leisure, and with light."

"But, Milord –" Ingmar stammered.

Holding up his hand, Oldar silenced the older man. "I need time to collect my thoughts if I am to be addressing my people tomorrow. I don't need you to accompany me, the tunnels will protect me." Ingmar looked as though he wanted to protest, but kept his mouth closed. "Besides, if anyone is able to reach me, that'll mean that they killed you lot anyway, so there's not much point in worrying."

"As you wish," Ingmar acquiesced. "I will alert the guards of your travels."

Oldar smiled as he walked away from his guard.

The halls of Ånchal were a bit crowded as the weary men of Alocar set up camp in the tunnels. The wounded were carried inside while the dead were left in the wain in the courtyard of the fortress. A circle of smoldering incense surrounded the fallen, making sure that their spirits did not try and leave their bodies and travel through the mortal realm once more. In the stable, the horses munched on hay and took a much-needed break.

Men spoke tiredly to their countrymen, relating all of their adventures from the last. Guards from the outpost spoke animatedly to each other and rushed to bring a measure of comfort to their exhausted counterparts. A meager meal was served by the army cooks, supplemented by some of the outpost rations. Ånchal didn't experience much in the way of action, so the available food consisted of hardier meals that were meant to last for two fortnights before they needed to be replenished.

As soon as everyone was safely within the stone walls and had settled down a bit, Oldar cleared his throat. The noise died down almost immediately. Soldiers who were stationed at the outpost stopped their nightly routines to listen alongside their exhausted brothers.

"I'll keep this brief," the king said. "I leave you all tonight to get a good night's rest. I will be moving on, using the tunnels to return home, and their protection will allow for me to safely travel at night with a light. I expect to have confirmation that all of you reach Madden by mid-day. Until tomorrow."

A muffled response from his men filled the halls. Guards returned to their duties while the others sat down and tucked into their evening meal before falling asleep. Oldar met Ingmar's eyes and gave a slight nod before leading his horse through the torch-lit tunnels.

XI

Hroth opened his eyes. A groan escaped him as he struggled to prop himself up on his elbow.

"Relax, Hroth," Pram said gently. The general's hand rested on Hroth's shoulder, pushing him back down onto the bed.

A slight breeze passed through an open window, ruffling Hroth's hair. He felt miserable. His insides throbbed, as though his organs were burning. Laying down, Hroth covered his face with his hands, the mage's teeth gritted as his arms ached from the movement. A hiss escaped him.

"Where is Len?" the Flame asked. "And Wyrd?"

"Evenhand is... trying to figure things out right now," Pram said slowly. "Wyr-raji is speaking with Viir and some of the Pshwani at one of the taverns. He's starting to amass a bit of a following after his outburst."

The general looked discomfited, which made Hroth uncomfortable. He'd never seen Pram shaken before. The man always maintained an air of composure and control. Hroth's attention was pulled from the general when Len walked in the room.

"Evenhand," Pram greeted, nodding his head in respect to the leader. "What are your thoughts on the matter?"

"Wyr-raji has convinced Viir and his followers to accept him as the new leader," Len replied. "Our people want nothing to do with this conflict."

"Especially since so many of Xan are recovering from the last campaign," Zaa'ni added.

"However, I can see a number of our brothers joining him out of fear of his demon fyre," Len admitted. "I need to speak with my Eyes and Hands before word gets to them of our return. The Thurlish and obviously Qu-ari are some of our strongest allies. If we can secure their loyalties then I believe we can turn enough of the others to keep Wyr-raji out of power."

"Evenhand," Pram said, "do you really think that the Thaylan or the Hanzo would truly side with the Pshwani, even with Wyr-raji's unholy powers?"

"Fear drives men to do irrational things," Len replied. "If Wyr-raji threatens them or their kin, it's almost guaranteed that they will betray us."

Hroth tried to speak, but he could only cough.

"Hroth, how are you feeling?" Len asked.

Struggling for his voice, Hroth was able to reply. "I feel like shit, but I'll live."

"Thank you for dedication," Len said, nodding his head in respect. A rare gesture of gratitude from the young man.

"Tell me, Swordbane," Hroth croaked, "if chaos breaks loose, what will you do?"

"Wyr-raji can't possibly overthrow Len," Zaa'ni spoke out. "Len has shown time and again that –"

Len held up a hand, quieting his wife. Looking around at those in the room, the young general took a deep breath.

"Pram, I need you to speak with our Thurlish brothers. Now. I will speak with my brothers."

Pram nodded silently and made to exit the room. Len motioned for him to wait.

"Pram, will Zaa'ni and Bermet be safe here?" Len asked.

"Though we are outside the capital proper, I would feel safer if they went to Honorable Intan's home. Despite his influence, I do not see others assaulting her or her home."

Len's brow furrowed as he closed his eyes. "I would prefer not to involve Mother, but I believe you're right." Turning to his wife, he said, "Take Bermet and head out to her home immediately, before Wyr-raji comes looking for you two. Pram, have Altansari, Berkah, Elok and Kemala join them. I can't have your family becoming pawns."

"Thank you, Evenhand," Pram said, bowing.

"Hroth," Len continued. "I want you to go with them, just in case."

The Flame struggled to nod his head as another fit of coughing overtook him.

"Can he protect us from Vahnyre?" Zaa'ni asked. "Wouldn't Wyr-raji be able to find us?"

"Wyrd most likely can do some form of fire scrying," Hroth admitted. "However, I can block Vahnyre from entering my mind to an extent. I've been doing it for years. We should be safe there, as long as they don't figure out where we went."

Zaa'ni let out a sigh of relief.

Bermet and Kemala ran into the room, the two girls giggling as they hurried by.

"Let's head out," Len said. "Time is not on our side."

XII

OLDAR EXITED the tunnels and found himself in the familiar streets of Madden. His feet ached and his eyes were heavy after almost a full day's trek. Waving over the nearest soldier, Oldar handed his mount to the boy and gave instructions for the horse to be groomed and fed. Tossing the remnants of his torch to the young man, Oldar rubbed his eyes, shooing the soldier away. Once the soldier walked off with the animal, Oldar made his way towards the castle proper.

Morning had come and people bustled around in the city proper. It was a subdued commotion, however. Instead of the streets being filled with a riot of color, black silks adorned the women and hung from the storefronts. The usual cheery chatter that filled the air was gone. Instead, it was replaced with a soft murmuring. The stores that were once a riot of color from the flowers and bright tapestries were a shadow of their former selves in this time of mourning.

The young king's stomach rumbled, reminding him that a warm meal would be most welcome after all of the energy he'd spent the last couple of days. Looking around, Oldar spied a bakery. Making his way to the shop, he caught the attention of many citizens of the capitol.

I must look like quite the sight, he mused groggily. *To think that their king would be so disheveled.*

His thoughts were interrupted by someone shouting his name. Looking around tiredly, Oldar tried to spy the source of the voice. After scanning the streets, he noticed a young man quickly approaching him. The man had a baby face and blonde hair. His pink cheeks were almost comical on his cherubic face when one noted how tall and lanky the man was. He waved towards the young king and called out his name once more.

Do I know him?

The young man walked up to Oldar and clasped his hands. "By the gods it *is* you!" he exclaimed. "I'd heard that your whole family had been wiped out during the battle at Pharn. I'm so glad to see you alive!"

Oldar blinked slowly several times before his brain worked out who was wringing his hands.

"Schaed, is that you?"

"Of course! How could you forget me so quickly?" The youth's blue eyes twinkled as he feigned hurt. "I knew Alastaire was lying when he said that you'd fallen to those bastards from Xan."

"Wait, what? My uncle?" Oldar stared at his friend, perplexed.

"Didn't you hear?" Schaed asked. "When word came back that your father and mother had died, your uncle came to claim the throne since there was no one else to rule."

Oldar stared at the man in shock.

"We'd not heard anything about you, so we all assumed that you'd been killed as well. Then the queen of Zanir issued a proclamation offering sanctuary to any who'd seek it. Alastaire said that she was trying to show sympathy so that they could take over. You know how those Greys have eyed our lands for centuries."

Oldar's sleep addled brain struggled to process everything. He opened and closed his mouth several times without any sound coming out.

"But you're home and now we can go back to having a proper ruler again," Schaed continued. Clapping the exhausted king on the back, Schaed led Oldar towards the bakery with a huge smile plastered on his face.

"Come, you look famished. Let's get you something to eat before you pass out."

Oldar allowed himself to be led towards food by his friend. People gave the pair a wide berth, bowing to the king as he made his way to the bakery.

"Now I don't want to concern you," Schaed whispered, "but your uncle won't be too happy to see you. That'll mean that he has to give up his claim to the throne."

Holding up a hand to stop the babbling man, Oldar said, "Please, Schaed, let me eat and rest before we discuss what will happen next. Ghan knows I've had blessed little of either since my parents died."

"Of course, of course," Schaed said with a bob of his head. "Come, let's go."

Schaed walked a few steps ahead of Oldar and opened the bakery door. Almost instantly, the scent of freshly baked bread engulfed the king. His mouth watered and his stomach rumbled in anticipation. Blushing furiously, Oldar tried to maintain his dignity by covering the rumbling with a cough.

The shop owner pretended not to notice the noise and rushed forward to greet the king.

"Your majesty," he said with a bow. "It warms my heart to see that you've returned. Please, what would you like? I believe I have some fresh cream in the back if it would please my king."

Oldar browsed the pastries that lined the shelves. Loaves of bread, straight out of the oven, tempted him. His eyes passed over the breads and sweet breads, and landed on the braided breads. Braids with tomato and sage, some with cheese, plain ones with butter, and spiced braids called out his name, begging him to take a bite. There were even sweet ones filled with either fruit or chocolate a little further down on the shelf.

Oldar picked up one of each of the savory twists and an apple plait, the baker placing each of the braids into a cloth as the king selected them.

Reaching for his pouch, Oldar realized that he did not have any money on him.

Seeing the king move to pay, the shop owner waved his hand and pressed the bundle into Oldar's hands. "Please, your majesty, take them. After all that you've done for us, this is the least I can do for you. Eat and enjoy."

"Thank you," Oldar replied warmly. "You've made my return much more pleasant."

The baker bowed low and thanked his king once more for patronizing his shop.

Oldar turned to walk out of the bakery. He noticed that Schaed stood near the door, almost like a guard, in silence as he waited for Oldar to finish selecting his food. As Oldar started towards the door, Schaed opened it once more and led the king out into the streets.

Opening the bundle, Oldar took a deep sniff of the breads that he just got. He decided on the tomato and sage braid and pulled it out of the group. His mouth watering even before he took a bite, Oldar took another deep sniff of his meal before tackling it with ravenous hunger. He groaned softly as he savored the bread. Its soft loaves were twisted together and then reheated, giving it a crispy crust. Steam trickled out of the plait as he bit through the crust.

"My favorite is the spiced one," Schaed said while Oldar ate. "Whatever they put into it, they created something fantastic."

"I believe it's cumin," Oldar said with a full mouth. "Father got the spices from one of the clans. He had an agreement with them in exchange for our furniture or something."

"What a great trade," Schaed mused absentmindedly. "Your father was always finding the best deals for Alocar. Remember when he got us the exclusive rights to wine from the Hanzo? So many people come to us for a chance to sample our exotic wines."

"You're just saying that because you own the store that serves the wine," Oldar said with a grin.

"Yeah, I suppose that could play a part. So," Schaed said with an air of mock pompousness, "I believe that m'lord has arrived at his destination. I would love to have a chance to talk with you later, once you complete all of your royal duties and whatnot. Would you care to join me for dinner?"

"That would be most welcome," Oldar replied. "Now, if you'll excuse me, I need to unwind."

"Until tonight," Schaed said with a wave before turning around and making his way into the crowd.

Oldar suppressed a chuckle and walked in through the door.

Still as much of an empty pot as I remember.

The young king made his way through the hallway, his mind in a daze. The warmth he'd been feeling from the ale he'd consumed earlier in the morning disappeared with his snack. Now, all he felt were the aches and pains of his near constant travel over the last few days. Servants and guards snapped to attention as he walked by, but he barely noticed their presence. The beauty that he would normally stop to admire after such a long period away from home faded dully into the background.

"Welcome home, your majesty," a matronly woman greeted with a low curtsy. Her deep voice broke through the young king's daze and brought him back into the present. "If it will please my lord, I can have a bath drawn immediately for you to soak in. I can consult the herbalist to see what we can add to it to help soothe you, as well. Would that please my lord?"

Forcing his eyes to focus, Oldar realized that the voice belonged to his childhood caretaker, Pruvencia. The older woman waited patiently, her eyes crinkled as she smiled at him. She stood in front of him, her heavyset frame now besieged with wrinkles. Just like she had done when he was a child, she wore her hair in a neat bun, the grays occasionally giving way to streaks of white.

"That would be wonderful, Pru," he replied. "I would also like my night clothes laid out on my bed for right after."

"As you wish, your majesty." Pruvencia curtsied once more and bustled away as quickly as her arthritic knees would allow.

"Pru," Oldar called after her. "I would also like a set of day clothes to be laid out in my room as well. I plan on going out later this evening."

"Of course, your majesty. I will see to it that everything is to your expectations." Pruvencia hobbled her way down the hall, snagging a couple younger serving girls on her way to help her heat the water.

Oldar continued on until he found himself at his bedroom. Pushing open the mahogany door, he slunk into the room. Sloughing off his clothes, Oldar laid down on his bear skin rug. He let his body melt into the soft fur and his exhaustion consume him. He closed his eyes and gripped the pelt.

XIII

OLDAR WALKED through the hallway, refreshed after his nap and bath. Now that the grime was off of his body, he almost felt like a new man. A faint aroma of lemon wafted off of his skin, reminding him of the pleasures he'd missed the last few days. As he made his way to the throne room, Oldar strode in confidently. He wore his best silks and his father's crown that he'd retrieved after the battle at Pharn. The crown, a simple band with sapphires inlaid around the periphery, sat lightly on his head. It filled him with a sense of power to wear his father's symbol. Servants bowed as he walked by, but he barely acknowledged them.

Outside the throne room, two guards stood at attention, spear blades pointing at the ceiling. Once they noticed his approach, the pair saluted with their free hands and stepped to either side of the door. The one on the left pulled the heavy door open as he moved off to the side. The glow from a fire flickered into the afternoon light in the hallway. With a deep breath, Oldar straightened his shoulders and walked into the room.

Sitting on the throne, his uncle Alastaire rested lazily in the chair. Upon seeing his nephew, the man scrambled to straighten up, his hand flying to the armrests in an effort to look more dignified. He wore fine silks and a fur-laced cloak fastened with golden clasps. To his side, his wife, Constance, sat lightly on Gwyn's throne.

"Well, well, Oldar. What a pleasant surprise to see you. Praise be to the Fallen for your safe return," Alastaire exclaimed. His oily voice did not match the brief flicker of shock that flashed on his face.

"Darling," Constance purred, "you have no idea how worried we were about you. Blessed Zemé has answered our prayers."

"Zemé, Aunt Constance?" Oldar asked. "You've never been religious before. Then again, neither of you have been worried about me before, so I shouldn't be too surprised. Tell me, how have my people been during my absence?"

Alastaire's eyes narrowed, but his voice remained steady. "Alocar has flourished, no thanks in small part to my and your dear aunt's efforts. I don't believe that our pains deserve your hostility." He leaned forward, resting his elbows on his thighs, and tented his fingers just below his chin. "In fact, I believe that we should be honored for our energies."

"We understand that things have been difficult for you, darling. I know that after my brother's death, I found myself struggling with figuring out my place in the world. With the grief that you must be feeling, I'd imagine that coming back to rule a nation would be quite daunting. Nobody would judge you for your weakness," Constance purred.

"In fact, it would be seen as a noble act to allow for those who have Alocar's best interests in mind to govern her people," Alastaire added.

"We wouldn't keep the throne from you forever. Just until you're ready to assume the mantle," Constance said softly. "Zemé will guide you once you are ready."

Oldar stared at his relatives in disbelief. His mouth moved as he tried to sputter out something, but nothing seemed to come out.

Constance chuckled gently. "Oh, Oldar, you look like a fish."

The young man's cheeks flushed as anger filled him. A muscle twitched in his cheek as he stared at his aunt and uncle. He felt his pulse quicken as he struggled to keep his temper. "Aunt Constance," he finally managed to say, "I don't believe that it is your place to assume that I would need help managing my empire. I am more than capable of ruling Alocar without your interference."

Constance stopped laughing and narrowed her eyes at her nephew. Her hands gripped the arms of the throne so hard that her knuckles turned white. Alastaire leaned back in the chair, his arms crossed across his chest and his lips pursed.

Fueled by his emotion, Oldar plowed on. "Thank you for your interest, but I will have to ask you to leave Madden at this moment. You dishonor my parents by sitting on their thrones as false prophets. Zemé? When has any-one spoken of that ancient deity? We have moved past such obscure gods, thanks to our knowledge of the Fallen. Zemé is a myth, and one that you are foolish enough to believe in."

"Do *not* speak of the gods in such a disrespectful manner," Constance said, her tone sharp. "You have no idea of what you speak. Alocar relies on her protection; we have for many centuries."

"Aunt Constance, I do not know why you remain on my throne. We are not here to debate the existence of gods. I have asked you both to leave. Do not make me summon my guards and have them remove you two." Oldar straightened his back and jutted out his chin slightly in an attempt to make himself appear more intimidating.

Reluctantly, the two slid out of the chairs and made their way past the young king and out of the throne room. Alastaire stepped on Oldar's cloak as he passed, tugging ever so slightly at the bright fabric. His lip curled up as Oldar turned to look at him, but the man did not make eye contact with his nephew. Constance walked by with her head held high, her dark ringlets bouncing lightly with her step. Her ruby lips were plastered in a smirk, though her eyes were frosty.

As she walked past the young king, she said without turning to address him, "Be careful, dear Oldar, of how you speak about the gods. They reward those who serve them faithfully. I believe that we will be crossing paths again."

Oldar's head spun to face his retreating family, but they left the room before he could come up with a retort. The door shut with a solid thud, leaving him feeling hollow despite his efforts at rousting his relatives. Walking over to his father's throne, Oldar slumped onto the wooden seat, reluctantly pleased at the warmth that his uncle provided to the seat. He ran his hands through his hair, knocking his fingers into his father's crown and almost toppling it from his head in the process.

By the gods, this is a mess, he thought with a sigh. *Uncle won't be deterred that easily. And when did Aunt Constance get so brazen? I almost fear that she's the one pulling the strings for this move.*

Oldar took the circlet off of his head and placed it delicately in his lap before burying his face in his hands. A cry of frustration escaped his lips, only to die out as it filled the empty old stone room. The flames in the hearth crackled in response to his anguish. Other than that, no sound could be heard. Silence greeted him, a silence that did not comfort him.

I will not be cowed. I am Iron Fist. I'll show everyone what I can do.

Lifting his head from his hands, the young king placed his crown back on his head. Standing, he smoothed out his pants and strode through the throne room out into the hallway. He held his head high and kept his face composed as he passed people.

One of his servants called out to him as he moved briskly past the man, wondering where the king was going in such a hurry. Without looking back, Oldar barked out, "Gilded Rose" and continued his journey out of the castle.

∽∾∾∽

Oldar entered the Gilded Rose and looked for his favorite table. Back in his school days, he and his friends would frequent the tavern after class. His eyes scanned the bustling bar for his spot. Bobbing from side to side, Oldar smiled as he was rewarded with his table, empty, at the back of the room near the stage. He deftly wove his way between patrons and bar maids as he headed towards his prized darkened corner. Once at the table, he unclasped his cloak and hung it off of the back of his chair before placing his crown on the mahogany surface. As soon as the crown left his brow, he felt a large weight leave him. He brushed off the feeling, however, and raised his hand to summon a serving girl.

After a few seconds, he caught the eye of a young woman with dark, wavy hair. She smiled and made her way over to him. As she walked, her hips mesmerized the young king. He noticed that they also managed to entrance a number of patrons in her wake.

"What can I get ya, love?" she asked once she reached his table. She rested her hand lightly on his shoulder, causing his heart to flutter momentarily. "Something to warm you up perhaps?" The woman winked at him, squeezing his shoulder.

"I would like a glass of red wine and a hearty meal," Oldar said, swallowing as he began speaking to her.

"Of course, love. Be right back."

The bar maid gave his shoulder one last squeeze before she wandered off to get his order. Oldar found himself watching her retreat, his head tilting to the side. He was startled by a loud smack on the table right in front of him.

"I see you've met Rez'maré," Schaed said with a boyish grin as Oldar spun back to face him.

"When did they bring her on?" Oldar stammered.

"Oh, I think she's a new hire from earlier this year. Geez, Oldar, did they not let you out of your king classes?" the lanky youth nudged his friend with a smirk. "They still have Faedra, you know."

Oldar blushed as he thought of the woman he used to pine for. Grabbing Schaed's arm, he shushed the man. "Not so loud," he begged. "What if somebody heard you?"

"You mean that it's still supposed to be a secret that you became a man when you bedded her last year?" Schaed asked before breaking into raucous laughter. He slapped the table in his mirth, drawing a couple curious glances. "That's not a secret I'm afraid, my friend."

Oldar noticed that a number of patrons were looking their direction. "Please," he begged, "keep it down. Tell me that no one knows of that."

Schaed wiped a tear from his eye as he tried to stop laughing. "Of course, no one knows," he finally conceded. "They were just rumors. I'll say that our friends were quite close to what actually happened, but Faedra managed to deflect everything with grace. She was a good choice, honestly."

Oldar let out a sigh of relief and clutched his chest. "Good, I was so worried that people would find out. It wasn't my most... uh... dignified moment and I was so afraid that Father would find out. It can't get out now. My aunt and uncle would pounce on the opportunity to usurp my power."

"I won't say anything," Schaed said, raising his hand. "You have my word."

Oldar ran his hand through his hair as he took a deep breath. Schaed, noting his friend's anxious demeanor, gently thumped the young king on his arm, his boyish smile not extending to his eyes.

"I was only giving you a hard time, Oldar," he said. "Come now, don't worry about anything. Everything is fine."

Oldar struggled to smile in an effort to appease his friend. The resulting half grimace caused Schaed's to falter.

"Come, let's get a drink. You could use something to help you relax."

Oldar nodded mutely at his friend's suggestion. Almost as though she knew she was being summoned, Rez'maré returned with his meal. Placing it down on the table with a flourish, the bar maid gave him a wink as she made eye contact with him.

"Here you are, love. Can I get you anything else?"

"Rez'maré, would you fetch me a nice ale?" Schaed asked. "I could use something a bit earthy to round out my evening."

"Course you can, love," she replied. Turning her attention back to Oldar, she said softly, "Let me know if you need anything else tonight."

With a swish of her hips, Rez'maré turned to head into the back. Schaed leaned over the table and gave her backside a little pinch, causing her head to twist around quickly. Schaed grinned and pointed at the baffled Oldar, causing him to blush profusely. Her eyes narrowed momentarily before she gave the young king a coy smile. Regaining her composure quickly, she continued to wiggle her hips as she made her way to the backroom.

Once she was out of earshot, Oldar spun to face his friend, his mouth opened in shock. Schaed laughed and held up his hands.

"I couldn't help it," he tried to reason. Seeing that the king's expression didn't change, he continued, "It's what we do. We give each other a hard time. Just watch, when she comes back, she'll get her revenge."

Oldar shook his head in disbelief.

"Things have changed, Oldar. We've all got our own interests now. Cassius disappeared a short while ago after meeting a pretty one. We haven't heard from him since he left Madden with her."

"What of the others?"

"Disappeared. Probably married, but I haven't been able to stay in contact because they didn't leave me their address to write. Theros was the first to leave; wandered out to try his luck in Ro'thre he said. Then there was Cassius, followed by Xia'neth, Lang, and Erymous. Lang and Erymous headed out to the Bone Coast. No idea what happened to Xia'neth."

"I didn't think the group would change so much once I left," he mumbled.

"No one did."

"An ale for the mister," Rez'maré said as she plopped down Schaed's ale. A bit of liquid sloshed out of the mug and landed on the table. "Apologies, good sir," she said as she pulled a rag out of her skirt to clean up the mess. As she finished mopping up the spill, she flicked the moist rag at Schaed, causing more than a few droplets to splash him. "I hope you both enjoy," she said with one final wink before sauntering off.

Oldar and Schaed stared as Rez'maré swished away to attend to her next patron.

"I told you she would do something," Schaed said before breaking out into laughter.

Oldar hesitated for a moment before joining in. It felt good to laugh, lifted his spirits higher than they'd been in a long time. The two shared a hearty chuckle, catching the eyes of some of their neighbors. Oldar wiped his eye before picking up his glass of wine. Raising it up as if in toast, Schaed lifted his mug as well.

"Here's to the start of a long and prosperous reign," Schaed said with a smile. "To the King of Alocar."

Oldar closed his eyes as he smiled. He tried to envision a future where people respected him. His body filled with warmth as he saw his people staring at him with adoration. Cheers erupted as he walked by, as did several people calling out his name. A new age was dawning.

"To me."

XIV

BODY ACHING, Cienna stumbled through the gates of Pharn behind a contingent of her soldiers. Her muscles begged her to just lay down, but she knew she must check in on her mother to see if the queen was well. As she broke off from the group, she heard Brody giving instructions to the men. Her senses were startled as she made her way separately towards the caer. Muted colors, a shadow of their former glory, greeted her eyes as a dull chatter filled the air. An occasional tinkle of a lady's laughter broke through the constant noise.

A yeasty aroma filled the air, causing her stomach to rumble. It broke through the stale scent of sweat that she'd become accustomed to over the last few days. Had the musky scent of man always been around her, or did she just never notice how pleasant things could smell in the city? Blushing slightly, she noted a faint musk followed her.

By the gods, this is embarrassing. I need to bathe. Has it really been that long?

The hurried pounding of boots on stone caught her attention.

"Princess, I don't think that it's best for you to wander around on your own, even if it is in Pharn," Brody said as he caught up to her. "We need to figure out how best to address all that's happened since we've left."

"I know, Brody. I just want a good meal and some sleep though." Her eyes burned as she struggled to keep them open. "Where is Caitlyn?"

Brody's eyes dropped briefly. "I think she went to be by herself."

A lump formed in Cienna's stomach as she thought of the feisty redhead and her journey in silence. "She's been through so much," she muttered. "Brody, once I've had a chance to refresh myself, I need you to go and check up on her. Make sure she doesn't leave Pharn until I've had the opportunity to speak with her. I want to thank her for all she's done."

"I'll see what I can do. She's pretty good at slipping away."

"All we can do is be there for her. I got the feeling that she doesn't have much in the way of family."

"You'd be right about that," Brody admitted. "Let's get you taken care of and then I will go look for her."

Lightly touching Brody on the forearm, Cienna attempted to smile. In her tired state, it looked more like a wince. Her eyes blurred the scenery in front of her as she turned back around and began trudging toward her home. The princess' feet scraped on the worn cobblestones as her boots barely lifted off of the ground. Her body ached from the combination of riding and walking for the last few days. Muscles that she didn't even know she'd used throbbed with each step. Finally, the entrance to the citadel loomed overhead.

"Blessed Aria, I never thought that home would look so beautiful," Cienna breathed. "I could just melt into the first chair I see."

Leading the way, Brody motioned for the guards to open the doors and let them in without any questions. As the princess crossed the threshold, Brody directed her through the halls. At one point, he stopped a servant to find out the queen's whereabouts. The two chatted briefly as Cienna leaned against the smooth stone wall. A gentle breeze played with her curls, tickling her nose with a strand of hair. The servant glanced towards the princess on several occasions, concern etched on her face. After a getting the information he needed, Brody dismissed the girl and lightly directed the princess' body to start moving down the hall again.

"How are you not dead tired?" Cienna asked, not even bothering to cover her yawn.

"I've been on a couple missions during training," Brody said. "All of the new recruits are made to undergo a three-day extensive training trip, kind of like the one Al went on at the spice mines. We get one or two of the older guys to lead us in groups of five or so. Most of the time, we just spend our time tracking a boar or some game like that. Very rarely do we actually have to worry about combat."

"What was your first outing?"

"Don't you remember? Bannen took me to the Isles with Al and the others." Brody's normally twinkling eyes grew dark as he recalled the experience. "I was only nineteen, and Zanir hadn't seen any real action in a long time. Sure, the pirates raze the coasts from time to time, destroying everything that the people worked to build, but for the most part they contained themselves to tavern brawls. This was different."

His voice trailed off until he fell quiet. Cienna walked alongside him in uncomfortable silence. The haze that clouded her mind momentarily cleared as her concern for the man took over. Tentatively, she reached out and touched his hand. His calloused fingers wrapped around her hand, but he did not look at her. Squeezing him, the two continued on.

After rounding a corner, Brody broke free from the princess' grip. Ahead of them stood Hera and her hand maiden, Aeliana. The queen stood in front of a tapestry, her hands clasped behind her back as she stared at the image in front of her. Aeliana turned at the sound of approaching footsteps and dipped into a curtsy at the sight of the princess. The hand maiden's attention was brought back to her lord when Hera spoke.

"Aeliana, have we received any word about my daughter?"

Cienna strode hastily towards her mother and embraced the queen roughly from the side, startling the woman. The princess buried her head into her mother's shoulder, willing herself not to cry. All trace of exhaustion vanished when she saw her mother.

"By the gods," Hera swore. "Cienna, you're home." The queen's voice shook somewhat as she brought her hand to her daughter's head, burying it in Cienna's curly hair. "Praise be to Freyna that you've been brought home to me safely."

Taking a steadying breath, Cienna forced herself to lift her head from the queen's shoulder. A wave of dizziness threatened to overwhelm her as she moved, leaving her lightheaded for a fleeting moment. She worked to maintain her composure as she righted herself. Once the dizzy spell passed, she tried to speak to her mother. However, Hera cut her off.

"I take it that everything has worked out in our favor?" Hera's eyes were hopeful as she stared at her daughter. "We didn't have too many losses, I hope?" Turning to Brody, Hera smiled. "Thank you for keeping my Cienna safe."

Brody bowed deeply. "My pleasure, your majesty."

"Mother," Cienna interjected, "I think we need to sit down. There's much to discuss about the last few days."

"Oh? Yes, let's go find a quiet room. Aeliana, fetch Cienna and her guard something to eat. You two must be famished after your travels."

Aeliana nodded as she dipped into a curtsy.

Hera glanced at the two standing before her. Noting the dirt and blood that caked their bodies, she added: "I think that both could also do with a nice hot cloth to wipe themselves down with while they wait for their meal. It looks as though they could really use it."

"Yes, your majesty," Aeliana said before scurrying off down the hall.

"Mother, please. I just need a chair to sit in so I can rest my feet properly," Cienna whined. In her state, she didn't care that she sounded like a child. All she wanted was to be able to relax.

"Now, Cienna," Hera tutted. "Cleaning yourself will do more good for you than you realize. Come, let's go to the library."

Cienna closed her mouth and moved to follow her mother.

Brody cleared his throat softly to catch the queen's attention. "If it is all right with you, your majesty, I do have some matters to attend to down in the city. Perhaps I can send someone in my stead? Perhaps Thol or Ronan to recount what happened?"

Holding up her hand, Hera shook her head gently. "I will send somebody to fetch you once I've finished talking with Cienna. Do not go too far into the city. I don't want to have to look too hard to find you."

"Of course, your majesty. You should be able to find me in the Hoary Oak. I'll be stopping by there to grab a bite to eat while I finish my business."

"Very good. We'll see you soon."

Brody bowed once more before turning smartly on his heel and making his way out of the caer.

Once he rounded the corner, Hera turned to her daughter. "I suppose that it'll be just the two of us for a while then. Come."

The two women moved through the keep at a leisurely pace, Cienna still falling further and further behind her mother with each corner they rounded. Tapestries and statues blended together into a blur of taupe and other earthy tones. Any color in the bright pieces only appeared as a splash of pigment against the neutral backdrop. The breeze from earlier that morning brushed against her face, waking her out of her stupor for a few seconds before the warmth of the day lulled her back into her daze.

Hera's voice droned on in the background, the words lost on Cienna. Occasionally, she heard praises to the gods or something about the headmistress, but nothing more. Hera seemed content to carry on while the princess trudged in silence. Cienna struggled to focus on what was being said. She missed all of her mother's ramblings about how the headmistress helped her find her voice right after the king died, and how Hera's praise to the gods was about Cienna's safe return. She did notice, however, the small effigy with periwinkle hair that her mother carried with her.

Mother seems to have recovered from the shock of losing Father, Cienna mused. *I never would've imagined her to be this excited over anything other than gowns and jewelry. Too bad she has no idea what we're all about to experience. And why is she carrying a doll with her?*

After what felt like an eternity, Hera stopped outside an oaken door. A brass knocker rested against the worn woodgrain. The plate was worn from where the ring struck against it. Splinters were starting to form in the middle of the door. A rune of knowledge was carved into the stone at the top of the door arch.

Cienna forced her mind to focus as she stood behind her mother in front of the entryway. Vaguely, she thought she heard her mother talk about the centuries' worth of wisdom that lay behind the doors. Or was it about diplomacy? Everything sounded so muted and far away.

Blessedly, Hera pushed open the door and walked over to her chair. Cienna trailed behind, her eyes catching on a nearby chair with a pillow leaning against the back. Hera continued speaking as Cienna scurried over to the chair and sank into it, her head coming to rest on the cushion that she grabbed as she sat down. Hera's eyes widened as she watched her daughter melt into the seat before smirking. Pulling a book off of the window sill, Hera sat quietly.

How can she be reading at a time like this? Cienna thought indignantly. *One would think that Mother's sensibilities would change now that the fate of Zanir rests in her hands.*

Cienna fumed mutely. She didn't even realize that her eyelids drooped ever so slowly with each second until she fell asleep.

XV

CAITLYN WANDERED into the Hoary Oak. The heady scent of mead coupled with Fren's stew made her mouth water. Her stomach growled as she made her way through the tavern towards a table in the back. Fren stood behind the bar counter rubbing a tumbler with a rag. He looked up as she walked by, eliciting a wide grin on his cherubic face.

"By the gods, I haven't seen you in a long time, Caitlyn," he exclaimed. "How have you been, my dear? Come, come. Have a seat and tell me about all that you have been up to."

The portly man put down the glass and pulled out a flagon and two short glasses. Pouring the amber liquid into both of the glasses, he proffered one to the redhead. Caitlyn grabbed the drink and half-heartedly pulled herself onto a stool. She downed the contents of the cup fairly quickly, drawing a bout of raucous laughter from the barkeep.

"Some things never change, do they?" he asked with a wink. "I always said that you could drink almost any man under the table. I see you haven't lost that talent."

Fren refilled her glass before taking a drink of his own. With a contented sigh, he took a look at his drink. Satisfied with everything, he smiled and placed the glass down on the counter. Picking up his rag once more, he waved it in the air to catch the bar maid's attention.

Averna sauntered over once she spied the movement. Several poorly disguised cries of disappointment erupted from the patrons in the tavern as she sashayed away from them and made her way to the bar. Throwing a seductive look over her lightly freckled shoulder, Averna purred, "I'll be back in a minute, boys. Don't you fret none." A wink sealed the deal and the men reluctantly returned to their food and drinks.

As she made her way to the bar, she called out to Fren. Caitlyn turned around and was pleased to see Averna's smile falter when she spied the archer. *I'm glad she at least has the dignity to seem abashed in my presence.*

Not wanting to appear frazzled, Averna leaned against the bar counter and pressed her bosom against it. "You called, Fren?"

"Yes, my dear." Fren beamed at his bar maid. "This," he said, gesturing towards Caitlyn, "is someone very special to me. Why don't you fetch her a plate of duck and vegetables? She looks famished."

"Please, Fren, you don't have to do that," Caitlyn protested.

"Nonsense," the portly man said with a wave of his hand. "I insist. Averna, darling, please be a dear."

"Of course, Fren." Averna replied. "I'll be back in a moment." Turning around, Averna walked towards the back of the tavern to get the food. Her hips swayed gently back and forth as she glided between the tables. More than one pair of eyes looked up in longing as she passed by.

Caitlyn watched the retreating bar maid, a knot of disgust forming in her stomach.

"She's such a sweet girl," Fren said to the back of Caitlyn's head.

"Yes, yes she is," Caitlyn replied distractedly as she turned back to face him.

"So, my dear, tell me what you've been doing these last few years. I've missed you."

"Well," she said, taking a deep breath, "a lot has changed since I last saw you."

Fren leaned his elbows against the counter top and rested his chin in his hands.

Caitlyn took a long draught of her mead, trying to think of a way to continue. "I've been working with the king's horses out in the moors near the border. It's been quite the challenge breaking some of them."

"Oh, I can only imagine," Fren replied. "A little thing like you working to tame them. I always knew that your stubbornness would help you go far. I never realized that it would lead you to working for King Jaste though, may he rest in the Halls of the Fallen for eternity. Alverick sure knew a winner when he met you."

Fren beamed at Caitlyn. She smiled weakly back at him, her eyes dropping to stare at her mug, unable to look at the man.

"Here we are," Averna's voice rang out behind her. Sliding the plate in front of Caitlyn, the bar maid gave her a wink. "As an esteemed guest of Fren's I figured that he wouldn't mind me bringing you a little dessert with your meal." Averna presented a bowl of mixed berries to Caitlyn. She placed the fruit next to the hot plate of food. "I hope you enjoy."

"Averna, stay with us for a moment," Fren said. "Caitlyn is about to tell me more about what she's been up to lately. I'm sure she has some news about Alverick as well."

Averna daintily smoothed her skirt before taking a seat upon one of the bar stools. She combed out her wavy red hair with her fingers and let it come to rest over her bare shoulder. Her eyes stared demurely at Caitlyn, avoiding prolonged eye contact with the redhead. Fren leaned forward, waiting for her to continue.

Dammit, I can't do this.

Suddenly, she wasn't hungry anymore. Her stomach felt hollow, but she forced herself to take a bite of potato to buy herself more time. The delicately spiced potatoes tasted bland to her. Caitlyn struggled to swallow down the morsel, finally taking a long drought of mead to help wash it down.

"I... Fren... I don't know how to say this, but things have been a little... stressful the last few days," Caitlyn began.

"Ah, yes. King Jaste, may he rest in the Halls of the Fallen, was a great soul and has left us too soon," Fren bowed his head in reverence. "I'm sure that there's been much mourning in the outer villages as news has spread."

"It's more than that," Caitlyn replied. "We went out to confront the man who killed our king, to confront Swordbane, and in the process lost Alverick."

Fren's jaw dropped. Averna let out a stifled gasp as she quickly brought her hand to cover her mouth.

"Lost, my dear?" Fren stuttered. "Like, he's split up from your party?"

Caitlyn shook her head.

"My boy," Fren groaned into his hands. "No."

Averna covered her mouth with both hands, her body trembling slightly. The color had drained from her already fair face, leaving her skin an ashy color.

The noise from the other patrons seemed muted to Caitlyn. Though they talked and laughed in the background, it felt as though she was in a bubble with Fren and Averna. The tavern owner's moans went unnoticed by his customers. He rocked back and forth, his elbows atop the bar, cradling his face in his hands. The bar maid's whimpers fell on deaf ears.

"I'm so sorry," Caitlyn whispered.

"My boy. My boy."

Tears welled in Caitlyn's eyes as she watched the grieving man. She tried to pull her eyes away, but couldn't bring herself to do so. Her hands shook as she interlaced her fingers in an effort to keep them steady on the counter surface. Caitlyn's eyes burned and her breathing became ragged.

After several long minutes, Fren lifted his tear-streaked face out of his hands. His eyes, usually so happy and full of joy, were filled with a pain that Caitlyn couldn't even fathom. His shoulders shook as he tried to take deep, steadying breathes. Looking up, Fren made eye contact with Caitlyn.

"Oh, sweet girl. Come here."

Fren walked around the bar towards Caitlyn and wrapped her in a tight embrace. As though a dam had broken, Caitlyn found herself sobbing softly into his shoulders. The barkeep rubbed her back and made soothing noises to calm her down.

"It's all right," he whispered into her ear. "Thank you for letting me know."

How can he be so sympathetic at a time like this? I can't even forgive Dez for what she did, and here he is treating me like his daughter. Al was so lucky to have him.

Caitlyn steadied herself and pulled away from his embrace, wiping a tear as she did so. Tears ran down Fren's cheeks, the only sign of his grief now. Glancing to the side, Caitlyn watched as Averna sat numbly in her seat. Her eyes were red and puffy.

She must have truly loved him.

Wiping her eyes on the back of her sleeve, Caitlyn straightened up in her stool and cleared her throat. It was suddenly so dry. She brought the mug to her lips and took a long pull on her mead, allowing for Fren to make his way back behind the bar and for Averna to smooth out her skirt.

Caitlyn's eyes darted around the Hoary Oak, no one seemed to really notice the trio. Several pairs of eyes scanned the tavern, searching for the young bar maid. Once they spied her sitting at the bar facing away from them, they dropped their heads and continued their conversation. More than one moved to get up from their table, only to be grabbed and shamed into sitting down once more.

Returning her attention to the duo, Caitlyn addressed them again. "He may not be completely lost," she said softly. "I have to hold out hope that we will be able to bring him back."

"Is that possible?" Averna squeaked.

"There you are!" Brody's voice managed to ring out, pulling Caitlyn from her muted bubble.

Heads swiveled towards the entrance and the general din subsided briefly as curiosity took over. Caitlyn watched as Brody made his way towards the bar where she sat. As he wove his way through the tables, the men returned to their meals and conversations. However, several soft conversations about the arrival of the disheveled soldier sprung up. Furtive glances were shot towards the group as Brody joined them.

"I'm so glad I could find you, Cait," Brody said. "I thought I'd find you here. Fren, I take it you've heard the news?"

The portly man nodded his head, wiping his cheek with the back of his hand. "I found out about Bannen right after you left. I know Alverick was like a brother to you, so this must have hit you especially hard."

"Thank you, Fren," Brody said, returning the gesture. "I haven't really had time to process everything properly. I mean, yes, I thought about it during our return, but I expect the next few days will be quite difficult."

Brody trailed off, his eyes looking into the distance. Caitlyn noticed that it took some effort for Brody to bring himself back and focus on the three. In the dim light of the tavern, his hollow cheeks and haunted eyes gave him a haggard appearance. The effect was enhanced by his sudden weight loss over the last few days.

I probably look just like him, she mused.

Caitlyn brought her hand to stomach and rubbed her hand up and down. She noted that her ribs felt a bit more prominent than she remembered. As if on cue, her stomach rumbled loudly, drawing the attention of

Fren, Brody, and Averna. Caitlyn's cheeks flushed and hastily grabbed her fork, spearing a piece of duck on the tines and shoving it into her mouth.

Fren cracked a smile. Averna jumped off of her stool as though she had been burned.

"Oh shit!" she swore softly. "My tables. I'm sorry to leave, Fren, but I have a couple people waiting on me to bring them new drinks." Straightening up her skirt and brushing a drop of moisture out of her eyes, Averna scurried off towards the back to fetch the drinks. Despite her haste, she managed to maintain her customary wiggle with each step, much to the delight of those she walked past.

Fren picked up his rag and resumed his cleaning of the mugs. He tried to mask the pain, but his eyes betrayed him. Caitlyn fiddled with the food on her plate, pushing it around with her fork. Fren noticed her actions and gently touched her hand.

"Eat, my dear," Fren said warmly. "Your food will go cold if you don't hurry." Seeing Caitlyn's hesitance, he added, "I don't blame you for anything. You tried to let an old man down gently, and I appreciate that." Reaching over the counter, he cupped her cheek. "You're a good girl. I hope you can find my boy and bring him back to me. But first, you need to eat and regain your strength."

Tears welled in Caitlyn's eyes as he removed his hand. Placing the clean cup down, Fren nodded to Brody and then hurried out from behind the bar to help Averna as she emerged from the back with a tray of drinks. Caitlyn watched as the pair worked to distribute the beverages to their patrons. She absentmindedly took another bite of food, her stomach enjoying the warm meal. She reached for a berry and plopped it into her mouth. As she bit down, the bittersweet juices exploded, providing a welcome treat to the redhead.

Brody placed his hand on her shoulder, startling her as she watched the people in the tavern. Spinning her head around, she locked eyes with the young man. Brody gave her shoulder a squeeze and moved a strand of hair out of her face and behind her ear.

"Are you going to be okay, Cait?"

She shook her head in a non-committal response. "There has to be something we can do," she said finally.

"We are. Cienna is in a meeting with her mother right now. I need you to help me talk to the queen about what else needs to be done and how to handle the new alliance with Swordbane and the crumbling one with Oldar."

"Not them, Brody. Al. There must be a way to bring Al back from that other dimension."

Brody sighed and ran his hand through his matted hair. "Cait, who could possibly have any information about the other re— Vashe. She may know." His chest welled in excitement as he felt a surge of hope.

Putting her fork down, Caitlyn stared at Brody, hope shining in her eyes. "What do you mean?"

"Think about it. She's headmistress of the Mageri and has a close relationship with Dez. In fact, she refers to Dez as her master, I think. I also know that she has some Shadow tattoos, so she'd be able to open a portal, I would imagine. She's the best chance we have."

"Wouldn't it be better to look for Dez? We know for sure that she can cross into the other realm. We saw that with our own eyes," Caitlyn tried to reason.

"Dez is unreliable. She shows signs of Snapping and it's impossible to get a straight answer from her."

"She seemed to be more forthcoming as we returned."

"She's acting in her best interest," Brody hissed. Dropping his voice and leaning in towards Caitlyn, he motioned for her to do the same. "I spoke with Dez the day she started to tell us of some of her history. I admit, I believe she was forthright with me when we talked. She spoke of voices in the wind, that they warned her of danger."

"What do you mean?" Caitlyn asked, her voice barely a whisper.

"Ancient powers are stirring. We've just touched the surface of the matter. She said —"

Brody paused as the door of the Hoary Oak opened. Caitlyn's eyes followed his as they looked to see who entered the establishment. In the light of the doorway, a voluptuous figure with thick, wavy hair cast a lengthy shadow. Brody shielded his eyes in an effort to protect them from the sun. Closing the door, the figure looked around. As his eyes readjusted to the light he froze. A sharp intake of breath could be heard next to him as Caitlyn watched Dez make her way into the tavern proper.

The woman's eyes scanned the building. Her eyes passed over Brody and Caitlyn several times before she made her way to the bar. A few of the patrons paused their meal to stare at Dez as she walked to her seat. One of the men wolf whistled at the woman, but she did not seem to notice.

"Did she not see us?" Caitlyn breathed. "I could have sworn she looked right at me."

"As did I," Brody muttered.

Dez sat down at the bar a little way from the two. She spoke softly to herself and looked down the entire time. Brody and Caitlyn shared a glance.

"*What's going on?*" Caitlyn mouthed.

Brody shook his head subtly.

"Zemé is lost," Dez said. Caitlyn and Brody looked over at the woman, startled. She continued to talk to herself, her hands gesturing as she spoke. "If I could find her, I would, but right now we need to speak with the queen."

A brief silence followed before she started speaking once more.

"Honestly, sometimes you pull me in different directions. I don't know what you want."

Fren approached the babbling woman from behind the bar and greeted her warmly. Sweat beaded on his brow as though he moved quickly to serve her. "Good afternoon, Miss." His demeanor, though still a bit despondent, regained much of his previous enthusiasm. "What brings you to the Hoary Oak?"

Dez gradually looked up, her eyes focusing on the man in front of her. "Why, I believe that I would like a strong drink." Catching the stares from Brody and Caitlyn next to her, she added, "And maybe something sweet, like my friends over here have."

"Are you a friend of Brody and Caitlyn's?" Fren asked.

"Oh, yes. We've been through a lot together," Dez said with a wink at the two. "Although, I would wager that they would say that I can be a bit of a nuisance at times."

"Well, any friend of these two is a friend of mine. Let me work on getting you that drink." Fren turned and busied himself with pouring Dez her beverage.

Dez got off of her stool and made her way towards Brody and Caitlyn. "Well, well. I didn't expect to find you two here," she said with a smile. "Things seem to be looking up for me."

"What is going on, Dez?" Brody asked in hushed tones. "You wander off as soon as we reach the city gates, and now you show up here talking to yourself. Who is Zemé?"

Dez's smile faltered. "Where did you hear about Zemé?"

"You were talking about her being lost," Caitlyn said incredulously. "Not to mention, she's the patron goddess of the farmers of Alocar. Not many speak of her though," Caitlyn admitted, "since the arrival of the Siblings during King Ilom's reign. She is seen as somewhat of a relic by those who speak of her."

Dez's face relaxed. "So, people are still worshipping dear Zemé. That warms my heart."

"Dez," Brody said, trying to keep the eccentric woman focused. "Does this have anything to do with what you told me a few days ago?"

"I'm afraid it does," she said with a sigh. "Zemé is just one of the powers that stir. She's quite fragile though, despite her age. I was hoping to meet up with her before she's captured."

Caitlyn looked at Brody, confusion etched into her face. *"What in the hells?"* she mouthed.

Brody held up his hand to silence her.

"The winds speak of a great darkness that is slowly beginning to cover Corinth. If Zemé is walking amongst Man like the winds suggest I must act fast to try and stop it. This is why I wanted to meet with your queen," Dez explained. "Not only should she be warned, but so must young Vashe. Although, I feel as though she may already be aware of what's happening."

"Brody," Caitlyn muttered. "Maybe she should be brought to Queen Hera. It may also be helpful if Cienna hears this too."

"I suppose you're right," Brody reluctantly agreed. "All right. We leave as soon as you finish your meal."

"Thank you, Brody," Dez said.

"Here we go," Fren said, almost on cue. "A tankard of our strongest ale and a bowl of mixed berries for you, Miss. I hope you enjoy."

"They look delightful. I'll savor them," Dez replied. As Fren walked away to return to his duties, she winked at Brody and Caitlyn, "To a tasty meal." Raising her tankard in salute, she took a long pull on the earthy beverage.

"Oh, what the hell," Caitlyn sighed. She raised her mug as well and took a drink before digging in to her meal. The duck and potatoes, though they had cooled, satisfied her hungry stomach.

Brody watched awkwardly as the two women tucked in to their respective meals. Occasionally, he snatched a berry from Caitlyn's bowl, earning a disapproving scowl from the redhead. Finally, the two finished their food and were ready to go.

Almost as if on cue, the door to the Hoary Oak opened and a young page covered in sweat called out panting, "Is Sir Brody in here?" The boy clutched at his side, massaging a stitch as he struggled for breath.

Brody waved his hand and stood up. Relief flooded the boy's face as he realized that he found who he was looking for. The two women followed Brody's lead and stood up as well. Caitlyn and Dez dropped a few coins on the counter to cover their tab before walking behind Brody out of the tavern. Waving good bye to Fren, Caitlyn also caught Averna's eye and gave a little nod to her as well. The young bar maid smiled faintly as she went about her duties.

The sun shone brightly as Caitlyn followed the others out of the tavern. She shielded her eyes as she walked out into the street. Ahead of her, Brody spoke with the young boy quietly. The muted noise from earlier that morning gave way to the familiar chatter and bustle that she remembered. Though the vibrancy of the people and shops was still subdued, there was an occasional splash of color either on a young lady's ensemble or in a shop window to remind her of the beauty that was once Pharn.

"Her Majesty, Queen Hera, needs you rather urgently," the boy was telling Brody.

"Understood," Brody replied.

As the group headed towards the caer, Caitlyn looked around. Everything reminded her of Alverick. Shadows of him walking through the streets, a dessert pastry in his hand, by her side flashed in front of her. She watched as he crouched down to scratch a stray dog behind the ear in the shade of a doorway. A smile tugged at her lips as she watched Alverick run down the street and launch himself into a maple tree as a pig chased him. The beast growled at him as Caitlyn, Bannen, and Brody laughed at Alverick from the safety of a clothier's shop.

The silhouette of the keep loomed ahead, dissipating the images that she saw and bringing her back to the present. Looking ahead, she saw Brody trying to engage the page in light conversation to distract him from Dez talking to herself once more. The boy stared at the woman uncomfortably, edging ever so slightly closer to Brody as they walked.

I've started keeping some unusual company thanks to Al, Caitlyn mused. *Gods, if we get him back, I'll never let him live it down.*

XVI

OLDAR HOBBLED out of the Gilded Rose with Schaed, his stomach full from the large meal he'd just consumed. He was pleased that his friend had pushed him to get an order of the honey cakes after all. Oldar couldn't remember the last time he'd enjoyed the treats. The king licked his fingers as he walked, savoring the sticky residue that stuck to them.

"That was divine," Oldar sighed contentedly. "I don't remember the Rose having desserts like that. If I knew they served stuff like that, I'd be three stone heavier. Like I need another excuse for people to mock me."

"It's because you have bold ideas for one so young," Schaed replied absentmindedly. He too licked the sticky honey off of his fingers as he walked through the streets. "People don't like change. They can't take people seriously when they talk about it. It's all a load of shite, really. In the end, change happens and they either adapt or they flounder. No middle ground."

"But I want to make sure that we succeed," Oldar said. "Alocar is only as strong as her people. If too many falter, she will fail."

Schaed walked in silence next to his king, giving Oldar time to think about his next plan of action. Much needed to be done to ensure an effective and smooth transition.

I'll probably need to meet with Rolaire and find out all that Mother and Father were doing. Perhaps I should bring Pru with me. It would feel odd to not have her around as much if I start listening to Rolaire as my main confidante. Oldar brought his hand to his mouth, but hastily forced it down to his side. He wouldn't chew on his fingers anymore. A leader did not show weakness.

As the sun began its descent below the horizon, the lamp-lighters made their rounds through the capital. As little balls of light began dotting the streets, the children and animals wandering about started to disappear. Instead, they were replaced with young couples walking arm in arm. Occasionally, an older couple would go by, nodding politely to their king.

Schaed began whistling a jaunty tune as he walked, his arms folded behind his head as he strolled leisurely next to Oldar. Oldar watched as the man's eyes lingered on the backside of several young women as they ambled along with their male companions in the early evening. Schaed caught Oldar watching him and winked in his direction as a shapely brunette passed. The king couldn't help but chuckle.

Ahead, Oldar watched a finely dressed couple walk out of the Moon Shine Inn, an inn that catered to the higher-class patrons. The man wore a crimson silk cloak and black breeches, while the woman dressed in a cobalt blue gown with a fox fur shawl draped over her shoulders. Her short hair was twisted into a low bun. The man turned to speak with his wife and Oldar saw the short beard and angular nose of his uncle.

"Ghan's mercy," Oldar swore quietly.

Schaed stopped whistling and arched an eyebrow. Oldar shook his head and brought his finger to his lips. Pointing towards his relatives, he looked around for a way to bypass them without being seen. An alley caught his eye and he motioned for Schaed to follow him. The two moved stealthily towards the passage, attempting to keep a casual gait without making too much noise. Schaed made his way through the mouth of the side street and Oldar moved to follow. The king let out a sigh of relief as he almost disappeared from the main street.

Almost as if on cue, a drunken bellow rent the air. "Lawds above! Yaaahr majesty!"

Oldar froze, his body stiff at the mouth of the alley. Turning his head in, what he hoped, a casual manner, he looked to see who addressed him and if anyone else noticed. A couple of people stood gawping at the king, leaning precariously to the side as they struggled to keep their balance after a night of heavy drinking. Scanning further down the road, Oldar noticed that his uncle and aunt stood staring at him. Alastaire's lips curled slightly at the edges as he watched the interaction.

"Gawds be bless'd as seein' yew aaaht 'ere," the drunk rambled on. "Happy ter 'ave yew back."

A general grumbling of agreement could be heard. The muttering was quickly drowned out as the door of the Moon Shine opened and the merry chatter from the inn filled the streets. Glasses could be heard clinking as a harpist played distantly in the background.

"Why yes," Alastaire cut in. "It is wonderful seeing you here, Oldar."

The king's uncle made his way towards Oldar, bumping into the drunk as he approached his nephew. The inebriate staggered as he worked to maintain his balance. Failing, the man dropped to the ground in a tangle of arms and legs. He protested his treatment incoherently as he attempted to return to his feet. The task took several endeavors before he managed to right himself.

"Why, hello, Uncle. Aunt Constance," Oldar greeted stiffly. "It's a surprise seeing you out in this part of the city."

"We've always treated ourselves to a show at the Moon Shine," Constance said in her sickly-sweet voice. "We used to go with your parents on several occasions, in fact."

A lump formed in Oldar's chest at the mention of his parents.

Did they really come here?

"We also thought it would be a good way to give you time to cool off from this morning," Alastaire continued. "Your aunt and I know how difficult it is to try and maintain a level of decorum when you're exhausted and starving. Don't you worry, your little outburst from this morning has been forgiven."

Alastaire spoke loudly and clearly, his voice echoing down the street. Several more people stopped walking to watch the interaction. Most just moved on, pretending that they didn't see the king and his family as they talked amongst the undesirables stumbling about.

"We're just glad to see you have recovered so quickly," Constance added. "You're strong, like your mother."

Oldar's head swam as he tried to process everything.

What's going on? What are they playing at?

"It's late out," Alastaire resumed. "Why don't we go back and continue our previous conversation next to the hearth. There's a slight bite in the air and I would hate for your aunt to get sick. Her health hasn't been as strong since her brother's death."

"Besides, darling," Constance purred, "you don't seem to be in a shape to be wandering out in the city by yourself right now."

"I'm perfectly capable of caring for myself, Aunt Constance," Oldar shot back. "I thank you for your concern though."

Those who had been previously stopped in the street all made to leave. Even the drunken man who was hovering behind his uncle and rambling belligerently wandered off. Oldar felt his face flush as he thought he caught someone mumbling about the state of Alocar's affairs as they walked away. Glancing towards the alleyway, Oldar saw Schaed, watching just out of his uncle's range of vision. The lanky man raised an eyebrow, as though asking if he should step out of his hiding spot, his hands held up in a questioning manner. Oldar shook his head imperceptibly.

"Come, Oldar, listen to your aunt. She only has your best interests at heart," Alastaire said. "Let us go to the castle and rest our feet."

Oldar turned to face his family, his face resigned. His shoulders dropped as he started walking towards the couple. He held his head level, but his eyes would not meet his relatives' faces as he approached. Glancing up, Oldar noted the smug look on his uncle's face. Alastaire's eyes twinkled and a hungry smile tugged at his lips.

"Oy, Oldar!" Schaed called out as he emerged from the alley. "Is that really you?"

Oldar turned, confused.

"I can't believe it. It really is you!" Schaed walked up to the king and clapped him on the back. "When I heard that you and your parents were involved in that fight at Pharn, I was afraid that we wouldn't see you again. I mean, you were never one for combat."

Schaed grinned at his friend and looked up to face a scowling Alastaire. Constance chewed the inside of her cheek as she narrowed her eyes. Schaed's eyes widened in surprise and exclaimed, "Oh! I'm so sorry. Did I interrupt anything?"

"N-no, Schaed," Oldar stuttered. "I was just talking with my aunt and uncle when you walked up."

"I don't want to interrupt," Schaed said waving his hands awkwardly. "We should catch up sometime. It's good seeing you back."

Slapping Oldar on the back, the lanky man grinned at the king before turning to Alastaire and Constance and doing the same to them. Schaed then made his way past Oldar, in the direction of the castle. Oldar watched as his friend started to disappear. Struck with the strangeness of it all, Oldar managed to pull himself out from his uncle's power over him and focus his thoughts.

"Thank you again, Uncle, for your concern, but I meant what I said earlier today," the king said with the same resolve that he had earlier that morning. "I do not need your help to run Alocar. I am more than capable of ruling on my own."

Alastaire looked at his nephew, disgust etched onto his face. Constance's lips were pursed and her arms crossed tight against her chest. She shot daggers at Schaed's retreating form as her fingers drummed against her forearm. Oldar thought he heard a snort of annoyance come from her direction, but he wasn't sure if it was someone scuffing their boot against the cobblestones.

"Don't be ridiculous, Oldar," Alastaire groused. "Obviously you are in over your head. Your people don't believe in you. Hells, they openly mock you. You are not fit to be king."

Alastaire tapped his foot impatiently as he struggled to maintain his composure. Oldar, however, was not going to let his emotions control his actions. Squaring his shoulders and looking his uncle in the eye, Oldar took a deep breath before speaking.

"Uncle, I am more than fit to rule Alocar. In fact, I am probably the only person in our family with the proper moral character to care for our people." Stepping closer to his uncle and dropping his voice, Oldar added, "I'm sure that Aunt Constance would love to know about late Aunt Vera or Miss Jaella." Constance's brows raised at the mention of her husband's first wife and mistress. "I'm sure that Aunt Constance has some inkling about your first wife, but she doesn't strike me as the type who would appreciate being misled. Mother's not the only one who has a sharp tongue."

Alastaire's eyes blazed as he stared his nephew down. His hands clenched at his sides as he struggled to maintain his composure. His first wife's mysterious death and trists with other women were still subject to gossip. Closing his eyes, Alastaire took a moment to relax his body before opening them and hissing to the king. "I would not do that, if I were you. You can try and play games, but you'll soon find that all you hold dear will be taken from you. If this is the way you want it, so be it. I hope you enjoy your solitude."

Straightening up, Alastaire turned and beckoned Constance to follow him. "Come, Constance. I believe that the king has made his decision. We've worn out our stay and it's time to leave."

Constance gaped at her husband. "But what about our efforts? Are they to be wasted?"

"Oldar appears to have everything under control, dear," Alastaire replied simply.

Alastaire made his way back to their room. Constance stared at Alastaire's back with her mouth agape. She turned briefly to shoot Oldar a nasty glare before following after her husband. The heels from her boots clacked on the worn cobblestones as she rushed to catch up with him.

Oldar sighed in the darkness once his relatives were out of sight. The whole ordeal left him feeling strangely drained, much like when he first arrived at Madden. His body slouched and his head dropped. A young boy walked by to light the lamps for the night. As he passed, he called out to his king. Oldar managed to mumble and give him a half nod in recognition.

Chatter in the city seemed to be amplified as more people took to the streets. The clear sky and warm weather made for a lovely evening. A myriad of stars winked at the people below, glowing gently against the dark sky. A gift from the gods to help Man travel and chart the passing of each year.

If only my evening were as beautiful as this night, he mused. *Alas, things never seem to go my way.*

A heavy thump on his shoulder caused Oldar to jump, his hand reaching for the dagger on his hip. Cold sweat broke out on his forehead as his breath caught in his chest.

"Did you see the looks on their faces?" a jovial voice called out behind him.

Oldar turned and saw Schaed standing behind him, a boyish grin taking up most of the space on his chubby face. Taking his hand away from his weapon, Oldar let out a deep breath.

"Ghan's mercy, Schaed, you scared me. I was ready to run you through," Oldar gasped.

Schaed roared with laughter. "Oh, come now, Oldar. I meant what I said. You're no good for combat." The lanky man grabbed a stitch in his side as he tried to control his mirth. "I wear a light layer of chainmail under my shirt on a daily basis," he wheezed as he tried to stop laughing. "Gods only know what would happen in my line of business if I was unprepared and an outlaw accosted one of my caravans. You may have seen battle, old friend, but you're no match for someone like that."

Oldar stood silently, grateful that the flickering light from the street lamps did not illuminate his face too much. His face burned with embarrassment. "I didn't realize that things were that dangerous for you," Oldar replied.

"I wouldn't trade it for the world," Schaed answered. "A life of fine wines and an exclusive trading right is bound to have a little danger. Let's just say that it keeps me on my toes."

Schaed winked at his friend out of habit. The action was in the shadows, but Oldar imagined the gesture and could picture it in his mind.

"How did you end up behind me?" the king asked.

"Oh, I just looped around a few streets once I hit the main road. I figured you needed a little help earlier." Schaed folded his arms behind his head. "I waited until they walked past me. Boy, you must have said something horrible. I've never seen someone so angry."

"Oh?"

"They were grumbling and shoved right into me as they went by. I don't think they even stopped to see who they ran into."

Oldar felt a slight twinge of regret for treating his aunt the way he did. The guilt was quickly replaced as he pictured the pair storming off. The tightness in his chest loosened as he recalled his actions. "You know," Oldar said sheepishly. "I've always wanted to tell off my uncle for being a complete thorn in my side ever since I was a child."

"I don't blame you," Schaed replied. "He's a bit of an arsehole."

The pair wandered off in the direction of the castle proper. People greeted the king as he walked by. Oldar's previous fatigue melted away as butterflies filled his chest. The night suddenly seemed much brighter to the king. In the distance, he heard a soprano singing an aria in theatre. Muffled conversation from one of the shops could be heard as he walked by. Schaed began whistling again as the two continued on. The jaunty tune was infectious and the king found himself humming along even though he didn't know the song.

Oldar turned his head as he walked and watched as young couples strolled down the street, arm in arm. His breath caught in his throat as Cienna's face looked his way. Blinking his eyes, Oldar tried to get the image out of his head. He felt Schaed nudge him with his elbow and looked over. Schaed's eyes darted to the young couple and Oldar realized that he had been staring at the woman. Her expression was confused as she attempted to scurry by without offending her king, her curly hair bouncing down her back as she quickly moved past. Oldar felt his heart drop as he returned his gaze forward. The heaviness he'd been feeling earlier returned full force.

"Are you okay?" Schaed asked.

Shaking his head, Oldar mumbled a half-hearted response. "It's nothing. I thought I recognized her from somewhere."

Schaed stared at his companion. "I think I should call it a night. Good night, old friend."

Oldar nodded mutely. "Good night, Schaed."

The king watched as the lanky man retreated into the shadows once more. People trickled down the streets around him and Schaed, talking lightheartedly amongst themselves. However, around Oldar, there was no happiness. All he could see was darkness.

XVII

CIENNA OPENED her eyes and lifted her head as bright light filtered through her eyelids. She looked around groggily. Finding herself sitting in a chair, she brought her hand to her head to move some of her hair out of the way. The princess rubbed her cheeks and noted with a hint of embarrassment that she had been drooling as she slept. Hastily, she wiped the slobber off. She groaned as she leaned back into her chair. As if on cue, her stomach followed suit, rumbling loudly as it complained about being empty.

"It's nice to see you finally awake, Princess," Brody said. "Your mother has been waiting for you."

Cienna's head swiveled over to where the sound was coming from. Her face flushed as she observed her bodyguard leaning languidly against the doorframe. Brody's eyes twinkled as he gazed at her. Cienna's hands flew to the knotted mess on her head and ran her fingers through her curly locks in an attempt to make herself more presentable. Her fingers got caught in the tangle as she tried to comb her hair.

Brody laughed at his charge, drawing a glare from the disheveled princess.

"Why didn't you wake me sooner?" she snapped. "There's so much that we need to go over. I shouldn't have fallen asleep like that"

"I would disagree," Brody replied as he strode over to her. "Clearly, you would have been too exhausted to think straight. I'm sure your mother would agree that this was probably for the best, even if it was a bit ill-timed."

Brody gave Cienna's nose a light tap as he smiled at her, causing her to flush once more. The princess brought her hand to her hair once more and began twirling a curly strand around her finger nervously. She dropped her gaze, unable to look at her guard for some strange reason.

A loud crunch off to the side caught her attention. Cienna's eyes snapped up, looking for the source of the sound. Standing in the doorway was Caitlyn. The redhead's eyes were swollen and she had dark circles underneath. Cienna spied an apple, the source of the noise. Her mouth watered at the sight of the fruit. Caitlyn brought the green apple to her lips and took another bite. The crunch elicited another gurgle from Cienna's belly.

Caitlyn arched an eyebrow at the sound. Taking a look at the snack in her hand, Caitlyn held it out to the princess with an amused expression on her face. "Hungry, are we?"

Cienna dropped her eyes momentarily in shame before snatching the apple from her hand and greedily taking a bite. The crisp skin and sweet juices of the fruit exploded in her mouth. Cienna closed her eyes as she savored the welcome treat. She felt her grogginess leave as her mind became more alert. Taking another bite, Cienna raised her arm up and slurped the juice that ran down her wrist.

"Thank you, Caitlyn," Cienna said. "I needed a little something to wake me up."

"Of course, Waterbug. What kind of person would I be if I let my fair princess starve while I dine on the bounties of our land?" Caitlyn smirked as she spoke. "I can only imagine the scandal it would cause."

"Come now, Cait," Brody broke in. "Surely you wouldn't want to put our beloved princess in a compromising situation."

"Not like some people we know," Caitlyn replied with a wink.

"My point exactly," Brody said with a laugh. "Poor Waterdrop has a lot on her plate already. We must be more considerate of her plight."

The two burst out laughing as Cienna watched on while eating her apple.

"By the gods, you two are so immature," Cienna sighed as she rolled her eyes. "If you'll excuse me, I've got a rather important meeting with my mother."

Cienna made her way out of the room, squeezing between the still-chortling duo. The princess stepped out into the hallway and made her way down the hall towards the stairwell. She took another bite of the apple as she walked, sucking the sweet juice as it welled up in the indent of her bite. As she reached the staircase, she reached out for the rope that dangled from the top of the ceiling to help her keep her balance as she descended the steep steps.

Her foot touched down on the first step before she realized that she didn't know where her mother was. Grumbling under her breath, Cienna pivoted around and pulled herself up the stairs and re-entered the hallway. She took a few more bites and finished up her breakfast. Looking around for a place to dispose of the core, Cienna was unable to find a servant walking through the hallway. Pulling a cloth square from her bodice, she wrapped the core in the fabric and set it on a small table that lined the hallway.

There should be someone by soon to clean up here, she reasoned to herself as she guiltily left the mess in the hall.

Down the hall, Cienna observed Brody and Caitlyn strolling down towards her at a leisurely pace. Both still had a wide grin on their face as they chatted. Brody glanced down the hall and noted Cienna's presence. Elbowing Caitlyn, he tipped his head in the princess' direction. Caitlyn looked over and made eye contact with Cienna.

"What can we do for you, Waterbug?" she asked.

Trying to overcome her awkwardness, Cienna replied, "Where did Mother want to meet with me?"

Brody and Caitlyn sped up to close the distance between themselves and the princess. Her guard noted the cloth-covered apple remnants and picked it up off of the table. Handing the mess to Caitlyn, Brody placed his hand on Cienna's shoulder and guided her back to the stairs.

Caitlyn stared at Brody in disbelief. "And what am I to do with this?"

Grinning at the redhead, Brody replied, "Find someone to give it to, obviously." His eyes twinkled as Caitlyn scoffed at him. Turning to the princess, he said, "Your mother wanted to speak with us too. She's waiting in your father's war room," Brody said.

"War room?" Cienna asked.

"Yes. It's where he went to plan out his strategies and get a break from things when he wanted a moment of quiet to himself. Bannen used to spend a lot of time with Jaste in that room going over drills and training expeditions over the years."

"I think Alverick spent some time there as well," Caitlyn added.

"I wonder why Mother never spoke of that room before." Cienna pondered. "Then again, I'm surprised that she knows about a room like that."

"Cienna," Brody said with an uncharacteristic use of her name. "I really wish you would give your mother more respect. Jaste was a sharp man, and he looked for an equal to take as a wife. Do you truly think your father would have taken a woman who was as empty as a pot as a wife?"

"Sure, she may be good at fashion, but how does that help us in times like this?" Cienna asked.

The trio went down the stairs, one-by-one, making sure to wrap the rope loosely around their hand several times to make sure that they didn't fall down the stairs. As they walked down the stairs, occasionally a servant would be traveling up. This resulted in everybody doing an awkward shuffle as they maneuvered themselves through the narrow staircase without losing their grip on the rope.

"Have you learned nothing from your classes?" Brody asked. "And here I thought I was the only one who didn't pay attention."

Cienna craned her neck to look at her guard briefly. Brody gave her a wink and motioned for her to turn back around and watch the stairs. With a pout, Cienna listened to him and continued down several steps without speaking.

Why are they so insistent on supporting her? Yes, she's queen, but I've been the one who has been preparing to rule. I'm the one who's gone out and actually tried to be diplomatic with the other nations. It's not like I'm just trading pretty fabrics...

"Oh," Cienna said faintly. "I see what you mean now. She *has* done a good job at maintaining relationships with the various guilders in other lands."

"I think she deserves to be given a little more leeway. Who knows? Maybe she'll wind up being a better ruler than you imagine. Ah, here we are," Brody said.

Cienna stopped on the landing, unraveling the rope from her hand. Behind her, Brody and Caitlyn followed suit. The three passed through the doorway and headed out into the hall. A serving girl dressed in a simple brown dress walked past them towards the staircase. As she walked by, Caitlyn shoved the covered apple core into the girl's hands before moving past her. The girl turned in surprise, but didn't say anything as the trio moved through the caer.

The group walked down a long hallway that Cienna didn't remember. The walls were covered with woven tapestries of scenic countrysides. Green hills dotted with red and orange poppies stretched out along the wall. Scenes with deer drinking from a lake or laying down to rest were interspersed between the hills. Statues made from granite carved in the likeness of King Jaste or one of his ancestors lay sprinkled throughout the hallway.

Cienna took in the serenity of her father's secret hallway. Warm sunlight streamed through the stained-glass windows, creating a pleasant multi-colored glow along the dull stones. The granite statues stood silently, a reminder of her father's stoic nature. Her eyes honed in on the statue of her father. The late King Jaste towered over the princess and her companions. His eyes were cast downwards and his lips were relaxed. It was almost as though he were staring wistfully down at her and all who walked past.

"Ah, here we are," Brody mumbled. Turning to face the women, he stood off to the side and pulled open the door so they could enter before him.

Cienna ducked her head in thanks as she walked in.

The room was bigger than she imagined. Circular in appearance, the pelt of a solid white bear lay on the floor. A large maple table sat in the center of the room, a stack of rolled scrolls sitting on top. Several bookcases lined the walls. A plethora of scrolls and cracked leather tomes filled their shelves. In the center of the room, plush chairs were arranged around the table. A fire burned in the hearth on the wall behind the bear pelt. Cienna stared at the luxury with her mouth agape. She wandered over to one of the chairs and ran her hand across its soft felt.

"I've never seen chairs like this," she murmured. "The cushion covers not only the seat, but the backing and armrests."

"Yes, they are quite the rarity," Hera said.

Cienna's head snapped up as she looked for her mother. Hera sat in front of the fire, an open book placed gingerly on her lap. Cienna couldn't believe that she'd overlooked her mother's presence.

"He got them from the Great Heart years ago. The Great Heart wanted to show off his wealth, and your father wanted to extend Zanir's hand in peace, so he offered several of his prized warhorses to them. Unfortunately, the chairs aren't common in Xan either, so we could never get enough to begin proper trading. Still," she smiled fondly and rubbed her hand across the armrest, "I do enjoy these chairs."

"Perhaps we can work on getting more of these chairs, Mother," Cienna said as she straightened up.

Hera raised an eyebrow and waited for her daughter to continue.

"While we were in battle, Brody managed to secure an alliance with the new Great Heart."

"Is that true?" Hera asked, turning to look at the young guard.

"Yes, your majesty," Brody replied. "I spoke to Swordbane during battle and he promised peace. He even protected me during the battle when his men wanted to attack me. Though I am hesitant to believe, I do see this slowly blossoming into a promising alliance."

Hera rubbed her chin as she mulled over the information. "I do enjoy letting their people sell in the marketplace. The Thurlish are a lovely bunch," she said softly. "However," she said more loudly. "Do you truly see him upholding his end of the bargain? From what I understand, he prefers to follow his own rules."

"I wouldn't put it past him," Brody conceded.

"I got the impression that his right hand is more honorable than him," Caitlyn added. "The man did save my life when Queen Gwyn was about to kill me. I would wager that as long as that man is around, we can expect Swordbane to be somewhat a man of his word."

"We can send out an official treaty," Cienna said. "If we can work with him and give in to some of his wishes, we should be able to keep him from stabbing us in the back."

Hera nodded. "I think that'll be a good idea. Now that your father has been properly mourned, we can devote more attention to this new union. I would like to think that in death, he managed to earn the respect of his enemies."

"What do you mean he's been properly mourned?" Cienna asked. "It's just been a few days. Surely there's more that needs to be done?"

Hera shook her head. "I took care of everything while you were away. The headmistress is a very valuable resource. She helped me with the viewing and mourning ceremony. I don't think I could've made it through the last few days without her."

Cienna opened her mouth to speak, but found no words strong enough to convey her displeasure. Her eyes began to burn as tears formed at the corners.

"His ashes are still in the shrine waiting for you to say your goodbyes," Hera said gently. "I would've saved his body, but protocol dictates that everything be handled in three days or else his spirit would be trapped with us and he would be unable to enter the Halls of the Fallen."

Cienna sank into the chair, unable to meet her mother's gaze. Brody and Caitlyn stood silently in the corner. She grabbed the skirts of her dress and absentmindedly began ringing the fabric in her hands. Her face felt flushed as she struggled to maintain her composure. She felt a soft touch on her cheek. Looking up, she saw her mother brushing her cheek with the back of her hand. Hera's eyes were soft and glistened as moisture welled around the edges.

"Your father loved you very much," Hera whispered. "He came to me the night that he died. He told me that he thinks that you're ready to take on a more active role in leading Zanir. That your determination will compliment my style." Tears rolled down Hera's cheeks as she spoke. "I would love it if you shared your ideas with me. We could enact so much change if we worked together."

Cienna nodded, tears streaming down her face and her nose dripping. Rising suddenly, Cienna straightened her skirts. Wiping her face with the back of her hand, she moved towards the door. "I think I'm going to visit Father," she said, her voice husky. "I need to clear my head before we sit down and draft anything to Swordbane.

"I'll be in the Great Hall when you're ready," Hera replied.

Cienna ran out of the room, wiping her eyes. Brody made eye contact with Hera before following Cienna out into the hall.

XVIII

L EN PACED around the yard behind his mother's house. The red-clay dwelling backed up into a forest on the outskirts of Fa'Tinh. Trees obscured him from view to any who may have been traveling near the home, but allowed for him to keep an eye out for people approaching. Off in the distance, Bermet ran about, spinning in circles with her arms outstretched as she wove through the trees. She giggled as she played near her father.

He paced, his arms clasped behind him, his brow furrowed in concentration. A thick cloth covered in salve was wrapped around his arm. The balm had been prepared by his mother and a local shaman. Len, though he wouldn't admit it, was pleasantly surprised with the potency of the cream and its healing properties. His arm was healing nicely and no longer pained him when he moved it. He raised his arm and flexed his muscles before resuming his previous posture.

A snapping twig caught Len's attention. Len gave a short, chirping whistle to Bermet, instructing her to be silent for a moment. She came over and stood by her father, hiding just behind him. Bermet's eyes were wide, both curious and frightened, as she peered around Len. Pram walked into the small clearing, his hands to his mouth making a warbling sound in response to Len's chirp. Len visibly relaxed, his body language providing comfort for his daughter and helping her to return to her cheerful state.

"Go on, Bermet," Len said to his daughter. "Everything's all right."

With a squeal, Bermet ran off and resumed spinning amongst the trees. Len watched her disappear behind him before returning his attentions to Pram. The man stood silently, waiting for Len to address him. Pram watched Bermet play, his eyes soft.

"It hurts me that she is forced to hide in the forest," Pram said. "Bermet should be running through the streets with her friends chasing the dogs."

"What news do you have?" Len asked.

"Hroth is still out gathering information, but people are reluctant to speak freely in front of us. Wyr-raji's little stunt in the square has many shaken up."

"Graak's mercy," Len swore. He clenched his hand as he spoke. "I thought you told me that Viir's group has quieted down?"

"They have," Pram said slowly. "However, Wyr-raji has been going around and declaring himself more fit to be the Great Heart. He says that he was chosen by Vahnyre himself to continue what you began."

"Chosen by Vahnyre," Len mumbled. "He's the reason we're in this predicament to begin with. If he hadn't been so hell-bent on summoning Alazi, we wouldn't have lost our only Shadow. We could've regrouped and used him to take our enemies by surprise."

"I agree. If his heart wasn't so corrupt, we could've prepared and better addressed Liir's death. Unfortunately, we're past that point."

Len crossed his arms across his chest and resumed his pacing. Pram followed in line, dropping a half step behind his leader. Len's mind raced as he processed all of the new information.

"There's only so much time that my mother can buy us," Len said softly as they neared Bermet. The young girl spun with dizzying speed in one spot, a small cloud of dust kicking up under her tiny feet. "I fear that our time is running short."

"What do you mean?"

Len turned to face Pram. "You've always been loyal to my cause," he said. "I need you to trust me now."

Pram studied his leader quizzically. "I swore my life to protect you, Evenhand. I don't plan on breaking my vow."

Len stopped walking and glanced over at his daughter, his face resigned, completely blank. "Watch over Bermet and my family," he said. Pram opened his mouth to speak, but Len held up a hand to quiet him. "We are low in numbers right now. The majority of the Qu-ari went with us on this campaign. The Thurlish do not involve themselves with the disputes of the other clans, nor do I wish to drag them into this right now. We need them to be seen as a neutral party, to be able to garner sympathy from the other nations. The Thaylan and the Hanzo will listen to reason, but let us assume that they will default to Wyr-raji's side in order to keep themselves safe. If we can get some spies in their tribes, we may be able to get more information. The Pshwani are angry, but I don't see them moving as a group against Fa'Tinh."

"We can gather a few people to serve as informants," Pram replied. "I know more than a few who would follow you to their deaths. I'm sure I can convince them to act as your Ears."

"I need to leave Xan for a while," Len continued.

Pram's jaw dropped.

"I've been talking with Mother, and she mentioned that there may be some mercenaries we can hire out of Thallysis. With our troop of Myrani depleted, we need some outside help if we're to quash Wyr-raji's ambitions."

"Why don't we utilize our new alliance with Pharn?" Pram asked. "Surely, we can call for aid and use their men as fodder to Wyr-raji's blood-lust while we pick away at him and his numbers."

Len shook his head. Bringing his finger to his lips, he motioned for Pram to stop talking. Bermet, still spinning, bumped into Len's legs. Giggling, she looked up at her father.

"She spoke to me," Bermet said breathlessly.

"Who, my pearl?" Len asked. He placed his hand on her head and gently smoothed down some of her flyaway hairs.

"The blue-haired girl. Freyna."

Len paused, his hand still atop her head. "What do you mean, Bermet?"

"I was playing with Freyna earlier, and she told me that she can't stay too long. She said you need her."

Len glanced at Pram before responding to his daughter. Looking around as he spoke, Len tried to find any trace of the goddess. Nothing.

"I think that she would have more fun playing with you," Len finally said. "After all, you are much more fun than I am." Raising his voice just slightly, Len looked up once more and said, "I would hate to have anything bad happen to you, my pearl. I would give anything to keep you and your mother safe."

A gentle breeze ruffled his hair and played with the bottom of his shirt. The air smelled of lavender and a few small leaves danced around their feet. Len smiled down at his daughter and pat her head. Pram watched on, his eyes wide. Bermet shot her father a quick smile before running off to weave through the vegetation once more. As the girl dashed off, the draft left with her. The leaves that had been circling their feet fell to the earth, kicking up a small puff of dirt as they landed.

"Evenhand," Pram gasped. "The gods protect you! Do you know what this could mean for us?"

With a smirk, Len replied, "It spells trouble for Wyr-raji."

"You don't need to leave now."

"Wrong," Len retorted. "If we confront him now, he will attack with his flames. I don't know the extent of our protection, but imagine the devastation we could rain down upon him if I were to return with a force from Thallysis."

"Couple that with our allies within the clans, and not only would you teach Wyr-raji a lesson—"

"But I would show any potential rivals what happens to those who challenge the Great Heart," Len finished. "This can only benefit us."

Pram clasped Len on the shoulder in a fatherly fashion, squeezing the young man lightly. "I'll give my life to protect your family."

Len scratched at the cloth that wrapped around his exposed arm. It'd been itching a lot since he received his mother's salve. He then grasped his general's arm and returned the sentiment. The two broke apart and headed towards the house. Bermet rounded a tree and saw the two men leaving. She ducked behind the trunk for a moment before popping back out and trotting over to her father.

The back door opened and Zaa'ni waddled out with her hand on her stomach. Her wavy hair was tied in a high tail, while her dress of loose cotton barely covered her large belly. Bermet ran to her mother when she saw her, embracing her around the knees. Len walked over and gave his wife a kiss on the cheek before ushering her back inside. Pram followed the group, closing the door behind them.

"I just wanted to let you two know that lunch is ready," Zaa'ni said. "Wash up, Bermet."

Bermet raced to the wash basin to clean her hands as the smell of spiced lamb and fresh flatbread greeted their nostrils. Pram bowed his head in respect to Zaa'ni and followed Bermet to the bowl. Len touched the small of Zaa'ni's back before heading over to the table.

Intan sat at the table talking quietly with Altansari. Pram's children, Berkah, Elok, and Kemala, sat on the floor eating lunch. Bermet rushed over to join them, her hands dripping. She grabbed a pear from the bowl of fruit in the middle of their little circle and greedily took a bite while she waited for her mother to serve her. Almost as if on cue, Zaa'ni placed a plate on the ground in front of her daughter. Bermet tore off a piece of her bread and used it to wrap up some of the lamb. She managed to include some onions and a sprig of rosemary in with her meat. Shoving the handful into her mouth, Bermet grinned as some of the sauce that her meat was sitting in dripped down her chin.

"Bermet, wipe yourself," Zaa'ni chided. "You know better than to make a mess in Honorable Grandmother's house." Swooping down, Zaa'ni dropped a cloth in Bermet's lap and gave her a meaningful look.

Bermet finished chewing and swallowed her food before wiping off her chin. Kemala made eye contact with Bermet and the two burst into a fit of giggles. Elok rolled his eyes at his little sister as Berkah nudged her brother.

Pram and Len sat down at the table, Zaa'ni right behind them with a plate of food for each. Altansari stopped speaking with Intan and they all began eating. Zaa'ni lowered herself slowly into her chair, her hand gripping the back of the chair as she sank into it. The room was silent except for the sound of fresh bread ripping apart and jugs making contact with the table.

"How is everything progressing?" Altansari asked. "I've noticed that your Flame has been coming in at all hours of the night these last three days."

"We've made some good headway," Pram replied. "I would hazard to say that we should be able to return home soon." Turning to Intan, Pram bowed his head in deference and said, "Your hospitality has been most appreciated, Honorable Mother."

Intan smiled, her eyes wrinkling. "It has been my pleasure to host a man with a reputation such as yours," her faint voice cracking slightly. "I am grateful that you devote so much to my son."

The children finished eating and all popped up to leave the room. Berkah lagged behind to gather the dishes off of the floor before joining the others. Altansari gave Berkah a little pat on the bottom in thanks for cleaning.

Once the children were out of the room, the adults finished up their meal in relative silence. Zaa'ni and Altansari made light conversation about the unborn child while the men ate. Intan dined leisurely, closing her eyes as she chewed. Occasionally, her soft voice would interject into Altansari and Zaa'ni's discussion.

As the meal wound down, Zaa'ni got up to clear the dishes. Altansari got up to assist her, picking up a towel and beginning to wipe the dishes in the wash basin. Zaa'ni went to take over the cleaning, but Altansari shooed her away.

Len took a drink from his mug. As he set the cup down, he said, "Pram will be acting as our leader for a while."

Altansari turned around, a sopping towel in her hand. Zaa'ni froze, midway through lowering herself into her chair. Intan sat quietly.

"I have some business that I need to attend to at the eastern coast that cannot be delayed."

"Do you really need to leave?" Zaa'ni said as she finally managed to sit down. "You've only just come back. We need your leadership right now."

"It's too dangerous for me to stay here. Wyr-raji wants my blood, and if he finds out that I'm here with you, he'll come looking for us."

"Surely Honorable Mother would be enough to deter him from bothering us," Altansari said. She walked away from the basin and stood over Zaa'ni, wiping her hand on a dry cloth.

"Wyr-raji has never been one to follow proper protocol," Pram responded. "I fear that he would not respect the sanctity of Honorable Mother's home and bring his grievances to her door."

"I'll be leaving tomorrow from the main square. I want to make sure that people see me leave Fa'Tinh. You'll stay here. Pram and Hroth will still be around to keep you all safe. I'll be back once my business is done," Len said.

"Len —" Zaa'ni said, but her husband held up his hand to interrupt her.

"You'll stay here. There's no discussion about this matter." His expression left no room for argument.

Zaa'ni stared at her husband dejectedly, eyes dropping to the ground. Len walked over to his wife and gently cupped her face in his hand.

"This isn't the Zaa'ni I know," he said tenderly. "I need the strong woman I married to help keep everyone in line. They'll listen to you, probably moreso than me, right now. If you can work to keep our people calm, we will be able to keep control of Xan and keep Wyr-raji from sewing more chaos."

"The girls and I will have a wonderful time, Len," Intan said to her son. "We'll see you when you return."

All eyes turned to the soft-spoken matriarch of the clans. Zaa'ni nodded in agreement, her jaw clenched as she walked over to a chair and sat down.

Len walked over to Pram and clapped him on the shoulder. "Keep an eye out for everyone. I'll see you when I get back."

"I live to serve," the general replied.

Grabbing a bag that he'd left by the front door, Len turned one last time to look at his family before heading out the door, closing it lightly behind him.

XIX

B IRDS CHIRPED as Oldar gradually woke up in bed. He kept his eyes closed as the sun shone through the windows and onto his face. With a groan, he rolled over and threw his throw over his head to shield him from the light. The heat from being under the blanket was stifling and sweat began beading on his brow. He slid the cover down to just below his nose and buried what remained of his head under his pillow. The birds continued to sing outside his window, their symphony heralding the new day. The king gnashed his teeth in an attempt to drown out the sound.

A knock on the door caused Oldar to throw the pillow off of his face and rip the blanket off of his body. The warmth of the sun beat down on his bare flesh. A second knock rapped against his door.

"In a minute," he hissed.

Looking around, Oldar spied a cobalt silk robe dangling over his reading chair. A gift from Pru, no doubt. Stomping over to the chair, he grabbed the cloak and wrapped it around his body, cinching it closed tight. Oldar then stormed over to his chamber door and flung it open as hard as he could.

"What do you want?" he asked through gritted teeth.

Outside stood a startled Rolaire. The former king's advisor stood in a burnt orange tunic and brown pants with puffy legs. He wore a lighter shade of brown leggings under the trousers. His beard was neatly trimmed and ended in a distinguished point at his chin. Unfortunately, the hair on his head was not as generous. A bald patch in the middle of his head reflected the morning light. In his hands, Rolaire held a length of parchment, a quill behind his ear.

"Why, I've come to begin your day, your majesty," the man stammered. His nasally voice caused a vein in Oldar's temple to throb. "There's much to be done and little time to do it."

Bringing his hand to his head, Oldar held back a sigh. "Give me a moment to make myself decent," he told the man. "I will meet you in the Great Hall for breakfast. Keep all but Pru out."

"As you wish, your majesty," Rolaire replied. With a flurrying wave of his hand, he spun sharply on his heels and strode quickly towards the hall.

Closing the door, Oldar moaned. The birds could still be heard warbling off in the distance, their symphony never ceasing. Touching his temple gingerly, Oldar muttered, "I think I have a headache coming on. What a brilliant start to my day."

With a sigh, Oldar shucked off his robe and began rummaging through his chests and wardrobe for a suitable outfit. After a lengthy period of time, he settled on an ivory shirt with a ruffled collar and sleeves, in addition to simple, black bottoms. He threw on a ruby cloak to add a splash of color before placing his crown on his head. Standing in front of his bedroom mirror, Oldar took in his appearance. Before him stood an imposing figure. Turning his head side to side, he admired the scruff that covered his chin. He'd never allowed himself to be anything other than clean shaven. Now, seeing himself with the beginnings of a beard, he noted how it made his jaw look stronger.

Satisfied with his appearance, he spun around with a flourish, his cape fluttering in the air behind him, and headed for the Great Hall to have his first meeting as the new king of Alocar. As he crossed through the halls from one side of the castle to the other, Oldar ignored his servants, brushing past them as they scurried to get out of his way.

In less time than it took for him to get ready, Oldar found himself standing outside of the Great Hall. The doors stood open, revealing the veritable feast that lay spread out on the table. Oldar found his mouth watering as he looked at the savory breakfast that waited for him. Fruit and pastries sat in the middle of the table while plates with quail and salmon lay in between. A goblet of wine waited in front of the king's chair. Falling into his seat, Oldar pulled the chalice towards him and took a long drink of its contents. The fruity beverage warmed him and helped alleviate his headache.

"Good morning, your majesty," Rolaire said.

Oldar slouched over his wine, swirling the contents of the cup slowly, not lifting his eyes to acknowledge the man. The sound of a throat clearing caught the king's attention. Raising his eyes, Oldar saw Pruvencia sitting at the far end of the table knitting.

"Good morning, Rolaire," Oldar mumbled. Reaching out, he slid a plate of fruit and bread over towards him. Oldar ripped a piece of bread and stuffed it into his mouth. "What do you have for me today?"

Glancing over at Pru, Oldar saw her eyes return down and focus on her knitting. Her needles clinked together as her withered fingers worked the instruments. She nodded faintly as she worked.

Was that towards me? Oldar wondered as he arced an eyebrow.

Rustling his parchment, Rolaire cleared his throat. "As I am sure you're aware, your majesty, Alocar has experienced great turmoil these last few days. Though but for the grace of Queen Hera of Zanir, our people would have been directionless. It is also worth noting that your uncle has helped keep our kingdom running."

Oldar let out a snort. He noted that Pru's eyes shot up once more in a disapproving glare. Oldar quickly tried to turn the noise into a cough. Bringing his goblet to his lips once more, Oldar took another long draught of the intoxicating liquid.

Rolaire pretended that he did not hear the interruption. "Thanks to their combined efforts," he said, pushing on, "Madden especially has been able to maintain her production levels of silks and other fine fabrics. The guild masters are wondering on when your union will be. They are hoping to have enough time to create a sensational dress for your betrothed, as well as yourself."

The king's eyes hardened and his body stiffened. "There will be no union between our two lands," he said crisply. The clinking of Pru's knitting needles could no longer be heard as he spoke. "She has broken her family's word and dishonored my father's good name."

Rolaire's eyes were opened wide in shock at the news. "Certainly, your majesty, the royal family of Zanir, our allies for the last few centuries, I might add, would not go back on their word."

"They have. Our treaties and agreements are now worthless in their eyes," he fumed. "Their queen obviously acted the way that she did in order to save face in the eyes of our allies."

Rolaire scribbled a note on the bottom of his parchment before feebly squeaking out, "Are you sure, your majesty? This is a serious betrayal, the likes of which hasn't been seen in centuries. The ramifications are huge."

Oldar seethed as he grabbed a quail leg and tore into it. Gnashing his teeth, he glowered at his father's advisor. Emotions that he'd been feeling for the last week bubbled to the surface, threatening to consume him. Images of Cienna fawning over her bodyguard filled his head. Laughter from her people rang in his ears along with the Alocarans' as snippets of previous conversations between the soldiers overlapped with the mirth. Almost as though to spite him, a phantom image of Cienna leaning in to kiss Brody filled his mind's eye. In the background, his uncle's face and mocking laughter punctuated the scene.

He saw red.

Oldar took another bite of the leg and forced himself to slow his breathing. Taking his time to properly chew and swallow, he cleared his mind to regain control. Once he'd emptied his mouth, he spoke evenly, "It brings me great pain to say this, but unfortunately, it is true." Pruvencia's eyes widened slightly before she dropped them back to her lap. Her needles did not move, however. Swallowing, Oldar continued. "When I first arrived at Pharn, I was greeted warmly by their king, but, alas, the queen and her daughter did not share the same sentiment. I believe that it was all a ploy to humiliate Father at my expense."

Rolaire wrote furiously on a clean sheet of paper as he struggled to keep up with what his king was saying. Ink splatters dotted his face. The man tried to wipe his face clean several times, but gave up quickly. Occasionally, he would nod his head, urging Oldar to continue speaking.

"To add insult to injury," Oldar said, "the princess chose to ally herself with my father's killer and not impose any punishments to the man. I tried to talk reason to her, but her bodyguard insisted that they'd made the right choice. It was at that point that I knew that I needed to withdraw Alocar's forces, for our own safety."

The frantic scratching of quill nib on paper remained unbroken as he sat silently. Looking for something to do, Oldar ripped off another piece of bread and munched on it. He popped a few grapes in his mouth shortly after. The burst of their bitter juice accentuated the fruity flavor of the wine.

"How would you like to handle the matter, your majesty?" Rolaire's nasally voice asked quietly once he'd finished writing.

Oldar thought for a moment before answering. "Perhaps we should draft a proclamation to our other allies informing them of the situation. I wouldn't want them to feel as though they need to choose sides between our two kingdoms. Let us sort out the matter ourselves."

"That is a most diplomatic solution," Rolaire said, nodding his head as he spoke. "The other nations will see that you're a magnanimous leader, not one looking for violence. People will speak highly of you." Gathering up his materials, Rolaire dipped his head in respect to his king as his rolls of parchment threatened to spill out of his arms. "I'll complete the draft today and bring it to you for your approval, your majesty."

"Thank you, Rolaire."

The advisor scuttled out of the Great Hall, his plate of food untouched and surrounded by splotches of ink. As soon as he left the room, Oldar sank back into his chair and downed the remaining wine. A servant walked by the door and spotted the king putting down his empty glass. Rushing to supply his lord's needs, the man whisked the cup away and poured a new glass from the decanter on the periphery of the room. Just as quickly, the man returned the full glass to Oldar and deftly placed it in front of him.

Oldar looked down at the newly replenished drink and downed it once more. Wiping his mouth on a cloth, Oldar motioned for another glass to be brought to him. The servant acquiesced and took the chalice away once more. While he waited for his wine, Oldar finished off the remaining loaf of bread that sat in front of him. He also snacked absentmindedly on dates and grapes. The process was repeated several more times before Oldar needed to stop.

With the fifth glass sitting in front of him, Oldar waved the servant away. The man exited the room soundlessly. Once he was alone in the room, Oldar let out a sigh and leaned back in his chair. His head swam. Pushing away the remainder of his meat and fruit, Oldar closed his eyes. His head throbbed as his headache from earlier in the morning came back full force.

The sound of a chair scraping across the floor caught his attention. Opening his eyes a crack, Oldar watched as Pruvencia got out of her chair, bundle of yarn and knitting needles in hand, and moved closer to him. Disappointment shown on her face. As she sat down next to the king, she placed the yarn in her lap and resumed her knitting. After several long minutes of the needles clinking against each other, Oldar pushed himself upright in the chair and faced his childhood caretaker.

Without missing a stitch, Pruvencia asked, "Do you believe you made the right decision today, your majesty?"

"I do."

"Everything you said was the truth?" she asked. Her deep voice was strained as she spoke.

Oldar nodded.

With a groan, Pruvencia pushed herself out of the chair and began shuffling towards the door. Oldar thought he heard her hip crack as she made her way to the exit.

"Pru," he called out.

Pruvencia turned to look at her king. "Yes, your majesty?"

Oldar's voice caught in his throat as he stared at the older woman. "Don't... don't you believe me?"

The woman turned and began walking back to Oldar. She cupped his face in her hands once she reached the table. Staring fondly into his eyes, she replied, "It just doesn't seem like something she would do."

Kissing Oldar on the forehead, she dropped her hands and shuffled towards the door once more. Oldar's stomach fell as she lumbered along. He could have sworn that he heard her joints creak once more as she moved. As she entered the doorway, she turned one last time to face him. Pruvencia leaned against the doorframe for balance and support as she looked at the king.

"I *do* believe that you're doing what you think is best. Please try and eat some more food, your majesty. If you need me for anything else, just let me know."

With effort, the woman pushed against the frame and hobbled out of the room and down the hallway. Oldar felt sick to his stomach. He buried his head in his hands, hoping that it was just the alcohol that made him feel that way.

Several minutes passed before he lifted his head from his hands. Grabbing his glass, he downed the last of his wine. Pushing himself out of his chair, he wobbled a bit before he managed to steady himself. Oldar grabbed a savory pastry off of the table and made his way out of the Great Hall, taking a large bite of the snack in the process. If he was going to deliver the proclamations, he would need to find someone he trusted to help him practice. Someone who would speak freely about any issues there were with his speech. He needed a friend.

XX

SOLVEIG STRODE through her cave, her fox pelt cape fluttering behind her. Tyr, her dire wolf, followed closely on her heels. The chieftainess' seal skin boots thudded dully on the cavern floor. Those who happened to be in her way quickly moved to clear a path. Tyr snarled at any who didn't move fast enough. Flames from the fire pits crackled, creating long shadows on the stone walls as people sat near them on carved wooden benches eating.

"Konugrr," Henrik called out. The wizened man fell in step behind the chieftainess. "We've received word from Jytte that all is in place for your emissary."

Solveig's lips tightened as she continued on. Her blonde hair swung side-to-side in her high ponytail. Her leather jerkin and brown breeches covered her lithe frame. At her hip, a battle axe lay strapped on. "Send Hegvaldr out before the sun falls below the mountains," she instructed. Her voice was deep and sharp. "He should be able to see eye to eye with the Fyre worshipper."

"Do we want to send a party with him?" Henrik asked. "I don't trust that man as far as I can throw Eivind."

Solveig chuckled as she passed the stocky Eivind. The man sat contentedly in front of a fire eating a chunk of meat on a bone. Juices dripped down his chin as he gnawed on the bone. The man's wild hair frizzed out in an unruly tangled mess. As she walked past, the man turned to look at her. She noted his eyes lingering on her chest.

"Like what you see, Eivind?" she asked loudly.

Several heads turned to face their leader. Some of the older men chuckled softly as they sat around a second fire drinking ale. Tyr growled at the slovenly man.

Eivind looked around the cave before speaking. "If Hegvaldr isn't around, I may." He took a bite of his food and leered at her as the fat dripped down his chin. "I can give you stronger kids than he can."

"Is that so?" a deep voice asked.

Eivind's eyes hardened as Solveig's crinkled up in a smile. From the depths of the cave, Hegvaldr strode up to the large man. Hegvaldr leaned over the seated man and picked up a chunk of deer leg from his plate. Bringing it to his lips, Hegvaldr smirked at Eivind before taking a large bite into the tender meat. Wiping off his mouth with the back of his hand, Hegvaldr threw the partially consumed meal onto the ground before walking away.

Solveig's eyes twinkled as she watched the two, waiting to see what Eivind would do.

"Oh, come now, Hegvaldr," Eivind groaned. "You're wasting perfectly good food." The man picked up the leg and gingerly plucked a pebble off of it before ripping off a large hunk of meat. Mouth bulging, Eivind gave Hegvaldr a baleful glare. "Should be a crime to do something like that," he muttered.

Solveig and the older men laughed. Eivind paid the group no mind as he returned to his original meal and started gnawing on the bone once more. A loud crack announced his success and the man proceeded to slurp the marrow out from within.

"I think a guard, at the very least, would be a good idea," Solveig said to Henrik. "I don't fully trust the man either."

Henrik nodded. "Should we bring Jytte back as well? I would hate to leave her as a temptation for his dark heart or the interests of his followers. Who knows how voracious his appetite is?"

"Leave Jytte," Hegvaldr said. "She's more than capable of taking care of herself. Besides, it's not as though the man is god-blessed. He poses no threat to her."

"I wouldn't underestimate one who is so tempted by Fyre," Henrik warned.

Solveig weighed the options silently. After a short period of time, she replied, "Hegvaldr, bring her back if she wants to return. Otherwise, let her stay and continue her work. It would be suspicious to pull her out after all of these years once you meet with him."

"Gods' will be obeyed, Konugrr," Henrik said.

The wizened man walked over to the group of older men and grabbed a mug from one of them. Taking a long draught, Henrik roughly shoved the jug back into the original owner's hands. Henrik then walked over to Eivind, who sat facing the fire once more as he sucked on his bone, and smacked him on the back of the head. Eivind gave the man a withering look and moved to turn back to his meal. Henrik snapped at him to get up and follow him. With a glare, Eivind reluctantly got up and threw his chewed bone into the fire. As they walked out of the cave, the larger man began gnawing on the meat in his other hand.

"I don't need Eivind, Solveig," Hegvaldr said. "Sure, he's good, but my name should be more than enough to keep that traitor from doing anything to me."

Solveig held up her hand to silence her mate's protests.

"He *needs* you," Hegvaldr continued. "Without you, his plan is doomed to fail."

"I know that," Solveig replied. "However, I don't want to take any unnecessary chances. He's already shown that he's more than capable of turning on his own people. What's to say that he won't turn on us?"

"The Almighty Re'nukh would never abandon you," Hegvaldr insisted.

"It's better to be safe than sorry," Solveig retorted. "Come, let me soothe your worries."

Turning to the older men in the cave, Solveig barked at them to leave. The group quickly got up and exited the cave, clutching their furs closely to their bodies as they walked out into the cold. Once she was satisfied that the room was empty, Solveig led Hegvaldr back to her room.

Her room consisted of an alcove off to the side from the main part of the cave. A fire roared in the corner, a circle of stones surrounding a large pile of wood and kindling that burned. On the floor lay her bedding, covered by several thick pelts, mainly bear. Leading Hegvaldr by the hand, Solveig directed him to her bed.

Hegvaldr smiled as he sat down on the pelts and pulled her into him. Solveig let her body melt into his until their two became one. Shadows lengthened on the walls as the chieftainess dominated the warrior. The flames of the fire were burning low in the stone circle before the pair pulled away from each other. Solveig climbed off of Hegvaldr and rolled onto her back.

"I am a benevolent leader," Solveig said as her mate breathed heavily next to her. Sweat beaded her brow and her chest heaved, but she spoke deliberately, keeping her breathing steady. "But I am not without my resources. I would hate to lose your company; however, I require your obedience in return for my favors."

Hegvaldr remained silent.

"I don't believe that I am asking too much from you. If you believe otherwise, I'm more than happy to replace you."

"Gods' will be obeyed, Konugrr," Hegvaldr said. "It would be my pleasure to travel with Eivind."

Solveig smiled. "I am pleased with your decision."

As the burning tinder began to go out, Solveig rolled over onto Hegvaldr once more. The chieftainess nibbled on his ear. With a breathy voice, she whispered, "It is better to please me than displease me, no?"

Hegvaldr let out a grunt as he flipped her over on her bed and settled on top of her. Solveig knew how to keep the cold nights from being unbearable.

XXI

Cienna wandered through the royal gardens behind Caer Grey. Purple, orange, and yellow chrysanthemums bloomed, creating a riot of color. Vines trailed up trellises alongside the caer's stony walls, heavy with green and red grapes. Occasionally, Cienna picked a grape or two from the plants as she walked by. Popping the little morsels into her mouth, she smiled at the explosion of flavor inside. A hummingbird darted in front of her, its iridescent wings flapping manically as it went from flower to flower in search of a little bit of nectar. Cienna stopped walking and stood where she was. She didn't want to scare away the little creature.

A bee buzzed by her ear, making her jump slightly, before dropping down and gathering some pollen. Laughing soundlessly to herself, Cienna watched as the two wove through the flowerbeds. It was hard to imagine that just a short time ago, something as mundane as this would be such a welcome sight. After watching the fauna for a while, Cienna continued through the gardens.

In the heart of the garden, a pond with a number of large goldfish swam around lazily. They moved in figure eights as they wove between the lily pads that floated on the water's surface. Cienna managed to catch a frog perched on the pad before it dove into the water, rippling the surface. The fish appeared undisturbed by the intrusion into their home.

Crouching down at the edge of the pond, Cienna dipped her fingers into the cool water. She swirled them around, making a little whirlpool in the shallows of the pool. As she moved her fingers, she was struck with an idea.

Closing her eyes, she focused on the water at her fingertips. Slowly, she pulled her hand out of the water, maintaining her circular movements. The water moved with her, rising out of the pond and spinning around through the air as it mimicked her hands.

Cienna smiled as she continued to control the water. Looking down at her hand, she noticed that more of her arm was covered in tattoos. Pride welled inside her as she saw her skill as a Stream increasing right in front of her.

I never would've thought that I could grow this much without more practical training. If only Father were here to see this. He would be so proud.

A heaviness filled her stomach as she thought of her father. When he died, it felt as though a piece of her went with him. The two shared a strong bond. It was going to be a while before she got over losing King Jaste. As she thought of his passing, her concentration broke and the water went crashing back down into the pond, startling the fish. Those closest to her darted away to the safety of the other side of the pool. The lily pads moved around in the water, displaced by the splash from the returning liquid during the fall.

Her hand frozen in mid-air, Cienna gradually got up and walked away from the pond. She crossed through the remainder of the garden in a haze, moving swiftly. She no longer took in the beauty of nature as she traveled. Instead, her mind fixated on the late king. Before she knew it, she was out of the garden and standing in front of the steps of the shrine. Seeing the large structure brought her out of her fog and focused her attention once more.

The shrine of the Fallen was an ancient structure. Although originally created to honor all of the gods, Ghan and Aria became the main emphasis for the temple once they fell to Corinth, while gods like Zemé, the wind siblings, Vahnyre, and the Ancients were forgotten. Their reliefs were faded and decaying in the marble structure, while the Fallen were maintained reverently. Silver leaf plated Aria's hair, making it stand out against the white marble.

With a deep breath, Cienna lifted her leg and placed her foot on the first step. She let out a sigh of relief when her world didn't come crumbling from out beneath her. Steeling herself, she began her climb towards the shrine proper.

At the top of the stairs just outside of the temple doors, there was a small well filled with cool water. Cienna walked over to the fount. Using the wooden ladle, she filled it and poured the cool water over her hands, washing them with the sacred liquid. After she'd washed her hands, she brought them together in prayer and said a quick word to the gods of the temple, begging for them to carry her message to her father as he traveled through the Halls of the Fallen. Once finished, she clapped her hands together three times before opening her eyes and walking into the building.

Inside the shrine, incense burned in little burners that hung from the ceiling between the temple's pillars. Cienna moved sluggishly through the sanctuary towards the little altar with her father's ashes on it, which were stored in a lilac urn with black and gold filigree decorating the outside. Once she reached the base of the dais, she knelt down on her knees and closed her eyes. Bowing her head, she clapped her hands three times and brought them up to pray. The air around her was stale, the fire from the hearth and the burning incense making her drowsy as she sat.

"Holy gods," she began, "please take my words to my father, Jaste Grey. I hope to receive his guidance, as well as any you may deem me worthy of receiving." Cienna took a shuddering breath and paused for a moment. After counting to ten to herself, she decided that she'd given the gods enough time to hear her plea and that they were ready to accept her message.

"Father, I don't know what I'm doing. I'm trying to keep Zanir afloat, but Mother seems to be managing things in her way. I'm so unsure of what to do. Do I follow her, or do I try and take the lead?"

Cienna felt the urge to open her eyes, but kept them closed. It had been a long time since she'd been in the temple to pray. Her parents didn't believe that it was a necessary ritual for her to regularly partake in. The last time she was there was when her grandmother died. Unsure of what to expect, Cienna decided to continue.

"I led - Alverick and Brody led Pharn to victory against Swordbane and the demon, Alazi," she babbled. "We lost Alverick in the process, however. Now, we are on thin ice with Oldar Storm. I don't know what to do. It's like we've gone from one enemy to another in such a short period of time. I'm trying to follow your ways, but I'm not you."

Cienna paused. An image of her and Brody popped into her head. Though she didn't want to admit it, the trouble with the Storms was her fault. She had to give her father all of the information.

"I, uh, I hope you won't be mad, Father, but I turned down Oldar for good. I needed to follow my heart. So," her voice caught in her throat as she tried to get the last words out. It took several attempts, but she finally succeeded in blurting out: "I love Brody, Father. I've chosen to give him my heart. Please don't be angry."

Cienna squeezed her eyes shut, as though she expected her father to yell at her. Did the air around her became heavy, or was that just her imagination? It almost felt as though Jaste's disappointment filled the room. As quickly as it came, however, the tension left. In its wake, Cienna felt a sense of calmness surround her. The chains of the burners clinked softly as they moved in a non-existent breeze. The princess opened her eyes at the sound of the rattling metal, her eyes landing on the one closest to her. The incense and its burner rocked slightly back and forth.

Her breath caught in her throat and she quickly pressed her eyes closed once more. Cienna's heart raced as she tried to rationalize what was going on.

"Father, I want you to be proud of me. I'm doing my best," she said. "Please, I just need a little guidance on how to proceed."

Cienna's hands trembled as she struggled to maintain the proper holy posture. Her legs had fallen asleep a while ago. They tingled as she knelt, a sharp needle sensation poking into them. A single chime from the bell out-side of the shrine sounded. Its high-pitched sound pierced her to her soul. With the single note, a sense of calm washed over her once more. The sound of clinking chains ceased immediately. Satisfied with the answer, Cienna muttered a quick thank you to the gods before clapping her hands three more times and opening her eyes.

The flame in the hearth burned low. As she struggled to stand up, the pain from the needle-like pricks into her dead legs caused her to stagger slightly. She noted that the sun had sunk lower on the horizon.

How long was I here? she wondered.

Taking one last look at her father's urn, Cienna found that her spirit felt a little lighter. "Good bye, Father," she said. "Until I see you in the Halls. Rest easy."

A heaviness pressed down on her head, moving to her cheek. It almost felt as though a hand patted her on her head before moving to cup her cheek. A small smile crept onto her face. She had a feeling that things would get better.

As she walked out of the temple, she saw someone running towards the steps. The princess stared at the incoming man, nonplussed. As he reached the steps of the shrine, he looked up and saw her about to descend.

"Your majesty!" he called out, breathlessly. "Queen Hera requests your presence immediately. We've just received word from our allies. They're withdrawing their support from Zanir."

∞⌒∞

"What is going on?" Cienna asked. She clutched at a stitch in her side as she tried to catch her breath from running back to the Great Hall from the shrine. "Are they really abandoning us?"

Hera sat somberly in her chair and motioned for a servant to bring Cienna a glass of water. "Take a moment, Cienna," Hera said. "The problem won't disappear in the next couple of minutes."

Cienna took a cup from the servant and took a big gulp of water. She held the liquid in her mouth, forcing herself to steady her breathing and keep from choking. After a moment, she allowed herself to swallow. She repeated the action a second time and found that her breathing had stabilized considerably.

Hera noted the change in her breathing as well. "What you've heard is true," she said. "I've received word from Tenzen that Oldar is going around telling people that we allied with his father's murderer. In order to avoid choosing the wrong side, Tenzen's taking an oath of neutrality. Ayobami has sent something similar."

"What about Ro'thre and Quallyah? Surely their leaders have not abandoned us? We've maintained peaceful relations for generations."

Hera shook her head. "I have not heard from them."

"We need to draft a response," Cienna said. "If we can get our side out to them, the true account of what happened, I'm sure that we can reclaim our allies."

"I've already sent someone to draw up something," Hera replied. "Now, we must wait."

"How can we sit idly by while he besmirches our good name?"

"We cannot push others into believing us. The stronger we come on, the more they may begin to believe his lies."

Cienna slammed her glass on the table in frustration, spilling some of the cup's contents onto the surface. A couple servants jumped at the sudden movement, startled by the normally calm princess' change in disposition. Brody walked up to Cienna and put his hand on her shoulder.

"If I may, Waterdrop," he spoke into her ear, "perhaps you should look into finding another way to handle the matter. What if we were to come up with a way to show our good will towards King Storm and his people? They say that actions speak louder than words."

"I like that," Hera chimed in. "If we remind them of how good we've been to them through thick and thin, we may not be able to sway the king right away, but we can get his people talking. Once we get them remembering the good days, they'll begin to question his statements. We might be able to get a dialogue going or even a meeting out of it."

"What can we possibly do to change his mind?" Cienna snapped. "He's so unbelievably stubborn. Not to mention, he's already made up his mind about us."

"He's not the only stubborn one, dear," Hera replied shortly.

"I could leave the city for a while," Brody said.

Cienna and Hera looked at him. Cienna in surprise, and Hera with interest and confusion.

Brody continued quickly, hoping to stave off any comments from Cienna for a moment. "What I mean is, King Storm is *mainly* angry at me. Sure, he says it's because of the princess, but I know it's because of me. If I were to go out on a mission or to, let's say, attend to some personal business, perhaps he will see my absence as a more favorable time to open up the lines of communication and work with us."

"Brody, no," Cienna said. "It's *actually* me that he's upset with."

Hera raised her hand, silencing her daughter. Looking at the guard, she narrowed her eyes. "Are you sure that you want to leave? You will be a hard person to replace while you are away."

"I'm sure that Thol and Ronan can keep Pharn safe in while I'm gone," he replied. "I just need a few days to get my head on straight. I can find someone to keep an eye on her. Ronan would probably be a better choice out of the two."

"I trust your judgement. Don't be long," Hera said.

Brody turned to leave. He caught Cienna's eye and noted the confusion. Her brow furrowed as she tried to appear unbothered. She chewed on her bottom lip unconsciously. Brody turned to face the princess before he walked out.

"Keep your chin up, Princess," Brody told her. "I'm sure you and your mother will be able to think of a way to get us out of this mess. Let me make this easier for you."

"You leaving isn't going to change anything," Cienna retorted. "He's mad at everything, not just you."

"I'm giving you an opportunity to speak with him one-on-one." Brody's voice was firmer than she was used to being spoken to. "Don't waste this chance. We may never get one like this."

Cienna opened her mouth to speak, but closed it as Brody turned from her and walked out of the Great Hall without another word to her. Unsure of what to do, she picked up the glass once more and absentmindedly started swirling it around in her hands. As the cup moved in its circular pattern, the liquid within moved dangerously closer to the lip until some of it crested over the brim and splashed out towards the floor. Without thinking, Cienna held out her other hand to catch the water, her mind yelling at herself for being so careless and making a mess.

As though listening to her thoughts, the water stopped just short of the floor, puddling into the air as though it were on a solid surface. Cienna and Hera stared at the floating liquid, astonishment etched on their faces. The servants standing at the periphery of the room gawked, attempting to hide their surprise by covering their mouths with their hands.

Cienna gazed at the puddle. It slowly spread as it flattened out in the air. She watched as it went from an amorphous blob to developing an abstract shape. Her mind flew back to her time in the temple as the feeling of calmness took over her once more. A heavy presence settled on her shoulders, like two hands placed comfortingly over her. Her mind raced as numerous ideas fought for her attention. Finally, one reached the front and began to take shape. Slowly, it grew, much like the floating puddle before her, until she had a plan.

Hera watched Cienna, noting her daughter's concentration, quietly. A slight smile played on her lips as she watched Cienna come up with a solution to her problem. After an undisturbed period of time, the queen observed her daughter reach a conclusion. Taking her cue, Hera got up and made to leave the Great Hall.

"Where are you going, Mother?" Cienna asked, surprised by the sudden movement.

"I think I'm going to get some air. Why don't you come find me in the garden when you have an idea on how we should move forward with this King Storm predicament."

Hera left the hall, leaving Cienna to think in peace. As she stepped into the hallway, she heard the telltale splash of water hitting the floor. With a smile, she continued on down the hallway.

XXII

HER BELLY FULL, Dez wandered through the streets of Pharn. She paid no attention to where she walked; she just let her feet guide her to wherever her destination was meant to be. People moved out of her way, grumbling in annoyance as she passed by. However, she was unaware of their grousing. The wind spoke to her, captivating her attentions as she traveled. It had been a long time since she lost herself in its words.

You can hear it, can't you? the voice in her head asked. **They're calling to us.**

"How can I not hear it?" Dez replied. "It's so loud and they babble so incessantly. I haven't known peace in a while now."

You aren't curious about what they say?

"If I paid attention to everything they said, I would go crazy."

The voice in her head chuckled in concession. **As if you didn't think you weren't a bit touched already?**

It was Dez's turn to have a quick laugh. What the voice said was true. She knew how people stared at her as she walked through the streets, holding a one-sided conversation with herself for all they knew. It'd been like that for as long as she could remember.

"Are you sure I haven't Snapped?" she asked.

We're having this conversation again?

"One can never be too sure with my condition."

Really now. Don't you think that you would know when you've Snapped? The day you Snap is most likely the day that I am no longer able to speak with you. Until then, think of my melodic voice as a boon. I give you the gift of sanity, dear Dez.

"Now I know you're full of it," Dez replied laughing.

The two walked on in silence for a while. Dez tried to ignore the ramblings of the wind, but sometimes it was just too hard. In an effort to block it out, she tried to focus on the conversations that those around her were having. It had been a long time since she knew peace.

Focusing on the couple walking in front of her, she eavesdropped on their conversation. The first blathered away about the latest fashion in Madden, some wide-brimmed hat with silk flowers and a ribbon. The young woman chattered away about how wonderful it would be to have that hat, and how all of her closest friends were going to be getting one.

The man asked his companion what she would wear it with, noting that none of her dresses would match such a bonnet. She began pouting. The woman clutched his arm and pressed her chest against his body as she tried to make eye contact with him. He noted her touch and turned to look at her. Taking the opportunity, she stared into his eyes, batting her eyelashes as she got even closer to him. She brought her lips closer him, closing her lids halfway as she tried to convince him that she needed the hat.

Dez watched the exchange with a bemused expression.

Makes you want to find one of your own, doesn't it?

Dez shook her head with a wistful smile. "There's no greater fear, than the fear of losing someone you love," she replied quietly. "I couldn't bear the thought that I would be responsible for someone's death, not again."

That was a long time ago, the voice said. He would have gone to the Halls at some point. Seeing that Dez wasn't perking up, the voice added, You did all

that you could. The plague would've taken you too if you hadn't left to find a treatment.

"It still stings," Dez explained. "Just like it will when young Vashe's time finally comes. I told myself that she's the last one that I'll ever open my heart to. No more."

I hope you don't mean that.

The pair walked on in silence once more. The young woman in front of Dez finally managed to convince her partner that the hat was indeed a necessity, and the two broke off to the nearest hatterie to look for one. The crowd thinned as Dez moved aimlessly through the streets. She would walk down a main road, only to turn down a side street and backtrack a bit.

Eventually, she found a well-worn stone next to a dressmaker's shop and decided to sit down and rest. She closed her eyes and listened to the conversations around her as people walked by. Their voices carried on the gentle breeze. Her hair tickled her forehead as it was ruffled in the wind. Pushing away the voices of the people, she focused on what the air whispered to her.

Chaos.

Pain.

Death.

The darkness...

Time.

Too short.

They're coming...

The Ancients.

Those that slumber.

They're coming...

Dez's breath caught in her throat as she brought her hand to her head as she tried to process the multitude of voices talking in her head. They all spoke at once, vying for her attention and overlapping with each other. Some whispered, some shouted. The warnings were always the same, repeating in her head.

Are you okay?

Dez straightened up and began walking once more. She ignored the strange looks that her sudden movement brought on. Taking a deep breath to steady her nerves, Dez continued with the flow of the street.

"Things are bad," she whispered. "The warnings are getting stronger. I thought things would settle down once we helped with Alazi."

I've felt a strange energy as well. I just assumed that it was things settling down from earlier.

"I think we may have been mistaken," Dez replied. "It seems as though we've only just scratched the surface here. The winds, they mention the Ancients and those that slumber. I don't know what that means."

The Ancients? Are you sure?

"Yes."

"I'm sorry?" a voice asked.

Dez looked around and saw a young man standing in front of her, staring at her in confusion. He was disheveled, dirt smeared on his face and all over his body. His clothes were torn, scraps of cloth dangling on his shoulders where the sleeves used to be.

"Pardon?" Dez asked.

"I asked if you would please step aside," he gestured to his lame leg weakly. The left leg was twisted inwards, the result of a broken leg that never healed properly. His mangled foot was bare. "I was hoping that it wouldn't be too much of an imposition."

Recognition dawned on Dez's face and she stepped to the side. "I'm sorry for not moving sooner. Have a pleasant day."

The young man nodded his head to her in thanks and hobbled on down the road. Dez watched as people gave him wide berth as he walked by, looks of disgust on their face.

What a shame to be so disregarded at such a young age, the voice in her head lamented.

"A tragedy," Dez agreed.

Dez continued walking down the streets, not paying attention to where she was going. Her eyes darted around, unseeing, as she walked.

Dzeara, if the Ancients are waking, we're in for a tough time ahead.

"But who are the Ancients?"

Before the aethren, there were the Ancients. The Ancients roamed the land of Enlil, creating new life and providing harmony to the realms. Apophmet, younger brother of Re'nuhktet, desired the world's balance to tip towards chaos. His brother sought to keep it even. After a time, the Brothers decided to create children, and thus Earth, Ayr, Water, and Fyre were born. The Brothers taught the aethren how to maintain the balance.

Once the Ancients were sure that their children could keep harmony between the realms, they created Man. After Man was born, the Brothers disappeared into Enlil, which was now empty of all life, and joined Seti and Maeyu'dana, their younger siblings. They watched as their creations worked together in the universe from the shadows. Apophmet, always craving chaos, began to sow discord amongst Man. He also influenced Fyre. As Fyre's mind slowly moved from a desire for balance, Apophmet sunk back into the darkness to watch his children fight.

"What does this have to do with us?" Dez asked.

My people are Awakening, the voice in her head replied. Soon, I will need to join my siblings and fight. This means that by default, so will you.

"Your siblings?"

Yes. We are closer than you realize.

"Is there a way to keep them from waking? Perhaps I just need to travel to Ein's home, Aramaine, or another dimension?"

I wish it were that easy. My people don't reside in Aramaine. I'm afraid there's no way for you to speak with them directly. We need to find the source of the disturbance before things get out of hand.

"Then I think we should head east. I'm sure we can find something out there. Perhaps we can even find something back home if we really need to."

Dez turned and began heading towards the city gates. She moved with a renewed vigor as she wove between the other city residents. People scrambled to get out of her way, but they didn't need to as she deftly moved between them. Keeping her ears open to the wind, she listened for any changes that it carried. By the time that she reached the city gates, she was satisfied that there was no new information to be learned and returned her focus to figuring out her travel plans.

At the gate, Dez was stopped by one of the guards, an older man with a grizzled beard. He walked over to her and held up a hand to stop her.

"I'm sorry, my lady, but we are not allowing any people to travel through the gates at this time," he explained.

"It's the middle of the day," Dez exclaimed. "Surely, there's no reason to keep travelers from leaving at this hour."

"My apologies, but those are my orders," he replied.

Dez opened her mouth to protest, but a faint noise caught her attention. Straining to pick it up, she thought she heard a familiar voice carried on the wind.

"King Storm?" she muttered.

"How did you know?" the guard asked. "That information was just received not even an hour ago."

"I just –" Dez began. A loud screeching in the distance captured her attention. The high-pitched screams, accompanied by snarls, carried over from the east.

This must be the beginning, the voice said.

Pushing her way past the gate guard, Dez ignored his protests as she headed out of Pharn and made her way towards the King's Forest. She strode swiftly down the road. Time was running short, and she hoped to avoid whatever destruction lay ahead. Dez rounded a curve in the road and turned to look at Pharn. A memory of Vashe as a little girl popped into her head, bringing warmth to her face as she held back a tear.

"I have to stop whatever this is. I can't lose Vashe, or anyone else," she murmured.

You're not in this alone, the voice in her head replied. **I'm here with you.**

XXIII

VASHE LED a bay-colored horse along the outskirts of Pharn. The stallion swished his tail lazily as he followed her lead. A pack and small pouch hung off the beast. In the pouch were travel pellets and a bit of produce. The pack contained her leather tome, some victuals, and an array of herbs and creams. On her hip, a short sword lay strapped against her black breeches. Hidden in her boot was a small dagger. Her hair bounced against her back, tied in a high tail. A necklace with a brilliant fire opal, her mother's necklace, adorned her slender neck. On her hand was the ring she had taken from Queen Gwyn with the House Madderoux crest on it. The stones on each piece of jewelry felt warm on her flesh.

As they walked, the horse's ears twitched. It had been a while since he walked amongst the populace. He tensed as he waited for commands to race through the streets. Vashe found herself whistling as she moved. Though she was not on the main streets, a surprising number of people bustled by. One such duo was a chestnut-haired male and a short-haired redhead. The two paid no attention to the statuesque woman as she stopped in front of them.

Clearing her throat, Vashe waited until the pair looked up from their conversation. When it seemed as though they would pass her, she spoke: "Well, I see that my salve has worked wonders on your leg, Master Brody."

Brody looked up as he heard the husky voice. His eyes widened as he gazed upon the Headmistress. Caitlyn furrowed her brow, trying to remember where she'd seen the slender woman before.

"Oh, it has indeed, Headmistress," Brody replied.

"Vashe," she prompted.

"Yes, of course. Thank you so much. We would've been hard-pressed for victory if it weren't for your gift. What are you doing walking down this street?" he asked. "Taking a shortcut somewhere?"

Caitlyn let out a soft "ooooh" as she realized who they were speaking to. Vashe smiled as she ignored the sound. Vashe studied the young man's body and noted that he was putting his full weight on his leg, not favoring his normal one.

"I'm on my way out. Where are you two headed?" Vashe asked.

"We were actually heading towards the Mageri in hopes of finding you," Caitlyn replied.

"Well, isn't that convenient? I can't stay long, Gods know I've already prolonged my stay, but I can spare a moment for you."

Vashe motioned for the pair to join her off to the side of the streets, out of the way of the populace. Her stallion meandered behind her, trying to sniff Brody and Caitlyn as he passed by them. His ears twitched as a fly attempted to land on it while he walked. Caitlyn gave the beast a pat on the nose as they moved.

Once in the shade of the city walls, Vashe dropped the horse's lead, commanding him to wait. The stallion flicked his tail, casually looking around for something to nibble on. He found some blades of grass poking through the worn cobblestones in the street and busied himself with them.

"What did you want to talk about?" Vashe asked.

"It's a tricky subject," Brody began.

"How do we find Alverick and bring him back?" Caitlyn said bluntly.

Vashe rubbed her chin as she thought about the question. "You do realize that he is beyond our realm, in the realm of the damned, don't you?" she asked. "Aramaine is inhabited by wyrms and dragons, and those are the more pleasant things that you'll find there."

"I don't care," Caitlyn insisted. "Surely, you know a way to bring him back to us, even if it means us crossing through the abyss and pulling him out ourselves."

Vashe crossed her arms. "I admire your determination, but this is no simple task."

"Aren't you a Shadow though?" Brody asked.

She nodded. "I am, but it is still quite dangerous, even for me. The only person that I know who has successfully traveled through Aramaine is my *naran*. I've never tried it."

Brody looked slightly crestfallen at the news. However, Caitlyn's eyes glowed with determination.

"We'll do whatever you say," Caitlyn said. "As long as we can bring him home."

Vashe, her arms still crossed, thought for a moment before taking the necklace from around her neck and proffering it to Caitlyn. The redhead looked puzzled at the trinket, but took it from the headmistress.

"I can't guarantee that you'll find him," Vashe warned. "I can't even guarantee that you'll make it back here, but if we're going to try, you may as well have this. I have twinned this necklace to the ring I am wearing, it should let me remain in some form of contact with you, even across great distances."

Caitlyn thanked her and put the chain around her neck. The pendant sat lightly against her skin. Caitlyn noticed that where the stone touched her flesh, a slight warmth emanated from the area. Nonplussed, she kept her mouth closed and didn't say anything. Anything that Vashe gave them to aid their journey would undoubtedly be important.

"Head south, towards the lower border of Zanir," Vashe continued. "Stop once you see the river. Do not cross it. If you do, your life will be forfeit. Scrymme lays on the other side of the river and their soldiers will not hesitate to kill any who venture too close to her borders."

Brody and Caitlyn shared a glance. He didn't know much about Scrymme, and she knew even less about anything beyond the northern moors of Zanir.

"When you see the river, follow it until you see a willow tree with a smooth stone underneath. That is where you can find a portal to Aramaine. I should be able to help you open the door from afar, but I cannot help you once you go through."

Walking to her stallion, Vashe dug around in the pack. Pulling out a handful of dried herbs, she returned to the pair and handed them to Caitlyn to put in her own pouch. The duo looked at the aromatics, but remained quiet. Caitlyn gingerly took the plants and carefully placed them into her hip pouch without crushing them.

"You'll need some blood from each of you," Vashe explained. "Place the herbs in a circle; not too big, but big enough that the two of you can comfortably stand within. You may also want to layer it with smooth stones from the riverbed. Once you're there and you've offered your blood, I may be able to open the portal from wherever I am. I must warn you, though. I've never attempted this before, and I don't even know if it's possible. There's no guarantee that anything will happen. You very well can end up taking this journey for naught."

"But you can help us once you come back, right?" Brody asked. "I mean, you're a Shadow. Surely, you could open a door upon your return. We could just wait for you at the spot."

Vashe shook her head. "I could open a portal, yes, but I couldn't tell you if everyone could go through or if it's only for me. This is my best guess on a way to let you both enter the realm of Aramaine."

"It'll have to do," Caitlyn said forcefully. "What next? Where do we go from there?"

"You then travel until you find a treasure beyond all your imagining. You will see plenty that take your breath away, but only one will be great enough to belong to Ein. I would assume that Alverick would be near there, but I cannot be sure."

"Find a mountain of treasure," Caitlyn said. "Got it."

"One last thing," Vashe added. "Aramaine is filled with all kinds of horrible creatures that you will most likely encounter, so stealthiness is vital. However, should you run into Ein himself, unless he doesn't see you, Aramaine will be the last thing you ever see. So, travel cautiously. Ein is not forgiving, especially if he thinks you're trying to steal what's his."

Brody and Caitlyn nodded.

"Thank you for everything, Vashe," Brody said. "If it weren't for you, we wouldn't even know where to begin."

"Yes, thank you," Caitlyn added. "We'll see you upon your return."

"And you'll have to tell me all about Aramaine," Vashe said with a smile. "I've always been fascinated by that realm. Take care, young Brody. I wish you and your friend a successful journey."

Taking up the reins once more, Vashe led her mount through the streets and toward the city gates. She turned and watched as Brody and Caitlyn stood off to the side of the street, discussing their travel plans for a moment.

"I hope I didn't send them to their deaths," Vashe mumbled. "It'd be a shame to lose them both. There's so much fire in their spirits. No wonder *naran* took such a liking to them."

~∞~

Hera stood facing a window, her hands clasped behind her back. She watched as a dark-haired woman walked towards the city gates with a bay-colored horse. The figure below her looked up at the window as though she knew the queen was looking. The queen recognized the headmistress and waved. She could've sworn she saw Vashe smirk in response.

Hera watched as the woman led her mount toward the gate. The guards attempted to turn her around, only to be met with magical paralysis, bringing a chuckle from the queen. The headmistress held up her hand as she walked past the soldiers. Though they were frozen, their mouths moved frantically, their eyes panicked. As soon as Vashe exited the city, the men were suddenly freed. Talking amongst themselves, Hera watched as they dispersed, heading back to their posts as Pharn's gates closed behind them.

Looking away from the gates, Hera went back to watching the people below her. Men and women strolled around, no longer in garments of mourning. Occasionally, she spied an older citizen wearing an article of black as a sign of respect for the fallen king. Hera found her heart warming as she saw her people's love for her husband.

How she craved that love and loyalty, to be adored like Jaste had been. What would happen once her people found out about the allegations against her and her daughter? Could she protect Cienna from any backlash? Hera didn't worry about herself, as she knew that she would be able to absorb most of the blow. But Cienna, she was too young for the politics of Corinth. She didn't know the games that were played.

"Oh, Freyna, protect my people. Give me strength to fight this battle so that Cienna doesn't have to. This isn't her fight," Hera prayed. On the window ledge, her little effigy of the wind goddess sat perched against the window. "With you behind me, I know I can bring peace to Zanir and Alocar once more."

The figure on the sill tipped over, almost falling to the floor. Hera jerked to catch it, bringing the doll up to her chest to subconsciously cradle it against her like a babe before placing it back on the ledge. Smoothing the white dress on the totem, she resumed her post. A pale blue feather fluttered in front of her, drifting through the air, catching on the eddies of the current and hanging in front of the window at eye level.

"How strange to see such a brilliantly blue feather," she mused to herself. "Must be bluebirds nesting somewhere nearby."

Hera's eyes traced the path of the feather as it moved along her line of sight. The gentle swirling brought her a measure of comfort and peace. It was the same feeling that she felt when she watched her people honor their king. It left her with hope. Hope that she was leading the nation in the right direction.

Eventually, the feather dropped below her vantage point. Children ran through the streets, chasing each other with sticks. The general din of laughter could be heard, even from where she stood. Their innocence brought a smile to her lips.

Scanning down towards the gate, Hera noticed a brown-haired male accompanied by a red-headed female leading a roan horse towards the exit. As they arrived at the gate, the man pointed to himself and the woman, gesturing outside. The soldiers on duty exchanged an animated conversation with the young man before they began laughing. His partner crossed her arms, looking less than amused.

The young man turned, patting it on the rump. He gesticulated with his arm some more before pulling himself up into the saddle. The woman swung herself onto the horse behind him, wrapping her arm around him. Speaking to the guard, he steered their mount towards the city gates. The soldier motioned to the duo before snapping into attention and saluting.

Hera smiled as she watched Brody and Caitlyn ride off. She didn't know where he was going, but she was happy to know that he did all of this to help protect her daughter's reputation. Jaste knew how to read people. Hera only hoped that in time she would be able to as well.

XXIV

Hroth walked through the streets of Fa'Tinh, his eyes constantly darting to view his surroundings. He wore a loose-fitting cream-colored shirt and brown breeches. His light brown hair had been dyed a darker shade to help complete his look. Changing his hair color wouldn't keep him unrecognizable from Wyrd, but it would help him travel without being harassed by Wyrd's followers. Viir and his group of Pshwani were still upset about Liir's death, but their outbursts were becoming less frequent. That worried Hroth.

"Move," a voice said gruffly, bumping into Hroth's shoulder.

Hroth staggered forward slightly from the force of the shove. The source of the voice strode past, completely ignoring Hroth's presence now that he was out of the man's way. Dressed in vibrant clothes, he strut through the street with pompous aggression. As he neared others in his path, he would bark out a command for them to move as well. Most just moved out of his way, shooting dirty looks at his backside. Some would grumble, but not make too big a deal of the matter. One older woman, however, did not take kindly to his brusque treatment.

"Just because the Great Heart has left us for a while doesn't mean that you get to go around treating people like offal," she called out. "We demand an apology for your actions."

"Grandmother, you are tricking yourself if you think that the Great Heart is coming back," the man replied. He turned and glared at her in mock pity. "He's been run out of town by one of his own. Does that sound like a capable man to you, Grandmother?"

The elderly woman glowered at him. Pulling herself up to her full height, which was still considerably shorter than the younger man, she marched over to him and poked him in the chest with her finger. "The Great Heart will be returning to us. There is no one who is equal to him. Now, I would like my apology."

Sweeping his cap off of his head, the man dipped into a mock bow in front of the wizened woman. "My humblest apologies, Grandmother," he said. His voice dripped with contempt as he maintained eye contact with her. "I did not realize that his departure was anything more than his failure to admit defeat at the hands of one of his inferiors. I hope that I can be forgiven, not only for my harsh criticism of our beloved Great Heart, but also for my actions against you, Grandmother. I did not mean to disrespect one such as yourself."

The aged woman's eyes burned as she bit back her tongue. Several people walked up to her and put their hands on her shoulder in an attempt to calm her, but she shook with rage. A young woman walked up to the pair and stepped in front of the older woman.

"You must be so proud of yourself to speak to this Grandmother like that," she scolded.

The man's gaze turned to her and his expression soured. "I would keep my nose out of other people's business, if I were you," he said coldly.

"What more can you do to disrespect us?" she asked. "You strut around like you are some high lord, yet we all know that you are merely a man with more money than fashion sense."

A loud smack split the air as the man slapped the younger woman across the face. Gasps from the crowd rang out. The woman brought her hand to her face and delicately touched her stinging cheek. Anger burned in her eyes as she shot daggers at the man, but she did not speak.

Hroth had had enough. Striding forward, he placed himself between the man and the two women. The man was taken aback to see yet another challenger in front of him. Composing himself quickly, he straightened up and placed his hands on his hips.

"And what do we have here?" he sneered. "Some foreign beggar man standing up for the women? No wonder the Great Heart left. There's no standards for the type of people we allow to walk our streets anymore." He laughed at his own words as the crowd glared at him.

"Why don't you just move on," Hroth said. His gravelly voice carried, despite the harsh laughter from the man.

"What could you possibly do?" he asked.

Throwing caution to the wind, Hroth casually brought his hand up and snapped his fingers. A small flame flickered in his hand. The garishly dressed man's eyes widened in fright as he stared at the magical fire. Hroth gave the man a smug look and extinguished the flame immediately.

"I'll let you imagine what I can do," Hroth said softly. "Now why don't you just move on and not bother anyone anymore? I would bet that you would make many people happy if you did."

The man stammered and staggered as he turned to briskly walk away. Hroth looked around and saw uncertain eyes watching him. With a shrug, he continued on his way down the road.

"It's going to be a long day," he mumbled.

⁓⦿⧉⁓

Hroth pushed open the door to Intan's house, slinking into the dwelling. Looking for a chair, he sat in the first one he saw. With a sigh of contentment, he stretched out in the seat and let his body melt into it.

"Hroth, is that you?" Pram's voice called out.

"Yes," he replied.

Pram rounded the corner, waiting for the Flame to push himself out of the chair. Pram looked stressed. Bags rested under his eyes and his cheeks appeared gaunt. Waving his hand, Pram motioned for Hroth to remain in his chair. Spying one nearby, Pram sunk down into the chair. His arms lay on the armrests, gripping the ends until his knuckles turned white.

"Who would've thought that Wyr-raji could stir up such discontent amongst our brothers," the general breathed. "I've just spent the morning talking the Pshwani clan out of a rebellion. Luckily, though Viir is angry, his people are more willing to listen to reason."

"Are you sure that you've managed to persuade them though?" Hroth asked. "I would imagine that they're not very happy with not being told that we're in an alliance with our enemies."

"I've done what I can for now," was all Pram could say. "Who knows if they're truly pacified? I'm just content with the thought that I've staved any rash action for another day."

Hroth nodded. He resumed his stretching, closing his eyes once more.

"How was your day?" Pram asked.

Cracking open an eye, Hroth replied, "The people of Fa'Tinh are agitated. Even those not directly involved in Liir's death are starting to listen to Wyrd. I ran into a little popinjay earlier today who seemed quite assured that Great Heart is not returning. If I didn't know any better, I'd say that Wyrd's amassed a bit of a following."

Pram frowned. "This is troubling."

"How were your people before the campaign?" Hroth asked. "Sword-bane doesn't seem like the type to leave loose strings lying about."

"He doesn't. Everything was orderly. The transition into his reign went smoothly. All accepted his rule. There were no cracks, no flaws." Pram's hands left the armrests as he began to rub his knuckles. "I've never seen anything like this, actually."

Hroth opened his eyes, watching the general. His stomach felt uneasy. He'd seen this before. It never ended well.

"That was before my time," Pram continued. "Sure, there was more isolation in the old days, but we didn't actively try and conqueror one another or call for the removal of a leader. Even if we were following the old laws, Len would still be the head of his people, and respected by the others as an equal."

"Can you invoke the old laws?" Hroth asked.

Pram arched an eyebrow questioningly.

"Think about it. In this time of uncertainty, if we can remind the older generation that Swordbane is still the rightful leader, we could find a way to quell the minority for now until he comes back and sorts everything out properly. It's the younger generation that is pushing for this fight, and that's primarily because Wyrd has stirred up their emotions and made them forget that whether we follow the new rules or the old, Len is in charge."

"I fear that Wyr-raji is trying to use this as an excuse to usurp power. If he can convince the elders that he is truly fit to lead, we may be cutting off our own nose in spite of ourselves. He will try and turn this around in his favor."

Hroth straightened up and pursed his lips.

Wyrd is making my job much more difficult, he mused. *I almost feel as though we need help from the Myrani. Too bad they won't bother to join in unless the price is right, especially against one of Wyrd's current skill. Damnation! How do we move forward?*

"I think I have an idea," Pram said, breaking Hroth's line of thought. "It's risky, but I think that it could work. My only concern is that it involves Honorable Mother." He looked towards the heart of the house, where Intan would be.

"I wouldn't use her," Hroth replied. "My little peacock from earlier today showed no sign of respect for an older woman. What makes you think that she would have any other result?"

"Because, Honorable Mother knows the old ways better than anyone else in Xan. She is well respected, both amongst our people as well as with the gods. If we can get the gods to show that they favor her over Wyr-raji, we can hopefully regain our footing and hopefully end this peacefully once and for all."

Hroth struggled with the idea. "I don't know, Pram. What if this backfires in our face?"

"Then she becomes the martyr we need to push our allies to join our cause. If Honorable Mother is killed, it will mean war for Xan."

Hroth stared at the general. The Qu-ari man's gaze was steely as he gazed ahead at the wall in front of them. His jaw was set tight as his hands returned to the armrests and resumed their previously white state. Hroth knew better than to speak with the man at the moment. The Flame knew that if he said much more, Pram's resolve would break and they would not have a chance at stopping the coup from gaining momentum.

"It appears to be the only way," Hroth muttered under his breath, just loud enough to be sure that Pram heard him. Hroth noted that the general's grip on the chair lessened ever so slightly at the words.

Pram leaned back in his seat and closed his eyes. After a short period of time, his breathing became rhythmic. Satisfied that the Qu-ari general was asleep, Hroth stretched out in his chair once more and closed his eyes. He wanted to shut off his brain, but his head was spinning after all that had happened that day. It was hard to sleep when his mind was so full. Slowly, he formulated a plan for when he next had to go out amongst the people. Finally, after a long period of time where he just sat there with his eyes closed, Hroth felt himself starting to doze off a bit.

Unbidden, an image of Intan floated into his head. She stood in front of her people, demure, but strong at the same time. Her faint voice ringing out for all to hear as she addressed the crowd. She would indeed be a critical piece in this scheme.

I'll have to keep an extra close eye on Len's mother, if only to give Pram a little more peace of mind.

XXV

LEN WANDERED off the main road with a determined step, trying to figure out where he was going to go. He couldn't just return home while Wyrd and his followers threatened bloodshed. But he couldn't just abandon his people to the mob. All he could do was try and figure out a way to regain control.

His departure from Xan had gone as planned. Dressed in his battle gear, he quietly walked through the streets and out of the capital, head held high. Len remembered the looks of surprise he received as people realized that he was leaving.

It's dangerous enough leaving Pram and Hroth there.

He took in the scenery as he headed south towards the coast. The tall grasses waved gently in the breeze. At knee height, Len kept his eyes out for snakes hidden in the grass. Occasionally, he'd startle a small quail into flying out into the open as he slipped on a loose stone in the dirt.

After walking for several hours, the grass got shorter and a warm breeze rustled his hair. Len looked around for a spot to sit and rest. He spied a tree trunk that had fallen long ago and was now reduced to petrified wood. Making his way to the log, he sat down and stretched his legs.

Pulling his sack onto his lap, he reached in and pulled out a bit of dried meat to eat while he rested. He'd traveled for several days and his rations were running low. Taking a bite out of his food, Len tried to gather his thoughts. They hadn't been able to give him any answers in the previous days.

Will Wyr-raji truly honor the elders of Xan and leave Mother out of his conquest? Viir and the Pshwani will. They fear the old laws. Or do they fear Wyr-raji's unholy powers more? Can Hroth...

Len started as he heard the crunch of underbrush in the not too far distance. He took a bite of his snack and sat quietly, waiting to see who came around the bend. It didn't take long before Len heard a large group of people talking merrily. Keeping his eyes down, Len took another bite of his food, finishing off the strip. Reaching into the sack, he dug out another bit of dried meat and pulled it out.

A tan woman with long red hair tied in a ponytail rounded the bend. She wore a white tunic that hung off of her right shoulder with black pants and boots. A tri-cornered hat sat lightly on her head while a short sword rested against her hip. A group of fifteen trailed behind her.

Len sat quietly on the petrified wood as he chewed his morsel.

"Well, well, what do we have here?" a feminine voice called out. "Looks like we've got a stranger in our territory."

Len glanced up and saw the redhead tilting her head towards him. Ignoring her, he took another bite of his food.

"Doesn't look like a very smart one either if he's sitting on my log," one of the men chimed in.

"'S'not your log, it's the Scourge's,'" another said as he addressed the first. "You know how the Scourge likes to think. He likes his peace an' quiet, ya know."

Len heard the crunching of grass get louder as someone approached him. Shortly, he saw a pair of black boots standing in front of him.

"Why don't you look at me, friend," the feminine voice asked. When Len didn't look up or answer, she continued. "You know, it's not polite to ignore someone when they're talking to you. Why don't you show us some manners and look up for a bit?"

Len felt a slender finger grab his chin and tilt his head up. His eyes locked onto the red-haired woman's emerald ones. He noted that freckles dotted her face and a small scar ran down the length of her left cheek. Len grabbed her hand and pulled her finger off of his chin. He stared coldly at her, daring her to try that again.

"Well, well. We got a lively one here," she smirked. Ripping her arm out of his grip, she leaned over and grabbed him by his hair, forcing his face to stare into hers again. "If you're as smart as you look, you won't try that anymore," she said softly. "I don't like being roughed up."

Pushing his head down, she walked around him and sat next to him. Len looked at her out the side of his eye. The young woman had her hands on her knees and was looking at him. Before he could react, she snatched the dried meat out of his hand and took a big bite. She grinned widely, her teeth not exposed, as she chewed the morsel.

"Freyna's mercy, you're insufferable," Len sighed. "Leave me be, woman."

Len grabbed his food back from the woman. He ripped off the portion where her teeth marks were and threw the little bit back at her before stuffing the remainder of his snack into his mouth.

Several of the men in her group moved to rush forward, their hands reaching for the swords on their hips. The woman held up her hand, staving off their advance. Placing her hat onto the fallen trunk, she reached up and tightened her ponytail before drawing her sword.

"Why don't we settle this like men?" she asked. "I do not take your disrespect lightly."

Len smiled and slowly stood up. He pulled out his warhammer and spun it idly from hand to hand.

"Tell me, who do I have the pleasure of killing?" Len asked, his voice cold.

"Kayna, queen of the pirates."

With a smirk, Len assumed a defensive stance, holding his hammer in front of him. His opponent returned the smile, her eyes hard, and motioned for him to move away from the fallen tree. Maintaining his defensive posture, Len stalked forward. Once they were back on the main road, Kayna lunged forward, her sword close to her body.

Len braced himself for the strike, placing his weight on his back leg. Kayna feigned a mid-level slice, but changed it up at the last moment to a stabbing motion towards his stomach. Surprised by the speed of her attack, Len quickly adjusted his weight and used his front leg to jump back, his weapon dropping down to parry her strike.

Regaining his balance from the evasive movement, Len dropped his weight and dashed to the right. He carried the hammer in his left hand, raised close to his chest. As he neared her, he twisted slightly and brought his weapon up with a large, strike. Kayna reacted almost a moment too late and barely dodged the slice. Her arms raised above her head, leaving her exposed.

Len took that moment to reverse his momentum and pivot on his front leg to deliver a hook punch to her side. Kayna doubled over as the blow landed against her ribs, gasping in pain. Len wasted no time and used his back leg to kick out her front leg from underneath her, bringing Kayna to her knees.

Smirking, Len readjusted his stance to stand over her.

Too easy.

No sooner had he thought those words, then Kayna spun around with her leg extended, sweeping Len's feet out from under him and causing him to fall flat on his back. He gasped as the wind was knocked out of him. His side ached dully from where he'd been injured in his fight against the Avalanche a week prior.

In an instant, Kayna had managed to climb atop of the young general and began raining punches on his face. Len brought his arms up to protect his face from her blows. The ones that she did land may have lacked the power that his would have, but they flew in sharp and quick. He let her hit him for several seconds before he found an opening. Using her open posture to his advantage, he bucked his hips up to throw her off balance before grabbing her in his arms, pinning her to his body.

Kayna grunted in annoyance.

Taking the moment to catch his breath, Len struggled to figure out his next move.

I need to get off the ground.

Looking around, he saw his warhammer laying several feet away from him. Kayna's short sword lay a little further away. Taking advantage of his current position, he clapped his hands together and squeezed his arms, crushing the woman against his chest. Kayna grunted once more.

Len prepared to roll her off of him when a sudden impact to the side of his temple stunned him. He groaned as a second strike came at his temple. In a swift movement, Len pulled Kayna into his chest in a tight squeeze before rolling over onto his side and releasing her, pushing her off of him. The young general scrambled to his feet, his head still throbbing from the strike. As he rushed to his weapon, he picked it up and noticed Kayna pick up her sword. Her hair was messy, the ponytail coming undone. Placing the hilt of the sword in between her teeth, Kayna hastily tightened her hair before resuming her stance. Her eyes sparkled with mirth.

"Talk about usin' yer 'ead," one of the men joked with his comrades. "Kayna's not gonna go down that easy."

Murmurs of agreement could be heard from the rest of the gang. Several of the women in the group jeered at Len as he stared down his opponent.

The two stood at a standstill, neither moving to attack until they could spy an opening in their opponent's defense. Len crouched down, his hammer held out in front of him. Kayna stood at an angle across from him, her left arm closed with her fist facing in and her sword poised to strike. She bounced slightly, keeping her muscles loose and her legs ready to move.

Len searched her body and after several long seconds, finally found an opening by her thigh. As her legs moved side to side, he noted that her hand was too far away to block a strike. Taking a subtle, steadying breath, Len forced his eyes to look higher up on her body, trying to give the impression that he was searching for an opening higher up than he actually was.

Widening his eyes as though he located a weakness in her defense, Len adjusted his stance a bit. In an instant, he launched himself forward toward the young woman. He covered the ground between them in seconds and feinted towards her hand. Kayna recoiled slightly. At the last moment, she darted to the side and came in with a low, swiping slice towards his hamstring.

Taken by surprise, Len raised his leg higher than he normally would have. He stumbled forward, landing awkwardly on his knee. Gritting his teeth, he spun around while he was still on the ground and brought his hammer up to block an overhand strike from Kayna. Sword blade met handle with a *clank*. The force of the hit jarred his body.

Len hooked the edge of his warhammer around her blade. He smiled as Kayna's eyes widened in surprise. Using his weight to his advantage, Len pushed himself up until he regained his footing. He then pushed her away using his foot. Len made sure that he leaned into the kick that he planted in Kayna's stomach.

The redhead grunted as she staggered back. Narrowing her eyes, she moved a strand of hair out from her eyes. With a growl, Kayna launched forward with a wild flurry of strikes. Len was startled at the ferocity of her attack, her movements concise with no wasted movement.

Len staggered backwards as he worked to dodge her blows. His usual composure all but forgotten as he fought this terror of a woman. Little by little, she drove him back towards the petrified trunk. She wound around his swings and delivered blows that would have been devastating, had he not been able to block at the absolute last minute.

However, several strikes did find their mark. One cut found its way to his thigh, while several landed on his arms. Luckily, they were shallow and did not bleed much. They were, however, a bit of a distraction as he fought. It'd been a long time since he'd been met such a formidable foe. Calls from her comrades only emboldened her actions. Her strikes came faster and faster, pushing him back.

Suddenly, Len found himself up against the tree trunk with nowhere to go. Kayna stood in front of him, angled in a way so that he couldn't move without receiving a blow from her sword. The jeers from her group became more raucous.

"It looks like we've come to the end," Kayna said with a wide smile. She inched her way closer, but kept herself outside of easy striking range.

"This is far from over," Len replied coolly.

Steeling himself, Len darted to the left, his warhammer in his left hand. He feigned a strike towards her knee, causing her to shuffle back. As she dodged his ruse, she managed to bring her sword around and score a shallow wound on his hand. He almost dropped his hammer, but he succeeded in maintaining his grasp on the handle.

It was a small price to pay to get him out of that corner.

This is far from over, he thought.

Taking a deep breath, Len controlled himself, pushing away his adrenaline and replacing it with a measured calm. Sweat dripped off of his head and his side ached. Pulling out his dagger in his right hand, Len took a brief second to glance at the intricate carvings in the pommel.

By the gods, I never thought I'd be struggling against someone who was not an elite. Oh, Freyna, grant me the strength to defeat not only this woman, but her group as well. I can't fall here.

A cool breeze from the west mixed with the warmer one from the east. Dust swirled at their feet, encircling the two fighters. Kayna stood facing Len, breathing heavily from her exertions. The young general focused on steadying his. A feeling of peace filled Len, bringing him strength. Len looked up at the blue sky and watched the white clouds churn around.

This is the end.

Metal clanged against metal as the two launched into a final flurry of attacks. Len wove his hammer in dizzying arcs, utilizing both his right and left hand in an effort to confuse his opponent. She matched his moves, dancing in and out of range as she avoided his strikes. His strikes with the dagger were short, but true. He managed to score a handful of small cuts on the young woman's arms and side, causing her to hiss in pain with each strike.

Kayna came at him with a wide sweeping strike. Len blocked the blade with the handle of his hammer. He spun around and managed to elbow Kayna across the bridge of the nose. As he pulled out of his spin, he used his dagger to cut her cheek. Jumping to the side, Len put distance between himself and Kayna's group.

Silence filled the air as Kayna's friends stared in disbelief. The redhead brought her fingers to her cheek, then to the gash on her nose. Blood flowed from both wounds. She tapped on her nose, relieved to find it wasn't broken. She spat on the ground before putting her sword away.

Len watched her with wary eyes as she motioned for her followers to put their weapons away. With a smile, Kayna turned to address Len.

"Well now, it seems that I underestimated you."

Len stared at her, his weapons still clenched in his hands.

"Tell me, what are you searching for?" Kayna asked. "Surely a man doesn't travel out to the Bone Coast on their own."

"I thought I was heading towards Thallysis," Len said.

"Thallysis is a ghost town. After the pirates from the Eastern Isles burned the city, everyone left. There haven't been people there in almost ten years."

"I have business there. If my journey ends in vain, at least I can say that I tried." Len made to head down the road behind Kayna. Passing the woman, Len maintained eye contact with her band of followers. None moved to oppose him.

"Wait," Kayna's voice called out.

Len paused, not turning around.

"I think I have someone that you may be interested in meeting. If you have some time, why don't you come with me?"

Len turned to face Kayna. She stood silently, waiting for his response.

"Who are you going to introduce me to?" Len asked.

Kayna smiled as she walked down the road to catch up with Len. Whistling to her men, she set off towards the coast. Len watched her group follow. Looking over his shoulder, he saw no one behind him.

"What the hell," he muttered as he trailed behind the group.

XXVI

LEN FOLLOWED behind Kayna and her troupe for longer than he thought. The dirt road they walked on seemed to go on forever as the trees began to blur together. Len's feet began to hurt and his stomach grumbled before they came to a burnt down building. Len stopped, observing the charred wood and rubble. As he turned away from the destroyed structure, Len was greeted by several more. The trees that lined the path, though they had originally been lush, were now burned bone white. Some were strewn on the ground, their blacked remains decaying with time since the bugs could not be bothered to break down the wood themselves. The young general marveled at the destruction. He noted the damage extended further than just the general area where he was standing. Every building, every house, was completely destroyed. Even the ground they traveled on was burnt. Occasionally, a weed grew out of the dead earth, the dirt dry and without any nutrients. The land had been razed beyond recovery.

"Holy Freyna," Len murmured as they walked through the carnage. "Everything's gone."

Kayna turned around when she heard his voice. Len nearly ran into her; he was too busy taking in all of the damage around him.

"I told you," she said softly. "The guys from the Eastern Isles really ruined the town. Thallysis used to be beautiful. It's a real shame that she ended up like this."

"Why did you take me here then?" Len asked. "Simply to waste my time?"

Kayna shook her head with a smile. "No, I told you that I had something that I thought would interest you. We need to head down closer to the coast."

Len walked in silence next to Kayna. Her men led the way, talking and laughing loudly as they trekked. Their laidback attitude surprised Len. While his eyes scanned his surroundings as he walked, the band of pirates barely paid any attention to theirs. Several even walked around with open hip flasks, taking sips of whatever was inside regularly in between shouts of mirth.

"Your men," Len said to Kayna. "Why are they not more alert?"

"Oh, they are," Kayna replied. Turning her attentions to her companions, she barked out, "Status?"

A heavy-set man in a sleeveless top twisted his head to address the woman. "Nothin' to be seein' here, Kayna. Although we did catch us a thief not too far from here the other day. Tryin' to sneak down to our ship and cut our lines, he did."

"Put his feet to the coals," another man added. "Told him we'd do much worse if we found him anywhere near the Bone Coast again."

The two shared a chuckle before passing around the flask and taking a sip. Pleased with the report they gave her, the two returned to their conversation with their friends. Their raucous laughter pierced the group.

"That tells us nothing of what's going on around us now," Len said dryly. "For all we know, your little thief could have returned with reinforcements."

"Oh, I don't think that's very likely," Kayna replied.

"And why is that?"

"Maya," she said simply. "Most likely they had to deal with her. She's not one to cross."

Len gave her a bemused side-eyed glance. "I find it hard to believe that you are one to bow down to anyone," he said.

Kayna threw her head back in laughter. "Maya isn't my master or anything like that. She's my second-in-command."

The group continued on, Kayna and Len walking in silence. The Qu-ari man wanted to get more information about this fearsome second-in-command, but Kayna never made eye contact or gave any indication that she was willing to speak further on the matter.

Destroyed homes became more frequent as they entered the heart of the town. As they rounded a corner, Len was surprised to see a wild dog sleeping in the sun, surrounded by rubble. The shaggy canine was surprisingly healthy looking for one roaming through desolate streets such as this. Kayna whistled sharply and the dog's head popped up. His eyes found her and the dog eagerly got up and bounded over to her.

Kayna scratched the scruffy beast behind the ears before patting her hip, signaling the dog to follow her. He trotted along next to Kayna, his tail wagging and tongue lolling out the side of his mouth. Occasionally, he gave an excited little bark, double-stepping as he tried to get her attention once more. Kayna absentmindedly scratched him again. Len's mouth turned upwards slightly at the sight of the stray and his affection for this rugged group of pirates.

The tangy scent of the sea caught Len's attention. The salty air proved to be a pleasant surprise as it cleared his head and refreshed his tired body. He felt rejuvenated in the briny air. Seagulls squawked in the distance, getting louder as they moved closer to the ocean. Len noticed that several buildings in the area were roughly reassembled, wooden planks fashioned together to create ramshackle buildings on the edge of the water. The crowned jewel on the coast took the form of a well-maintained tavern. A crude sign bearing a skull at the top and a sword and rose crossing underneath hung over the door.

Len admired the emblem as he walked under it. He barely paid any attention as he walked through the tavern doors until he noticed how dark it was. Len blinked several times, trying to adjust to the darkness after the brightness outside. As his eyes became accustomed to the dimness, he noticed that he walked into a room filled with pirates, all of whom were staring at him as he stopped in the doorway. Reaching for the sword on his hip, Kayna placed her hand over his.

"You're safe here," she said. "My people will not hurt you without my command."

Len slowly withdrew his hand from his weapon. However, his eyes darted around the room rapidly, watching for any sudden movement from the twenty or so men who sat drinking in the room. After the initial disbelief of seeing an outsider enter their bar, the men returned to their conversation and drinks. Len relaxed minutely as he saw they began to ignore his presence. He continued to look around, but not as fervently as before. His eyes fell on the figure of a lone woman sitting at the bar.

Though she sat, Len could tell that she was a tall, slim woman. A wide-brimmed hat sat perched on her head. She wore a simple white blouse and tight black pants. At her side, a thin sword lay strapped on her hip. Len was surprised when Kayna began making her way towards the woman.

"All right, I assume?" Kayna called out.

The dark-skinned woman turned around. Her face remained impassive as the woman addressed the redhead. "Other than a singular nuisance yesterday, things have been pleasantly tedious." Her voice matched her regal appearance. She spoke with a slow cadence, her voice as sweet as honey.

Kayna clapped the woman on the shoulder. "I heard about our little visitor just a short while ago. You must have done quite a number on him, Maya, for me to not even know that he'd been here."

"I just advised him that it was in his best interests to leave and never return," Maya replied, nonchalantly. "He seemed to take it rather seriously and took off running out of town."

Kayna gave Maya a wide grin. Looking at the plate on the bar, she spied a bit of deer meat on Maya's plate.

"May I?" she asked, pointing to the meat.

Maya nodded before burying her face in her tankard of ale. Kayna picked up the meat and tossed it over her shoulder to the scruffy stray. The dog gave a happy yap before devouring the morsel on the floor, his tail wagging rapidly as he ate.

"Who's your friend?" Maya asked as she put her mug down.

"Oh, this is Len," Kayna replied. "He's looking for Thallysis, but I promised him something much more interesting."

Maya arched an eyebrow inquisitively.

"You being one," Kayna said with a mock bow. "I think the two of you will become quite close."

"I'm honored that you think I would find him intriguing," Maya said sardonically. "I can't wait to spend more time with him."

"I knew you would like him," Kayna replied. "I also thought that he'd be interested in meeting the Lord of the Western Isles."

Maya paused at this news. Putting her tankard down, she took an appraising glance at the Qu-ari man. Her eyes swept up his body, starting at his dusty boots, stopping briefly on his wrapped arm, until she landed on his face. Her eyes studied his, piercing his eyes and staring deeply into his soul. Finally satisfied, she gave a silent nod and returned to her drink.

"Am I up to your standards then?" Len asked, annoyed at being both simultaneously judged by the woman and dismissed.

Maya shot a look at him out of the corner of her eye for a brief second before returning to her drink without another word.

Len scowled at the woman, but didn't say another word.

Kayna, amused at the interaction, pulled Len aside and steered him towards the back of the tavern. "I think you and Maya will become fast friends, if you don't kill each other first," she said.

"Who is she?" he asked.

"Maeyu'dana, but we call her Maya. She's my right hand, if you will. I leave all of my important business to her."

"And you speak so freely of your relationship with her? Don't you worry that I may use that information to my advantage?"

"You can try," Kayna replied nonchalantly. "Unfortunately, you wouldn't make it back to your people alive if you did. So, I'm not particularly worried about telling you this information. I would hope that you don't give me a reason to regret it, though. Like I said, you intrigue me."

The pair wove through tables and the crowd until they reached the back of the building. Worn doors leading to a back room blended into the dilapidated wall. Though the main front of the tavern was sanded down to give a polished appearance, the back of the pub, the part that lay hidden in the shadows, bore more of a resemblance to the rest of Thyllasis.

Len stopped as they neared the door. As Kayna went to open it, he grabbed her hand, stopping her from doing so. A sense of foreboding flooded his body, unlike anything he'd ever felt before. It was a primal dread. His brain screamed at him to turn and run, but he pushed down the emotion in an attempt to steady himself.

What is this? I am a son of Xan. I shouldn't fear anything that may lie behind this door.

Despite his assurances, he still could not work up the nerve to move forward. His eyes darted around the wall and door, looking for any runes or sign to explain his apprehension. Nothing. He glanced at Kayna and noted that she stood patiently beside him. She did not seem to share his unease.

"Are you ready to move forward?" she asked. "If not, perhaps we should just return you back to where we found you."

Len caught her eyes and shook his head. "We will move forward, but you'll go in first." Pulling out his sword, he moved his arm so that the weapon was not visible by the rest of the tavern. "Should you take me to my doom, be forewarned, I will take you to the Halls with me."

Kayna smirked. "A fair trade, I suppose."

Len released her hand. The red-headed pirate reached for the doorknob once more and gradually turned it. She then pushed the door open, revealing a darkened room. Len paused outside of the door, waiting for her to make her move. Kayna, ignoring the blade inches from her neck, strode confidently through the door and into the room. Len watched her bend down and pick up a lantern, lighting it with a piece of flint that she found next to it.

As the gentle light of the flame flickered on the walls, Kayna moved further into the room. Len looked around him once more before following her into the room and shutting the door behind him. He made sure to leave the door cracked slightly in case he needed to make a quick escape. As he turned to face Kayna, he saw her observing him with an amused expression.

"You really don't trust easily, do you?"

"Not people who've tried to kill me the same day we met," he replied.

"Fair enough," she shrugged.

Kayna crossed the room and walked over to a painting that hung on the wall next to a bookshelf. Lifting the frame out of the way, she reached into a hole that was hidden behind the picture and pulled out a brass key. She fitted the key into a lock next to the bookshelf and turned it. Len heard a faint click as the lock opened. He waited for the stand to be pushed aside, revealing a door, but that never happened. Instead, Kayna opened a door that he didn't even notice next to the shelf.

The door had the same texture as the aged wood in the room, blending in and obscuring any seams between it and the wall. Behind the door lay a long, windy corridor. Kayna ducked her head as she entered the hallway. Len, checking his surroundings yet again, followed suit.

The two traveled through the darkened passage, the lantern providing the only source of light to guide them. Len kept his weapon at the ready, muscles tense and prepared to move should the need arise. Kayna whistled a tune as she walked, the light of the flame causing her shadow to bounce against the wall in time with her ditty.

Their journey passed quickly, as after what felt like only minutes, Len noticed the tangy scent of the ocean that hung in the air. Despite his trepidation, the smell soothed his nerves, if only barely. As they continued on, Len realized that not only was the smell of the sea getting stronger, but there appeared to be an additional light source apart from the lantern. His suspicions were confirmed when Kayna blew out the flame and placed the lantern on the floor a short time later.

"Are we almost there?" Len asked.

"Shortly," came her curt reply.

As they rounded a corner, the sound of the coast could be heard. Seagulls cawed outside and the sound of the crashing waves could be heard. Len took a step forward and felt his foot slip a little. Looking down, he saw that the floor of the tunnel had been replaced with smooth rocks. Between the rocks lay moist sand.

"What's this?" he asked.

"High tide must not have been too long ago," Kayna said. "Looks like the stones are a bit slippery. Tread carefully."

"High tide? What do you mean?"

"Look around," she replied, gesturing to their surroundings.

Len looked up and saw that the corridor expanded, revealing a great cave that opened out into the ocean. At the mouth of the cave, the silhouette of a grand ship cast a shadow in the grotto. It bobbed gently in rhythm with the waves. Stalactites dripped briny water from the ceiling, several droplets landing on the Qu-ari's head. He let out a gasp of wonder.

Kayna smiled. "I knew you would be impressed."

"I've never seen anything like this," he replied. "There's a simple beauty to this cave. Easily defendable, a good place to hide."

"It can be a bit tricky if you need to make a hasty escape though," Kayna explained. "Especially if the tide is coming in. The water level rises fairly high in here."

"How is it that the tunnel hasn't flooded?"

"This used to be an oceanside collection of shops and the beach. When they were destroyed ten years ago, all that was left was the cavern. Our leader found this place, a burnt tavern with two entrances. He found this shell of a building and thought that it would be a good idea to rebuild part of the coastline. On the outside, that hallway was just an empty building that sits behind the tavern. Inside, it's a way to travel in secret."

Len stepped toward the left-hand side of the grotto and made his way toward the water. His feet crunched on the moist sand as he walked. He looked down and saw how his boots sunk into the sand. *Bermet would love this place,* he thought. *This could actually be a way to help my brothers escape, should I fail and Wyr-raji manage to assume control.*

"Len," Kayna called out, breaking his train of thought. "I have someone I want you to meet."

Len spun around and noticed that Kayna had walked up to a large figure. Though he couldn't see the person, the sense of foreboding that he'd felt earlier returned. His feet stuck in the sand as he tried to will himself forward. Taking a deep breath and counting to ten, he managed to force himself to approach the pair.

As he neared, Len saw that the red-headed woman stood near a monster of a man. Though he sat, Len saw that he must be close to seven feet tall. His body was chiseled muscle and covered in scars, the most prominent being one under his right eye. A shock of dark hair with silver streaks lay on his head, while a bit of stubble covered his jaw. His eyes were a deep chestnut and stared through Len, into his soul.

"Who do we have here, Starfish?" he asked.

Len expected a gruff voice for one so imposing, but he was surprised to find that it was actually quite smooth.

"This is Len, Papa," she replied. "I found him by your tree earlier just sitting there. He wanted to go to Thallysis."

Papa? This brute is her father?

The man grunted. "Why do you come to the Bone Coast, young warrior?"

Len took a step back, wary of the man.

"Come, come," the man said, standing up and taking a step forward. "I see your weapons on your hip. Do you take me for a mystic or something?"

"No," Len replied slowly, "but that doesn't mean that I trust you."

"Fair enough," he replied, sitting back down. After a lengthy pause, the man continued. "You still never answered my question though. Trust me or not, you are in my land. Now, tell me. Why did you seek the Bone Coast?"

Weighing his options, Len decided that he needed to answer. A strength radiated from the man in front of him like no other. Even the Avalanche or the Tempest that he'd met during his campaign paled in comparison to this beast.

"I came looking for aid." The seated man raised an eyebrow at Len and motioned with his hand for him to continue. "My people are being threatened by one who has the power of the gods. I have a Flame, but he doesn't seem to be on the same level as the god-blessed."

"God-blessed?" the man asked.

"I don't know how else to describe it," Len said honestly. "At his suggestion, we went into battle with the demon Alazi. Alazi tried to kill him, but instead of perishing in the god fyre, he emerged, stronger, with the gifts of Fyre himself."

Kayna stood open-mouthed. The large man swore quietly under his breath.

"I have seen blessed Freyna," Len continued. It was almost as though the man was pulling this information out of him against his will. "I know that she protects me and my family. I believe she has blessed my quest in search of aid." Taking another deep breath, he said, "I come looking for the help of the pirates. I've heard that they are fierce. I could use their forces."

The large man ignored Len's last statement. "You've *seen* the Ayr sister?" he asked incredulously. "And you believe that she's supporting your cause?"

"I do," Len replied confidently. "She's come to me on several occasions. Kept me safe in my dealings with the demon. The bones are in my favor."

Kayna looked to her father, who fell silent as he mulled over everything that was said. After a lengthy period, he finally spoke.

"Starfish, what do you think of him?"

"He intrigues me," she answered. "I don't think you'll regret it if you consider working with him further."

"Leave me to think," he instructed. "There is much to consider."

The large man got up and walked over to the right side of the cave where he perched himself on a rock.

XXVII

AGELESS ZEMÉ WALKED through the streets of Pharn. Her dress of pale yellow contrasted against her faint olive-green skin. As she wandered through the city, the confused goddess' bare feet gripped the worn cobblestones. Her unkempt sheet of auburn hair hung limply down to the middle of her back. Her emerald eyes gazed blankly ahead of her. People walked around her, barely acknowledging her presence as she moved through the busy streets.

"A land of stone and wood. The ground cries," she muttered as she roamed. "Can't stop the bleeding. Torn trees. Beyond me, beyond me."

No one batted an eye as the girl spoke to herself. As she walked, a trail of moss was left in her wake. Occasionally, a single red flower grew out of the moss once it sprung up between the stones. A robin swooped down and landed on her shoulder.

"What news do you have?" she asked it.

The bird chirped in response before taking off once more. Zemé watched the bird fly through the sky, his red breast a bright speck against the clear blue.

"Death in the north. Pain in the east. Too much, too much." Zemé shook her head violently as she walked. "Where am I? Why am I here? Death, pain, blood. Too much."

People continued to walk past Zemé, ignoring her. One person walked straight into her, knocking her backwards a step. Without looking down to see what he hit, the man continued on his way.

Groaning, Zemé shook her head and continued her directionless journey. The young girl talked to herself as she staggered. As she moved deeper into the heart of Pharn, she noticed more shrubbery and potted plants. Her eyes began to clear a bit as she spotted the flora. Chickens moved through the streets, sometimes followed by a stray cat crouched low, looking to pounce. As Zemé approached, the poultry scattered with indignant clucks.

People began to give her strange looks as she went by. Her pale dress became more translucent as her eyes became clearer, taking in her surroundings.

"Pharn, it's been too long," she muttered to herself. The looks became glares as people no longer ignored the young girl. "The trees, they cry. The ground burns with their mangled corpses. At least they weren't put to waste." Zemé glanced at the city walls and noted that there was a dense copse of trees surrounding one of the walls. "At least the forest still stands, healing the scars of the earth."

The moss that trailed behind her as she walked was becoming dotted with more flowers. Yellows and pinks sprung up along with the reds. The moss itself was becoming thicker and more vibrant. The city folk began commenting on the moss' arrival, trying to figure out how it managed to grow between the heavily traveled cobblestones.

One woman spotted Zemé and gave her a wide berth, thinking her to be some homeless urchin. More people began doing that as Zemé wove through the throng.

The wandering became less aimless, and more focused. Zemé watched as a stray dog walked up to her, tail wagging.

"Why hello, friend," she greeted the dog warmly. "What can you tell me about this city?"

The dog barked excitedly as Zemé nodded along with it. People cast dirty glares their way, muttering amongst themselves about the filthy child playing with the stray. Zemé ignored them, much like they'd previously ignored her, and continued listening to the dog yap away. After several long minutes, Zemé thanked the dog and made her way to the center of the street.

She stopped right in the middle and looked around until she found the caer. She ignored the angry mutterings from the people who moved to go around her. Holding out her hand, Zemé didn't have to wait long until a warbler landed on her palm. It chirped and sang to her for a long time, drawing curious stares from those around her.

Once the bird quieted down, Zemé whispered into its ear. The bird took off and flew to a window on the tower that overlooked the city proper. It settled on the perch and puffed out its feathers, getting ready to settle down for a long time.

Zemé nodded to herself in silent approval of what she'd done. "There's too much death and pain in Pharn. Hopefully there isn't too much for me to fix."

XXVIII

BRODY SLOWED their mount down to a leisurely walk. Caitlyn sat behind him, dozing off in the saddle as they traveled. After a day and a half of hard travel, the change of pace was a welcome break. The sun hung low in the sky as the afternoon turned into evening. Brody's stomach rumbled. He leaned over, reaching into his saddlebag, and pulled out a strip of dried meat to chew on. As he ripped a bite off of the morsel, he looked around, keeping his eyes peeled for the river.

How hard is it to find a river? he groused. Despite his outward demeanor, the idea of accidentally running into Scrymme unnerved him. *It's getting dark soon. We probably should stop for the night.*

As he scanned the area for a good resting spot, a soft burbling caught his attention. His roan horse also perked up its ears at the sound. Brody urged his mount into a trot as he set off in search of the source. He didn't have to travel far before he spotted the river. The water ran gently, the lack of rapids resulting in the water being crystal clear. Brody could see small fish swimming languidly in the current.

Caitlyn's head dropped heavily onto his shoulder, startling awake. Brody's head snapped around to see if she was okay just as she brought her hand to her head, groaning at the rude awakening.

"Ghan's mercy," she swore, "what's going on?" She rubbed her temple with the palm of her hand. "You'd think that a girl could get some sleep while she travels. Apparently not."

Brody chuckled. "You hit your head against me," he teased. "I've been doing important work over here, making sure that we don't run into the religious fanatics and whatnot, and you're over there sleeping like we're on a leisurely journey."

"Come now, Brody. I offered to switch spots with–" Caitlyn trailed off as she saw the river they walked next to. "Ghan's mercy, we found it," she breathed. "I was afraid that Vashe had sent us on a wild goose chase, but here we are."

"Not yet," Brody said. "We still need to find the tree."

"I don't imagine that it'll take long to find it though."

The two slid off their mount, stretching their legs a bit. Brody walked over to the river and filled up his waterskin. He took a deep drink from the skin before refilling it and tying it back on his hip. After securing the sack, he cupped both of his hands and filled them with the frigid water. He vigorously splashed the water onto his face, refreshing himself and clearing off the grime from their journey. Caitlyn walked up beside him and refilled her water pouch, repeating the same motions that Brody had not even a moment earlier, before walking the stallion over to the river to quench its thirst.

Once the trio was well watered, they continued walking along the bank. Caitlyn gave the horse a bit of a lead, allowing for him to graze on the grass as they looked for the tree. The horse nickered as he leaned down and began chewing on the long greens as they strolled. Brody made his way to the saddlebag once more and pulled out another piece of dried meat to munch on. Caitlyn watched him devour a large chunk of the snack before following suit.

The group traveled in peace, listening to the gentle babbling of the river and the buzzing of cicadas. Brody wondered how he'd never found this place before. Though it was outside of Zanir's borders, he'd been far from home before.

I don't think even Al knew of this place. He would like it here. It's so serene; he needed something like this. Brody's stomach dropped as he remembered his fallen comrade. It'd been a while since he felt this way when thinking about Alverick. *This must be what Al felt after a bad campaign. I don't envy him for his position if this is what comes with it.*

"Brody, are we still in Zanir, or are we in another land?" Caitlyn asked.

"To be honest, I don't know. I think this is unclaimed land. From what Vashe has said, it's not part of Scrymme. The only possible explanation is that it's some uninhabited portion of Zanir, but I've never seen this place on any maps."

"I wonder how many other places there are in Corinth that we don't even know about because it's hidden like this?"

"There can't be that many," Brody replied.

As the sun sank lower in the sky, Brody scanned the horizon for a place to sleep for the night. The tall grasses did not show him any good spots to settle down for the night. Their shadows lengthened as they searched for the stone and tree. Brody worried that it would be too far away and they wouldn't reach it that night when suddenly, Caitlyn let out a yelp.

"What happened?" Brody asked as he whipped his head around.

The roan stallion nickered uncomfortably as he eyed the redhead, pawing the ground. Caitlyn tried to soothe creature, but at the same time, she rubbed at her neck, exposing the necklace that Vashe had given her.

"The necklace, it started getting warm," she stammered. "It just caught me by surprise is all. I'm fine." Caitlyn whispered softly to the horse, trying to calm him down. "I wonder what it means."

"I do too," Brody replied. Scratching his head, he tried to think of a reason why it would get warmer. "Didn't Vashe say that the necklace is connected to her somehow?"

"Yes, I believe she said that she had a ring or something that she'd found a way to link with it. It's supposed to let us remain in contact or something."

"Perhaps it's a warning of sorts?" Brody wondered. "Or maybe it's a sign that we're getting close?"

"But how would she know where we are?" Caitlyn asked.

Brody shook his head. "I don't know."

With a sigh, Caitlyn managed to finally relax their mount and the group continued forward. She rubbed her neck occasionally as they walked. Brody thought he saw the stone glowing faintly, but figured it must just be his imagination.

Where in the hells is this place?

Streaks of orange, pink and purple tinged the heavens as the sun began its descent below the horizon. Brody resigned himself to the fact that they would not be able to go much further that evening. He just about called out to Caitlyn when he noticed something in the distance.

"Is that a tree?" Caitlyn asked. Her hand shielded her eyes from the setting sun as she looked ahead.

"I think it is," Brody replied. "There's something under it too. I think we may have found our spot."

"Hell's horses," Caitlyn swore. "It took long enough."

The two broke into a light jog, horse in tow, and headed towards the tree and whatever lay underneath it. As they neared, they saw it was indeed the smooth stone. The stone was so smooth, in fact, that it appeared to be polished.

"We found it," Caitlyn breathed. Her face flushed with excitement.

Brody nodded.

"I can't believe it's actually here," she continued. "I mean, who would have thought that a portal to another dimension would be here, in this beautiful clearing?"

Brody stood silently, listening intently. The air around them felt wrong. He couldn't tell why, but there was something unsettling about the area.

Must be because the door is here, he reasoned. *We must be near some ancient magic. But how can I feel this?*

"Do you feel it too?" Caitlyn asked.

Brody's thoughts were pushed aside as he looked at her. "The heaviness?"

"Yes." She pointed to the necklace, which shone brightly in the evening light. "It started getting warmer as we walked. It's about as close to hot as it can get, without burning me."

"Shall we get started then?" Brody asked.

Caitlyn nodded. Leading the horse, she walked to the tree and tied the guide rope around the trunk. Her fingers moved deftly as she worked to secure the knot. Brody walked off towards the river in search of some stones to use for their summoning circle. He wasn't sure if he'd find what he was looking for exactly, but he went anyway.

At the riverbed, he found that the floor was covered with smooth stones. Rolling up his pants legs, Brody waded into the cold water and began scooping up stones. In short order, he managed to both fill his arms and soak his shirt. Satisfied he got a decent number on his first trip, Brody trudged out of the river and returned to the little crest by the tree. He saw Caitlyn had already started crafting the circle out of the dried herbs. Placing his load on the ground, he looked around for some kindling.

"Do you think I got enough rocks?" he asked.

As she finished making the circle, she eyed the pile. "I think so."

"Good. Then I'm going to start a fire for us."

Brody walked off and started to pick up small branches and other bits of kindling to use. It wasn't long before he had a decent sized bundle in his arms and had to head back. He was surprised to see Caitlyn had completed the circle in its entirety.

"There were enough stones," she said.

Brody dropped the brush onto the ground and wiped off the stray bits that clung to his wet shirt. "Should we get the fire started?"

"I would like to try opening the door tonight, if you don't mind?"

Running his hands through his hair, Brody looked from Caitlyn to the circle. "Do you think that we are in any shape to do it tonight?"

"I don't think I can wait much longer," Caitlyn said. When Brody didn't look convinced, she added, "We can't put this off. Every day that Al stays in that realm probably weakens him and brings him closer to death. He wasn't in that great of shape to begin with, if you remember."

An image of Alverick, face bloodied and body leaning to one side, popped into Brody's mind. Alverick had been close to death before he was pulled into Aramaine by Ein.

"Fine," he replied.

Caitlyn beamed at him. She walked over to the horse and pulled out some of the travel pellets to feed it. The stallion munched happily on the supplements out of her hand, his nose hairs tickling her hand as he ate. When he finished, Caitlyn gave him a pat on the neck. The horse took that as a sign to resume his grazing, and did so with much vigor.

"We'll need some blood," Brody reminded her.

Caitlyn pulled out a small dagger from inside her boot. "I'm one step ahead of you."

Brody and Caitlyn stepped into the circle and stared at the dagger in Caitlyn's hand. "Are you ready?" Brody asked.

Caitlyn nodded.

Brody grabbed the weapon out of her hand and unsheathed it. Pulling up his damp sleeve, Brody found a spot on the back of his arm that was more muscle than soft flesh. Gritting his teeth, he ran the blade quickly across the back of his forearm. Bright droplets of blood quickly welled up from the wound and dripped down his arm. Brody opened and closed his hand, testing the muscles to make sure that he didn't cut too deeply. Caitlyn took the dagger from him and quickly followed suit.

Once their blood landed on the ground, the stones outlining the circle glowed brightly. The necklace around Caitlyn's neck first shone a blinding white before turning red.

◦◦◦◦◦

Vashe felt the ring on her finger burn and looked down. The stone blazed in the evening light.

"They must be waiting for me," she mused.

Closing her eyes, Vashe concentrated on connecting her body with Caitlyn's. Her ring's sister stone helped her find what she was looking for quickly. She felt two spirits pulsating inside a circle, surrounded by a red throbbing light. The more slender of the two figures shone with a greater intensity, reaching out to her ring through the stone around her neck. The two stones released a crimson beam of light, connecting them together in a singular ray.

Vashe felt Caitlyn's heart racing while the two were connected, how the redhead's breath caught in her throat as they joined. A tingling sensation filled the Scrymmen woman's ring hand. It almost felt as though it was humming with energy.

There isn't much time, Vashe told herself. *The connection will only last a few minutes.*

With a deep breath, Vashe pictured what she wanted to do. She visualized opening a door into the other dimension, one that was hopefully free from any unsavory creatures in the immediate area. Drawing on her knowledge of the realm, Vashe found, what she believed to be, a clear spot. Chanting softly to herself, the Scrymmen woman focused on opening the door.

A vibrant green circle filled her mind's eye. As she continued to chant, the ring became a tube, engulfing the two red objects within. Vashe felt more than saw the green light surround her. Its warmth soothed her, attempting to coax her into dropping her guard. Beads of sweat dotted her brow. It took a great deal of concentration to exert her willpower over the force cajoling her, as well as work to open up the portal. In her mind, a second door opened, inviting her to enter through a closer entrance.

Shaking her head, Vashe chanted faster, urging the gateway closest to Brody and Caitlyn to provide them egress. A tightness formed in her chest, making it difficult to breathe. She felt the energy around the first green circle letting up. As the heaviness disappeared from the area, Vashe gave a mighty push and commanded the door to open for the two.

A brilliant flash nearly blinded her mind's eye before the tightness in her chest disappeared. Vashe felt a strong surge of relief as the light around her vanished. The crimson beam that connected Vashe and Caitlyn dissolved and her hand stopped humming. She looked down at the stone in her ring and saw that it returned to its normal, dull state.

Vashe slumped over, her hands resting on her knees as she took deep breaths.

I hope that worked.

～∞～

Brody and Caitlyn brought their hands to their face, shielding their eyes as a bright flash of green light nearly blinded them. When the light died down, the two were faced with a portal to Aramaine inside of a green ring.

The two shared a look. As one, the duo steadied their nerves and walked into the gateway.

XXIX

Alastaire stormed through his manor. He knocked servants aside, pushing them roughly as he moved through his home, his cape fluttering behind him in his wake. His help scurried to get out of his way, bowing in apology when they couldn't move fast enough.

"Move!" he roared.

Those remaining in his way darted off to the side, terrified of his wrath.

Alastaire reached the end of his manor hallway and came upon an unimposing wooden door with a brass knocker. He pulled a key out from under his tunic. The key hung loosely around his neck on a piece of string. Yanking the makeshift necklace from around his neck, he shoved the key into the lock and roughly turned it until he heard a click. Gnashing his teeth, he stuffed the key and string into his trouser pocket and thrust open the door.

He walked into a darkened room. Fumbling with the torch in a sconce on the wall, Alastaire managed to wrench it out of its bracket and carry it to the hearth on the other side of the door. He shoved the torch into the flame and grumbled to himself as he waited for it to light. After what felt like forever, the torch caught fire.

"Finally," he groused.

Alastaire stormed back into the darkened room and used the light from the torch to help him navigate the winding staircase and into the lower level of his home. The wooden steps soon turned to dirt and stone as he descended further into the darkness. Soon, the top of the staircase disappeared into blackness once more, and all that remained was the orange bobbing of his flame.

As he reached the bottom of the steps, Alastaire walked around the room, lighting the remaining torches before shoving the one in his hand into a sconce on the wall. Alastaire stood in a nondescript room with dirt walls and floor. A rough wooden table stood in the middle of the room. On the walls, there were chains with shackles. In a gloomy corner, iron bars were evenly spaced and went from the ceiling to the floor, making a makeshift prison underground.

Alastaire tore off his cape and threw it onto the table. With a primal roar, he slammed his hands down onto the table. Various metal instruments that lay on the table gently shook with the force of his action.

"Now, now," Constance chided as she walked down the stairs, torch in hand. "You'll never be able to complete your project if your head is not in the right place."

"Quiet, Constance," Alastaire snarled, "or you may not have much to say for much longer. I have never been so mistreated in my life."

Constance found an empty bracket and placed her torch into it. She then walked over to her husband and removed her own capelet and laid it gently on the table.

"You may be upset, but I will not be spoken to this way," she said sharply. "Now, why don't we be productive?"

Growling, Alastaire stormed off from the table and made his way to the steel cages, grabbing a pair of tongs as he walked by. As he walked up to the bars, he banged the tongs onto them, disturbing the inhabitants. Several pairs of white eyes glared at him from inside the cage. Though none ventured out of the shadows, Alastaire was pleased to note that he could distinctly see their different shapes.

"How are you treating your new friend?" Alastaire asked.

More than one of the shadow creatures let out an ear-piercing shriek in response. Long, thin fingers, more like tendrils of smoke, snaked their way to the bars and wrapped themselves around them. The bars rattled, but held steadfast. The creature hissed in frustration and withdrew his hand.

Alastaire smiled. He banged on the bars once more and called out, "I know you hear me, boy. Why don't you come closer so I can get a better look at you?"

One of the monsters, his body more solid than the rest, hissed at Alastaire and tried to slink into the shadows, but Alastaire wouldn't allow it. He walked away and grabbed a torch from the wall before returning to the prison. Shining the flickering light into the gloom, Alastaire was pleased to note that the majority of his children faded away into the shadows. One remained, standing in the light, his black arm shielding his face from the light.

The creature had an elongated form, like the tongue of flames, but as dark as night. Claw-like fingers tapered off from his hands. His jaw stretched out so that it could accommodate his thin fangs that filled his mouth. White eyes glared at Alastaire from behind his arm. Instead of the normally amorphous top to its head, there were still remnants of the curly hair that the creature once had.

"How does it feel to be proven wrong, Cassius?" Alastaire sneered. "You told me that the Faceless were just an old wives' tale. I believe that I've proven you wrong."

Cassius replied with an ear-piercing shriek. The creature dropped his arm and reached out towards Alastaire, his long, slender fingers struggling to grip his captor. The claws stopped just short of reaching their goal, the light from Alastaire's torch causing them to bend back like smoke just shy of his body. Cassius hissed, his white eyes narrowing and fangs bared.

"You'll thank me once you reach maturity," Alastaire told him. "Until then, you can help your newest friend acclimate to the changes that they're about to experience. You remember what it was like to be reborn when I brought you and your little lady friend here from Madden, don't you?"

Cassius watched as a trio of Alastaire's servants brought in a young woman with mousy brown hair. Her small nose was covered with freckles and was currently a bit red, like her puffy eyes. She staggered as the servants led her to the wall. One of the men roughly took her arms and locked them in the shackles. Once she was securely fastened, the three turned and made their way back up the stairs in silence.

Cassius screeched in dismay as he saw his fiancée, Ellie María, struggle against her bonds. Her eyes scanned the room frantically as she tried to find some shred of hope. Her bottom lip quivered as she fought back tears.

"Cassius?" she whimpered. "Cassius?"

Alastaire strode over to the young girl and roughly grabbed her chin, lifting her head up to look him in the eyes. "How are you holding up, my dear?"

Ellie María blushed and looked away from him. Alastaire shook her face roughly, drawing her eyes back to his face. Tears welled in the corners of her eyes and her breathing became ragged as she struggled to maintain control of herself.

Alastaire waited for her to respond. When nothing was forthcoming, he slapped her hard across the face and glowered at her. "Do we want a repeat of the other day?" he asked.

Her bottom lip trembled, but she remained strong. She averted her eyes once more. Ellie María glanced into the prison and happened to spot Cassius. He locked eyes with her and tried to call out to her. An eerie wail filled the room, causing the color to drain from her face and her knees to give way. Ellie María slunk to the ground as she stared, unblinking, at the nightmare creature nearby.

Alastaire smirked as he watched her discomfort and Cassius' distress. It wouldn't be long until Cassius' transformation was complete. Cassius struggled to form words, to try and reassure his love that he was okay, but his mouth could no longer make those sounds. His lips fumbled over his elongated jaw, his razor-sharp teeth blocking his tongue from making human speech.

"Constance," Alastaire said. "I think she's almost ready to begin the first step in her new journey. Why don't you go upstairs and send Pellek down? I need his help with something."

"As you wish," his wife replied.

Constance turned and made her way up the stairs. Alastaire watched her retreat for a while before returning his attentions to Ellie María. He walked over to the table and returned the tongs. Looking around, he found a whip. Picking it up off of the table, he made his way back to his prisoner.

"I see that you've reconnected with your fiancé, my dear," Alastaire said. He stretched out the whip in his hands, making it go taut. "Don't fear. You'll be reunited with him soon enough."

In one swift motion, Alastaire cracked the whip, bringing it down against her cheek. Ellie María cried out in pain as blood seeped from the wound on her face. Alastaire snapped his arm once more, this time bringing the crack of the whip against her chest, causing her to cry out again. The sound of footsteps could be heard coming down the stairs as Pellek came, as summoned.

Cassius felt his insides rage as he watched the men beat the love of his life. With every cry, his fury grew, threatening to break free and consume his consciousness. The darkness around his body roiled as he became less distinct, less solid. After a particularly heart-wrenching cry from Ellie María, Cassius felt his mind snap. He screamed out in a frenzy, his body rushing the steel prison, trying to break free. His curly hair disappeared completely, only to be replaced with the swirling blackness that was the rest of his body. He tried with all his might to escape his cage, shrieking his blood-curdling cry in anger.

Alastaire took a break from his beating, looking up at Cassius from the limp form of Ellie María who lay on the ground. A wicked smile lay plastered on his face. Cassius tried to reach out through the bars and tear the expression off of his face. Alastaire hung back, watching Cassius lose the last remnants of his humanity as he completed his transformation into one of the Faceless. He felt a deep swell of pride as he saw that his army was growing.

XXX

GLANCING AT EACH OTHER, Brody and Caitlyn clasped hands and entered the dimensional door, their breaths held in anticipation. As soon as the two crossed the threshold, they slowly let out their breath. The acrid stench of burning sulfur assaulted their noses.

"By the gods, this is foul!" Caitlin exclaimed.

Brody nodded his head and motioned for the two to continue further into the abyss. They walked stealthily into the darkened world. Faint green firelight was all they had to see by. Unfortunately, the light also caused a myriad of flickering shadows, making it was difficult to tell what was actually shadow and what was alive. Images danced on the walls, catching their attention out of the corner of their eyes as the tendrils of flame burned without a fuel source.

"How are we going to find him in this?" Caitlyn asked, her hand covering her nose and mouth. "My lungs burn and my eyes are watering."

"Vashe said that we need to find the great wyrm's horde and we'll find Al. Surely there aren't many of them in this realm," Brody reasoned.

Caitlyn's eyes widened. "You do realize that he is the Great Wyrm, don't you?"

Brody nodded mutely.

"Then you remember what she said. Ein is the oldest of the wyrms. He leads a legion of wyrms and dragons."

"Then we'll search until we find him," Brody said. "This is our only chance to get him back. I would face a thousand of the beasts if it meant bringing Al back. I'm sure you feel the same way."

Caitlyn's eyes dropped slightly before nodding.

"Then we need to be smart about this. Let's go. Quietly."

The two continued on, their senses heightened, straining to see in the faint light. Their hands covered their noses as they attempted to breathe in the acrid stench. The sound of dripping water echoed in the distance. What sounded like growling could be heard coming from all directions. Occasionally, Brody and Caitlyn saw the flash of what appeared to be two eyes staring at them in the darkness.

Time was impossible to judge in this realm. The surroundings appeared endless, branching off into tunnels of equal darkness. Fire flickered dimly, the green glow barely reaching thigh level, a faint light reaching the eyes and illuminating the realm only the slightest. Their stomachs threatened to empty themselves on several occasions thanks to the sulfuric fumes that filled the realm. If they were lucky, a light breeze would blow in from one of the side corridors, relieving them from some of the stench. When the pair found a passageway with fresher air, they decided to take the turn, hoping that they would run into something new.

Twice, they found a small fortune of gold coins in a cave that broke off from the main hall. The corpse of several small creatures lay at the base of the mound. Each time, the pair stopped abruptly, their breaths catching in their chests. As silently as possible, they backed up, never taking their eyes off of the treasure as they returned to the main tunnel.

While they backed away after encountering the second pile of gold, a soft hiss could be heard from the opposite side of the mound. Thin tendrils of smoke peeked over the top of the heap. The dull scraping of claws on rocks and sound of shifting coins followed shortly after, causing Brody and Caitlyn to spin around and sprint out of the niche. They raced blindly down the tunnel, turning right and left. Their feet pounded on the rocky surface, echoing eerily in the silence.

Once they felt safe enough to slow down, the two stopped to lean against a wall. Caitlyn clutched a stitch in her side as Brody massaged his wounded leg. Reaching into his boot, he pulled out a large leaf that was folded several times. As he unwrapped the leaf, the smell of Vashe's salve broke through the acrid stench of the other realm.

Brody dipped his fingers into the cream and grabbed some from the leaf. Wrapping the salve back up and returning it to his boot, Brody then reached into his breeches and delicately rubbed the ointment onto his wound. The pain in his thigh subsided almost immediately as the cool balm worked its way into his system.

"How long do you think it'll take to heal since you keep aggravating it?" Caitlyn asked between gasps.

Wiping his hands on his tunic, he replied, "Not sure. It's only been a handful of days. I'd guess a month if I wasn't using it so much."

Smiling, Caitlyn straightened up and began walking further down the hallway. "So, never then?"

"Sounds about right," he replied with a weary smirk as he moved to catch up with her.

The two moved through Aramaine without any other incident. The flickering flames appeared to glow brighter as they moved forward. Warm, stale air filled the cavernous space around them. Bones littered the ground, resting against the walls in small piles. As they continued on, the skeleton of a young drake came into view. Its body lay stretched out with one leg in front of the other. Large cracks in the femur and tibia, as well as the neck that lay skewed at a slight angle, indicated that the creature did not die a gentle death.

"Keep looking straight ahead," Brody whispered suddenly as his hand moved towards his short sword.

A shadowy figure stalked behind them, slowly closing the distance between them.

"Best to not make eye contact with them. Maybe they won't bother us."

"Not likely," Caitlyn whispered back.

Brody glanced at her from the side of his eyes, keeping his head facing straight ahead. Removing his hand from his nose and mouth for a moment, he mouthed, "*What?*"

Caitlyn's hand moved casually, as though she was reaching for one of her arrows in her quiver. "We have a friend who's been following us for a while now," she said softly. "Small looking thing. If we strike quickly, I think we can take it out before it can sound an alarm."

"Let's keep moving forward," Brody replied. "I don't like the idea of it trailing us, but perhaps we can lose it, or make it lose interest in us."

A rumbling growl sounded behind them.

"Let's stop and pretend to examine the bones," Caitlyn said. "Once it gets within striking range, I can make my move."

Brody thought for a moment before barely nodding.

The two made their way to the drake's body. Brody bent over the bones and pretended to examine the claws. His ears strained to hear the creature approach. If he held his breath, he could make out the soft scratching of claws against the stone. Caitlyn stood next to him, her body tense.

A hiss could be heard as the creature's pace picked up. Brody heard the beast break into a sprint as it charged the two of them. His hands went to his short sword, ready to pull it out when he spun around to face the monstrosity. Before he could react, Caitlyn whirled to around, her hand glowing with white electrical energy.

"Ghan's mercy!" Brody called out.

The creature snarled as it approached. Brody caught his first glimpse of the other-worldly beast. A sleek, furry monster the size of a cat barreled towards them. Its claws left furrows in the stone. Drool dripped from its opened maw; thin, razor-sharp teeth bared. A smooth, whip-like tail thrashed side-to-side as it approached.

Caitlyn moved quickly. Before the creature could process what the foreign light was, she released her energy and flung it towards the being.

The ball expanded until it connected with the creature. Once it made contact, it engulfed the monster in a bright light and began sizzling. The beast gargled weakly as its body convulsed. Within seconds, it lay on the ground in a smoking heap.

Brody turned to Caitlyn, his mouth hanging open, in time to see her collapse to the ground.

XXXI

Hegvaldr sat down in a tavern, his back against the wall. His green eyes scanned the room, a wide-bowled glass of wine in his hand. Hegvaldr brought the crystal to his mouth and took a sip of the dry wine. He made a face of disgust at the drink and placed the wineglass on the table, pushing it away from him.

"What these people need is a good ale. Something strong to warm all the way through their body," the blonde-haired man groused. "This is too weak. It'd never keep me warm back in Grimmrheimr."

Hegvaldr turned his attention to his plate instead. Rosemary lamb on the bone with lentils sat in front of him, steaming. A loaf of flatbread rested in the center of the table on a wooden board, a lump of butter and knife sat in the corner of the board. The barbarian ripped a piece of the flatbread from the loaf and scooped up a pat of butter to slather up the bread before shoving the food into his mouth.

"At least the food's decent," he conceded.

Using his hands, Hegvaldr picked up the lamb by the bone and tore a chunk out of the meat with his teeth. He eyed the vegetables on the plate in front of him before pushing the dish away from him towards the wine. The barbarian quickly consumed the meat as he watched the room. Once he finished his meal, he started gnawing on the bone absentmindedly.

The door opened, briefly bringing in the afternoon light into the dank inn. Hegvaldr kept his head down as he chewed on the bone. After a while, he achieved success as he cracked the bone and started sucking the marrow out. A body dropped heavily into the chair across from him, but the barbarian paid him no mind. Hegvaldr slurped the last bit of marrow out of the bone before looking up at the person at his table.

"You're late," Hegvaldr said. "You'd be wise to not do this with Konugrr Solveig. She is not as tolerant as I."

Wyrd took a sip of his wine and placed the cup on the table. "I don't appreciate your tone," he replied. "I'm doing your little queen a favor and here you are scolding me like some child. Remember, I don't need you. You're the one who needs me."

Wyrd made prolonged eye contact with Hegvaldr to emphasize his point. The barbarian met his gaze and didn't shy away. Wyrd barred his teeth in a menacing grin and snapped his fingers. A tongue of flame burst from his fingers, dancing in the semi-darkness. Hegvaldr's eyes widened in surprise and scooted his chair back from the table until it slammed against the wall.

"Almighty Re'nukh!" the barbarian swore quietly. "The mark of Apophos."

Wyrd leaned back and enjoyed the reaction. He opened his hand and the flame disappeared. Wyrd placed his hand flat against the table's surface. "Do you understand now?"

Hegvaldr nodded his head mutely.

"Now," Wyrd said, motioning for the man to scoot his chair closer to the table, "is Solveig ready to come down?"

"She is."

"Excellent," Wyrd said, clapping his hands together. "You couldn't have come at a better time. Len has left Fa'Tinh and no one knows where he went or when he's coming back. He's left a couple of people behind, but they're not anything we need to be worried about."

"His general is from the old days," Hegvaldr said. "Are you telling me that he's not a threat?"

Wyrd nodded.

"Then why do you need our help if you bear the mark of Apophos?"

"I've only recently been blessed with my gift," Wyrd explained. "Though I can handle any threat that Pram and the Flame may bring, if I'm going to bring unity to our brothers and sisters, I need an army to back me up."

Hegvaldr leaned forward, resting his chin on his clasped hands.

"Your people command as much respect in Corinth as Xan does. What gives you your edge though, is that the people of Grimmrheimr don't travel down from the northern wastes. Imagine the fear we could strike together."

"So, you're just using us? You promised Konugrr that we would get land."

"Well, since you're not going to be facing as much danger as we first thought, what with Len currently out of the way, I don't think that the stakes are high enough to warrant giving part of my homeland away."

Hegvaldr clenched his fist and brought it down on the table, causing the plates and glasses to rattle. "You cannot back out of your deal like this," he hissed. "Konugrr was promised land and that's what she demands."

Wyrd pulled out a dagger from his hip and laid it on the table. In the corner of the room, Eivind moved to get up out of his chair. He watched as Hegvaldr folded his hands together across the tabletop, his posture completely relaxed. Eivind eased back into the chair and placed his axe in front of him.

The Qu-ari man watched Eivind's motions off to the side with interest. "Your friend over there seems a bit antsy," he mused. "Perhaps we should invite him over to discuss his concerns with us."

Hegvaldr glanced over his shoulder and spotted Eivind observing the two with a keen eye, the axe resting on the table. Eivind shot Hegvaldr a pointed glance. Hegvaldr shook his head and returned his attentions to his host. Wyrd watched the interaction with a bemused smile, his arms folded across his chest.

Hegvaldr took a deep breath and leaned back into his chair. "What will you do if we withdraw our support?" the barbarian asked.

Wyrd narrowed his eyes and leaned forward. "Trust me, you don't want to do that."

"Why is that? You don't seem to have a problem with stabbing us in the back. Why should we risk our necks for nothing? We do not honor those allied with Apophos."

Wyrd picked up his dagger and returned it to his hip. He then leaned back and stared long and hard into the barbarian's eyes. A glimmer of bloodlust flashed in his eyes. Lowering his voice to a whisper, Wyrd spoke to Hegvaldr. The barbarian had to lean in close to be able to hear the Qu-ari man over the din of the tavern. As he tipped forward, Wyrd grabbed Hegvaldr by the collar of his shirt and roughly pulled him in.

"I've killed people for less," the Qu-ari man explained. "If you don't hold true to your word, you will want to watch your back. I was able to convince Len to ally us with a demon. In the end, I always know what's best for my brothers, and I'll do whatever it takes to keep them on the right path."

Shoving the barbarian back roughly, Wyrd resumed his relaxed posture as he leaned back in his seat. Hegvaldr rubbed at his neck, massaging the area where his collar dug into his flesh. Anger flashed in the man's eyes, but he held his tongue. The threat of god fire was enough to silence him.

"So, we'll keep to the plan?" Wyrd asked. Hegvaldr nodded. "Perfect, then I await your return to Fa'Tinh with your forces. I speak for my brothers and sisters when I say that we appreciate your commitment to our cause. The world will know to fear the sons of Grimmrheimr. Until next time."

With a tap on the table, Wyrd got up and downed the remainder of his wine before walking out of the tavern. As he walked out of the establishment, Wyrd threw a couple coins at the bar towards one of the bar maids.

The door shut behind him with a soft thump, leaving Hegvaldr alone at the table once more.

As soon as the Qu-ari man left the building, Eivind got up and crossed the room towards Hegvaldr. The burly man dropped into the seat previously occupied by Wyrd. Seeing the glass of wine and plate of lentils on the table, Eivind pulled both towards him and set off to clear them. Hegvaldr watched the man eat, numb after the exchange that they just had.

"That seemed to be quite the conversation," Eivind said between bites. "Doesn't look like it went very well though."

Hegvaldr gritted his teeth, his anger flaring inside. "He's using us as his pawns."

"I don't think the Konugrr would be too pleased with that."

"We're not going to tell her," Hegvaldr replied. "If we do, he's already said that he'll kill us."

"Do you really fear a small man like him?"

"He bears the mark of Apophos," Hegvaldr explained. "I am not going to tempt fate to see if he'll follow through on his word. I wouldn't doubt that he would give it a try. Besides, he only seems to be following his own selfish desires, despite what he says. He seems to be rather unhinged."

Eivind shrugged his shoulders as he shoveled the last bits of food into his mouth. He downed the wine in a single gulp, wiping his lips with the back of his hand. Spying the flatbread still sitting on its platter, the monstrous man snatched it up and proceeded to tear into it.

"I'm not one to go against Konugrr. I know she wouldn't hesitate to have Tyr teach us a lesson. Although, I'd rather face him than her," Eivind said nonchalantly.

"Leave it to me," Hegvaldr replied. "Now, let's go. We need to talk to Konugrr and prepare for a fight. Despite his assertions, I didn't expect there to be a second bearing the mark of Apophos that we'd be going up against. We'll need our best if we're to engage these people."

The large man looked up at the comment. "Two with the unholy mark?"

"Yes."

Eivind put down the small piece of bread that remained and looked directly at Hegvaldr. "I know that you are Konugrr's favorite, but I think that you should really consider this partnership. Let's go home and tell her that he's changed his mind. What do you think are the odds that he would really follow us up to Grimmrheimr? You know people like him wouldn't last in Re'nukh's land. Our god will protect us, and if not him, the weather will."

Hegvaldr sat quietly, absorbing the man's words. One of the bar maids walked by and cleared the plates and glass from the table pausing to demand that they pay the bill before she left. Eivind fished a few coins out of his pocket and placed them on the table. The girl snatched up the coins and counted them quickly before thanking the pair and walking off to the next table.

After several minutes, Hegvaldr shook his head. "I can't risk it," he said finally. "Who knows if he'll send someone to the bazaars and markets our people attend? He can pick them off one at a time until he's confronted. I don't want that on me."

"Shall we head out then?" Eivind asked with a shrug.

Hegvaldr nodded. Eivind picked up the last remnants of flatbread and popped it into his mouth. Chewing as he walked, he led the way out of the tavern and into the streets of Fa'Tinh, Hegvaldr following close behind. People stepped out of their way as the two large blond men moved through the streets. They were an imposing duo as they walked around with their weapons strapped to their bodies, not bothering to hide the fact that they were heavily armed. The furs that lined their shoulders and boots, along with their long, wild hair, completed the look.

As the pair picked up their horses at the local stable, they looked around quickly to make sure that no one was following them. Satisfied that they were on their own, they kicked their heels into horseflesh and rode off towards Grimmrheimr.

XXXII

SCHAED FOUND OLDAR sitting in his study just like the old days. The king lounged in a dull green chaise reading a book, a decanter and glass of whiskey sitting on a small table right next to him. The decanter, Schaed noticed was half empty. The lanky man softly pushed open the door so as to not disturb his friend. He needn't have worried, however. Oldar swayed slightly as he propped himself up to reach his glass, laying his book across his lap.

"Think they can make me look like a fool," Oldar slurred as he grabbed his tumbler. Schaed struggled to make out the rest, but all he could hear was "Iron Fist..." and "that'll show them..."

The whiskey sloshed in the cup as the king dropped back into his seat. By some miracle, none of it spilled as he lurched back. However, as he drank from it, he managed to dribble some down his front. Oldar swore under his breath as he tried to wipe up his mess with the back of his hand.

"Excuse me, Oldar," Schaed said tentatively, speaking in a low tone to not startle the drunken king. "I have a handkerchief, if you need one. It looks like you could use a little help." He held out a pale yellow square of fabric to Oldar.

The king leaned forward and took the proffered cloth. Returning to his original position, he began vigorously rubbing the front of his shirt. Schaed took this opportunity to speak with Oldar further.

"Oldar, what happened?"

"I just needed to unwind a bit. My uncle, and now my proclamation is starting to sink in for Pharn."

Schaed looked at the king, nonplussed. "What?"

"My uncle wants to take over my power and I had to kick him out of my home," Oldar struggled to get out.

"Did he come back after the other night?" Schaed asked.

Oldar shook his head.

"Oh, so he's not here now. This is because of that one night."

Oldar nodded vigorously. "Also, the alli- the," Oldar struggled to find the right word. "The pacts with the mountain people and others are starting to break. They don't want to be part of our troubles."

A flash filled Schaed's eye briefly, but the drunken king missed it. "So, the princess is starting to regret her actions then? Has she come and apologized to you?"

Oldar shook his head. "Cienna and her mother sent a letter wanting to sit down and talk, but I told her that I need an explanation first. I deserve that much."

"Have they responded to you since you told them?"

"No, but I'm still waiting."

"How long have you been in here, uh, drinking?" Schaed asked delicately.

Oldar held up two fingers, swaying slightly as he brought his glass up and took another drink. "I'm not too bad though. Pru brought me something to eat this morning."

"How about we put the glass down for a while and just sit and talk. It'll be like the old days." Schaed reached over to grab the tumbler as he spoke. He was pleased when his friend didn't fight him, letting the glass slip through his fingers.

Oldar leaned back into his chaise and closed his eyes. "I don't want them to belittle me," he moaned. "No one respects me. What did I do to deserve this?"

"It's not easy being a leader, you said so yourself," Schaed said. "Just remember, no one has the ideas that you do. You're a visionary. Can your uncle honestly say that he'll do a better job ruling Alocar than you? I don't think so. You've spent so many years studying and writing. Who knows your people better than you?"

"You've already tried those points," Oldar slurred. "Clearly, they mean nothing to the others. Dreams, visions, ideals, what good are they at the end of the day if no one is willing to listen to you? What good are they if no one trusts you enough to let you try?" The king reached out towards the table for his glass of whiskey. When all he grabbed was empty air, he gave a despairing look at the table before turning back to his friend. "All I get is disrespect, and I'm tired of it."

"As you should be," Schaed agreed. "Come, come. Why don't we talk about other things, more positive things? You need to take your mind off of this right now. Otherwise, once you speak with the princess and her mother, you will be too upset and you may not be able to get your point across clearly."

"That's a good point," the king said, nodding. He turned to reach for his glass again, but was disappointed once more. "I can't make a good argument if I spend too much time dwelling on it."

Schaed slid onto the chaise next to his friend's feet. The lanky man subtly placed the whiskey on the floor on the other side of the chaise, just out of the king's line of sight. He then sat on the edge of the chaise, leaning on his knees with his hands.

"Tell me," Schaed began, "what do you think about going to the tavern again? You had a good time the other night. Let's grab a meal and spend the evening taking in the city. We can check out some of the shops like we used to in the old days after class. Not to mention, some of the shopkeeps have started hiring street performers to attract customers. I've heard that the glassblower employs a firebreather and theatre sends some of their singers out to serenade the passersby."

Oldar perked up at the news. It had been a long time since he'd taken a leisurely stroll around the city just to enjoy Madden's beauty. "That sounds nice. Why not?"

"Excellent!" Schaed exclaimed, grinning boyishly.

"Do they do this every night?"

"They do."

"I would love to take Cienna around an' show her the sights," Oldar explained.

Schaed blanched at the idea, but didn't say anything at first. As the king struggled to push himself out of the chaise, his friend gently reminded him, "Why don't we think of something to do with her another day. We're not thinking of Cienna or any other royal duties tonight, remember?"

"Oh, yes, yes," Oldar replied absentmindedly. "I don't know where the thought came from. Tonight is our night."

⤞⤟

Oldar and Schaed staggered through the streets. Oldar felt much better after getting food into his stomach. Though he no longer slurred his speech or swayed as he moved, he still felt a bit lightheaded after drinking a couple glasses of red wine with his dinner. Schaed wobbled a bit as he walked, but he wasn't too badly off either, having consumed several pints of ale along with his wine.

The street lamps were lit, along with the shop windows, providing a pleasant glow to the pedestrians walking through the streets. Young couples strolled arm in arm down the worn cobblestone paths, chatting happily amongst themselves. Teenaged boys jostled into each other as they moved in packs. Schaed nudged his friend and pointed to the carefree group of lads.

The two snickered as they recalled their youth, as though they were two old men whose childhood had long since become a distant memory.

Schaed hadn't been exaggerating when he spoke of the street entertainment. Jugglers stood under lamps at the street corners. Some left their hats down at their feet in hopes of earning a few coins, while others directed onlookers into toy shops or a nearby tavern. In the distance, Oldar thought he heard a vielle or a lute playing a haunting melody in the distance, but he couldn't discern the source between the excited chatter of the bystanders and the shouting from the performers.

As they walked, Oldar stopped a few times to look into shop windows. His eyes darted from window to window, taking in the brightly colored outfits in the clothier's to the multi-colored sweets in the local candy shop. In no time at all, he'd forgotten all about his troubles from the last few days. He felt lighter than he had in a while. Schaed watched the king's reflection in the store windows, smiling to himself at the drastic change in Oldar's attitude.

Moving further along the streets, the pair were practically stopped by a large crowd. Cheers of amazement could be heard from all directions. Standing on his toes, Oldar endeavored to see what everyone was looking at. Schaed tapped the king on the shoulder and pointed towards the sky. Oldar looked up just in time to see a pillar of flame shoot over the crowd's head, only to be greeted with more roars of applause.

"We must be at the glassblowers," Oldar said. "It's been a while since I've looked in his shop."

Schaed nodded, his eyes twinkling. "Follow me," he told the king.

Oldar watched dumbly, trying to figure out what Schaed was up to. The taller man began tapping people on the shoulders and saying, "Make way for the king" in a commanding voice. The crowd parted easily as he wiggled his way to the front of the throng. Oldar fought to hide a smile as he followed his friend through the group.

As they neared the inside of the circle, Oldar felt curious eyes on him. He glanced around and watched as his people moved for him without a second thought. They didn't glare at him or roll their eyes in his direction as he passed by. Instead, they gave a respectful nod or curtsy and returned to the show. In the center of the group, Oldar observed the firebreather pausing his demonstration while the king found a better vantage point. Once he could properly enjoy the performance, the man resumed his routine.

Oldar marveled at his art. The firebreather took a sip of alcohol from a non-descript bottle before spraying it at a lit torch. The resulting pillar of flame was blinding and resulted in a round of applause from everyone. The man then motioned with his hands for everyone to step back. Oldar heard several people talk about the grand finale as they took large steps backwards to give the man more room. Following their lead, Oldar moved until he was even with them.

The firebreather pulled out a rope with a large knot at each end. He poured some of his alcohol on the knots before sticking each end into the fire. The balls blazed into life. Draping the rope across his back, the performer began clapping his hands in a steady rhythm, prompting the crowd to join him. Once the group was clapping to the beat, he took the rope in his hands and began swinging it around in dizzying arcs. They fire balls left mesmerizing trails of light behind them as they danced in the dark sky. The man whirled the balls faster and faster, the clapping reaching a fevered pitch before he spun around in a circle, the rope spinning in the opposite direction across his back before being snatched up when he returned to the front.

Thunderous applause broke out, signaling the end of the show. The man bowed to his audience and more than a few coins were tossed his direction. The owner of the glass shop stood in the doorway and beckoned onlookers into his store.

As the crowd gradually dispersed, Oldar looked around. People were happy. No one spoke ill of him, or even spared a negative glance in his direction. Surely, all of his worries had been in his head. His people couldn't think ill of him without giving some outward indication. It really was his uncle's and Zanir's poor attitude that had poisoned people against him. His people loved him.

XXXIII

L EN SAT on one of the stones, dragging his boots through the damp sand. He watched as he would make a small furrow in the ground, only to be filled up again with water. He'd been sitting there for a long time while the other man perched on his stone and meditated. Kayna played in the sand as well, running her sword's sheath into the sand. She drew circles and other simple shapes into the ground, waiting until they were erased by the tide before coming up with a new picture. Len waited quietly, unsure of what he was supposed to while the man mulled over whatever he needed to.

"Are you ever going to tell me who that man is, and why he's making me wait here?" Len asked Kayna. "If there's nothing for me to do, I will be going."

"You don't want to do that," Kayna replied. "That's Angh, Lord of the Western Isles, Scourge of the Seas." Seeing Len's blank face, she continued. "He's basically the lord of all pirates. He's responsible for the orderly division of territories between the groups. He's the one who sent me and my fleet to Chargyl, off of Corin, to handle some rogue pirates who were kidnapping and murdering innocents. Have you never heard of him?" she asked incredulously as Len stared blankly back at her. "He's a legend, even amongst our people."

"And he's your father?" Len asked.

"He is," Kayna answered.

She looked over her shoulder at Angh. Len noted that for the first time since he'd met her, Kayna seemed antsy and on edge. Her eyes would dart over towards his corner of the cavern, only to return to her line drawings.

She's hiding something, Len thought. *There's no reason for her to be so nervous right now. I probably should go if I want to make it out of here alive.*

A thunderous crash in the distance startled the two. Both turned to face the entrance of the cave and observed that the previously calm waters were now choppy. The sky outside turned a dark grey. A blinding flash shot across the sky, followed shortly after by another rumble.

"Foul weather," Kayna noted. "I wonder which of the Brothers are angry today."

"Brothers?" Len asked.

"Yes, Thuul or Graak. Surely you know about mighty Freyna's older brothers?"

"Ah yes. I've spent too much time with the Westerners and hearing more than I needed to about their own Siblings that I thought you were talking about theirs. Neither Ghan nor Czand have domain over the wind."

Kayna shook her head.

"Any adventurer who is worth their weight in salt knows that to anger the Ayr is automatic death out there. Sure, we respect Aria and her brood, but without the Ayr, we're dead on the water," Kayna explained.

A flickering light bobbed along the wall, announcing the arrival of another party to their conversation. The pair watched as Maya sauntered over to join them. Her black heeled boots clacked on the water-worn stones before they were muffled in the sand. Maya made her way over to Kayna and Len, her eyes scanning over the Qu-ari man every time she looked in his direction.

Without any preamble, Maya said, "I've just received word that Jylla and his men are heading over."

"What? Why would they be coming here?" Kayna asked, her shock evident in her tone.

"My guess is that the Bone Coast has always been alluring to them. They burnt it ten years ago, and yet people still live in the surrounding towns. Maybe Jylla feels as though he's not getting enough payment for his 'protection.'"

"Damnation!" Kayna swore. "Those bastards have been a pain in my ass for far too long."

A rival gang seeking dominance? Len mused. *This land is falling apart.*

"Maeyu'dana, Kayna, what is going on over there?" Angh called out. "You're interrupting my meditation."

"It's nothing," Kayna replied.

"Don't you lie to me, girl," Angh warned.

Pushing himself off of his stone, the imposing man made his way towards the trio. Len felt his unease rise as the pirate lord got closer.

"It's nothing to worry about, Lord Angh," Maya said. "I just surprised Kayna, is all."

"Now don't you cover for Kayna either, Maeyu'dana," the large man cautioned. "I know when the two of you are lying. You both seem to think that you need to hide the truth from me. You know that I do not appreciate dishonesty."

Len watched the interaction with great curiosity. Though Angh's tone was harsh, he didn't appear to be truly angry with the women. Kayna glanced over at her father sheepishly, while Maya maintained her regal air as she dealt with the towering man. Len couldn't help but admire the apathetic Maya in this situation. Kayna was right, she truly was an intriguing character. He was caught off-guard when he noticed that Kayna and Angh walked off a short distance away, leaving him with Maya.

"He seems to have a good relationship with her," Len noted. "In Xan, she would be seen as a bit on the disrespectful side with her attitude towards her father."

"He's not truly her father," Maya said. "He took her in when she was young and raised her as his own."

"Why would he do that? Someone as powerful as him taking in an orphan would've been a big distraction, especially one so young."

"Nobody challenges the Scourge," Maya said matter-of-factly. "If you haven't noticed already, Lord Angh is an excellent judge of character. He can tell when you're trying to deceive him and when you're being sincere. Who do you think helped gather this crew? Kayna has a good eye, but he's been in the shadows, weeding out the ones that she may have misjudged, which hasn't been many."

He does seem to have an uncanny ability to look into your soul. What is he looking for with me?

"Don't worry though," Maya continued. "If he hasn't ordered your death immediately, there's still hope for you. I mean, after all, he could've killed you on his own when he first laid eyes on you."

"Is that supposed to make me feel better?"

Maya shrugged. "It is what you make of it."

Len shot her a look of annoyance and returned to dragging his feet in the sand. He noticed that the tide crept closer to him. *Is the storm responsible for the higher waters?* The waves in the cavern were choppy, causing the ship at the entrance to bob violently in its surf.

"Looks like they're coming back," Maya said. "Kayna must have told him about Jylla."

"Is this Jylla really a threat?" Len asked.

"He's more of an irritation. His crew is the reason that Thallysis is a ghost town."

Len arched an eyebrow questioningly.

"About fifteen years ago, he came to the coast and started charging the townsfolk for his protection. He guaranteed that the brigands in the Eastern Seas would not bother them if they paid him tribute. Unfortunately for the townspeople, those were his own men he was protecting them from. He expected to be treated like royalty and be paid to control his men. Needless to say, once the people found out, they stopped paying. Jylla threw a fit and burned Thallysis to the ground as an example.

"By the time that we found out what he was doing, he'd already destroyed the city. Kayna took a group of men out and we had a nice talk with Jylla. Since then, he's been nipping at our heels, trying to find the right time to strike and resume his control over this part of the world. He's never been pleased that Kayna's managed to take over his territory."

"Why doesn't your Angh do something more permanent?" Len asked.

"Lord Angh prefers to keep himself out of such petty squabbles. Not worth his time. Now, if something big were to happen, say Jylla goes after another city, then Lord Angh may have to step in. Razing one city, though horrible, is not the end of the world. Thallysis could've rebuilt, they just chose to pack up and leave."

"Seems rather short-sighted to give up so easily on your homeland," Len noted.

"Yes," Maya agreed. "It makes much more sense to leave them in their time of crisis and set out on some journey of self-exploration in the name of trying to find aid."

Len gave Maya a sour look, but did not speak further. What did she know about his decisions? It's not as though he had a choice in the matter.

"So, Len, is it?" Angh asked as he approached with Kayna. "My little Starfish has told me that you're quite the fighter. What do you say to helping us take care of a little problem that we have?"

"Unfortunately, I will have to decline your offer," Len said. "I have more pressing matters back at home that I need to handle at the moment."

"Then why are you here?" Angh asked. "The Bone Coast is not the place that someone on a mission usually visits."

Len hesitated.

He's going to know whether I tell the truth or not. Might as well speak freely here. Whether he believes me or not, if he wants me killed, he'll be the one to do it.

"I came here looking for a crew to bring back to my homeland."

Angh narrowed his eyes as he studied the Qu-ari man.

"My brothers are in a bit of turmoil, and I... I cannot handle this on my own," Len continued. "One of my own kin has decided to use the power of the gods for nefarious purposes. My people are divided; some desire only peace, some side with him, others are scared to choose a side. I need more than just what I can command if I am to protect my own from this man."

Angh stared into Len's eyes. It almost felt as though he was sifting through the general's memories, searching for something.

"A little one, and one yet to join us," Angh murmured. "You fear for these two more than even your own safety, am I right?"

Len nodded, a lump in his throat and a slight headache developing. "They are a big reason why I came out here," he admitted. "However, there's more than just them. My brothers need my guidance. I have a vision, and I need them behind me if I am to show Corinth the greatness of the sons of Xan."

"Yes, of course," the pirate muttered. "And what are you willing to give in exchange for our service?"

Len paused. He didn't expect for the man to be so blunt. "What is your price?"

"Your service," Angh replied with a grin. "I see a lot of potential in you. I desire your skill amongst my crew. Promise me that you'll submit to me and I'll give you all that I can."

"No," Len replied quickly. "I serve no man. I wouldn't bow down to Pharn when we were facing the demon, and I won't do so now."

Len turned to leave before things got violent. As he made his way to the passageway, he heard Angh call out to him:

"You would sacrifice your wife and children just to save your pride?"

Len stopped abruptly. It took all of his willpower to not turn around and face the man. He felt his resolve draining with each moment that he stayed in the great pirate's presence. He knew that in order to preserve his dignity, he must leave.

It didn't matter though. None of it did.

"If I were to join you, what would you ask of me?"

Len could feel Angh smile at his back.

"You'll know when the time comes."

Len remained frozen in place, unable to turn and face the pirate, unable to walk away. A knot formed in the pit of his stomach as he swallowed his pride. It was a humbling experience to find himself in this position. The young general forced himself to turn around and confront the man.

Without a word, he nodded. He felt the tension in his stomach loosen a bit and some of his trepidation about the man melt away. For the first time since he stood outside of the passageway door, Len did not feel a suffocating heaviness around him. Angh nodded, pleased with Len's decision.

"Kayna, Maeyu'dana, gather the men," Angh commanded. Let's go and meet Jylla out at sea instead of letting him get his footing on land. He won't expect us to intercept him. We should have the edge."

A wide grin spread on Kayna's face and she turned to inform the others. Angh went off to his corner of the cave and started rummaging around through a large chest. Occasionally, he pulled out a sword or mace, inspecting each weapon before putting it back and picking up another. Len and Maya stood together by the shore.

"You're not pleased," Maya remarked bluntly.

"You're quite astute," Len retorted. "How long did it take you to figure that out?"

Maya smirked. "Not that long."

Len scowled and stormed out of the cavern towards the tavern.

"Where are you going?" Maya asked.

"I need a drink," he grumbled.

As he disappeared into the dark passageway without a light, Maya crossed her arms with a self-satisfied smile. Glancing over in Angh's direction, she remarked, "And so, he finally appears."

XXXIV

Vashe crouched behind some bushes and pulled a bit of bread from her travel sack. She stared straight ahead as she chewed, watching the land in front of her. Between the leaves, she saw several men walking around, chatting amongst themselves. Their lanky bodies and black hair contrasted against their alabaster skin, which shone in the sun. Though they didn't carry any sort of weapon, Vashe knew that they were part of the royal guard, scouting the area.

Their shirts were sleeveless, showing off their tattoos that wound all the way up to their elbows. Glancing around to both sides, Vashe slunk down to her stomach and slowly crawled her way through the grass.

Thank you, Blessed Aria, for your tall grasses that cover the land of Scrymme.

Inching her way down the slope of the hill, Vashe tried to figure out what tattoos each man had. The one with short cropped hair had the hazy tattoos of a Shadow that went all the way up his right arm to his elbow. The man with shaggy hair and the one with hair that went down to his mid-back were both Liches. Neither had tattoos that went as far up their arm as the Shadow, but they covered almost as much of the body. The longer haired one wore his hair in a low tail and his markings covered more of his body than his counterpart.

Looking around, Vashe sought another way to enter her home country. She didn't want to engage in combat with those three. It would arouse suspicion and set the guards off looking for the intruder if the bodies were discovered. Twisting the ring on her finger, Vashe contemplated her options. A cloud moved in front of the sun, creating larger shadows. Vashe smiled as she watched the trio laugh, hardly paying attention to their surroundings.

Scooting her way down, Vashe worked to angle herself behind a tree near the three guards. She waited until the cloud moved and sunshine filled the area once more before she began focusing on her magical energies. She looked around for her first target. The Shadow walked near where she was hiding, and Vashe had an idea. She reached out with her shadow magic and waited until he stopped moving. Once he stopped and leaned against the tree, she reached out and immobilized him. Praying that he didn't try moving any time soon, Vashe snuck up behind him and raised her hands to his temples.

Once her hands were in place, Vashe began whispering in his ear, suggesting to the body that it should be resting instead of working. Slowly, the man's eyelids began to droop and his knees buckled. Within a minute, he dropped heavily into Vashe's arms, sound asleep. Working quickly, she dragged the unconscious body up the slope and hid him in the bushes. Satisfied that the man was hidden, she quietly returned down the slope and made her way back to the tree.

The Liches were chatting away, not even aware of their comrade's disappearance. One leaned against the tree that Vashe hid behind, resting his hands behind his head.

"I don't know why they stuck us on patrols," the long-haired man groused. "Our time could be better spent infiltrating the Mageri."

"I've heard that the Head of the school is the most knowledgeable they've ever had, Dzorath" the other one said, lowering his voice. "I've even heard that they're dabbling into the forbidden magics."

"What do you mean, Dzmara?"

"I've heard from Dzeketh that Her Holiness has blessed their Head with knowledge that even our people know. Using that information, they found a way to travel between the realms and speak with the gods."

Dzeketh? Does he know that I'm in Pharn?

"Dzeketh has been trying to create a reason to strike those heretics for the last decade," Dzmara said, waving his hand in dismissal of his partner. "No one takes him seriously."

Vashe let out a silent sigh of relief. She would be able to return to her sanctuary in peace, assuming she managed to escape Scrymme.

"Dzvroth listens to him," Dzorath muttered.

"Dzvroth is a power-hungry man who is always looking for his next kill. I wouldn't be surprised if he doesn't come after you for your careless watch," Vashe said as she stepped out from behind the tree. Time was running short, and she needed to deal with these men before she could move forward with her mission.

Both men stared at her in disbelief. Dzmara craned his neck so quickly to see who was speaking that Vashe could've sworn that he pulled a muscle by the way he was rubbing his neck.

"You there! Identify yourself!" Dzvorath demanded. His eyes grew wide as he realized that she was one of their own, traveling into Scrymme from the outside world. "Traitor!" he cried.

"Now, now," Vashe said, lifting her hands over her head in an effort to show that she wasn't armed. "Surely we can forget this little meeting ever happened."

Her flowing sleeves fell down as to her elbows as her hands were in the air, revealing her intricately tattooed arm. The mixture of markings that covered her limb, clearly moving further up the arm, caused both men to pause. Dzmara spun around to face her while his partner stood rooted to where he stood.

The two managed to regain their composure shortly after and moved to confront Vashe. With her hands still in the air, Vashe took a step closer to the men until her she was within striking distance. The sun beat down overhead, causing the shadows to elongate along the earth. Both men froze midstep as she moved forward.

"I have no weapons in my hands," Vashe told them. "Just let me pass through and we can all be done with this ridiculousness."

Dzvorath turned to his companion, uncertainty in his eyes.

"In the name of Dzvroth Ari, we will be bringing you into custody to await judgement from His Highness," Dzmara replied.

He made to grab Vashe by her wrist, but she stepped back quickly out of his way.

"It's a shame that we have to do this," she muttered.

With her hands still raised, she closed her hands. Both men stood in shock as they were suddenly unable to move. Cries of frustration broke through their lips as Vashe walked over to them. Looking deeply into the eyes of Dzmara, Vashe began whispering to him. The man tried to break eye contact with her, but she grabbed his head and held it steady in front of her. Once he looked into her eyes, he was unable to stop her. He tried to close his eyes, but before his lids were sealed, she had him.

Softly, she spoke to him. Occasionally, she stroked his hair, soothing his suspicious soul and replacing it with a feeling of contentedness. His eyes began to droop as they got heavier until he was sound asleep. Vashe gently laid him down on the ground and made her way to the second man.

"Please," he whimpered. "Don't do this to me. I don't want to die."

Vashe looked at Dzvorath and realized that he was just barely more than a boy. Running her hand through his hair, Vashe sighed.

"Who do you report to? Dzvroth or Dzeketh?" Vashe asked.

The young man shook slightly as he spoke.

"Dzvareliah Ari."

That wasn't the answer she expected. Vashe stood silently, trying to process the information. Dzvareliah ruled Scrymme with an iron fist. She enjoyed punishing all who dared to displease her; it was almost a sadistic pleasure for her. She was also Vashe's mother. Both Dzvroth and Dzvareliah taking a hand in how the military functioned was a bad sign. Dzvroth was bad enough, but throw in his wife and that was a recipe for disaster.

Walking over to Dzvorath, Vashe placed her hands on his temples and stared deeply into his eyes. Unlike Dzmara, he made no effort to try and avoid her gaze. Instead, he actually relaxed his body and allowed for her to have full access to him.

Images of a raven-haired woman in a flowing silver gown popped up. Soldiers scurried around as they tried to complete whatever task she barked out at them. A young woman carrying several bundles of sleek silver chain-mail accidentally dropped her load as she tried to avoid colliding with a man who was walking backwards as he directed a small group struggling with a large chunk of marble down the hallway.

Dzvareliah honed in on the young woman and quickly strode over. With a movement like lightning, the queen slapped the other woman. The smack was so loud that it caused a momentary pause form all of the others in the hallway. Just as suddenly as they stopped, they returned to their work. The queen did not tolerate a disruption in duty. The woman who was on the receiving end of the punishment quickly picked up her mail and continued on her way as though nothing had happened.

Vashe pulled away from the visions and instead began murmuring into the young man's ear, inviting him to give his conscious to her. His eyes drooped and his knees buckled as his weight dropped downwards. Within seconds, Dzvorath was sound asleep in Vashe's arms.

Looking around, Vashe sought a different hiding place for this soldier than the last two. Something about him spoke to her, and she didn't want him to suffer any punishment because of what she was about to do.

There's about to be plenty of chaos soon enough.

Spying another grove of bushes off in the distance at the bottom of the slope, Vashe hefted the lad over her shoulders and gradually made her way towards them.

Thank Her Holiness that he's a wiry little thing, she mused.

After finally reaching her destination, she gently laid the body down and made sure to adequately cover it with brush. Once satisfied that he was properly hidden, she made her way down the road, off the main path, and towards the fortress that she used to call home. She hadn't gotten very far when she felt a nagging in the pit of her stomach. Turning around, she backtracked towards the brush and young Dzvorath.

When she reached the spot covering the young Liche, Vashe knelt over his unconscious body once more and whispered into his ears. Once her message was completed, she straightened up and resumed her journey back towards Caicyne Ari, her home.

XXXV

CAICYNE ARI LOOMED in front of Vashe. It was a thing of nightmares. Twisted spires jutted into the sky, stabbing the heavens themselves. Memories of tortured screams rang in her head. She'd spent so many years struggling to block it out, swearing to never return. And yet, here she was. Vashe blessed Aria for the darkness of night that engulfed her. The *jyarls* would not be able to do anything with the moon hidden behind the clouds. It left her at a disadvantage too, but she wasn't too bothered at the prospect of not being able to use some of her magic.

Glancing around, Vashe squinted and strained as she tried to locate the guards. After several tense moments, she caught a couple of voices carrying on the wind. She stealthily took a few steps forward, trying to discern the precise location of the voices. The noise got closer and Vashe noticed that they were coming from her right. She wasn't able to see the source yet, but she knew that they were approaching quickly. Checking both directions, Vashe darted from the treeline and sprinted towards the castle. Once she was inside of the doorway, she paused, crouching down as she waited to see if the voices would pass.

Eventually, she watched as two bored guards sauntered by. They spoke amongst themselves, unconcerned with their surroundings. Vashe held her breath as they passed her hiding spot. They may not be able to see her very well, but if the guards turned to enter the castle, they would surely run into her. She said a quiet prayer to Aria, hoping that the duo wouldn't be calling it a night. Luck appeared to be on her side as the guards continued on their rounds, oblivious to her presence.

As they passed her, Vashe slowly got up and flattened herself against the arch of the doorway. Glancing behind her, Vashe made a mad dash in the opposite direction towards one of the castle walls. She stopped when she reached a trellis that was covered in ivy. Taking a moment to catch her breath, she looked around to see if there were any other guards coming her way. Satisfied that there was no one in the immediate area, Vashe began scaling the trellis.

The lattice didn't go very high, but it allowed her enough purchase to reach the kill holes that were hidden in the stone. Using her fingers, Vashe inched her hand along the worn stone until she found the small holes. She then used the slots to position her hands and feet along the castle wall to support her weight. If somebody looked up, they would see her crouched form hanging from the walls. Moving slowly, Vashe scaled the wall, looking for a window to squeeze through.

The climb was painfully slow. Her fingers began aching shortly into her ascent, not used to having so much weight placed on them, and her toes started to cramp in her boots. Inch by inch, she moved up the wall. On one occasion, her hand slipped and she found herself scrambling to grab onto some crumbling stone that plummeted to the earth. Her heart froze as she looked down below her to see if there was anyone approaching. Mercifully, there was no one around to notice the debris.

Finally, she found a window positioned several feet above her. Steeling herself, Vashe repositioned her hands and launched herself up towards the window. She managed to get a grip on the sill and gradually pull her body up. Vashe peeked through the window to see if there was anyone in the room. She was pleased to find that the room was empty. With a determined grunt, she pulled her arms through the window and managed to get one of her legs placed on top of the windowsill before dragging the rest of her body into the room.

Looking around, Vashe tried to get her bearings. She hoped that the layout of the castle hadn't changed too much; she didn't think that her parents would do anything that drastic, anyway. In the room, she noted that there were rolled pieces of parchment and maps strewn on a table pushed to the side of the wall. There were also a few affixed to the wall above the table.

Vashe walked over to inspect the drawings. She expected to see detailed charts of various parts of Scrymme. Instead, she observed thorough diagrams of various defenses for the other nations. There were two maps, one of Zanir and one of Xan, that both outlined strategic strongholds. In Xan, she noted that there were several circles surrounding innocuous spots at random intervals. She scanned the drawing more and noticed that there was a cluster of smaller circles at the top-left corner of Fa'Tinh.

Isn't that the ore mine? Vashe wondered as she stared hard at the map.

Her eyes moved to the map of Zanir. She noticed that there was a circle at the northern border, and several other ones in Pharn, Loast, and near the southwestern corner.

Those are the spice mines and iron ore pits in Zanir, she realized. *It looks like they're mapping the resources for each realm. What are they trying to accomplish?*

Vashe heard an arrogant voice in the hallway and straightened up. She moved towards the doorway and flattened herself against the wall. She strained her ears, trying to hear what was being said.

"Go," the voice commanded. "I've seen enough of you for now. Why don't you bring me one of the serving girls for some entertainment for tonight?"

Vashe heard a soft mumbling through the door, but couldn't make out what was being said. A loud smack followed, then silence.

"I don't care how old they are," the louder voice said. "Just bring me one who's had her monthly bleed. That's how you'll know they're old enough."

More mutterings. The sound of scurrying feet could be heard moving swiftly in the other direction.

"Gods' mercy, these servants don't know what they're talking about," the voice muttered.

Vashe listened as the footsteps paced the hallway. She quietly let out her breath as she resigned herself to a long wait.

Why does that voice sound so familiar?

"What is taking them so long?" the voice groused. "It can't be that hard to find me a girl for the night."

Aria's mercy, that's Dzvri. I should've known that my dear brother would turn out to be such a disgrace. He was following in Father's footsteps so nicely growing up.

Vashe felt an emotion that she hadn't felt in a long time, anger. She'd worked so hard to push the actions of her family out of her head, but she struggled right now.

Blessed Aria, give me the strength to finish what I set out to do.

The footsteps stopped outside of the door. Vashe held her breath as she waited for Dzvri to do something. She heard him muttering to himself, unable to make out what he was saying through the thick wooden door. After a lengthy period of silence, the door opened and Dzvri strode in.

Vashe crouched down as her brother passed right by her and made his way to the cartographs. He leaned over one of the drawings on the table, studying the images on the paper. Vashe glanced around frantically before slowly slinking away from the door and towards a corner of the room behind him. As she moved, she removed a dagger from the sheath on her thigh and palmed the weapon. The cool blade rested on her forearm as she grasped the lacquered handle tightly.

Vashe gripped the pommel tighter as she tensed her body. She watched as her brother finished fiddling with a lantern before returning back to the charts. The flame danced weakly along the wall, providing minimal light. Vashe thought about temporarily using the light from the fire to freeze her brother, but the mention of her name caught her attention.

"Dzvaresh must still be out there somewhere, the traitorous bitch," Dzvri grumbled. "I could probably take a side expedition once we take the ore and handle her. Father would be so proud to know that her disgrace will no longer taint our name."

Vashe caught her breath. Remaining crouched, she slid one leg out to the side, positioning her weight on the outstretched leg before pushing off with her bent, base leg to maneuver herself closer to the door. She repeated this process two more times while Dzvri hunched over the maps, talking quietly to himself. Vashe wormed her fingers into a crack between the door and the wall, trying to inch it open. Her fingers struggled to get a good grip on the entrance, but couldn't move it subtly enough. Her eyes never left her brother.

Left with no other choice, Vashe utilized the power of the flame to grab on to Dzvri's shadow and trap him at the table. Once she was sure that he was immobile, she popped up and ripped the door open, dashing out of the room as her brother cried out in shock.

Vashe sprinted down the hall. She heard the crash of the iron lamp and the shattering of glass in the cartography room.

Well, it couldn't last forever.

"Stop!" Dzvri roared as he tore after his sister.

Vashe looked around and was surprised to see that the hallways were blessedly empty. Gripping her dagger in her hand, she slowed her pace just enough to let her brother think that he was gaining on her. As his footsteps neared, she steeled herself to move.

Well, so much for subtlety now.

XXXVI

Planting her left leg, Vashe pivoted and swung herself to the left. Her momentum took her a step or two up the stone wall, running along the side. With a kick from her right foot, Vashe took out the lamp that lit their section of the passageway, plunging them into near darkness. Dzvri cried out as the shattering glass flew at his face.

Vashe managed to land on the ground in a crouch. Her legs tensed briefly before she flung herself at her brother. Vashe managed to catch Dzvri off-guard, catching him in the stomach with a knee and causing his legs to buckle as his lost his breath. She brought her arm back and punched him in the head, her hand still clasped around the pommel of the dagger.

Dzvri grunted as the blow landed against his jaw. Dropping to his knee, he quickly spun around, extending his leg and catching Vashe's in the process. The motion caused her to stumble back, barely managing to keep her feet beneath her. As she stutter-stepped her way to balance, Dzvri straightened up and launched on the offensive.

With both of their magic subdued, Dzvri cocked back his arm and swung at his sister. She barely had time to block, his blow landing solidly on her forearms and knocking her back a step. He brought back his left and swung. Vashe rolled with the wide hook and let the force of the hit absorb into her body as she dove into a forward roll. She came up with her back against the other wall, his side exposed.

Vashe threw a quick one-two punch combination at her brother, scoring a hit on his arm then ribs. She brought her knee up quickly and jammed it into his thigh. Dzvri grunted as his leg muscle spasmed. Vashe went to hit him with a tight hook punch in the head, but Dzvri managed to turn and catch her strike in his hand. Vashe's eyes widened in surprise as she struggled to pull her hand back.

Dzvri grinned as he stood up, her hand still clenched in his. He pulled her close to him and headbutted her across the nose. A cut opened on the bridge, causing blood to drip down the side of her face. He pulled his hand back and punched her twice, catching her on her cheek. Vashe felt the warm blood fill her mouth. She stomped on his foot, causing him to release her hand, and danced out of his grip. She spit a mouthful of blood onto the floor as she moved.

"Getting slow, dear sister," Dzvri taunted. "I guess all those years with the heathens have turned you soft. You're a pale shadow of what you used to be."

Vashe's mouth hung open. She wasn't able to breathe with it closed because of her nose. She narrowed her eyes and shifted her weight. Vashe brought her hands up in a defensive position that she'd seen some of the soldiers of Pharn assume during their training.

"So, you want some more, Dzvaresh? Didn't they say that you were smart?" Dzvri sneered.

"Let's finish this, Dzvri," Vashe said coldly.

Dzvri jeered and attacked. He threw a flurry of punches towards her ribs in quick succession. Vashe parried his strikes and threw in a few counters herself. Both managed to land several blows on their opponents, but nothing that stopped the other long enough to score another hit.

The two danced around each other in the tight hallway as they exchanged blows with each other. During one exchange, Dzvri managed to knock Vashe off balance. As she stumbled, he pursued her with a renewed vigor. He landed several strikes against her body and head in quick succession, knocking her back further.

With a mighty punch, Dzvri managed to catch her in the stomach with a heavy hit. Vashe doubled over, clutching her stomach, as she struggled for breath. Dzvri loomed over her, smirking. He grabbed a handful of her hair and lifted her into the air. Her knees left the ground as he pulled her. Vashe grunted, one of her eyes closing in pain as he tugged at her roughly.

Leaning down until he was eye level with her, Dzvri looked into her eyes with a smirk on his face. Blood ran down her face from several cuts, staining her alabaster skin. Pulling her in, he whispered in her ear, "Long live Her Holiness." He drew back his fist and punched her throat.

A startled gasp filled the quiet hallway as the pair stood, motionless. Vashe's dagger was jammed into Dzvri's throat, his hand inches from her own. His eyes bulged as he struggled to breathe through his severed windpipe. He tried to speak, but no words came out. Instead, all that she could hear was him gasping.

"Long live Her Holiness, indeed," Vashe whispered.

She pushed herself to her feet as her brother dropped to the ground. Reaching down, Vashe pulled out the weapon from his neck. She wiped the blade nonchalantly on his cream-colored tunic before returning it back to the sheath on her thigh.

"Now, if you don't mind, brother, I need to be going. I have much to do, and I don't plan on staying here long."

Stepping over Dzvri's fallen body, Vashe backtracked towards the cartography room and began searching for Dzvareliah's personal shrine to Aria. She crept through the deserted halls, unnerved at the lack of servants or other bodies hustling around.

It's been a while, Vashe thought to herself. *I guess that they've taken drastic measures to keep the staff out of their way.*

Almost as if on cue, Vashe heard the sound of approaching footsteps. Scanning around for a place to hide, she began to panic as she realized that there were no statues or side rooms for her to duck behind. Her mind racing, Vashe took a deep breath and assumed an imposing stance.

A male servant came up, dragging a young girl behind him. Tears ran down the girl's face, her eyes wide in terror and faint whimpers escaping her lips. The male kept speaking softly to her, trying to soothe her as they sped through the hallways. As they neared Vashe, the pair slowed down, unable to place the slender woman with the royal household.

"Miss, miss!" the man addressed Vashe. "Are you okay, miss?"

Vashe turned her bloodied face to him, trying to keep an imperious air about her. She watched as he first recoiled at the sight of her face, then scanned her in an attempt to place her.

"Do you have a cloth?" Vashe asked. "I seem to have misplaced mine after my evening training class." She was dismayed at how easy it was to resume her former act.

The man held out a pocket square with a shaking hand. Vashe took the cloth with a thank you and wiped off her bloodied face. Once she was satisfied that she was able to get all of the blood that she could, she stuffed the square into her blouse.

"Thank you," she told him. "Tell me, it's been a long time since I've admired Lady Dzvareliah's sacred shrine. How much farther is it?"

The man eyed her, uncertain of who she was, but dared not to disobey one of the family. "It's around the corner, miss. Once you make it around, you'll stop at the third door on the right."

Vashe nodded to him and headed towards the corner.

"Miss," the man called out. The young girl whimpered softly as she stood silently during the exchange.

Vashe turned. She raised an eyebrow, silently prompting him to speak.

"Begging your pardon, miss, but I'm not able to place your name with your face. I would like to properly address milady in case we run into each other in the future. May I know your name?"

Vashe hesitated for a moment. Taking a gamble, she decided to be honest. "You may call me Dzvaresh. Although, I would prefer if you didn't mention seeing me. Lady Dzvareliah doesn't approve of my training classes. She thinks that they are too intense, even for one of our family."

"Of course, Miss Dzvaresh. Is there anything else I can do for you tonight?"

"Yes. I think that you should let her go back to the kitchens for a quick snack," Vashe pointed to the young girl waiting quietly at his side. "I'm sure she has a big evening ahead of her and could use a full stomach." Turning to face the girl, Vashe asked, "You know where you need to go, yes?"

The girl nodded mutely.

"But, Miss Dzvaresh, I have orders from Lord Dzvri to bring her right away," the man protested.

"I just ran into Lord Dzvri," Vashe explained. "He hinted at a strenuous evening. I'd hate for him to be upset with you for not bringing him someone who isn't up to his standards."

The man's face blanched as he thought of the implications. "Yes, of course, miss. You're absolutely right. If there is nothing you require, I bid you good evening."

"Good evening," Vashe replied with a curt nod.

The man scurried off down the hall towards the kitchens. Vashe watched as he dragged the young girl behind him. Once the two disappeared down the hall, Vashe checked the passage. Once she was sure it was clear, she continued down towards her mother's sanctuary.

⚬⚬⚬

Vashe pressed her ear to the ornate mahogany door. Intricate swirls were carved into the frame, depicting the ethereal nature of the gods. In the center of the door, a smooth carving of a young woman with flowing hair lay amid the whirls. Her hair was covered in thin silver leaf. Vashe waited for several minutes before she felt comfortable that the room was empty. Glancing around quickly, she grasped the door handle and pushed open the door. Opening the door just a bit, Vashe slipped through the cracked entryway into the darkened room.

Vashe waited a few moments for her eyes to adjust to the darkness before she moved further into the room. As she acclimated to the blackness, Vashe felt thankful that the clouds moved in the sky, providing some moonlight through the window for her to see by.

The room was almost completely empty. Smoothed stone with veins of gold and silver leaf flowing through it covered the entire room, even the walls. In the center of the room were two marble pedestals with a stone dais in between. On the dais sat a silver bowl of holy water. It was positioned so that it caught the moonlight perfectly through the open window. The marble pillars stood shorter than the dais. On each of the platforms, three relics were placed on top.

Vashe walked up to the shrine, a feeling of trepidation filled her. She hadn't been in the holy room since she was a little girl when her mother initiated her into the world of sacred magic. Despite her hatred for her family, she still felt a sense of guilt as she was about to defile such holy artifacts. A sense of reverence quickly replaced her nervousness as she stepped up to the altar into the moonlight. Her silver eyes reflected against the water in the brilliance and she felt at peace.

She looked at the sacred items on both pillars, trying to find what she was looking for. One the left-hand side she found a crystal vial filled with dark red liquid sitting between a ragged doll with a few strands of hair attached to it and a silver dagger with a shining sheath. Vashe picked up the vial reverently and held it up in the light. The liquid refracted against the crystal, sending small sparkles onto the walls and floor. Vashe pulled out the bloody cloth from her bosom and wrapped the vial in it before placing the wrapped artifact into her hip pouch. She quickly picked up the dagger and slipped it into the back of her bodice, securing it snugly against her back.

Vashe took a quick look at the sacred items on the right pillar. A second vial sat in the middle between a worn stone with a splatter of blood and an ancient stone knife. On an impulse, Vashe grabbed the second vial and the bloody stone, shoving them into her pouch, before glancing furtively around.

She suddenly felt uneasy. The feeling of eyes boring onto her gave her a heavy feeling in her stomach though there was no one in the room. With a deep breath, Vashe dipped her index finger into the holy water and swirled it around three times. Pulling her damp finger out from the bowl, she then drew a rune of protection on her forehead. As the water dripped down her nose and cheeks, she felt a warmth engulf her.

With a final glance around the room, Vashe turned to the window and looked below her. The ground was clear. Straining her ears, she was surprised to find that she still hadn't heard any cries of alarm in the halls.

Have they not found Dzvri's body yet? She wondered. *Surely someone would have noticed the broken lantern and the mess by now.*

Crossing the room to the window, Vashe climbed onto the sill and flung her leg over. Carefully, she climbed down the side of Caicyne Ari and made her escape from home for the second time in her life.

XXXVII

VASHE TRAVELED through the darkness towards the border of Scrymme. Her body coursed with adrenaline as she struggled to process everything she'd just done in the last few hours. She blessed her luck that no one had ever snuck into Scrymme before. If anyone from one of the other nations dared try to enter, they would've died quickly at her border.

Dzvroth surely will be sending out his assassins once they find out it was me. If those two know what's good for them, they'll stay quiet and pretend that we never met. Letting out a wan laugh, Vashe shook her head as she moved quickly through the land. *I've signed their death warrants, and probably my own in the process. Father will be furious. No matter, I'll be ready for them.*

Toron's moon peaked and slowly began his descent. The clouds in the sky cleared, revealing a beautiful heaven with a multitude of stars twinkling. Despite her haste, Vashe looked up and admired the constellations that she knew she could only find in Scrymme. Since she was in the lower part of Corinth, there were three star clusters at this time of year that only they could see.

She saw the Siblings, a cluster of stars that represented Her Holiness Aria, Ghan, and Czand. The star for Aria was the largest of the three, shining the brightest in between her two brothers. Next, she spied the five stars that made up Ramarda, the archer. He stood to the left of the Siblings, protecting them in the heavens as they enjoyed their lives together, unlike their tragic time amongst the gods.

Vashe smiled as she watched the happy family and their guardian. Having them watch over her as she escaped from her homeland filled her with hope — a hope that she made the right decisions and was doing their work. The moonlight washed over her, bathing her with an ethereal glow.

Looking up to find the last constellation, Vashe was surprised to see that she could not see the great panther, Maah-res. The spot where the powerful feline once stood was startlingly empty. Vashe paused, craning her neck to see if maybe she misjudged the stars. She was gone. The panther completely disappeared from the sky.

This is bad, Vashe worried. *Maah-res watches over all of us. If she's disappeared, that can't mean anything good. I fear this is an omen.*

Vashe broke into a jog, her discomfort fueling her already emotion-filled journey. Toron's brilliance shone on the open expanse that she now traveled. Being so exposed put her on high alert. As she looked ahead, she saw a shadowed figure standing on a knoll. Vashe slowed to a stop and crouched down. She looked around her for a place to take cover and noticed a small copse of trees off to her right. Glancing back at the figure, she made the decision to run for the thicket.

As she reached the safety of cover, she took a moment to collect her breathing and thoughts. Sweat covered her forehead. She wiped her brow off with a tattooed hand as she steadied her breath.

Who is he? Did I miss a new nightwatch when I snuck in? Has Dzvroth sent his soldiers out to intercept me?

Vashe sucked in her breath as she watched the figure turn and start walking in her direction. She ducked down behind a trunk and prayed that he wouldn't get any closer to her location.

The shadow walked leisurely towards her. As it neared, she saw that it was a man. Her breath caught in her throat as she observed that he wasn't a Scrymmen native, but a foreigner with dark skin and brown eyes. She grabbed the dagger on her thigh and palmed the hilt in her hand. Glancing around to make sure that no one was sneaking up behind her or from her sides, she stood up and rested against the tree. Her slim frame was able to be almost completely concealed by the trunk. She readied her energies so that once he was in range, she could immobilize him like she had the others earlier that day.

As the man approached her hiding spot, the light of the moon suddenly illuminated her position, exposing her against the darkness. Vashe steeled herself and swallowed her nerves. If she was going to need to fight, at least she would have the ability to use her magic against the stranger.

"Greetings," the man called out. "Isn't it a lovely night tonight?"

"It is," she replied warily. Tightening her grip on the pommel, Vashe stepped out from behind the tree; it wasn't hiding her anymore. "What brings you out to Scrymme? Surely you've heard about how dangerous it is for one who is not of their blood to travel through their lands."

"I have heard of that, but it was so beautiful out that I couldn't resist taking a stroll and observing the stars. Aren't they wondrous? It is a little distressing that Maah-res is missing though."

Vashe scrutinized the man's face. He had dark skin, high cheekbones and dark, short-cropped hair. A gold band encircled his left arm, contrasting against his skin and the cream-colored clothes that he wore. His top was sleeveless and his bottom resembled a skirt. He wore black sandals, the straps tied halfway up his calves.

"Scrymme has been blessed with beautiful heavens," she said, her body still tense.

How does he know about Maah-res?

"Tell me, friend, where do you hail from?" Vashe asked.

"Ah," he said with a smile, his eyes crinkling, "I am a wanderer. Not unlike yourself." The man winked at her, as though they shared a secret. "You know what it's like to lose your home, am I right?"

Vashe had a sudden urge to leave the copse. Her adrenaline started pumping once more and she couldn't explain why. The air around her was heavy, similar to the way she felt in her mother's shrine.

The man must have noted her discomfort because he smiled at her once more. "Tell me, what is a lovely daughter like yourself doing at this time of night?"

Vashe didn't speak.

"Oh, forgive me," he said with a chuckle. "My name is Dseti." When Vashe didn't answer, he stared at her quizzically. "Do you not trust me? We are kindred spirits, believe it or not."

"I trust no one who travels in Scrymme," she said simply. "No good can happen to anyone while here."

"I see. Are you thinking of the two from earlier this evening? The ones who helped you?"

Vashe's mouth dropped open slightly, but she managed to maintain her shock. "I have encountered many on my trip."

Toron's light shone on Dseti's face. In the light, it almost looked as though his brown eyes had turned a milky silver. "Yes, yes you have," he said with a knowing nod. "I too have run into a number of people tonight. But enough of that. I can see that you are an astute woman, would that be accurate?"

Vashe did not respond right away. She fiddled with the knife concealed in her hand, debating on whether or not to use it. She tried to reach out with her magic and freeze him, but found that she could not take control of his shadow, even in the brilliant light. A knot formed in her throat as she panicked at her inability to use her magic, but she forced herself to keep her expression neutral.

What is this? Why can't I grab onto him? It's almost like talking to naran. He's all over the place.

"I enjoy a good riddle," Vashe replied cryptically, taking a step back and to the side. "As I'm sure that most do."

Dseti clapped his hands together in delight, a wide smile breaking out on his face. "Excellent! We're of the same vein, you and I. What if I told you that I know of a place that would satisfy your curiosities unlike any other?"

Vashe cocked her head. She was intrigued, but she didn't want to let him know it. Vashe felt as though she needed to maintain a neutral countenance when speaking with this man. Showing fear or interest did not seem like a good idea.

The man leaned closer to her so that Vashe could see that his eyes were indeed brown. The change in color must have been a trick of the light. He beckoned Vashe to lean in as well, but she did not.

Not put off in the slightest, Dseti continued. "I've just come from a place, a place that I think would make even you nearly faint with excitement."

Unable to hide her interest, she asked, "Where?"

"Enlil," he said conspiratorially.

"Enlil? The ruined city of the gods?"

"Yes, my daughter. One and the same."

"That land is nothing but overgrown vegetation," Vashe replied skeptically. "After the great shake centuries ago, nothing has been able to grow on her soil since. Not even animals live there."

"Ah, but that's because they don't know where to look," Dseti said. "If it intrigues you, let me show you where to find the door."

The heaviness in the air melted away at the promise of a chance to explore the ruined city of Enlil. Few had heard of the place, and those who did only dreamt of it. People had died trying to find the city, and here was an opportunity to discover it. However, Vashe was still leery. She knew absolutely nothing about him, yet he promised her a treasure beyond her wildest dreams.

"What do you want in exchange for this knowledge?" she asked.

Dseti's eyes crinkled once more as he smiled at her. "All I ask is that you go and learn as much as you can before returning back to your home. Enlil is a beautiful place, and I would hate for her to be forgotten."

Vashe stood, conflicted. She gripped the pommel of her dagger harder until her knuckles turned white.

"Come, my daughter, what do you have to lose? You wanted to visit Enlil anyway."

She opened her mouth to respond, but was struck by a sudden question. "Why do you call me daughter? How do you know my desires?"

Dseti approached her hesitantly. Reaching out towards her, he lightly placed his finger tips on her forehead. Images flashed into her head, blurring together. She struggled to get a cohesive picture, but from what she gathered, the man was an old soul who lived through a lot of pain, more than anyone ever could experience in a lifetime. When he pulled away, she found herself crying.

"I hope that answered your question," he said softly. After a pause, he asked, "Are you ready to find Enlil?"

Vashe wiped away the tears rolling down her face and nodded silently.

XXXVIII

CAITLYN SLUMPED to the ground. Her head throbbed and her vision swam red. Darkness threatened to consume her as her mind pulled in different directions. She brought her gloved hand to her face and tried to block out the blinding white light that burned itself into her retinas.

"*What's going on, Cait?*" Alverick asked.

"I made a mistake," she murmured.

Alverick stared at her quizzically.

"I'm tainted," she said quietly. Pulling the glove off of her left hand, she revealed the jagged tattoos of a Spark. However, many were broken, not connected to the others like one would normally find on a mage.

"Caitlyn!" Brody's voice sounded so far away.

Suddenly, she felt pressure on her shoulders and her head snap forward. Her vision slowly returned to normal, revealing Brody gently shaking her. Concern was etched on his face as he stared into her eyes. Blinking, Caitlyn struggled to clear her eyes.

"Caitlyn!" he repeated.

"Did I get him?" she asked weakly.

"Yes, it's dead," Brody said distractedly. "What's going on? Are you okay?"

"I'm fine," she said, trying to stand up. As she got her feet under her, her legs buckled and Caitlyn found herself kneeling on the ground once more.

Caitlyn spent several minutes breathing deeply, her lungs burning from the sulfur in the air.

Once she felt steady enough, she tried standing again. This time it was a success. Caitlyn rubbed her head to try and stop the throbbing. It seemed to help.

"Cait?"

Looking up, Caitlyn saw Brody holding her leather glove. She looked briefly at her bare hand, her tattoos exposed.

Shit!

"What's wrong with your hand?" he asked quietly.

With a sigh, Caitlyn faced him. "I thought I would try my luck with the gods." Waving her hand up for him to see, she showed off her tattoos. "Unfortunately, the gods weren't with me and I ended up tainted. Somehow, I've managed to maintain some semblance of sanity, unlike the other poor bastards who were rejected."

"How did you –"

"I don't know," she replied, shaking her head. "I've been looking into it, and I can't find anyone who's gone through the same thing that I have. I just thank the gods that I'm not completely tainted. Those souls are in a worse place than I." Her eyes dropped and she brought her tattooed hand to her head.

"*Cait.*"

Caitlyn looked around, trying to find the voice. "Did you say something?" she asked.

"No."

Frowning, she looked side-to-side once more.

Where did that come from? Who was that? It sounded familiar.

"Let's get moving. We made a lot of noise earlier. I don't want to see how the creatures of Aramaine respond to intruders in their realm," Brody said.

Caitlyn nodded in agreement and the two set off once more. They made their way past the remains of the drake as they headed deeper into the heart of Aramaine.

The green flames they'd seen earlier provided them with a faint light the deeper they moved in the tunnels. Their shadows dancing on the walls looked less like impish creatures, but more sinister. The feeling of being watched continued, and on more than one occasion, they turned around to see if anything was following them.

"Maybe we shouldn't have killed that monster," Brody mused on several different occasions. "I feel like I'm being hunted."

Caitlyn didn't answer. She felt it too.

Will we ever find him in this maze?

"Cait."

The voice seemed to be getting stronger.

Waving for Brody to stop, Caitlyn pointed to the right fork in the road. "We should go this way."

"What makes you say that?"

"I just, I feel that it's the right way."

Brody nodded and let Caitlyn lead the way. As they walked, the air began to clear up a bit, causing their lungs to not burn as much and their eyes to not water. Caitlyn took a deep breath of fresher air and felt her lungs clear.

"It's nice, isn't it?" Alverick said. He walked next to Caitlyn, taking in the minimalistic scenery.

"Nice isn't what I would call it," Caitlyn replied shortly.

"Come now, Cait. Why can't you take the time to just enjoy our time together?"

"How can I enjoy things when I'm in a world where everything wants to kill me?" she responded as she shot him a disgusted look.

Alverick walked beside her in silence. Caitlyn looked over at him and saw the pain in his eyes.

"What is it?"

"I never got a chance to just walk with you. Now that I do, you're not enjoying it."

"By the gods, Al, this is not some leisurely stroll. I'm trying to find you without losing my way out."

"It's not the location, but the company. Turn left."

Without thinking, Caitlyn turned left down a darker corridor. Brody called out in surprise behind her.

"Why didn't you tell me you were going to turn?" he asked. "You were talking to yourself and then you just changed directions. What's going on?"

"Sorry," she said sheepishly. "I just knew I should turn."

Caitlyn turned to look at Alverick, but he had vanished.

"Next time, please let me know."

A hiss sounded behind them. Two more sounded after. Faint scratching could be heard on the stones.

"Go, find Alverick," Brody whispered.

"I can't leave you," she replied. "Let me fight."

"No, you're in no shape to fight."

Reaching for an arrow in her quiver, she shook her head. "At least let me get one shot in. It sounds like there's more than one. You'll need help."

Brody chewed his lip as he worked furiously to plan a course of action. After several long seconds, he nodded resolutely. "No magic, just one shot," he said.

"One shot," she agreed.

Pulling his short sword out, he crouched down behind a rock and held his hand out for her to be quiet. Caitlyn positioned herself behind him so that she wouldn't hit him. She nocked the arrow and waited for the beast to round the corner and show itself. Taking deep breaths, she worked to steady her breathing and calm her heart. Red still played around her periphery, but she ignored it.

In short measure, she heard the raspy breathing of the creatures. Peering around the stone, she watched them approach. The lead monster was about three feet tall with long spindly limbs. Its knuckles dragged on the ground. Two more of its kin followed behind. Each one looked around with bulging eyes, trying to find the trespassing duo.

Brody's hand moved in her periphery, motioning for her to shot. Without waiting for another word, she loosed her arrow. The bolt flew straight and embedded itself in the head of the creature on the left. The one in the middle roared and rushed forward, his companion right behind him.

Brody stood up and made his way towards the creatures. As Caitlyn turned to run, she noticed that the creatures' fur appeared to change texture, becoming sharp tufts of hair. Reaching behind her back, Caitlyn grabbed another arrow and sent it flying into the beast on the right. As she turned to run, she heard the monster screech in agony.

Sounds like I hit my mark.

Caitlyn wound her way through the tunnels running as quickly as she felt comfortable in the dark realm. Several screams followed her, echoing down the halls. After running for what felt like several minutes, she found what appeared to be a dead end. As she approached the end of the tunnel, she saw that it emptied into a large hall. The scraping of claws sounded behind her in the distance. Looking back, she strained to see what was behind her. Unable to see anything, she darted forward.

Caitlyn rounded the corner. Grasping her chest, she leaned back against the wall and slowly lowered herself to the ground. Her heart pounded in her chest as she struggled to calm her breathing. Brody rounded the corner shortly after, his short sword bloody. A dark patch stained his sleeve. Ripping the other sleeve, Brody pulled up the bloody one and began bandaging his wounded arm.

"It's not deep," he said as he noted Caitlyn watching him.

"Let me help," she said, standing. Reaching over, she took the ends of the cloth. Caitlyn pulled the fabric tightly, tying it in a knot.

"Thanks," Brody said. He watched the redhead return back to the ground. "How are you feeling?"

"Things are a bit muddled, but I'll be fine," she mumbled. "I shouldn't have done it though."

"Well, I really appreciate it."

The two took a couple moments to gather their wits. Caitlyn leaned her head back and felt the wall behind her shift slightly.

What?

The sudden sound of coins moving caused her to snap her head back towards Brody.

"By the gods!" Brody swore.

The two looked at the wall behind them and saw that it was actually a mountain of coins, gems, and other riches. The peaks of the Res Mountains paled in comparison to the towering pile before them.

"Aria's mercy," Caitlyn whispered. "There's more wealth here than all of Corinth."

The pair moved slowly along the perimeter of the treasure. Green light flickered more strongly in the surrounding area. As they moved further around the base of the mountain, Caitlyn noticed that the air became heavier, but a bit clearer. The acrid stench of sulfur was not as powerful as the main corridors. A gentle breeze rustled her hair, breaking the stale heat from earlier. Caitlyn let out an involuntary sigh of relief as she relished the cool air.

Time seemed to be at a standstill as they moved stealthily. Occasionally, a few pieces of treasure fell from the mound, causing them to pause mid-step and strain their ears to see if they could hear anything. After several tense moments, they cautiously let out their breaths and continued on.

Finally, they reached the outermost corner of the pile. Brody held up his hand, signaling Caitlyn to stop behind him.

"Do you see anything?" he asked. "I don't want to move any further blindly. Ein is not someone I want to meet."

Caitlyn's eyes scanned the clearing in front of her. A warmth on her chest caught her attention. The necklace that Vashe had given her glowed faintly.

Why is it doing that?

"Hey Cait," Brody said softly. "Look at that smaller pile over there."

Caitlyn looked over to where Brody was pointing. In the shadows, she noticed a smaller mound that lay away from the main hoard. It looked different from the other stashes of treasure than they'd seen in Aramaine. Almost as though the riches were smoothed over.

"*Cait...*"

The voice seemed to call her name more strongly that it had before.

"It's moving," Brody gasped. "Al!"

Looking both directions, the young man quickly made his way across the open space to the smaller mound, crouching as he ran.

Caitlyn hesitated for a moment before following behind him. Out of the corner of her eyes, she watched, startled, as Cienna moved beside her. The young princess moved gracefully. Caitlyn quietly thanked the gods that the girl had agreed to forgo the royal garb in lieu of the more practical riding pants and pale tunic.

"*Are we sure it's him?*" Cienna asked. "*Mistress Vashe said that the creatures of this realm have been known to take the form of those we care for.*"

"It's him," Caitlyn replied softly.

"How can you be sure?"

"I can feel it. His heart beats with mine."

Caitlyn caught up to Brody. He knelt over the prone figure of his friend. Caitlyn looked back for the princess, but she had disappeared. Returning her gaze to Alverick, she let out a small gasp. His body was bloody, his clothes torn. The light from her opal pendant accentuated the wounds on his face.

"Oh, Al," she murmured.

She reached out a hand and tentatively touched his face. He groaned softly, but did not waken. Moving her fingers lightly against his flesh, she traced his forehead and cheek. She paused about halfway down his cheek, near his broken nose. A large gash ran across the bridge, but otherwise there was not much blood, which surprised her.

"He's in bad shape," Brody said. "I don't know how we're going to get him back. I don't know how we're going to get back..."

Caitlyn's head shot up and she stared at the young man. Up until this point, she hadn't thought of how they would return home. She'd been so preoccupied with finding Alverick. The burning on her chest from the glowing stone got hotter as she felt her fear rising within her.

Taking a deep breath, she replied, "Let's just figure out how we're going to move him. I don't want to stay out in the open like this much longer."

Alverick groaned again, this time, louder.

"Al," Brody called out softly. "It's us. Wake up, brother."

Brody rubbed Alverick's back gently in a desperate attempt to rouse him.

"Come on, Al," Caitlyn implored. "By Aria's grace, you need to get up."

She reached out and gingerly grabbed his filthy hand. Wrapping her fingers around his, she closed her eyes and gave his hand a squeeze.

You can't leave me like this. Not after what I've already gone through.

A solitary tear rolled down her cheek.

"Why are you crying, Cait?"

Snapping her eyes open, Caitlyn looked at Alverick. His eye was opened slightly thanks to some swelling from his fight with the elemental. Dried blood caked at the corner of his mouth and his hair was matted, but his amber eye stared deeply into hers.

"You can't leave us," she choked out.

"Leave you? Where would I go? Where am I?"

"Aramaine. You were pulled in by the great wyrm during the battle."

Alverick went silent, his eyes staring blankly ahead. After a while, he spoke.

"Where's Bannen? I saw him in the gorge."

Caitlyn choked back a sob as more tears ran down her face. "Gone," she whispered.

Brody worked frantically to wake the unconscious man, rubbing his back and murmuring to his friend.

"Oh."

Alverick's eyes went blank once more as he processed everything. A single tear trickled down his broken nose and puddled on the ground beneath him.

"Perhaps things are better this way."

"Dammit, Al!" she swore softly. "We need you. Zanir needs you. I need you. Oldar is turning the nations against us. We need you to help keep them at bay. Pharn will fall if you don't get up."

A low rumble caused Caitlyn's head to snap up. The ground shook, pebbles dancing on the surface, as heavy footsteps sounded in the distance.

"Caitlyn, we don't have time. We have to go, now."

Wrapping his arm under Alverick's shoulder, Brody lifted the man and flung him onto his shoulder; the Avalanche's head dangled on Brody's back. The two began a swift, but quiet, retreat towards the mountainous mound of treasure. As they neared the stack, a mighty roar broke through the silence.

"Ghan's mercy, we're in trouble!" Caitlyn squeaked.

"Keep moving," Brody instructed.

They made it behind the pile and worked their way back to the main corridor. Alverick's legs dragged behind Brody, causing him to slow down. A sudden burst of heat and light filled the room as the monstrous form of Ein entered.

The obsidian behemoth stared around with his crimson eyes, his nostrils working furiously in an attempt to figure out who dared approach his treasure. His claws raked long gouges in the stone floor as he curled his feet in anger. Black, acrid smoke began to fill the room.

"Go!" Brody hissed to Caitlyn. "We'll only slow you down."

"I'm not leaving without you!"

Another deafening bellow from the furious wyrm rang out as Ein stuck his head around the corner of his beloved treasure. With a cry of anticipation, the lord of Aramaine scrambled to round his hoard.

"Ghan's mercy, we're dead!" Caitlyn cried. Her voice sounded strange in the otherwise silent realm.

"Run!" Brody yelled.

Ein's eyes locked onto the trio, his neck darting forward in an attempt to snatch one of them. Brody and Caitlyn jumped back just far enough that his razor-thin teeth missed them. They could feel a burst of wind from the motion.

"Aria, protect us!" Caitlyn cried.

The ground beneath them began to rumble, with coins and other riches tumbling to the floor. Ein's claws dug into the earth as he prepared to lunge forward. The groanings of the land got stronger, as stones from the ceiling cracked and fell to the earth.

"What?" Brody exclaimed as he looked around, trying to figure out the source of the shaking.

Caitlyn's eyes locked onto his. She saw the fear in his eyes, a fear that she didn't see on the battlefield.

We're going to die here.

She glanced at Alverick one last time. His eyes opened and he lifted his head off of Brody's back slightly. His hand was clenched in a fist as he pulled at the earth's tectonic plates.

Alverick.

Ein gave a roar of confusion as he danced a little on the shaking ground. Coins and other fine treasures tumbled down from the gargantuan mounds and spilled onto the floor. The wyrm looked on in horror as his prized possessions were thrown around. Gravel and stones moved across the earth as the shaking intensified.

"No, no, no!" he roared.

Ein scrambled to catch the gold and jewels that strayed from their home. Scooping frantically, the great wyrm corralled his treasures and pushing them back to the foot of the mountain. Ruby eyes narrowing in anger, he turned to face the source of the shaking once more.

"I've had enough!"

The wyrm's chest glowed as an inferno built within. He braced his legs and lowered his head as he took aim.

Caitlyn turned to look at Alverick once more. His eyes were unfocused as he tried to create a larger earthquake.

"Al, it's not working!" she cried out.

Alverick's hand dropped and his head drooped once more as his fatigue overwhelmed him. The shaking gradually stopped. However, the fire within the wyrm continued to burn.

Ghan's mercy! Glancing towards the entrance to the room, she contemplated hitting the beast with a blast of electrical energy. The edges of her vision fuzzed as she concentrated on forming a ball of energy in her hand. *Please work.*

Caitlyn had never summoned her magical energies so quickly before. Her body ached, as though she'd run a long distance quickly. Forcing her eyes to focus, Caitlyn threw the ball at the wyrm as hard as she could.

The energy dissipated against his chest without leaving so much as a scuff on his obsidian scales. Ein didn't even blink as he arced his neck and let loose a wall of flame towards the trio.

A tear rolled down Caitlyn's cheek as she watched the flame approach. Glancing at Brody, she saw that he stared stoically ahead, his jaw set firm. A blinding light engulfed the three as a pillar of flame shot towards them. Caitlyn squeezed her eyes shut and waited for her death.

XXXIX

VASHE LEANED against a tree, nodding off when she felt her ring become warm. Looking at the trinket from House Madderoux, she noticed that the stone glowed a soft red. The crackle of her campfire enhanced the brilliance.

"Looks like I was able to successfully twin two objects together with my blood after all," she mused. "I wonder what else I can do with the god blood."

Her thoughts were cut short when the ring grew hotter and began shining a blinding white. Her adrenaline started pumping and beads of sweat formed on her brow as panic welled in her chest.

"Blessed Aria's mercy, this is interesting."

Getting up to quickly check her surroundings, Vashe returned to her spot by the tree and closed her eyes. She took a deep breath and began reaching deep within herself, pulling on her energy reserves. In her mind, she pictured Caitlyn and Brody, focusing mainly on locating the opal necklace her master had given her not more than a week prior. Her hand burned as the ring sought out its partner.

As quickly as the ring began to burn, it stopped. Vashe snapped open her eyes and stared at the flaming green portal that she'd created. The light from the dimensional door illuminated her surroundings in the darkness. Looking around once more, she tried to determine if anyone was nearby. News of her actions should have already spread in her home. Satisfied that there was no one around to follow her, she stepped through the door into the abyss with a smile on her face.

She was finally going to meet Ein.

The acrid stench of Aramaine assaulted her nose before she finished crossing the realms. A low rumbling sounded not far from her. Stepping into the abyss, Vashe was greeted with a wall of flame racing towards her. Before closing the portal behind her, she moved out of the way, allowing for the inferno to disappear into its darkness.

In front of her stood the mighty Ein, a behemoth of purest black. His ruby eyes blinked at her, surprised to see her in his presence. Dipping her head in deference, Vashe took a step forward towards the beast. Behind her, she heard voices sputtering in shock. A small smile played on her lips.

"At last, we meet, Great Ein," Vashe called out. "I've been hoping to speak to you for some time now, but you've always managed to elude me."

A snarl curled the mighty wyrm's lips at her words. "Why do you disturb me?" he growled, his voice gravelly as it spoke the human tongue. "All I want is to live in peace, but you and yours continue to bother me with your petty squabbles." His eyes narrowed. "And those pups behind you dare to steal from me. What have I done to deserve this disrespect?"

His chest glowed a dull red as he summoned the fire within him. Acting quickly, Vashe bowed deeply, motioning for those behind her to follow suit. She heard a thud and Brody swear quietly.

Looking up with only her eyes, Vashe addressed the venerable creature. "My humblest apologies, Great Ein. It was not my, nor theirs, to disrespect your wishes. My master was the one who roused you from your slumber to come to our world. I believe you remember her, Dez."

Vashe lowered her eyes to the ground and prayed that those behind her kept their heads down. Ein stood quietly for several moments, his claws digging deep gouges into the ground as he subconsciously flexed his talons.

Another low rumble.

"I do remember Dzeara, young one. The old magic flows through her." His voice was thoughtful.

Glancing up, Vashe was relieved to see that his chest no longer glowed.

That was close. How does naran do it?

"Why would Dzeara use me in her fight with the Ancients?" he asked.

Ancients? Does he mean their aethren children or the Ancients themselves? Just how old is he?

Before she could answer, Ein continued.

"I received a nasty burn from an angry Ancient as he escaped my grasp and disappeared." The wyrm raised his claws and showed her a shining spot amongst his scales. The area around the wound was already peeling, so it was healing quickly. "It took quite a bit of convincing to keep him from incinerating the human that came with him."

Ein motioned to the prostrated form of Alverick on his knees with his head on the ground. Brody and Caitlyn stood behind him, bowing low and keeping their heads down.

"The Ancient did not want to let him go."

So, he speaks of Vahnyre, one of their children.

"*Naran* knows that the ancient laws keep the Ancients from killing those from Aramaine. She knew that only you could've saved us from Vahnyre," Vashe said.

A rumbling laugh could be heard from the wyrm. "What is your name, young one?"

"Dzvaresh, Great One," she replied. "Although I have renounced my name and go by Vashe."

"Why do you throw away your history?"

"For the same reason Dez did." Vashe took a risk and looked look the wyrm in the eyes, raising her head slightly. "I would rather determine my own history, not have it dictated for me."

"Yes, Dzeara said the same thing to me long ago," he mused. "I see why she chose you to be her ward."

Vashe dared hope that she was making progress.

"But I still do not understand why she would send two thieves into my home?" his voice carried a hint of a growl. "I've spared the broken one, but I can't have others come into my sanctuary and take what is now mine."

His chest swelled once again as a dull orange filled the cavernous cavity. The wyrm braced his front legs as he arced his head back a bit.

Working furiously, Vashe quickly said, "Great Ein, we ask for your blessing to take Alverick with us. War is brewing and we need all the strength that we can get. We would love it if you joined us in our cause, but we would also like to not drag you into our insignificant problems."

Ein slowly returned his head to its previous position as he relaxed his body.

Carefully now...

"If you would be so gracious as to let us bring Alverick home to help us. We would be honored to have such a boon from one as great as yourself." Vashe dropped her head once more in supplication.

Silence.

After what felt like an eternity, the gravelly voice of the wyrm spoke once more.

"I do not want to be disturbed anymore. If I let you take him, will you leave me alone?"

"Of course," Vashe replied quickly.

"And you won't try and contact me through that magic puddle of yours?" he asked.

Vashe bristled slightly at the insult. Working to keep her voice even, she said, "I will not contact you via scrying, you have my word."

"Very well. Take the broken one and return to your realm before I change my mind."

Ein laid down on the ground in front of them and watched them with impatient eyes. His tail slid side to side as his claws dug into the ground, an indicator of his agitation.

"Come, you three," Vashe said.

She quickly hooked her arms around one of Alverick's and Brody rushed to the other side. The pair hoisted the injured man onto his feet. Alverick's eyes were slightly glazed as he struggled to focus on his surroundings. Caitlyn's eyes darted from the wyrm to Vashe may times in quick succession. Her face pale as she stood quietly.

Reaching within herself, Vashe tapped into her energies. Pulling as hard as she could, she worked to open a door back to their dimension. Behind her, she heard a low growl and the shifting of gravel. Genuine panic welled in her breast. This was not an emotion brought on by a magical artifact, but her own fears as she realized that the situation was dangerously close to getting out of hand.

Sweat beaded on her brow as she tried to steady her breathing and concentrate. She could see her campfire burning low in her mind's eye. Her heart rate started to return to normal as a she felt the door began to take shape.

It felt like it took longer than it actually did, but the green flames of the portal appeared in front of her. Darkness lay on the other side of the dimensional door, punctuated only by the twinkling of stars in the night sky. Smoke from the campfire drifted by, mixing with the sulfuric scent of the abyss.

Motioning for the others to go through the door, Vashe waited until Caitlyn and the boys had gone through before turning around to look at the great wyrm one last time. His eyes narrowed as he loomed above her.

"I've always gathered the best treasure for myself," he said, motioning towards his giant pile. "You would make a fine addition to my collection."

Vashe stood in shocked silence.

Naran said that wyrms don't go back on their word. But he's no ordinary wyrm.

Her heart caught in her chest as Ein made his way towards her.

"Great Ein, it would be an exercise in futility to try and keep me," she finally said, her voice tight. "You know that I could open a door back to my world whenever I wanted and just return to my realm. What would keep me here with you?"

Ein's lips parted in a wicked approximation of a smile. The low, rumbling chuckle from earlier returned. "I can see into your soul, young Dzvaresh. I can give you all that you crave if you will join my collection."

"You couldn't possibly know what I want," she retorted.

"Knowledge," he said simply. "A place where you can test out your theories in peace without having to worry about the ethics of your experiments. I can give you access to all that you need. Just say the word."

A hunger filled her. Oh, how tempting the offer was, and that hunger caused her to pause. To be able to study the mighty wyrm, among other things had been her life's ambition. Vashe took a step away from the dimensional door.

Opening her mouth to speak, she shut it abruptly as a series of images flooded her head. A field covered in the bodies of the fallen. Towns razed to the ground. Children roaming the streets crying, not only for the loss of their families, but because they had bellies that had been empty for far too long. Pharn lay in ruins, its flag crumpled on the ground in tatters. A man with a golden armband stood on a knoll, overlooking all of the destruction below him. His eyes were pained. They were also familiar.

Vashe's heart ached for the man. Behind his eyes was the pain of a thousand lifetimes.

Stepping back towards the door, Vashe looked back at the wyrm. "I'm sorry, Venerable Ein, but I'm afraid that I must decline your offer, as generous as it is."

The mirth behind the wyrm's eyes quickly disappeared as anger replaced it.

"Do you understand what you are throwing away?" he hissed.

Vashe turned and made her way into the portal. She stepped through as a growl reverberated in the cavernous room. She looked back at the room one last time.

"I'm afraid that I do," she said solemnly. "My humblest apologies, Great One. It was a pleasure to finally meet you."

XL

ALVERICK LAY CRUMPLED on the ground, barely conscious. His body ached, his bones freezing. Around him, he heard familiar voices, but he couldn't make out what they were saying. Gradually, he felt a warmth surround him. The cold that he'd been feeling for so long finally started to melt away and his aches subsided. He struggled to open his eye a crack, and was rewarded with Caitlyn leaning against a tree a few feet away in front of a fire. She looked tired. Drained. Closing his eyes, Alverick let his mind wander as he allowed the warmth of the fire soothe him.

A new set of voices caught his attention. Alverick opened an eye once more. His body was warm. With effort, he managed to lift his head off the ground and open his other eye. Gravel stuck to his face as he looked around to get his bearings. The fire that he'd seen just a moment ago was gone, as was Caitlyn. In its place, he saw several large pillars forming a columnade. Inside the columnade, he spied a roaring fire.

Pushing himself onto his feet, Alverick found that the action wasn't as hard as he imagined it would be. His ribs still ached from where the aethren had punched him, but he was surprised at how well his body responded to his thoughts.

Must have been the cold, he reasoned. *Maybe I'm not as bad off as I thought.*

Alverick limped towards the light. At one point he had to stop and take a quick break, leaning against the stone pillar while he rested. However, he was pleased with how quickly he moved.

I must've wandered off, half-conscious, looking for a place to relieve myself and passed out in the process. Patting himself down, he was pleased to not feel any wet spots. *Looks like I didn't embarrass myself at least.*

As he neared the camp, Alverick heard a deep voice and stopped in his tracks. He didn't recognize the voice at all.

Is this all a trap? Am I still in that wyrm's lair? I thought I saw Caitlyn – was that just a dream?

Straining his ears, Alverick struggled to make out what was being said.

"The balance is shifting," the voice explained. "We've bided our time, and now we are ready to reap the fruits of our efforts. In short matter, our pawns will be in place and we can strike."

"Are you sure that everything is ready to go?" a second voice asked.

"Maah-res is no longer guarding the heavens," the first replied. "There's chaos in the lands and brother is turning upon brother. Our brethren are scattered as well. Now is the time for action."

Alverick crept closer, hoping to catch a glimpse of the two speakers. Slowly, he staggered along, crouching as he moved.

Maah-res? Who are they guarding? This almost sounds like a military strike. As he inched along, he heard the second one speak once more. *Where have I heard that voice? He sounds familiar.*

"Are you going to be able to keep your brother out of this? We were so close the last time, but he managed to snag his first and thwart you."

"You have enough on your plate to deal with," the first replied. "Mind your duties, and I'll mind mine. The Faceless will not grow on their own."

Alverick noted the tone in the deeper man's voice and wasn't surprised when the second didn't respond. He finally reached a clearing where he could make out some of the features of the two speakers. Though he couldn't make anything out in great detail, he dared not get any further.

The first was a dark-skinned man with a white skirt and black sandals. His chest was bare. Around his neck, a thick gold chain hung down. Alverick felt his heart stop as he looked at the man. Dark energy radiated from him. The darkness was so heavy that it threatened to choke Alverick.

The second man walked up and Alverick felt his heart almost drop into his stomach. He recognized the aethren, Vahnyre, from his battle at the gorge. The aethren stood beside the other man, a full head shorter than his darker counterpart. Vahnyre was just as Alverick remembered. His hairless body was bare, except for the flames that licked his bald head and provided the trouser-like coverage of pants over his lower half. The aethren stood a half step behind the other, almost as though he was offering his respects to the man.

"Continue your work," the deep-voiced man told Vahnyre. "I'll fetch you when the time is right." The shirtless man then turned and walked off, ending the conversation. Alverick caught a glimpse of a red eye before the man disappeared into the blackness.

Once the man was gone, Vahnyre spun around with a hiss. The flame from the fire flared to an inferno as the aethren silently raged. He balled his fists and punched the nearest tree. The plant erupted into flame and disintegrated to dust in a matter of seconds.

Alverick felt his breath catch in his throat as he watched the power of the god. *How was I able to survive my encounter with him? I should be dead. I should be...*

Alverick's thoughts were interrupted by a hand on his shoulder. He almost cried out in shock, but managed to keep quiet. His eyes traveled to his side and a wave of relief washed over him. Crouching down next to him was Bannen. His friend held a finger up to his lips, warning Alverick to be silent. Motioning with his head, Bannen started to slink away from the burning camp. Alverick followed behind.

The return to where they started took an eternity. Alverick's thighs burned as he remained low to the ground, but he dared not stand up while the raging god lingered nearby. Once he reached the columnade, he pulled himself upright, unable to bear the strain on his muscles anymore. Alverick gasped for breath as he massaged the knots in his legs.

"Come on, Al," Bannen coaxed. "A little further and I think we'll be safe."

"Bannen, what are you doing here? How did you find me?"

"When we joined the guard together, we swore that we'd always protect each other. That's what brothers do."

"Yes, but I've been gone for so long. We were swept into the void. I don't know how you would've managed to find me."

"I remember," Bannen said softly. "I was there when it happened."

A lump formed in Alverick's throat. He opened his mouth to speak with his friend, but Bannen held up his hand to silence him.

"Now is not the time. We *really* need to leave this place."

Alverick nodded and the two continued on. It didn't take too long for them to reach the clearing where Alverick first woke up. Bannen stood around and took in the surroundings to make sure that everything was clear. Alverick found himself dropping to the ground roughly.

"Al," Bannen said quietly, a sense of urgency in his voice. "You need to get out of here. You must warn the others of what you saw. I've been listening to the talk around the Halls and they speak of the Ancients awakening while their children, the aethren, descend to Corinth. A battle like we've never known is coming."

"I know," Alverick muttered. "I should have known that when there was talks of a demon, but I, I wasn't in my right mind at the time. We'd just lost so much. I wasn't in a good place."

Clapping his friend on the shoulder, Bannen said, "Then I'll leave you to it. I have to check on something, but I'm sure we'll meet up before this is over."

"Do you have to leave now?"

"I'm sorry, but yes."

"I wish you didn't have to. Until we meet again."

Bannen glanced around furtively before disappearing into the darkness. Alverick felt a deep sadness as his friend's form retreated. Every time he lost Bannen, it felt like that day at the spice mines again. A warmth washed over Alverick, making him feel drowsy. He rubbed his eyes with the heel of his palm.

When he opened them, he found himself laying on the ground once more, Caitlyn and the crackling fire sitting just a few feet away.

Caitlyn glanced over in his direction and saw that he was awake. "Al! You're conscious. Thank the gods."

Brody and Vashe walked up and stood over Caitlyn's shoulder. Alverick felt a wave of relief as he saw his friends. Brody's eyes glistened gazing at his friend. Alverick noted that despite his happiness, Brody looked worn as well. Even Vashe, a woman whom he'd never seen so much as out of breath, appeared strained.

XLI

VASHE LOOKED OVER Caitlyn's shoulder at Alverick. The man had a glazed look in his eyes. He pushed himself onto his elbow so that he could lift his head off of the ground. As Brody and Caitlyn rushed over to help him up, she hung back, watching his movements.

"Al, I'm so happy to see you're awake," Brody said. "You scared us back there."

"Do you even remember creating that earthquake?" Caitlyn asked.

Vashe flinched at the information. "When did this happen?"

"Right before you came," Caitlyn replied. "That wyrm was bearing down on us and I thought we were done for."

Alverick let out a weak cough as he tried to speak. The women's attention snapped back to the unsteady man. Vashe noted that Alverick swayed lightly as he leaned against Brody.

"No," he said feebly. Alverick rubbed his head with the heel of his palm as he tried to center himself.

Vashe's eyes narrowed as she watched him struggle. His eyes still couldn't seem to focus on any one thing in particular. It was almost as though something else held his attention.

What's going on in his head? she wondered. *Has his mind been torn?*

Alverick gingerly released his grip on Brody, trying to force himself upright. He rocked, but managed to keep his balance. His eyes wandered over

Caitlyn and Brody, landing on Vashe. She locked eyes with him, and a sense of understanding passed between them. Alverick's eyes shifted into focus. Vashe felt as though she could communicate with him nonverbally. She felt a powerful bond with him that she'd never felt before.

"What is going on?" Vashe asked quietly.

"Something big."

"Tell me," she insisted.

Brody and Caitlyn watched the exchange with interest. Neither spoke. Caitlyn brought her hand to her mouth, her eyes wide in shock. Brody stared anxiously at his friend. Alverick seemed to hone in on Vashe, ignoring the other two who stood near.

In an instant, the connection was broken and Alverick's eyes lost focus once more. They began darting in all directions and he started mumbling to himself. Occasionally, he would gesture with his hands, as though he was speaking with someone. Several times, the group heard him mention Bannen.

Vashe sighed heavily. She then walked over to Alverick and placed her hand on his shoulder. Whispering softly in his ear, she said, "Are you able to protect us from this threat?"

He gazed at her, unsure, and shook his head hesitantly.

"Can you see it?"

Nodding, slower this time. However, there was a question on his face.

Vashe gently cupped his chin, her tattooed fingers resting lightly on his cheek. She stared deeply into his eyes and muttered softly. Alverick's eyes drooped. As he started to drift into unconsciousness, the Scrymmen woman appeared to be doing the same. Her eyes became heavy in sync with his, both of their chins dropping lower. They blinked the heavy blinks of one who is fighting off sleep. All the while, Vashe murmured to Alverick with a rhythmic cadence.

Finally, his eyes appeared blurred, not from his Snapping, but from fatigue. His lids were open barely a sliver. And then, he spoke back to Vashe. Most of it was incoherent babbling, but enough stuck out to hold her attention.

"Gods... attack... Faceless... gods... run..."

If there was any clarity in his eyes upon his return from Aramaine, it had all vanished. Whatever remnants of sanity were wiped out as Alverick's mind fully Snapped.

His eyes darted around, fully alert once more. Vashe no longer could hold his attention. She released her hold on him and led Alverick to the horse that stood tied to a tree a little-ways off. The broken man allowed for himself to be guided to the beast. Holding out her hand for the horse to sniff, she prompted Alverick to do the same.

The beast's whiskers tickled the pair as his muzzle moved over their hands. Alverick looked down at the gentle creature and patted the stallion on the nose. The beasts' dark eyes stared into Alverick's. A look of understanding flickered across the horse's face, as though even he knew that there was something wrong with the man.

After hoisting Alverick onto the horse and securing him in the saddle, Vashe returned to Brody and Caitlyn as they waited by the campfire. Brody's arms lay crossed against his chest while Caitlyn hugged herself. The postures took Vashe by surprise. Though she was not familiar with the duo's intimate movements, the actions did not strike her as normal for the pair.

"We've lost him," she said, shaking her head. "I thought I could peer into him and see if there was anything we could salvage, but there's nothing left. Whatever he's experienced, it's broken him."

Caitlyn's bottom lip trembled, while Brody's jaw became hard.

"So, you saw nothing that can help us?" Brody asked.

"I saw some things, but nothing that could save his mind," she admitted.

"What did you see?" he asked.

Vashe hesitated for a moment, unsure of how much she should say. As she stared at Brody's determined face, she knew that she should trust her gut.

"I think that his connection to the gods may have something to do with his current state. When I watched your battle against Alazi, I noted that he absorbed much of their energy into his body, damaging his mind in the process. While in Aramaine, he must have had another encounter with the gods. Whether a psychological attack or a physical experience, it did not help his mental state.

"Just now, he spoke of an evil that has long been gone from our realm. I don't know what it means, but I believe that you three must return to Pharn as quickly as possible. If the danger that's in his mind is as dire as he thinks, we could be in for a rude awakening."

"You're coming with us though, right?" Caitlyn asked, finally breaking her silence. "Surely, you wouldn't leave us to fend for ourselves. Especially after we barely scraped by the last time."

"I'm afraid that I can't go back with you right now," Vashe said.

"Ghan's mercy!" Caitlyn swore. "What kind of shit is this? Aren't you supposed to be some all-powerful mage? Why can't you ever be around when we need you?"

"Cait," Brody said, placing his hand on her shoulder in an attempt to calm her.

"No. We've been left at the mercy of people like her for far too long. If you're going to get involved in the struggles of us lowly common folk, the least you can do is lend your strength."

"I hear your concerns, and they are valid," Vashe conceded. "However, I have urgent business that I must attend to. In light of what I've just seen, both in Aramaine and within Alverick, I feel that I cannot put off the last leg of my journey. I'll admit that this part wasn't planned, but I feel as though fate has been steering me in the right direction. I'm sorry."

"You're sorry?" Caitlyn asked incredulously. "You're sorry? Did you hear that, Brody? She's sorry."

"Cait, come on. She's done what she can," Brody tried to soothe angry redhead.

"No! She has not done all she can. She's done the bare minimum. She's let her friend drag Alverick into some god-forsaken abyss. Then she almost lets us die before she decides to rescue us from said hell hole."

"Hey," Brody interjected. "Vashe told us of the dangers of Aramaine."

"Why couldn't she just go and grab him herself?" Caitlyn continued. "She's obviously strong enough to open the portal. She could have spared us all of that trouble."

"Listen," Brody finally managed to cut in. "She told us of all of the dangers associated with this mission. She told us that it may fail, that we may die, that we may not even be able to enter the other realm. It's not her job to fight our battles. Vashe has done all she can. Am I happy that it wasn't easier? No. However, we can't blame her for everything. For all we know, she's working on something that may save our ass."

Caitlyn crossed her arms across her chest and pursed her lips. She glared at Brody out of the corner of her eyes, but did not say anything else.

"I can't give you much hope, other than I don't plan on staying away from Pharn for long. If you guys can hold everything together until I get back, I promise that I will give you my full, considerable strength," Vashe said. "But first, I must journey east."

"Of course," Brody replied. Caitlyn chewed the inside of her mouth, but remained silent. "We understand. Well, as much as we can, I suppose. Please hurry."

"I don't plan on being gone long," Vashe promised. "Until then. I wish you safe travels."

Caitlyn stomped over to the horse and began untying his lead. Alverick, who up until that point had been having an animated conversation with the tree, looked over at Caitlyn and cocked his head quizzically before resuming his conversation with the shrub.

"Keep an eye on her," Vashe told Brody. "I fear that she's too unstable right now after seeing him."

"I will," he replied with a nod. "She just has a lot on her mind right now. I'm sure that as we travel things will calm down."

"Then, I wish you all a safe and speedy journey. Keep your ears open."

Brody reached over and clapped Vashe on the shoulder, startling the slender woman. She wasn't used to being treated with such a sense of familiarity and found herself smiling. She reached up and grabbed Brody's hand, squeezing it in response.

The two shared one last look before parting ways. Vashe watched as Brody and the group headed back towards Pharn, Brody leading the horse on foot with Caitlyn while Alverick rode. Once they'd disappeared from sight, Vashe turned and started heading out east. Enlil was calling her.

XLII

CIENNA COULDN'T BELIEVE that she was still expected to show up in Madden. It was bad enough that Oldar tried to sabotage their alliances, but now he wanted to bring her to his home and discuss their relationship. It had been three days since he'd asked her to meet with him, and she finally decided to comply. Now, as she sat on her horse outside of the city gates of Madden, she regretted everything.

"Seems like a waste of time," she groused.

"Come, Cienna," Hera chided. "If we are to salvage this alliance, we must be willing to at least hear what he has to say. No good comes from just ignoring his requests. If we're not careful, he could declare us to be traitors and sanction embargoes on all of our wares."

"And yet, even if we do meet with him, there's still the chance that he'll do the same thing," Cienna said.

"That's true," Hera conceded. "However, we must show good faith. Perhaps you are wrong and have simply misjudged the young king."

"I doubt it," the princess mumbled.

"What was that?"

"Nothing, Mother."

The two sat in silence for a bit before Hera's handmaiden, Aeliana, returned to them after speaking with the gate guards.

"They're opening the gates, your majesty," Aeliana explained. "Once we're inside, they've arranged for us to have a guard escort us to the castle. There, King Storm will be waiting for us."

"Thank you, Aeliana," Hera said. Turning to her daughter, the queen asked, "Are you ready?"

Cienna nodded mutely, steeling herself for what was to come. She didn't know exactly what Oldar had in mind, but whatever it was, she was sure it wouldn't be pleasant.

A guard in blue and silver livery approached the Greys and instructed that they follow him. The women got off of their mounts and followed the man, their horses trailing behind them. Once they crossed through the city gates, another couple of soldiers came over and took their mounts from them, leading them to the stables for grooming and feeding.

"What nice hospitality," Hera remarked. "Looks like things may not be irreparable."

Cienna grumbled an incoherent response. The princess folded her arms across her chest and started taking in the scenery. She marveled at the opulent buildings that lined the streets. More than one of the guilders used gold-leafed molding on the columns that preceded their shops. The decorative additions were quite stunning painted and maintained in pristine white.

"Come now, Cienna," Hera said. "Straighten up and act like one of your station. You wouldn't throw this attitude if your father was around."

Cienna's cheeks burned, but she uncrossed her arms. The group continued to walk in relative silence. Occasionally, Hera would ask their escort a question about some aspect of the city. Cienna gazed at the beauty around her. Madden not only was aesthetically superior to Pharn, but it was even better maintained. Compared to Pharn, the capital of Alocar was older, the former not being established until the migration of the Ghreyssons. However, the cobblestone roads looked to be polished, while the shops were adorned with luxuries like gold-leaf molding.

Instead of the pavilions that dotted the streets of her home, Madden only allowed for permanent, physical establishments. And the people who walked through the streets seemed to reflect the ostentatious facades that they passed daily. The women were gorgeous, their waists cinched tight and their skirts flowing behind them. Paint decorated their faces and their hair was intricately coiffed. Even the men were stunning in their tunics and socks, immaculately clear of any dirt or debris.

I never realized that Oldar came from such a place, Cienna admired. *Pharn must be so plain compared to everything he's used to. And yet, he was willing to disregard all that he's known in an attempt to win my hand. Too bad he's not as polished as his lovely home.*

After what felt like hours, the group entered the castle proper and continued down the halls.

"King Storm will be meeting you in the Great Hall," the soldier explained. "He's prepared a light meal for you all to enjoy after your long trip."

Queen Hera let out sounds of excitement and thanked their guide for the generosity of his people. Cienna tried not to scoff at the blatant display of wealth and continued to take in their surroundings.

Look at such waste, she mused. *Marble statues don't need to be covered in gold leaf like that. Nor do the tapestries need to be woven with golden thread. This is all just a show of power.*

Despite her grumblings, Cienna found herself begrudgingly enjoying the marble statues that lay dotted along the hallway. Apart from the usual statues of great family members, clothed in barely anything, there were several animal pieces. Cienna found herself drawn to a graceful stag standing on a piece of petrified wood. His antlers were plated in gold, contrasting beautifully against his white marble skin.

Cienna found herself stopping in the passage to admire the magnificent beast. Whoever carved the creature did so with a meticulous hand. She reached out to touch the smooth stone.

"Is the art to your liking?" a male's voice called out.

Cienna started and looked to her left. She saw Oldar standing in the hallway, her mother leaning out the doorway to look back at her with an amused grin on her face. Cienna blushed slightly before hurrying to join the group.

"It is one of my favorite pieces," Oldar explained.

"Cienna's been drawn to animals like that since she was a child," Hera said fondly. "As time went on, I assumed that it was because she was a Stream and could understand their gentle nature."

"It is quite lovely," the princess agreed. "I've never seen anything like it."

Oldar smiled. "I'm glad that something in my realm pleases you." His tone, though light, carried a bitter undertone.

Cienna walked into the Great Hall and took a seat at the maple table. On top, there was a wide array of food to snack on. In the center of the table sat a pheasant, its skin golden and smoking. A variety of berries rested in wooden bowls, a side of fresh cream next to them. There were also plaited breads, a regular loaf of bread, and sweet pastries.

"What a delectable feast you've provided us, King Storm," Hera exclaimed. "Surely you didn't need to go through this much trouble."

Oldar waved his hand and motioned for the ladies to sit. "Come now. What kind of host would I be if I did not offer my guests a fine meal? Please, eat and enjoy."

Hera smiled warmly at Oldar and smoothed her skirts before sitting down. Placing a cloth napkin lightly across her lap, she reached over towards a braid of cheese bread and ripped off a piece. She closed her eyes as she savored the flavors.

"What a delight," she said joyfully. "We don't have anything as lovely as this back at home. Cienna, you really should try this."

Hera reached out and grabbed the remaining plait of bread to munch on. Aeliana stood next to her mistress and stared longingly at the food. The queen happened to glance up at her handmaiden and saw the hunger. She motioned for the girl to grab a bite as well. Aeliana gave a grateful whisper of thanks to her mistress and picked up a pastry filled with fruit. She took a big bite and closed her eyes as she relished the treat.

Cienna glanced around the table before grabbing a bread plait with dried tomatoes and herbs baked in. She took a bite and was surprised to find how light the flavors were. "This is quite delicious," she told her host. The princess took another mouthful before addressing the king.

"So, King Storm, what brings us to your beautiful home?" Though she attempted to speak in a respectful tone, even she couldn't help but notice the hint of sarcasm that dripped from her voice. "The last I remembered, you were accusing me and my mother of purposefully breaking our alliance and threatening our relationship with Alocar."

"I asked you to come to see if we could possibly mend any misunderstandings that may have occurred since last we spoke."

Hera looked up from her meal, watching the two interact. She noted that Cienna sat stiff, her guard up, while Oldar had a more open posture.

"I think that clearing the air would be a wonderful idea. Our nations have been close for ages, and I would hate to see our bond severed over a simple misunderstanding," Hera said.

Oldar bowed his head to the queen. "Thank you, Queen Grey. I appreciate your kind words." Breaking off a leg from the bird and taking a nibble, the king continued.

"When we finally defeated that demon, I must admit that I thought you had authorized an alliance with my parents' murderer. To say that I was distraught, especially after losing so much in such a short period of time, would be a bit of an understatement. I do apologize for any harsh words that I may have said. I was emotional at the time."

Cienna nodded her head, acknowledging his words. "We all lost a lot, you especially. I understand that you may have been speaking more from the heart than your mind."

"Nonetheless," Oldar continued, "I believe that the best way for our people to remain unified is to strengthen the union between our lands."

Cienna blanched at the words.

"I don't think that forming a union with those bloodthirsty clansmen is the answer," he said. "I have a few ideas that will bring our two nations into the modern day, things that will make the two of us unstoppable together."

"Wait," Cienna interjected. "Why would we not want an alliance with Xan? They are not only strong, but they have valuable resources that our nations can benefit from."

"Such as?"

"Spices that we don't have access to. Salt. Gods know that they also have one of the biggest mineral mines in Corinth. Imagine what would happen if we anger them and they no longer wish to trade ore with us. The results would be devastating."

"There is ore elsewhere," Oldar said flatly. "Not to mention, I believe your people discovered a spice mine not too long ago on your northern border. The clans aren't as important as you are led to believe."

Cienna roughly put her food down, her lips pressed tightly together in anger. *How can he say these things? Is he trying to provoke me?*

"Is this really about the truce with Xan? I get the feeling, based on the way that you speak of our union, that you're actually talking about something else."

Oldar placed the pheasant leg on a plate and narrowed his eyes. "Are you trying to imply something, Princess Cienna?"

"I don't think we need to be so subtle and imply anything," Cienna said coldly. "You've managed to twist what happened at the gorge in such a way that long-standing alliances are now being broken. You are no better than those warlords in how you try and manipulate those around you. My father would not have stood for such treatment, and neither would yours, if the stories I've heard were true."

At her side, Cienna heard her mother curse under her breath.

Well, we seem to be making progress. Let's see how far this goes.

"If you're accusing me of having ulterior motives and acting in an improper manner, Princess, perhaps we are not as close to resolving our differences as I hoped. I thought that with a little time to reflect, you would see that your guard acted impulsively, but that doesn't seem to be the case. You seem to be content with defending him no matter what information is brought before you."

Cienna folded her arms across her chest and leaned back into the chair. She didn't say anything. Instead, she waited for Oldar to continue. The king leaned back in his chair as well, studying Cienna. He placed the tips of his fingers together and drummed them together.

"I see that we're not going to reach an agreement," he finally said. "Perhaps you all should leave."

Cienna pushed her chair back, causing it to scratch on the stone floor, and stormed out of the room. Queen Hera and Aeliana were much more graceful in their departure. Before the princess exited the room, she heard her mother thank the king for his hospitality.

⋘⋙

"I can't believe he called us out here just to waste our time," Cienna fumed. The princess marched towards the stables to retrieve her horse.

"I really wish you would've held your tongue a little better," Hera said exasperated. Cienna opened her mouth to retort, but her mother held up her hand to silence her. "I understand why you're upset, but we're treading a delicate line. We can't afford to lose any more allies right now. I only hope that those who have pledged neutrality will not be swayed to join his side."

Cienna glanced over at her mother. "Do you really think that they would do that?"

"Tenzen is not a man who is known for conflict," Hera replied. "We've been good to them, so I don't think that they will abandon us completely, but there's always a chance."

"Czand's damnation!" Cienna swore under her breath. "This is getting messy."

"There's no point in dwelling on the matter longer," Hera said. "What's done is done. Let's go home and come up with a plan in the event we need to fight for our allies."

As the women reached the stables, they picked up their horses and clambered on top. Keeping their composure, they rode towards the city gates. Cienna took in the beauty of the city once more. The elegant buildings mixed with the brightly colored populace created a combination that she found most intriguing.

Too bad I couldn't spend more time here under different circumstances.

As they neared the gates, the princess gave one last look at the retreating city before crossing through the entrance and heading towards Zanir.

XLIII

DEZ WANDERED AIMLESSLY through the burned rubble on the outskirts of Thyllasis. The voices in the wind pulled her closer and closer to the coast line. It had been years since she felt the urge so strongly. As she walked, she pulled out an apple from her hip pouch and took a bite, enjoying the crisp crunch and sweet juices. The wind blew through her wavy hair, causing a few loose strands to tickle her nose. She absentmindedly brushed them away before returning to her snack.

Are you sure that we're going in the right direction?

"It's coming from this direction," Dez replied in between bites. "They seem to get louder, at least, the closer we get. That has to be a good sign."

That is promising, the voice conceded. **I just worry that this long journey will have been for naught if you misheard.**

"You know, you would think that since you seem to be in my head, you could also hear what I do," Dez said with a chuckle. "Instead, it's like the blind leading the blind between the two of us."

I'm offended that you could consider what I do as leading you blindly, the voice said sullenly. **I would've thought that after all we've been through, you would consider me trustworthy.**

"Oh, you know what I mean," Dez replied. "You know that I value your company and input."

The voice in her head did not respond. Dez found herself feeling heavy and forlorn.

"Please, I'm truly sorry."

As she walked, Dez felt a lightness within. She found herself smiling as she went to take another bite.

I forgive you, little one.

The feeling of lightness got stronger. Dez almost felt as though she received a fond pat on the head. As the sensation grew, Dez found herself reciprocating the emotion.

The two strolled through the street. As she neared the shore, a sensation of unease. It felt as though there was someone, or something, watching her as she moved through the town. Dez stopped in the middle of the street and slunk behind a piece of burnt wood that used to be a doorframe. Putting her back to the structure, she took a final bite of the apple and gently placed it down on the ground.

What is it?

"Something in the air doesn't feel right," Dez muttered. "There's a feeling of foreboding, as though some fell creature is nearby."

The voice paused, reaching out to the world around them.

I feel it too. There's a presence not too far off. Let's be careful. It seems more powerful than I.

"Well, I feel relieved," Dez joked. "As long as you are feeling the same discomfort as me, we should be just fine."

The sound of crunching gravel caught Dez's attention. She spun her head towards the source of the noise. Looking around, she couldn't see anyone moving through the deserted city streets. The sound of displaced gravel told her otherwise. Dez's head moved side to side, trying to locate the disturbance.

Finally, she heard a crunch near her feet and looked down. A scruffy dog was leaning tentatively over by her, munching on the apple core she had discarded. Relief washed over Dez, but it was brief.

Kneeling down, Dez blew gently in the dog's direction, letting him get a sniff of her scent. Immediately, his nose began twitching as he processed the new smell. The stray looked up, his body still stiff, and made eye contact with Dez. She proffered her hand a short distance away. Her hand was far enough that he would need to get closer to her if he wanted to bite her, but not so far that she couldn't lean over and scratch him.

Once he relaxed just a bit, Dez did just that. Leaning over, she placed her hand on the dog's head and lightly rubbed his ear with her thumb. As he relaxed more, she incorporated more of her fingers until her whole hand was scratching the top of his head. The dog's tail wagged low between his legs.

"It's okay," Dez whispered. "I won't hurt you."

Reaching into her travel pouch, Dez pulled out a small strip of smoked fish and held it out for the dog. He sniffed eagerly at the morsel, his body tensing up as he stretched towards her. Dez made soft soothing noises as she held out the treat. After a bit of hesitation, the dog snatched the meat from her hand and disappeared into the ruins.

Dez chuckled as she straightened up. She dusted her hands on her pants, trying to get some of the dirt from the dog's fur off. Before she could turn around, she felt another presence nearby. It was behind her.

So, there are people here.

Turning slowly, Dez found herself facing a small group of rugged looking men. They sneered at her as she made eye contact with each one individually. Dez noted that each one carried a sword or long dagger, several of which were already drawn and pointing in her direction.

"Yes," Dez said slowly. "But this isn't who I was expecting."

"Why, hello there lovely," one of the men called out. "I wasn't thinking we'd find anyone like you traveling through our lands. Who were you speaking to just now?"

Assuming her usual air, Dez smiled coyly and replied, "Myself. I tend to do that when I have no one else around."

The man who first addressed her glanced at the man to his right. He was a large man, both tall and broad, and seemed to be the first man's muscle. The burly man smiled, revealing several missing teeth.

"She's a cutie," the second one remarked. "Can we keep her?"

Several of the men nodded in agreement, excited at the prospect of enjoying the pleasure of a woman.

The first man shook his head. He looked disappointed as he did so. "Nah, don't suppose we can. She looks like she should be brought to the boss."

"Oh, come on," a gangly man chimed in. "Just give us a little time with her."

Several of the men closed in on Dez. She maintained her composure, but tensed slightly. Glancing at the men, she picked out two people to include with the husky man that she may have to use her magic on.

I think we should go see their boss, her voice said.

Dez nodded imperceptibly as the men argued amongst themselves. Waiting for a break in their conversation, before cutting in. "Why don't we go and visit your leader? The sooner we visit him, the sooner I can continue on my travels."

More than one of the men gawked at her, surprised that she would ask to be taken to their superior. Low chatter broke out as they discussed how best to handle the situation. The muscular man and his gangly companion argued with their comrades about whether or not they should leave immediately or take their time.

Dez caught snippets of conversation, including words like "no time," "Jylla," and "distraction." Finally, the first man snapped at the group, bringing them back into focus.

"Sly, Tarv, we need to move quickly. The sooner we get her to the boss, the sooner you can become acquainted with her," the first man said.

The burly man and his gangly partner stopped arguing and grudgingly agreed. The larger man moved to grab Dez by the arms.

"Careful, Sly," the gangly man, Tarv, warned. "She looks to be a tricky one."

Sly roughly seized her and held on tightly, expecting a struggle. Dez stood loosely, allowing for her limbs to hang limply in his grasp. Confused, the husky man squeezed harder and gave her a small shake. Dez turned to look at him curiously.

"Is that really necessary?" she asked.

"I – uh – shut yer yap!" Sly commanded.

"As you wish," she replied serenely.

The group looked at each other in confusion. Sly shook her roughly once more and the started marching her towards the coast.

⤳⤳⤳

Dez was led into a dark cave that opened out into the ocean. The smell of the sea air felt refreshing on her skin. The breeze was stronger in the cave that it had been out in the charred streets. Dez relished the gentle rustling of her hair on her face and back. Sly still held her roughly, but Dez didn't mind.

Waves lapped up against her boots, splashing her with white foam. She looked out to the mouth of the cave and watched as a large boat bobbed in the surf. A number of people bustled about in the grotto, grabbing weapons and speaking hurriedly to a red-headed woman. The woman pointed to the different things that needed to be done, instructing the others to do it.

She must be the boss, Dez considered. *I wasn't expecting their leader to be a woman. This will be easier to handle than I thought.*

Dez was surprised to see the young Qu-ari general from the battle in the gorge sitting on a large rock. He stared at his blade as he turned the weapon around in his hand. As she passed, he looked up. Dez smiled as she saw the shock in his eyes.

I guess he remembers me. She chuckled softly as she moved forward.

Sly led Dez towards the red-headed woman. The woman was giving instructions to another man. Sly, Dez, and the first man waited patiently for her to finish while the other members of their party went off to prepare for whatever was happening.

"Well, well, well," the woman finally said, addressing the trio. "What did you bring me, Darron?"

"We found her skulking around in the main part of the town. We weren't sure if she's one of Jylla's spies or not. It seemed strange that a lone woman would be wandering through the Bone Coast like that."

The red-headed woman walked up to Dez and lifted her chin. She studied Dez's face closely. Finally, she removed her fingers from Dez's face. "Why don't we see what the Lord of the Western Isles has to say."

Dez raised her eyebrows in surprise.

It looks as though we may have underestimated the situation.

"So it seems," Dez muttered.

The other woman glanced over at Dez, nonplussed. However, she did not say anything to her. "I'll take it from here, boys," she said.

Sly released Dez and the two retreated back to their original group. Dez watched them stroll over towards the rest of their original group. They began talking animatedly with them, shooting glances at the two women on occasion.

"Now," the redhead said, "what are we to do with you?"

"Why don't we go meet this Lord of the Isles?" Dez replied. "He sounds fascinating."

"Aren't you a chipper one?" the other said. "I'm glad they brought you to me instead of taking you out to some dilapidated barn for an hour or so. I may not have been able to meet you otherwise."

"Is that really their usual routine?" Dez asked.

"Oh yes. Unless they think to bring someone to me or the boss, it usually never ends well."

"Well, I suppose that I owe you a debt of gratitude," Dez paused, waiting for the woman to introduce herself.

"Kayna."

"Kayna," Dez repeated. "If it weren't for your reputation, I would surely have been put in an awkward situation."

"You could say that," Kayna said.

The two walked over towards a large, polished stone. Whether it was polished by the waves over time, or man-made, the stone shone beautifully in the waning cavern light. A large man leaned against the stone, rubbing a whetstone against a blade.

"Papa," Kayna called out, "I have somebody I'd like you to meet."

The imposing man looked up. "Another one?"

"I think you'll like her too. Today seems to be a good day to meet interesting people."

Kayna sauntered off to oversee her crew. Dez faced the Lord of the Western Isles, waiting for him to speak. However, he remained silent, staring intently at her.

There's something about him, the voice warned. **I can't quite place it, but he's dangerous.**

"Who are you?" he asked. He ran his hands through his dark hair, weaving his fingers through the silver streaks. His chestnut eyes narrowed as he looked at her.

"Dez."

"No. There's more to you than you let on."

"I'm not sure about that," Dez replied. "I am what you see." Tilting her head, she asked, "And you are?"

Shaking his head, the man reached over and grabbed her face with both hands. "Like you, I, Angh, am not what I appear."

Dez gasped in surprise as she felt a strong, prying sensation digging around in her head. "Let go of me!" she yelped. Panic filled her chest as she struggled to pull away. She felt a powerful force seeping from his hands into her mind, probing her memory, reaching for her very essence.

Fight back! the voice commanded. **I... I don't think I can keep him out. He's too strong.**

XLIV

DEZ LURCHED BACKWARDS as she struggled to get Angh's hands off of her face. The silver-haired man held on tightly, his chestnut eyes staring into hers. She struggled to close them and finally managed to get them shut. The voice in Dez's head gasped as Angh separated the two. Grabbing on to the voice in her head, he dug deeper, looking within for whatever he was seeking.

Dez squeezed her eyes tight, but that didn't stop him from pulling out a vision. She felt a twinge of shock as the voice in her head fought to keep the man from probing further. Dez watched helplessly as Angh extracted the memory.

❧

Dzvre Ari-makh stood as the lone guard to the borders of Scrymme. His long hair was tied back in a low-hanging tail. At his hip, a thin blade lay sheathed. It had been a quiet day, as it usually was. No one strayed near the border, not even one of his own countrymen.

"How did I get stuck with security patrol?" he grumbled.

Reaching into the pouch on his back, Dzvre pulled out a piece of sweet biscuit and nibbled on it. He brought the snack up to his mouth for a second bite when he was surprised by the form of an approaching figure near their border. Slinking into the shadows of the trees, Dzvre carefully made his way down the hill and watched the arriving of the foreigner with interest. Most never found the Scrymmen periphery. They just wandered by. This person, however, was going to cross her borders if they continued their current trajectory.

Pulling his sword from its sheath, Dzvre prepared to intercept the stranger. As Dzvre crouched down, he noticed something that caused him to pause. The person advancing towards Scrymme was a young woman. Her dark brown hair trailed behind her as she sped towards the line of trees. He saw that she ran, eyes wide in panic. Occasionally, she would turn her head to see if she was still being pursued, never slowing down. As she neared, Dzvre noticed that sweat beaded on her umber skin.

Dzvre took his eyes off of her and looked behind her. A pair of men chased after her shouting lewd comments. Returning his silver eyes back to the woman, he saw that her blouse was torn around the collar. Taking a deep breath, Dzvre steeled himself. Jumping out from behind the tree line, the woman stutter-stepped in surprise. Her eyes were frightened as she tried to determine where to go now that another man popped out in front of her. The men behind her didn't register that a new party entered the scene.

Looking around for something to use, Dzvre reached out to the woman's shadow and pulled her off to the side, causing her to stumble. She cried out in shock as she labored to right herself. The men behind her shouted out as they finally noticed the dark-haired man standing before them. Flipping his blade in his hand, Dzvre stared the duo down, a smile tugging at the corners of his lips.

"Greetings, gentlemen," Dzvre called out. "You're approaching restricted territory. I'd turn around and head back to where you came from if I were you."

The two men stopped a way in front of the Scrymmen man. The larger of the pair stepped closer to Dzvre. He was a hulking man in a sleeveless shirt, his muscles bulging as he brought his arms up and crossed them in front of his chest.

"Outta the way, little man," the larger man sneered. "We gots business with the lady."

His friend snickered, leering at the panting woman. He licked his lips as his eyes traced the curves of her body.

"Little man?" Dzvre asked. The Scrymmen man looked down at himself. His slender frame didn't boast the large muscles like the two in front of him, but his body was toned after years of training. "I don't think I'm *that* little."

The larger man walked towards Dzvre and raised his arms in an attempt to shove him out of the way. The woman whimpered, but did not run away. As the man's hand lightly touched Dzvre's chest, he found that he could no longer move. Dzvre looked down at the man's hands before looking up at the figure who loomed over him. A smirk played on Dzvre's lips, his silver eyes narrowing.

"Whaddaya waitin' for?" the shorter thug asked his friend. "Push 'em outta the way. I can't wait much longer." His eyes rested on the petrified woman, fixating on her chest.

"I can't!" his companion cried. "I can't move."

"Oh, come now," Dzvre said. "Surely a 'little man' like me is no match for a beast like you."

Sweat started to form on the bigger man's brow as he struggled to move. He grunted as he strained himself. Veins in his arm began to bulge as his face contorted in a grimace. "What the hell is this? What did you do to me?"

"Gods' mercy! I'll do it myself," the second man roared as he charged at Dzvre.

The girl cried out as the shorter man shot out from behind his friend, arm raised and fist clenched. In a matter of steps, the gap between the shorter man and Dzvre disappeared. As quick as a snake, the Scrymmen man brought up his dagger and rammed in through the attacker's eye. Screams rang out as the rushing brute staggered over, his hands covering his wounded eye. The larger, frozen man watched helplessly as blood ran down his friend's face.

Dzvre reached down and pulled the weapon out of his opponent's eye, eliciting a scream of pain from the wounded. Shaking off the blood from the thin blade, Dzvre brought it up to the larger man's neck and pressed the blade up against it. The man's eyes followed the dagger's every movement. Sweat now ran down his face as he felt the cool steel on his skin.

"Let's try this again," Dzvre said. "Why don't you take your friend over here and go back to where you came from? We can just pretend that this never happened. How does that sound?"

"Y-yes," the hulking man stammered.

Behind him, his friend groaned in pain, still hunched over. One hand covered his bloody face while the other leaned heavily on his wounded knee. Dzvre looked over the giant's shoulder and smiled. The large man managed to turn his head just slightly, eyes wide and sweat dripping down his face.

"Smart choice," Dzvre replied.

Turning around, Dzvre walked over to the shaking woman and extended his hand. Tentatively, she reached out and gingerly grabbed his. Dzvre led hear back up the sloping hill into Scrymme. As they neared the crest of the knoll, the larger man suddenly staggered forward, no longer frozen. Glancing up at the Scrymmen man in fear, he grabbed his friend's arm and pulled the injured man away from the border. Dzvre steered the woman towards a tree and let her crouch down to rest as he watched the two figures retreat in the distance.

He stood silently, surveying the land in front of him, his silver eyes squinting in the bright sunlight. Dzvre tucked a strand of onyx hair behind his ear. Once satisfied that the threat was gone, he walked over to the tree and pulled a leaf off. Wiping the bloody dagger on the vegetation, Dzvre inspected the weapon, checking to make sure that it was clean once more, before putting it back in its sheath.

"Thank you," a breathless voice said feebly.

Dzvre turn to face the woman. Up close, he saw that she was barely a woman, no more than seventeen or eighteen. Her eyes were a deep chocolate, so dark the sclera was a pale sky blue. Her lips were full and parted slightly as she stared at him.

"Don't mention it," he muttered. "I honestly shouldn't have done that. You shouldn't be here."

"Please, I can't go back. Where am I to go?" her eyes were wide as she spoke to him.

"I don't know. My people are not kind to strangers."

"Chelia," she said.

"What?" he asked.

"My name is Chelia. Now we are no longer strangers."

"Why are you doing this?"

"If you turn me away, you sentence me to worse than what you saved me from. You may as well have let them capture me and have their way with me like they wanted. To send me back is almost a guaranteed death sentence."

"That is none of my concern," he replied.

"Then why did you get involved?" she asked.

Dzvre stood silently, trying to figure out how to answer her question. After a lengthy pause, he slowly replied, "I don't know."

"Please," Chelia begged. "Please don't send me to die. I can help you with house work." When Dzvre didn't respond, she added, "I can also be very quiet. Please." Chelia's voice trailed off as Dzvre didn't respond.

With her lips quivering, Chelia turned and began making her way down the slope. Dzvre watched her retreat, back straight and head held high, despite her obvious terror not even a moment before. Before she got halfway down the knoll, Dzvre cursed quietly and jogged down towards her. He grabbed her shoulder, startling her and causing her head to whip around to face him.

"Dzvre," he said as he touched his chest. "If you stay with me, your life is no safer than if you went home. Are you sure that you want this?"

"It can't be worse than what's waiting for me out there," she replied.

"Very well."

⤙⤚

Dez tried to pull free once more of Angh's grasp, but the man held on tightly. The tattoos on her arms glowed silver as she attempted to shake the pirate off of her. A maelstrom thrashed around her, causing those around them to cry out in fear. Angh stood firm, unmoved by the onslaught. Time seemed to drag on as Dez struggled.

She felt the essence of the voice in her head pushing back against the man, trying to keep him from whatever memories lay below her surface. After several long moments, despite their best efforts, she was unable to break his grip, even with magic. Angh's eyes were squeezed shut as he focused on viewing the visions. With a groan, another scene flashed in Dez's mind.

⤙⤚

Dzvre and Chelia sat in the shade of a tree. The leaves were a riot of color. The crisp air gently rustled their hair as they lounged about during the harvest season. Chelia leaned her head against Dzvre's chest, her hand resting gently on her stomach. A slight bump protruded from under her blouse. She let out a contented sigh and closed her eyes.

"Dzvre," Chelia said softly. "Do you think that Her Holiness will bless our little one?"

"Her Holiness blesses all of her children. It's the king and elders that I'm more concerned with. We can't keep hiding forever."

"We've managed to so far. I'm sure we can continue to do so. If not, we can always leave Scrymme."

"My people do not leave our home. To do so is instant death. If we were to leave, the king would send his best after us."

Chelia sat quietly for a while. After a pregnant pause, she replied, "Then we will stay here."

⤜⤛⤛⤚

The scene faded away quickly and a new one replaced it. Dez felt a burning sensation in her stomach and closed her eyes against the pain. Her tattoos were blinding as they glowed against her skin. Light emanated from her body, something that had never happened before. Dez whimpered as she finally stopped fighting against Angh's grip. The spirit of the voice in her head fought to keep the man out, but she was too tired, and let him in further.

As the gale around her died down, Dez's knees buckled. Her body sank down to the earth, but Angh delicately held her up, his gaze unwavering as he searched for what he wanted within her.

⤜⤛⤛⤚

Dzvre walked through the door. Chelia sat in a wooden chair, a small bundle wrapped in her arms. He approached her and kissed her on the top of her head. His hand cradled hers, lightly touching the cloth that their daughter lay bundled in.

"How was your day?" Chelia asked softly.

"We need to leave. Now."

Chelia turned to look at Dzvre questioningly.

"What's going on?"

Dzvre walked over to the wall and picked up his short sword and a few throwing knives. After strapping the knives to his thigh and his sword to his hip, he pulled off one last weapon, his dagger. Covering up his weapons with his cloak, he also pulled one off the hook for Chelia. He strode to his wife and carefully lifted the sleeping infant out of her hands. Once the baby was secure in his arms, he handed the dagger and cloak to Chelia.

"Strap it to your thigh," he told her. "You may need it."

"Dzvre?"

Shaking his head, Dzvre brought his finger to his lips to silence her. Chelia stared at the man, confusion etched on her face and fear creeping into her eyes, but remained quiet. The pair walked out the door and slipped into the night.

The air was chilly and the wind howled occasionally. Dzvre pulled his cloak tighter around himself as the edges flapped about. Keeping his child hidden within the folds of the cape, he led his wife through the wilderness of Scrymme. Stars shone brightly in the sky, providing them with a measure of light to see by. Cursing to himself, Dzvre lamented the brightness. The light only helped to make him and his fleeing wife visible to their pursuers.

In his arms, the child began to fuss. Dzvre looked around him, turning his head to see if anyone followed as he tried to soothe his daughter.

"Hush now, Dzeara," he whispered. "Her Holiness is here to protect you. The wind is her arms, embracing you, pulling you closer to her. Do not be afraid."

Dzeara settled down, staring at her father with wide eyes. Curls of chocolate hair framed her dark face, barely peeking out from the cloth. Her silver eyes stared up at him, wide and curious. She brought her chubby fist to her mouth and began sucking on it.

A muffled scream caught his attention. Whipping around, Dzvre came face-to-face with seven warriors pointing swords and a bow in his direction. Another held Chelia, his arm around her neck and twisting her arm behind her back. She whimpered in pain as he pulled her arm a little higher, putting her off-balance.

"Dzvre!" she called out.

"Don't move!" one of the men called out, raising his sword higher. The archer next to him nocked his bow and drew aim right at Dzvre's heart.

Raising one arm in the air, Dzvre tried to show that he was unarmed. His other arm pulled Dzeara closer to his breast.

"We should kill them," one of the guards said in Scrymmen. "He knows that to bring an outsider into our home is forbidden."

"Hold," the first man replied. He appeared to be the leader.

"Please," Dzvre pleaded, "let them go. You can take me, but don't hurt the woman and her child."

With a wave of his hand, the head of the group motioned for one of the men to grab the baby from Dzvre. The man who went, the one who suggested killing the three of them, walked over eagerly and ripped the babe from Dzvre's arms. As he walked back to his commander, the man looked down at the child.

"Dzvryth!" he exclaimed. "The child has silver eyes. She is an abomination to Her Holiness."

Chatter broke out amongst the group. Chelia watched on helplessly, unable to understand anything that was being said, her arm being yanked higher at the news. The captain of the group, Dzvryth, walked over to the other man and pulled back the cloth to expose the child's face.

His eyes widened as he stared at the half-Scrymmen infant. "Blessed Aria, forgive us," he muttered.

Dzvre felt his stomach drop as he watched the others inch closer to him, weapons poised to strike at any moment. Forced with no other option, he raised his other hand into the air and lowered his head. Keeping his eyes down, he sank to his knees in the long grass. The wind whipped around him, but he spoke with a clear, steady voice.

"*Nannohav,*" he said solemnly. "I request *nannohav.*"

"Judgement?" Dzvryth asked, incredulous. "What makes you think that Her Holiness will be on your side? King Dzveren speaks on her behalf, and his word is law. No person from Scrymme shall bring a foreigner across her borders. You've not only threatened Scrymme's safety, but you defiled the purity of her people by laying with this woman and producing a child. Do you not see the damage that you've done? Our killing you now will be more than you deserve."

"No man shall be denied *nannohav* once they've requested it," Dzvre replied. "If you don't believe me, why don't you consult with my father, Dzvrean?"

More than one gasp could be heard over the howling of the wind at the mention of the king's brother, the Host of Scrymme. The high priest was the mouthpiece of the gods and served as the gatekeepers of Scrymme's history. As the king's younger brother, he carried even greater influence over Scrymme's people.

"Prove that you are High Host Dzvrean's blood," Dzvryth challenged.

Pulling on a chain around his neck, Dzvre presented the seal of House Ari-makh. Engraved in silver, the sigil was of a solitary eye above two olive branches. The necklaces were passed on from generation to generation. If Dzvre wasn't family, the only way he could get one was by killing the necklace's owner and stealing it. The odds of that happening were almost non-existent.

Scanning the faces of his men, Dzvryth motioned for them to put down their weapons. Pointing to two of his soldiers, Dzvryth directed them to grab Dzvre and pin his arms behind his back. The men shared a hesitant glance, but moved quickly as they obeyed their commander's orders. One stood on each side of Dzvre and pulled his arms up behind his back, twisting his elbows in an uncomfortable manner. They lifted him slowly to his feet, not wanting to hurt him and face the wrath of the king. Once on Dzvre was on his feet, Dzvryth walked up to him and roughly grabbed his face.

"You'll get your judgement," he hissed. "I can't say that'll do you any good, however." Turning to his men, Dzvryth barked out, "Let's head back. Dzvrall, Dzvron, you two go first with the king's nephew. The woman and child will follow behind." As Dzvrall and Dzvron led Dzvre past Dzvryth and towards Caicyne Ari, Dzvryth said to Dzvre, "Don't try any tricks now. I've still got my bow trained on you. Not to mention, you wouldn't want anything to happen to your precious half-breed before she's been given a proper judgement, now would you?"

"You'll hurt neither of them," Dzvre said with an edge of defiance in his voice. "You know the law as well as I do. Those who interfere with *nannohav* are put to death instantly."

"Ah, yes. But you see, accidents do happen," Dzvryth replied with a sneer. "So many things can happen in the dark. It's always best to err on the side of caution."

Darkness engulfed the group as Dez slumped to her knees. Angh went down with her, crouching down to maintain eye contact with her. The silver glow that surrounded Dez traveled up Angh's arms and consumed him as well. His eyes went from a steely blue to a vibrant silver. Moisture glistened on his forehead as he focused on going deeper.

Dzvre stood in the holy temple of Aria, a pair of the king's elite soldiers standing on either side of him. Only the faint red glow of lamps lit the room. All the other windows were blocked to prevent any light from entering. Dzvre stood with his head staring straight ahead, his eyes moving from his father to Chelia to his daughter.

Dzvrean faced away from his son, his body stiff. Long black hair fell down to the middle of his back, and a pair of small braids ran down each side. The braids were loosely tied behind his head along with the rest of his hair. He wore silver silks with threads of gold embroidery snaking around his sleeves like his tattoos. A crimson cord wrapped around his neck and hung down the front of his robes. The cord's tassels covered a golden signet of the House of Ari-makh, dripping down from the eye like rivulets of blood.

On a stone dais in the center of the room, Dzeara lay bundled on top. Her cries echoed in the stone room, eliciting sobs of distress for Chelia. Chelia struggled against her captor, her face in a grimace as he tugged slightly on her arm to keep her from wiggling too much. The room was silent, waiting for Dzveren to arrive. Faint chatter from the guards ceased immediately as soon as the door opened and King Dzveren walked in.

Dressed in a pearl-colored robe, the king's sharp cheek bones were hidden behind a sheet of ebony hair. A white gold circlet sat atop his brow. At his hip, a thin sword rested lightly, enclosed in an elaborately decorated sheath. All in the room dropped to their knees, except for Dzvrean, who dipped into a bow.

"Tell me, Dzvrean," Dzveren drawled, "what have I done to you to warrant such a disgrace of a nephew?"

Everyone returned to their normal position as the king strode past, stopping at the dais. He pulled back the cloth and gave a revolted glance at the babe within.

"I am as disappointed as you are, brother," Dzvrean replied solemnly. "Never in my life would I image such shame would be brought to my family."

Turning his nose up at the child, Dzveren walked over to stand in the corner under a lantern. The faint light it provided gave him a gaunt appearance, accentuating his harsh cheeks even more. "Let's get on with everything," Dzveren said in a bored tone.

Dzvryth stepped forward and cleared his throat. "The accused stands charged with exposing a foreigner to the ways of Scrymme. He also has shared the sacred blood of Scrymme with the impure as well, threatening the future of our people by muddying our bloodlines."

Dzveren's eyes narrowed, the silver glinting in the faint light.

"He has requested *nannohav*, and by the laws of Scrymme under Her Holiness, Blessed Aria, he is entitled to be heard." Dzvryth turned to Dzvre and smirked before facing the king once more.

"What do you have to say for yourself?" Dzveren asked Dzvre.

"I ask that you spare Chelia and Dzeara," he replied flatly. "I am the one who broke the law. I brought her into Scrymme and filled her with child."

Dzveren stared through Dzvre, his gaze cold. "You're right. You broke the laws. As such, you must be punished."

Dzvryth turned to Dzvre and smirked. Dzvre tensed and looked for a way to escape. Searching for something to use, Dzvre cursed his luck that there was not enough light to draw on his Ghost skills. The men at his sides grabbed him roughly by the arm and held him in place. Dzvre yanked both of his arms into his body, knocking the pair off balance. Freeing himself from the grip of one man, Dzvre aimed a side kick at the second. His foot connected and Dzvre's other arm was freed.

Dzvre's eyes fell on his father momentarily. A sharp pain in his stomach brought his attention back to Dzvryth. The guard stood in front of him, a sword buried deeply in Dzvre's abdomen. Chelia screamed as Dzvre's shirt started to turn red around the blade. Dzvre's eyes were wide in shock, his breath caught in his throat. Struggling to breathe, Dzvre doubled over. Dzvryth pushed the sword deeper into Dzvre's body, shaking the man with the force of his push.

His vision began to swim as he struggled to hold his head up. Behind Dzvryth, he saw his father looking at him with pain in his eyes. The Host avoided making eye contact with his son; rather, he looked at Dzvre's face. Dzvre's gaze drifted to Chelia. Tears ran down her face as she hung limply in her captor's arms. She gasped for breath as she watched him die.

Dzvre felt his body go weak and dropped to his knees. The two men who previously held him stood just out of arms' reach, waiting to make sure that he died. With blurry vision, Dzvre's eyes finally landed on the bundled form of his daughter. Dzeara lay on the dais, her cries muted. Or was it all noise that sounded muffled and far away?

Dzvryth pulled the sword out of Dzvre and handed it to one of the soldiers who stood on the outskirts of the room. Dzvre watched as Dzveren gave some instructions, unable to hear anything that was being said. Dzvryth pulled out a dagger and approached the dais. Dzvre tried to call out and beg for mercy, but his voice would not come out. Chelia opened her mouth and let out a dull scream.

Raising the dagger above the baby, Dzvryth swiftly brought it down. A blinding silver light engulfed the child, protecting her from the blade. The dagger bounced off of the light and threw Dzvryth to the ground. The light's brightness continued to grow in intensity. Cries rang out in the room as people began shielding their eyes. The man holding Chelia released his hold on her, and she darted towards her child.

Scooping the baby up in her arms, she turned to look at Dzvre. Standing behind Chelia, Dzvre saw the form of a silver-haired woman smiling down at his daughter. The woman looked up at Dzvre and locked eyes with him. His breath caught in his throat as he stared at the silver-eyed form. A sense of peace washed over him as he watched the ethereal woman step through Chelia and meld with Dzeara.

Chelia didn't notice the figure as she surrounded the now sleeping babe and entered the infant's body. Before the woman's head disappeared into his daughter, Dzvre gurgled, trying to speak.

The woman looked up at him, pain in her eyes.

Fear not, the woman's voice rang inside his head. **I shall protect little Dzeara. I promise you.**

Angh's hands flew off of Dez's cheeks as though he were burned. Tears streamed down her eyes as she became overwhelmed with emotion. The glow of her tattoos that previously surrounded the two disappeared as soon as his hands left her flesh. Blinking rapidly, Dez tried to clear her vision from the bright flash she saw from the woman. Looking at Angh, his eyes were open in surprise, his lips slightly parted.

A hollow feeling filled Dez as the voice in her head worked to regain her composure. Dez took short, shallow breaths, as though she had run a great distance, in response to the distress of the essence within her.

The pirate blinked, attempting to clear his vision. Once his eyes were able to focus once more, he caught Dez's gaze. Moisture rimmed the edges of his eyes as he focused on her. He seemed younger to her now, as though more than a decade had been stripped away.

"Praise be to Re'nukh," he whispered. Tentatively, he reached a hand out and gently stroked her cheek. "I knew there was more to her. It really is you." His voice was breathless as she spoke. "I thought I lost you all those years ago."

Dez stared at the man, disoriented after everything she saw.

"Aria, Sister..." he murmured.

The voice within Dez gasped, as though in recognition.

Ghan.

XLV

OLDAR SAT SLOUCHED over in the Great Hall. In front of him, a flagon of mead lay sideways on the table, a small puddle of amber liquid spilled from the jug. A plate of partially eaten bread and fruit sat next to the young king. Across from him, Schaed leaned back in his chair, his eyes closed. A glass of wine sat in front of the lanky man.

A groan escaped the king's lips as he forced himself to sit up. His eyes were bloodshot. He hadn't left the Great Hall since the previous afternoon. The entire time, both he and Schaed sat at the table, drinking. On several occasions, Oldar found himself sick from all of the alcohol that he'd consumed and he needed to excuse himself as he went to empty his stomach. Other than that, he sat at the table and drank, lamenting the events of the past couple weeks.

His relationship with Zanir was all but destroyed, yet he could not stop himself from antagonizing the princess further. Nothing he tried seemed to be working. His desire to rule as the Iron Fist was quickly fading away with every drink.

Brushing his hair out of his eyes, Oldar leaned back against the oaken chair. The king's head throbbed. A gentle knock on the door sounded like a cannon boom to his sensitive ears, just as the slight sliver of sunlight managed to peek into the room when Pruvencia opened the door blinded his eyes.

The matronly woman cleared her throat before speaking. "Your majesty, it has been quite a long time since you've had anything substantial to eat. If it would please you, let me bring in some beef and vegetables for you to peck at while you prepare for the day's activities."

"Bring whatever you wish, Pru," Oldar said, waving his hand in dismissal. "I will be having a late start today. I... I wasn't able to sleep well last night."

"Of course, your majesty," Pruvencia said with a curtsy. "I shall have the serving maid leave it outside your door when it's ready, so as not to disturb you."

Oldar grunted in response.

Pruvencia delicately shut the door behind her as she made her exit.

Oldar groaned again. "By the gods, I have not had a night like that since I was in school."

Schaed shifted slightly in his seat, his eyes still closed. "Perhaps we overindulged a bit, my king," he mumbled.

"I... uh, I don't remember much of last night, Schaed. Tell me, did I do anything... uh, like I would've done back in the old days?"

Schaed cracked his eyes open a little. He sat quietly for some time before slowly responding. "I do not believe that you acted outside of your position. If I recall correctly, you did spend a lot of time talking about that Zanirian princess though."

Oldar buried his face in his hands and moaned. "I don't understand, Schaed. I barely know the girl, and yet, she truly has enchanted me. All those years of Father talking about how we'd be such a wonderful couple, how our union would create the strongest alliance in all of Corinth. While I was finishing school, I started dreaming about what kind of woman she would be. She was kind, intelligent, someone who cared for her people, and wanted to join me and enact change for all of Corinth. Think of the trade agreements we could make to keep any one nation from having an economic control over some item."

Schaed's eyes narrowed as Oldar spoke.

"I thought, when I first arrived at Pharn, that Cienna would be a woman who was nothing like what I imagined. And I was right. She was so much more than I could've hoped for. She's beautiful, but not only is she beautiful, she takes an active interest in her people. While I've only read treatises and discussed the philosophical merits of different changes, she's out there actually trying to enact change. She even threw herself into battle to protect her people." Oldar sighed dramatically. "I don't think I've met a woman in all of Madden who even holds a candle to her. I can only imagine what she would do with diplomatic issues."

"But she completely shamed you and even insulted you by expressing her interest in her servant, didn't she?"

"Her guard, but close enough," Oldar grumbled. "I have never been so embarrassed in my life. Completely disregarded for the help."

"That doesn't seem like something that a woman worthy of your affections would do," Schaed said slowly. "That almost seems like the actions of someone who wanted to throw away a perfectly good alliance for their own selfish gains. As though they were above you and all you have to offer."

"What are you saying, Schaed?" Oldar slurred.

A soft knock at the door heralded the arrival of their breakfast. Schaed pushed himself out of his chair and staggered towards the doors. Pushing them open, he found a pair of serving girls waiting outside with large platters laden with food. He held the door open for them as they scurried inside. The two quickly placed the platters on the table and then dropped into a deep curtsy before darting out of the room. Schaed smiled a lopsided smile as he watched the hems of their dresses disappear around a corner.

"Well?" Oldar asked.

The king, suddenly ravenous, pulled the beef towards him and speared himself a cube with a fork. He chewed vigorously as the juices dripped down the side of his mouth. Oldar wiped his face with the back of his hand as he reached for another cube.

"I'm just saying that maybe, this is Pharn's way of saying that they don't need our help anymore," Schaed replied as he stumbled back to his chair. He grabbed his glass and downed the remaining wine.

"Well, if they don't need me, then I don't need them," Oldar groused.

He pulled over the plate of vegetables and grabbed a carrot. Struck with a sudden idea, Oldar took the carrot and rammed it through a beef cube. He then ate the pairing with a satisfied crunch of the carrot.

"No, no you don't," Schaed agreed.

XLVI

SCHAED WAITED until Oldar passed out before getting out of his chair and swiftly exiting the room. He closed the door softly behind him so as not to wake the drunken king. He walked with a steady gait down the hall. After passing several corridors, he turned sharply, veering into the royal gardens in order to avoid being seen more than necessary.

Once he was in the garden, he slowed his pace a little. Looking around, he found a small stone bench sitting off to the side under the shade of a birch tree. Pruvencia sat on the bench knitting. Schaed thought he heard her humming in the warm morning. Not wanting to draw attention to himself, he backed up slowly before turning around and surveying the lush grounds for another way to exit the keep.

With a sure step, the lanky man managed to leave the keep without being noticed by too many. Glancing around, he watched as the castle guards stood lazily at their posts chatting with their partners as the people of Madden passed by. Not so much as a second glance could be spared on the populace. Schaed smiled as he quietly walked behind a group of guards and joined a swarm of people walking by. In one swift motion, he was able to blend in with the crowd and move on into the heart of the city.

Schaed broke away from the group several buildings away from the keep. The expansive storefronts and high-end clothing shops quickly camouflaged his lanky frame. He wandered a bit before turning down the cobblestone street and heading towards the local tavern. The large mahogany sign for

The Gilded Rose greeted him before the noise did. Even in the middle of the day, the tavern maintained a large clientele.

Opening the mahogany door, Schaed walked in and looked for the bar maid, Rez'maré. Despite his height, he had to crane his neck a bit to see over the sea of heads that bobbled around at the tables, laughing and enjoying a hearty meal. After a while, he spotted the dark-haired woman and made his way towards her.

Rez'maré stood bent over a table as she wiped it down. A cloth hung out from the back side of her skirt. Schaed grabbed the cloth out from her skirt and waved it in her face with a smile as she spun around.

"Hell's horses, Schaed. I told you not to bother me when I'm busy," Rez'maré said through gritted teeth.

She reached for her cloth, but Schaed jerked it out of her reach and held it over her head.

"Oh, come now," he teased. "You know that I make your life interesting. If it weren't for me, you'd be still on the streets whoring for your next meal."

Rez'maré bounced up on the balls of her feet and snatched the cloth out of his hands, her eyes burning holes into him. "At least I know how to make an honest living for myself," she spat out. "Bohumír has treated me very well, no thanks to you. He even promised me a chance to sing when the minstrels play. I have my own lutist to accompany me. I don't need you."

The young woman moved to return to her duties. Schaed grabbed her arm and held her in place. Rez'maré grimaced in pain as he gripped her arm. The lanky man shook his head, warning her not to make a sound. Though he was gangly, he was surprisingly strong. Rez'maré stood frozen, her eyes wide in terror as flashes from her past filled her mind.

Tutting, Schaed smirked at the bar maid. With his eyes not reciprocating the emotion, the expression looked quite eerie on his cherubic face. "Now, now, Maré. Do you really think that that attitude will help you? Come, let's find a spot to sit and grab a bite to eat. I'm famished."

Steering the young woman towards a secluded table in the corner, Schaed followed behind her, his hand still gripping her arm. Once he was seated at the table, he waved her off to get him some food. His eyes never left her as she went to grab something to eat. Rez'maré returned fairly quickly with a loaf of freshly baked bread and some chicken.

Schaed motioned for her to set the plate down and join him at the table. Looking around helplessly, Rez'maré joined him. He ripped off a chunk of bread and took a large bite, ravenous after his long day of drinking with the king. Despite the strips of dried meat and dried fruit that he stealthily ate during their binge, he still felt the effects of the wine.

"Why don't you be a sweet thing and bring me some water, Maré. I've had a long night and my throat is quite dry."

"I'd rather you choke on your meal," she muttered.

Before she could react, he reached over and slapped her across the face. "Oh, Maré, look what you've made me do. Why don't you just get me my damned water and quit your bitching?"

Rez'maré slunk out from the table, her hand gingerly touching her cheek.

Schaed let out a sigh as he took a bite out of the chicken. The warm food filled his stomach and helped with the slight headache that he had. He continued to eat while he waited for his drink. Rez'maré finally returned with a glass of water and placed it in front of him. Taking the glass, he took a long drink, quenching his thirst as he drained the glass.

"Ah, I feel so refreshed," Schaed remarked. "Thanks for the meal, my dear. I look forward to visiting you again soon."

Standing up in front of his empty dishes, he gave her cheek a pinch before making his way out of the tavern. Schaed wound his way through the tables and patrons. He joined in with several as he passed, sharing a joke or a laugh with them as he headed towards the exit. Before walking out, he looked around one last time and spied Bohumír, the heavy-set barkeep, grabbing something from behind the bar. The man turned around and caught Schaed's eye. Waving good bye to the barkeep, Schaed opened the door, bringing in the sunlight once more, and left the tavern.

XLVII

A BELL TINKLED as the apothecary door opened. The shopkeep, Drogo, walked out from his back room to greet his customer.

"Welcome, good sir. How may I assist you today?" Drogo asked with a smile.

"Thank you," the young man replied. He looked around the shop for a bit. "To be honest, I'm not sure." He smiled a boyish grin and ran his hand through his blonde hair in embarrassment. His lanky appearance contrasting with his cherubic face. "My pa asked me to get something to help our gran with her pain. She's been sick for a while and Pa said that maybe it's time that we help her out with her suffering."

Drogo's smile faltered as the man's smile became pained and his gaze dropped downwards.

"I mean, Pa would know best, wouldn't he?"

"Oh, my dear boy, I'm so sorry that you've been sent on this mission. Perhaps I could suggest a few sedatives? Opium will help keep the pain away and allow for her to rest. I think this may be the strongest that I have. I can recommend a few more if you would like."

"Oh, no. That sounds perfect! I would like some of that, please."

Drogo nodded and made his way to the back of his store to prepare a small amount of opium. He pulled down the clay jar and spooned out a little bit of opium before wrapping it up in a piece of cloth and tying it with a bit of string. Drogo returned to the young man and presented him with the herbs.

"That will be three silver," Drogo said.

The young man reached into his pouch and pulled out three silver coins. Handing them to Drogo, the man thanked him and exited the shop.

With a sigh, Drogo went to put the coins away. "Poor lad, I don't envy his position none too much."

The tinkling of the bell announced a customer. Turning around, Drogo saw that the youth had returned. His cherubic face was once again wearing that awkward smile.

"How may I assist you, my boy?" Drogo asked.

"I forgot that my Ma also made a request," he replied sheepishly. "Do you happen to have any daffodils?"

"I do."

"What about anything to keep out the evil spirits. Ma heard a rumor back when Queen Gwyn traveled to the Halls of the Fallen that there's wicked spirits walking in our world again. She asked me to pick up something to keep them away."

Drogo thought for a moment. "I do have some foxglove that she can make a black dye out of to keep out the evil. Do you think that would work for her?"

The boy looked blankly back at him for a moment before that goofy grin returned. "I think so," he replied as he ran his hand nervously through his hair once more.

"Let me go wrap those up for you. Please give me a moment," Drogo said.

Turning back around, Drogo headed to his back room to gather the herbs. He grabbed a glass jar and poured out a few daffodils into a square of tan cloth. He then returned the glass jar and pulled down another clay jar. Ladling the tiniest amount of foxglove into a separate cloth square, he worked to carefully wrap the herb. Once he'd tied the two squares with some string, he returned to his customer.

"This is a little more expensive than the opium," Drogo warned. "Because it's also dangerous, the foxglove is seven silver. The daffodil is another three. I can do ten silver or one gold."

The young man's face dropped as he dug around in his pouch for the payment. After searching for several seconds, he looked down at the floor, unable to make eye contact. "I, uh, I don't have enough for both. I'm sorry."

Drogo thought for a moment before asking, "What do you have?"

The boy pulled out eight pieces of silver. "This is all I have. Pa gave me his month's earnings to get the herbs for our gran. I don't think he or Ma realized how expensive it would be to keep the bad spirits away."

"I can do six, if that'll help you out," Drogo said. "I don't want your Ma to worry."

The boy's face lit up and he handed over the six silver pieces eagerly. "Thank you so much!" he exclaimed as tears welled at the corner of his eyes. "You have no idea how much it'll mean to Ma and Pa."

"Have a wonderful day, good sir. Take care of your ma and gran," Drogo said.

The young man waved to Drogo and exited once more. With a sigh, Drogo went to put away the nine silver pieces that he just made.

<hr />

Schaed walked out of the apothecary with a smile on his face. He whistled a jaunty tune as he carried his three small parcels. His coin pouch jingled as he walked, his bouncy gait shaking the coins with every step.

XLVIII

CIENNA WALKED through the market square, unable to unwind in the bustling flow of her people like she used to. The muted chatter of the crowds didn't help. Perhaps it was the lack of noise that unsettled her and kept her on edge. Things hadn't been the same since her father died. Now that she could take the time to think about it, she was finally able to let it sink in. It had been three days since she'd had her last interaction with the Alocaran king. Wandering aimlessly in the streets, she weighed everything.

I wish Brody would return, she thought. *This whole plan has been useless. Oldar is more manipulative than Mother realizes and he's doing a good job pitting us all against each other.*

Her people gave her a wide berth as she moved through them, shooting her glances as they passed.

How are we going to fix this mess? With Vashe and Brody gone, I feel so lost. At least he would've been able to fill in for Alverick and helped me lead. The princess sighed loudly as she walked. *Perhaps I've made a mistake.*

"Are you all right, Princess?" Ronan asked.

Cienna looked over at the guard. Ronan had taken it upon himself to act as her bodyguard while Brody was gone. Having him around her did put her at ease, but was not enough to help her in her despondency.

"I'm fine, Ronan," she replied. "I just feel overwhelmed with everything. I mean, who would've thought that Tenzen would have withdrawn the support of his people after everything that Oldar's said? With the tribes of the north in turmoil, as well as the clans in Xan, all we have left are the Isles who back us. Alocar was our strongest ally, and now we are down to basically nothing as Corinth is being torn apart. I don't know how Father managed everything. I'm struggling to keep my head above water with all of the politics."

Ronan nodded thoughtfully. "Have we sent emissaries to Kalimba? I'm sure we could get help from them. Thallysis may be lost to the pirates, but there's still Ro'thre and Quallyah."

Cienna walked in silence for a while. After a lengthy pause, she spoke. "I don't really know. I've always heard that Kalimba is like Enlil, completely abandoned." Turning to the man, she asked, "Are there really people still in Ro'thre and Quallyah?"

"From what I know, there are. Good people, too."

"Then perhaps we should look into sending out a messenger once Brody and Caitlyn return," Cienna said. "I'll draft something up with Mother once we get back home so that it's ready to go. I expect that they should be returning soon, but if they're not back in two days we'll send a rider out."

"Understood," Ronan replied.

The two continued on through the market in silence. Cienna tried to lose herself amongst her people, in their colorful dresses and the warm woods of the buildings. As she watched the people around her, she noticed that there was a tension between the vendors. The Thurlish merchants were subdued, not trying to attract too much attention to themselves as they worked to sell their wares.

Cienna walked over to one of the food vendors, the scent of spiced meat greeted her nostrils. Her mouth watered as she drew nearer. Cienna looked for something to eat at the stall while Ronan stood off to the side.

A man with a shaved head timidly approached her. "Good morning, my dear," he said, his hands rubbing each other at chest height. "Might I tempt you with something?" His eyes shifted side to side as he tried to smile.

Reaching out and touching the man on his hand gently as she smiled, Cienna replied, "Do you have any spiced meat buns? I had some from a lovely man and his wife a couple weeks ago and have been craving another one."

The Thurlish man returned her smile and nodded. "I do, my dear. Please, let me go and get it for you."

Spinning around, the man went to the back of his booth and picked out a bun for her. He wasn't gone long before he returned to her. Holding out the bun for her, he told her, "That will be one silver, my dear."

Cienna, hand grabbing the food from him, stopped. "One? But I paid three last time."

"Please, one is plenty," he said, holding up his hands.

Cienna reached into her pouch and pulled out three silver coins. Proffering them to the Thurlish man, she forcefully placed them in his hand when he tried to refuse.

"Take them, my friend," she insisted. "It's what you need."

"Thank you, my dear."

Cienna took a bite of the bun and enjoyed the warm meat marinated in a myriad of seasonings. She closed her eyes as she savored its flavors. Opening her eyes, she noted that the man was looking off to the side at his booth neighbor. He looked nervous.

"What's going on?" she asked.

Snapping his attention back to the princess, the Thurlish man smiled and tried to downplay his actions. His eyes didn't lie, however. Worry hid behind them, an emotion usually not seen on the jovial people of his land. Leaning his head towards the princess he spoke softly so that only she could hear.

"I don't want to speak ill of your wonderful people, but ever since the Great Heart of Xan attacked your beautiful land, your people have not been as, uh, hospitable as they used to be. Some of them have blamed my brothers for the Great Heart's actions. We've found our pavilions damaged and some of our goods missing."

Cienna's eyes were wide in disbelief. "I never realized that things were this bad. Please, let me help you and your people."

The man held up his hand and shook his head. "Please, sweet princess, do not trouble yourself with this. We know that this will all blow over. Pharn has always been good to us. She will be good to us once again."

"But..."

Another shake.

"There have been many who have helped us. You see my booth?" he waved his arm to emphasize his point. "Several of my neighbors have helped me in fixing it. Pharn is good to us. We just need to be alert in this time of trial."

Cienna's eyes dropped as she was filled with pain for the man. "I'm sorry that you have been experiencing troubles. Please, if you ever need my ear, you or your people, come and talk to me. Both the Queen and I do not stand for such actions."

"Of course, my dear."

The Thurlish man gently squeezed the princess' hand. His eyes were soft as he wished her well. As she walked away from the merchant's stall, she took another bite of her food. Her mind was pensive as she watched her people with a more critical eye. Vendors from other nations still attempted to sell their wares, but they were not as boisterous as they used to.

That explains the lack of commotion in the market.

As people walked by occasionally, one of the older citizens, usually from outside of the capitol, would shoot a suspicious glance at the foreigners. Nothing was said, but she took note of how the normally calm market square was now tense.

Father would be devastated to see this. I need to speak with Mother. We cannot allow for people to be treated this way in our city. If we can sort this out, we may be able to repair some of the damage done by Oldar's proclamation.

Cienna turned around and made her way towards the caer at a rapid pace, startling Ronan. Consuming her meat bun in three massive bites, the princess continued her determined march, ignoring the guard's call.

"Princess, what is going on?" Ronan asked as he quickly caught up.

"I must speak with Mother," she said simply.

"What is going on?"

"No time to stop. We must reach her, now."

Ronan followed her without asking anymore questions. He remained a step behind her, allowing for him to observe her from many angles. Cienna did not slow her pace as she wove through the crowd. The men and women parted in front of her, alarmed at her progress. Women grabbed their skirts and pulled them up above their ankles as they stutter-stepped out of her way. Occasionally, a startled cry would ring out as she passed them.

In short time, Cienna found herself at the caer doors. Taking a moment to catch her breath, she patted down her dress and ran her fingers through her curly hair. She dabbed at the light sheen on her forehead. Even though Hera was her mother, a queen is still a queen. Once she was presentable, given the circumstances, she walked through the door.

※

Hera sat in the library. A discarded book lay on her lap as she stared out the window. The warmth from the sunlight relaxed her and made her feel a bit drowsy. She closed her eyes contentedly and leaned her head back against the plush chair. In the distance, Hera could hear a bird warbling. A small smile played on her lips as she sank into the chair further.

Her mind began to wander as she drifted off to sleep. She worried about her daughter.

My stubborn girl takes too much upon herself. I wish she would let herself relax a little and let me be her queen, and her parent.

Hera knew that she hadn't shown herself to be a capable decision maker while Jaste was alive. Cienna obviously didn't realize what she was capable of.

The pages of the book on her lap fluttered as a gentle breeze came in through the window. A golden butterfly landed on the sill and began flapping its wings wildly as it cleaned its proboscis. It clung to the stone ledge as a stronger breeze came through the window.

Hera opened her eyes, suddenly alert and unsure of what bothered her. Looking around, she spied a little girl standing off in the corner. Her skin was pale white and her hair, periwinkle. What bothered Hera was that the girl's eyes were jet black. Despite being so dark, the little girl's eyes held a light behind them.

She looks familiar, the queen thought.

The little girl walked over to the queen and grasped her hand. Her eyes were earnest. The cream-colored shift that she wore moved as though it was being blown by wind. The scent of lavender seemed to permeate the entire room.

"What is it, my dear?" Hera asked.

The girl squeezed her hand. Her movements were more deliberate.

Hera struggled to figure out where she'd seen the girl before. A vision flashed before her eyes. The blue-haired figure standing watch over a battlefield. A dark-haired man. A figure shrouded in orange. She had seen that vision before, shortly after she made a prayer to her goddess; the effigy that she carried with her at all times.

"By the gods!" Hera gasped. "Holy Freyna!"

Moving to stand, Hera felt the little girl's hands upon her legs, pushing her down. She was deceptively strong. Freyna opened her mouth. It sounded like the time she'd gone to the coast with her parents and listened to the ocean through a seashell.

Stay strong, faithful one. As long as you keep me with you, I will protect you.

Hera reached into her bodice and pulled out the white and blue petal. She held it out for her protector. Freyna nodded and placed her hand on Hera's, causing her to wrap her hand around the petal. Tears welled in the queen's eyes as she took the holy relic and placed it back inside her bodice.

A knock on the door caused her head to snap towards the library entrance.

"Enter," she called out.

Turning her head back to Freyna, she saw that the goddess had disappeared. The golden butterfly that had been on the stone window sill also was gone. Hera placed her hand on her bosom and felt the softness of the flower petal against her flesh. A sense of calmness and warmth filled her once more.

XLIX

OLDAR PACED the halls of his keep deep in thought. After the previous day's spiral into intoxication, he woke up determined to maintain the promise that he had made to himself a few weeks prior. No longer would he allow for his emotions drive him to drink. If he was to be Iron Fist, he would need a clear head and would be a man of his word. The young king turned on his heels and continued his pacing.

How can I move forward for the good of Alocar? I've been going about this the wrong way. I need to be more pragmatic if I'm going to be Iron Fist.

The answer came to him almost immediately. Oldar stopped his pacing, almost running into one of his serving girls as she tried to squeeze behind him with her arms full of linens. She squeaked out an apology as she scurried past him. He paid her no mind as he made his way to his room.

Once he arrived at his room, he went straight to his desk and pulled out a few pieces of parchment as well as a quill and ink. He lit a couple candles to give himself more light and sat down. The blank sheets of paper stared back at him, waiting to fulfill his needs.

The best way to move Alocar forward is to do it with a strong ally.

Dipping his quill into the ink, he began scratching away at the parchment. He wrote feverishly, occasionally crumpling up a piece of paper and throwing it over his shoulder, torn between his royal duties and following his heart. After a long while, he stared at his completed work. Droplets of ink splattered his face, but the parchment was perfect.

Ever so gently, he rolled up the message after waiting for the ink to dry. Taking his wax seal stamp, he held it to a candle flame to heat the wax. Once the wax was hot and dripping, he pressed it against the parchment. The brilliant red image of the Storm family crest came out perfectly against the dun color of the paper. The Tree of Life, a sprawling tree that connected the holy land of the gods to the mortal realm, lay embedded in the wax. Satisfied with what he'd done, he grabbed his scroll and headed out of his room.

The sun hung low in the sky. He'd been writing for longer than he thought. Looking for a servant in the hallway, he spotted a young boy and called him over. The child looked up at the bespotted king and offered him his handkerchief. Confused, Older took the cloth and rubbed it over his face. When he pulled the handkerchief away, he chuckled at the darkened rag. Giving his face another wipe, he returned the rag to the boy.

"Take this message to our courier and make sure that it is received by the queen of Zanir. Use our fastest warhorse; I want it there before night falls. I want to make sure that she personally collects it, so do not leave if they make you hand it off to one of their staff. Understood?"

The young child nodded his head as he accepted the scroll. He stuffed the soiled cloth into his pants pocket. Without a word, the boy bowed to his lord and then turned and ran down the hallway. Oldar watched the child retreat, a feeling of contentedness welling in his chest. It had been too long since he felt truly at peace.

By Ghan's mercy, I'll be able to fix this mess.

Smiling for the first time in several weeks, Oldar turned around and started walking towards the kitchens. A hearty meal and a good book seemed like a wonderful way to indulge himself for the rest of the day. He hadn't managed to find the time to treat himself to a relaxing afternoon in a long time. Today would be the day that he returned to his old self and figure out what he needed to do to take over his father's mantle. For all his talk of change, he never stepped up to the challenge. Today, he would.

L

CIENNA STRODE into the room, Ronan right behind her. The princess' normally curly hair was a bit disheveled and her dress was creased. A little sweat beaded on her brow and her breathing was slightly labored. Behind her, Ronan stood at attention. His expression didn't tell Hera anything.

She rushed to get here. What happened?

Closing the book on her lap, Hera remained seated. She smoothed her dress before folding her hands neatly in her lap. Hera waited a moment for Cienna to compose herself. The princess ran her hands down the front of her dress a couple times and then through her hair. Lastly, she dabbed her forehead with the back of her sleeve. Hera noted that her daughter's breathing had slowed. Once she was presentable, Hera nodded her head, indicating that she should speak.

"Mother, we need to talk about the repercussions of everything that has happened since Father's died."

"Cienna, we know what has happened," Hera replied. "I hear about it almost daily from my spies. We are in a time of change, but we must remember that we are also in a period of transition. Our people are getting used to hearing our voices instead of your father's. We are trying to cope with our former allies casting doubt on our principles, which then trickles down to our own people questioning us. At the same time, we are balancing an act between appearing stronger than we truly are and hiding our weaknesses in our defenses. We are literally a spark away from being consumed."

Hera watched as Cienna processed everything. She felt bad for hiding the additional intelligence from her daughter, but with all that she had been through previously, she didn't want to burden her with that. Understanding filled Cienna's eyes as everything fell into place.

"I know that I don't come off as capable," Hera said gently, "but I actually have been able to keep things afloat. Your father already had the spies in place, so I've just been continuing their duties. Now, what is it that you wanted to tell me?"

Cienna's mouth tightened. She opened her mouth to speak, but was interrupted with a heavy knock on the door.

Everyone's head turned towards the sound. Ronan walked over and opened the oaken door. Standing behind it, a young serving boy stood with a bottle of wine and a message. Looking around timidly, the boy entered the library. He wasn't more than nine, the son of one of the staff most likely.

"Come closer," Hera said softly, beckoning the boy closer. "What do you have there?"

The child quickly crossed the room and handed her the bottle of wine, as well as the parchment. He then backed up just as quickly and stood in the shadow of the doorway. The boy stood awkwardly as he awaited further instruction.

Hera placed the bottle on the floor and broke the seal on the scroll.

"It's from the Storms," she told her daughter. "Perhaps there's good news contained within."

Cienna looked suspicious, but said nothing.

Opening the scroll, Hera read the message:

Greetings and warm wishes, venerable Queen Grey,

I have spent the better part of the last three days undergoing deep meditation of our last conversation. It pains me that our union has been struggling lately, partially at my hands. I cannot allow for my people to suffer because of my pride, as I am sure that you cannot allow yours.

Through my reflections, I have reached the conclusion that we can return to the way that we once were. All we need to do is swallow our ego and move forward. Your kindness to my people during the time of transition between my parents' death and my return to Alocar has not been forgotten.

In an attempt to garner good will, I have provided a bottle of our finest wine from the Hanzo tribe of Xan. As I am sure you are well aware, there is no sweeter drink than that of the Hanzo. It is my hope that you will enjoy this treasured gift and recall all of the good memories that our people share.

Yours faithfully,

King Oldar Storm of Alocar

Hera rolled up the message. She stood up and placed the scroll on the ledge of the bookshelf. The queen then turned and picked up the bottle on the floor. Looking at the bottle, it was indeed a rare vintage from the Hanzo. The burgundy liquid moved slightly in the bottle as she gave it a little shake.

"Why don't we enjoy a glass of this fine wine while we draft a response to King Storm?" Hera asked. "He's offered this generous gift in hopes of mending our relationship."

Cienna's eyes narrowed. "I don't know, Mother. I still don't trust him after all that he's done."

"Nonsense," Hera said, waving her hand. "No one would waste a fine vintage like this to lull their enemy into a false sense of security. It would be like giving away your prized warhorse. It's much too valuable."

She waved over to the child and asked him to bring her a glass. The boy bobbed his head in what could be construed as a nod of understanding and dashed away. Hera sent Ronan away to go and fetch an older servant to uncork the bottle and pour the drink. When the guard was gone, Hera walked over to her daughter.

Softly stroking the girl's cheek, Hera tried to read what was going on in Cienna's eyes. There was distrust, but also sadness. Hera saw a lot of herself in those eyes. All of the queen's insecurities and desires to be strong were reflected in her daughter's eyes.

"Cienna, I hope you can trust me," she said. "I know it's hard, but together we can make Pharn, and Zanir, strong."

Cienna grabbed her mother's hand and held it against her cheek. "I worry that the people outside the capital do not understand what we do. They're so used to being isolated, that when they finally come to Pharn they do not trust all we open our gates to."

"So, you've heard of the attacks on the people of Xan, I see."

Cienna's eyes widened. "You know?"

Hera nodded. "I've been sending out soldiers to make sure that their pavilions are not destroyed. A couple have been broken, but it's not something that's unfixable. Our people have also been more than giving and helped repair any damage as well. That is what drew me to Pharn when your father courted me all those years ago."

Hera's eyes misted slightly as she remembered her love. She pulled her hand back and brought it to her chest. Gingerly, she pressed with two fingers against her bodice, seeking comfort in the flower petal hidden within. Though it was not as strong as before, the feeling of peace returned. A warm smile appeared, providing a measure of calm to her daughter's worried eyes.

"Do you think we can overcome this?" Cienna whispered. Her eyes and nose were starting to turn red as she struggled to speak without her voice breaking. "I'm afraid we may have gone too far."

Pulling her daughter in tightly, Hera tried to soothe young princess. Her hand stroked the girl's hair, while the other kept her firmly pressed against her body. Cienna's body shook as she gasped for breath. Hera softly shushed her daughter, trying to calm her.

"Cienna, what's wrong? I haven't seen you this upset in years," Hera asked.

"I'm... fine..." she replied through broken sobs. "Everything's just catching up with me."

Hera pulled her closer, rubbing her back. "Let it out. Everything will be fine. This is just something that will make you a stronger ruler. It'll make both of us stronger in the long run."

Ronan returned with the serving boy and an older servant who appeared to be at least fifteen. The younger boy carried a chalice in both hands. Ronan had the two servants turn away from the women as Cienna backed up out of her mother's embrace, wiping her eyes and nose on her sleeve. Her eyes were puffy and red.

"Thank you, Ronan," Hera said.

Ronan and the boys turned around and faced the queen once more. The younger one held the goblet as the older one worked to pull out the cork in the bottle. After a bit of struggling, the cork came free with a loud *pop*. The earthy aroma of the wine wafted over towards those in the room. Moving towards the younger boy, the elder one poured a small amount of the burgundy liquid into the cup.

Handing the chalice to the queen, the two servants bowed deeply and then exited the room. The older one left the bottle on a table in the room before ducking out. Ronan moved to close the door of the room, but Hera held out her hand to stop him.

"It's a warm day. I don't want it to get too stuffy."

Holding up the glass, Hera swirled the aromatic drink, admiring the way that the wine caught the light. The burgundy liquid sparkled in the sunlight. Sniffing the wine, she nodded her head in approval. This was indeed a fine drink.

"To stronger friendships," she murmured before taking a sip.

"How is it?" Cienna asked.

"It's quite good," she replied.

She took a second sip and stared thoughtfully into the distance. A knock on the door heralded a courier in Alocaran livery. He pulled out a sealed scroll and presented it to the queen as she was raising the glass to her lips once more. She suddenly dropped it as her vision swam. A strong pain shot through her stomach. A groan escaped her lips before she fell to the ground unconscious.

LI

OLDAR STRODE out of his room in his riding clothes. It was a beautiful day. The sun shone in the cerulean sky. Birds sang out over the chatter from the people as they bustled about in the city below. The symphony of children laughing, women gossiping, and servants calling out to one another layered perfectly in the air with the music of the birds. Oldar took a deep breath, trying to suck in all of the splendor of the day.

"What a beautiful day to ride," he mused. Oldar raised his arms over his head and stretched his back. A satisfying crack let him know that he was ready to continue.

The king strolled down the hallway, heading towards the kitchens for a quick bite to eat before making his way to the stables. As he walked, he hummed softly. He didn't remember the words to the song, but it was a tune that his mother used to sing to him. Something about the winds bringing change, both good and bad, and that no matter what horrible things came his way, the wind would always be there to blow it away. He smiled to himself as he recalled the song.

In the kitchen, he grabbed a savory pastry and some grapes. He wrapped the food in a cloth before leaving. As he walked, he popped a few grapes into his mouth, savoring the burst of juice as ate them.

The stables were on the eastern side of the keep, close to the city gates. Oldar walked in and began admiring the horses. The stalls were filled with the majestic beasts, all in various states of readiness. Palominos and dun stood tied to a hook in their stall, chewing on hay. There were black ones pacing in their stalls or drinking water. Looking around, Oldar tried to find the one that he wanted.

At the end of the stable, he found Bells, his favorite mare. She was a dun-colored horse with a silky black mane. He made his way over to Bells and greeted her. Patting her muzzle, he smiled as she whickered at him in response.

"Hello, girl. Are you up for a ride today?" Oldar asked her as he scratched her nose.

She whinnied at him and stamped her foot as her tail twitched.

"I'm glad," he said with a smile.

"Can I help you?" the stable master called out. "Oh, your majesty! How may I be of assistance?" The portly man whipped off his hat and bowed.

"I will be going to Pharn today and need Bells to be ready. How much longer until she's able to travel?"

"Let me put on her tack and you can take her in a few minutes."

"Perfect," Oldar replied. "I will be waiting outside by the gates for her. I will need her as soon as possible."

"As you wish, your majesty," the stable master said.

He grabbed Bells and hurried off to get her ready. Oldar took his time leaving the stable before heading out to the city gates. He found himself enjoying the sights of the city. As he neared the gates, he spied a familiar face amongst the guards. Ingmar stood with the younger soldiers and delegated orders. The younger guards saluted the seasoned man and turned to assume their posts. One of the newer men looked over and saw the king approaching and snapped to attention. The others stared at him, trying to figure out who was heading over. Upon seeing the king, they too went to attention.

Ingmar, his back to Oldar, was giving someone instructions inside one of the towers at the city gates. Oldar nodded to his head to the soldiers, letting them relax around him. Holding his hand up to keep them quiet, he motioned for them to return to their posts. They did so and tried to covertly watch what the king planned on doing.

Oldar quietly approached the veteran and waited patiently behind him, just out of sight of whoever was in the doorway. Ingmar spoke sternly to the person in the tower.

"Son, if you don't keep to your post at all times, what good will you do you when you're needed? If you can't do something as simple as this, I will have you removed from the guard," Ingmar scolded. "You can't keep sneaking off to visit the girls, son. Just because a few are impressed that you are part of the royal guard, that doesn't mean that you'll be able to chase their skirts while on duty."

A mumbled apology could barely be heard from inside the tower.

"Now, son, I know that it can be hard. Hell, I remember when I was your age. It took me a good long time to stop going after the ladies, but..."

"I would've never expected you to be such a lady's man," Oldar interjected with a smirk. His eyes twinkled as Ingmar spun around in surprise.

"Your majesty," Ingmar said, startled. "Forgive me, I –"

Holding up his hand, Oldar shook his head. "There's nothing to forgive. I look to you to make sure that my soldiers are up to scratch. No matter what it takes."

Snapping to attention, Ingmar saluted his king. Turning back to the soldier in the tower, he waved the youth off back to his post. Once the soldier was gone, Ingmar returned to his king. The veteran approached Oldar and motioned for him to follow.

"Iron Fist, if I may, I would like to speak with you," Ingmar said softly.

"Let's walk," Oldar replied.

The two set off around the perimeter of the city gate, staying just within her walls. Oldar walked with his hands behind his back, something he'd seen his father do on many occasions. Ingmar strode next to the king, the soldier's body stiff as he moved.

"Iron Fist," Ingmar began, "since your last orders, we've secured our borders from both your uncle and his ilk, as well as those from Pharn. Alocar is a strong land and can survive without goods from Pharn considering that there are other nations to open trade with. On occasion, however, we have allowed for the rare merchant in so that they could sell their wares. I apologize for going against your orders, but your friend asked that they be let in."

"Schaed is familiar with the needs of the guilds, and I have been unavailable for a while." Oldar turned to face Ingmar, making eye contact with the veteran, "There's nothing to apologize for."

The two rounded the city gates, in silence. After a while, Oldar asked, "Have you heard any word from my rider? I was hoping that he would've returned earlier this morning."

"Unfortunately, we have not seen anyone. The day is still young though. Most likely, he'll be back by noon-day meal."

"Oh, I plan to be gone by then," Oldar replied. "I wanted to visit Pharn myself and hopefully speak with the queen and her daughter."

"Shall I accompany you?"

Oldar opened his mouth to respond, but was distracted by the arrival of the stable master and Bells. The horse was prepared to ride, a satchel of provisions for the king strapped to her side.

"No need," Oldar said distractedly. "I shan't be gone long. Father always said that Zanir is the closest thing to home when I am away. Her people will keep me safe."

Ingmar made an uncomfortable grunt in response, but dared not question his king outright.

The portly stable master ripped his hat off his head as he neared the king. Oldar turned to the seasoned soldier and motioned for him to follow.

"Your majesty," the stable master called out. "Bells is ready to go. She seems quite keen on taking this ride."

"Excellent." Oldar rubbed his hands in anticipation. "Ingmar, I trust that you will keep Madden, and Alocar, safe while I am gone?"

"Of course, your majesty."

"I have a feeling that Alastaire won't be denied what he thinks is rightfully his without a fight. I hope to be back by tomorrow at the latest," Oldar explained. Walking over to Bells, he swung himself up into the saddle and grabbed her reins. Bidding the two men farewell, he nudged the horse with his heels and set off towards Pharn.

⋘⋙

Miles passed as Oldar rode leisurely towards Pharn. A whirlwind of emotion filled him, most of the feelings surprised him. Instead of trepidation at seeing the queen and Cienna, he looked forward to the meeting. There was so much to discuss, he hoped that they would be receptive to his ideas.

The gates of Pharn loomed ahead, getting closer as he spurred his mount faster, until he was almost upon them. He stared at the portcullis in awe, noting the splinters in the wood from battering ram attacks. Spots of dried wax splattered against the entrance, another remnant of the fight almost two weeks prior.

On the wall walk, a pair of guards noted his arrival. They gripped their spears as he approached. Looking to the side, Oldar saw an archer that he didn't see before. The soldier hid in the shadows, or what remained of the shadows in the afternoon sun, with an arrow trained on the young king.

"It looks as though Pharn is not taking any chances with visitors," Oldar mused to himself. "Not that I really blame them though."

As Oldar drew closer to the gate, one of the guards on top called out to him.

"Halt! Who goes there?"

"King Oldar Storm of Alocar. I have business with Queen Hera and her daughter. I trust that you've already received my rider?"

The man on the gate stared at his partner in confusion. Both looked unsure of how to respond.

"Let them in," the archer said. "We can have them escorted by Thol while they are in the city."

His comrades nodded and quickly made their way down to the crank that opened the gates. With several groans, the gate gradually opened enough for Oldar to ride through. He was greeted with a number of soldiers, several with their weapons drawn on him, their faces showing a variety of emotion as they stared down the young king.

"What's going on?" Oldar asked, confused.

A gangly youth approached, spear in hand. "King Oldar?" he called out.

Oldar squinted his eyes, trying to better see the man. His dark hair hung around his youthful face like a mop. His hands were large and broad, the hands of a person who spent years working hard. The soldier neared and Oldar recognized him immediately.

"Cody? What is going on? Why am I being treated as an enemy? Surely you received my message?"

"I think you better follow me," he replied.

Oldar slid off of Bells, handing her reins to the man near him. "I expect her to be treated properly," the king told the soldier.

The man saluted the king sharply before leading the horse to the stables. Oldar watched as his mount disappeared into the distance. Returning his gaze back to Cody, he approached the youth.

"Take me to them," he commanded. "Leave the others at their posts."

"I'm sorry, m'lord, but I can't do that," Cody stammered in apology. "I don't have that kind of authority to order them around."

Shooting a withering glare at the remaining soldiers, Oldar replied, "Very well. Let's go."

The two walked away from the gates and towards the caer. Oldar looked at the scenery that had enchanted him just weeks before. The vibrancy that once separated Pharn from his home was now muted. Bright dresses and accent pieces like flowers or bangles were replaced with more earthy tones. Fewer children ran through the streets, laughing as they chased each other. Chickens wandered about, clucking contentedly as they wove through the populace without fear of being harassed by children.

"Ghan's mercy," Oldar swore quietly. "What's happened, Cody?"

Cody continued on, his gaze remaining forward. His eyes shifted as he looked around him. Though his posture was straight, his body was rigid as he trudged along.

"Cody," Oldar whispered, "why won't you talk to me?"

The youth did not answer.

"I know that I have been acting differently since we last saw each other, but I've always held you in high regard."

The king's voice trembled as he spoke, uncertainty creeping in. Raising his hand, he began nibbling on the skin on his thumb.

Did they not react favorably to my letter of peace?

He stopped chewing when he caught himself ripping off a small strip of skin around his thumbnail. Forcing his hand back down to his side, Oldar placed his hand on the youth's shoulder, causing Cody to turn to face him.

"The queen fell sick yesterday after drinking some wine that you sent her," Cody replied softly. "Why would you do this to us? Queen Hera is on death's door."

Oldar's breath caught in his throat as he stopped in his tracks. "By the gods, Cody, I would never do anything like that. I didn't send you any wine."

"We have the bottle," Cody hissed. "It's awaiting inspection by Headmistress Vashe."

Oldar opened his mouth to speak, but Cody cut him off.

"I saw the bottle. It's Hanzo wine. Who else has that?"

Oldar didn't reply. His stomach dropped as he realized the implications. Only one person had access to such fine wines, and they usually were reserved for special events.

"Come, m'lord. We must continue on."

Oldar forced his legs to move once more. The pair walked in silence until they were deep in the heart of the city. The caer loomed over them, her worn stones providing shade in the warm afternoon sun. The young king struggled to keep his nerves in check as they walked up to the gate. On several occasions, he found his hand hovering close to his mouth. Instead of letting his bad habit take control, he forced himself to rub his chin or his nose.

Two guards stood at attention as they saw the approaching duo. Cody waved his hands and they relaxed. Moving ahead on his own, he spoke quietly to the guards. Their eyes widened in surprise as they looked at the king standing in front of them. One of them answered Cody and shook his head, his face solemn. Cody pointed at the other guard with the butt of his spear and the man took off into the keep. Turning around, Cody motioned for Oldar to enter. Oldar walked through the caer gates. Passing the remaining guard, he noticed that the man stared at him with hateful eyes, but did not move from his post.

The two walked briskly through the hallway. They passed several servants, and, in their haste, ignored the cries of surprise. Cody led Oldar into the familiar Great Hall, shutting the door behind him. He motioned for the king to take a seat while they waited.

A low fire burned in the hearth despite the day's heat. Oldar sat uncomfortably in the silence, his hands gripping the carved armrest until his knuckles turned white. Sweat covered his palms as he waited. Cody stood stiffly by his side. The young soldier averted his eyes whenever Oldar tried to catch his gaze.

After what felt like an eternity, the doors finally opened. Cienna strode into the room, followed by Ronan and Thol. A courier in Alocar livery followed behind them. The messenger's eyes were dark and puffy due to lack of sleep. When the man saw his king, he rushed over and stood off to the side.

"Thank you for releasing my man," Oldar said as he stood up. He bowed to the princess.

"I wasn't holding your messenger hostage, not when he was so helpful to me," Cienna replied. Her voice was strained.

Oldar looked at her and noticed that she too looked exhausted, as though she hadn't slept well. Her gown was wrinkled, as though she had slept in it. His eye wandered to the two guards. They too appeared haggard.

"My condolences on dear Queen Hera," Oldar said. "Please know that I would never wish ill of her like that."

Cienna stared at the king coldly. "Thank you for your concern. You'll forgive me if I don't just accept you at your word."

"Understandable. Please, will she make it?"

Cienna arced her eyebrow, trying to figure out how much to tell him. "The head healer and his infirmary have worked non-stop to keep her from joining my father in the Halls of the Fallen. By the grace of Aria, we have been able to figure out some of the herbs in the wine. Perhaps you can tell me what the other one is?"

Oldar shook his head. "I'm sorry, Cienna, but I don't know what is in there."

Cienna scowled at him. Ronan looked at him warily, but Thol stared at the king questioningly.

"I do, however, have a good idea of where that wine came from." Everyone in the room perked up at this news. Oldar took a steadying breath before continuing. "If you would trust me, I will make sure that this is taken care of properly."

"Attempted murder of a queen is an act of war," Ronan snapped. "Punishment should be issued by –"

Cienna held up her hand, silencing the soldier. "How will you handle this? Ronan is right. I should be determining the fate of this person or group."

"If it pleases you, I can bring him to you. All I ask is that you spare his life. I would like to handle his future."

Ronan opened his mouth to speak, but Thol cut him off. "While I think that you make a reasonable point, I do believe that it is our lady's decision in the end. After all, it does appear that he is acting on your behalf."

"Did you not see *my* message?" Oldar asked. "I hoped that we could work at returning to the way that we once were. I know that my actions cannot be undone, but surely if you give me a chance, I can begin to make things right."

Cienna's eyes softened just the barely as she listened to her former ally's plea. She'd wanted nothing more in the last two weeks, but now that he was here in front of her, she couldn't bring herself to accept his offer. She had read his message and Oldar appeared to be genuinely interested in making their alliance work. His words now also led her to believe as much. But she just couldn't do it.

"I did read it," she replied slowly. "Your words were nice, King Storm. I would almost dare to say heartfelt." Oldar's spirit lifted a little. "However, you spoke with just as much passion not even a week ago when you condemned me and my people as dishonorable. You called me a harlot and my mother inept. You accused me of breaking a treaty that went back countless generations, all because you could not stand to be told 'no'. How can a man who has been so fervent about one thing have the same fire about something so different?"

Oldar's hope dropped into the pit of his stomach as he took in her words. He'd said some ghastly things about his father's best friend, about the people who had been nothing but nice to him and his family.

"I cannot take back the damage that I've caused your people," he replied softly. "I had hoped that once I told you that I'd already sent couriers to Chief Tenzen and Lord Qa'fan explaining how I was completely wrong about how I'd handled everything would be a start to the healing process."

Cienna's eyes softened some more.

"Cienna, the more I thought about you and how you handled everything with grace and dignity, the more I admired you and wanted you back in my life."

"Your words come too late," Cienna said. Her eyes didn't return to their original coldness, but her tone remained sharp.

Oldar's head dropped.

Cienna opened her mouth to continue, but she was interrupted by the oaken doors of the Great Hall opening abruptly.

LII

Caitlyn and Brody entered the Great Hall, Alverick following behind them, his gaze unfocused and muttering to himself. Their clothes were torn and dirty. Brody had a strip of cloth wrapped around his arm; a dark brown stain tainted the cream-colored fabric.

"By the gods!" Cienna exclaimed. "You made it!"

"I can't believe you brought him back," Thol added. "That was a fool's mission you went on."

"It was," Brody said tiredly. "Both the rescue mission and our trip back."

"When darkness falls, the gods will return to Corinth once more. Their followers will carry their sword and Man will fall to the Faceless once more," Alverick muttered.

All eyes turned to face the man; confusion etched on their faces. Alverick stood in front of the hearth, his hands dangerously close to the flame. A ball of electrical energy surrounded his hands as he moved them around the blaze.

"Bannen, I need you more than ever right now," he mumbled. "The Faceless grow stronger and we could use your skill."

Brody walked over to Alverick and placed his hands on his shoulders. "Al," he said softly. The electric energy encompassing Alverick's hands disappeared. "Why don't you step away from the fire? We've traveled a long way and you could use the rest."

Alverick turned around, his eyes wide and empty, and began making his way towards one of the chairs. Distractedly, he pulled out a chair and sat down. He continued to speak softly to his dead friend.

"Ghan's mercy," Oldar swore. "What happened to him?"

Brody looked tired. "His mind was torn during the battle at the gorge and he's now Snapped. We haven't been able to get anything coherent from him since we found him." Running his hands through his hair, the young head of the guards sighed. "Who knows if he'll be of any help to us in the future?" After a pause, Brody looked up towards the king. "What are you doing here? Is everything all right now?"

Oldar turned away sheepishly. He looked to the princess, who wasn't paying him any attention at all. "Well, not exactly," he mumbled.

Cienna, ignoring the conversation for the moment, walked over to Alverick and gently placed her hands on his shoulders. He absentmindedly reached up and grabbed one of her hands. "I'm so sorry that you've lost so much protecting our people," she said as she gave him a squeeze. "You'll never know what your sacrifice means."

Alverick looked around at the people in the room. His eyes seemed to gain clarity as he observed everyone watching him. "The darkness draws nigh," he said.

Caitlyn turned away, rubbing her eyes. They were puffy. Her nose dripped and she hastily moved to wipe it as well before the others could see.

Ronan stood speechless as he watched his friend and fellow soldier rapidly drum his fingers on the table. "All was for naught," he mumbled.

"Stay strong, Ronan," Thol intoned. "There's hope yet. I'm sure the headmistress can help him."

"What makes you say that?" Ronan asked.

"Well, I must admit that I'm not very knowledgeable about magic, but I would think that someone of her intelligence would be able to reverse the Snap or something."

Alverick began muttering to himself. Occasionally, "Bannen" or something about the Faceless could be heard. Everyone stared at the man, their faces displaying the various levels of despair that each felt. Caitlyn's eyes reddened around the edges as she sniffled.

The sound of the heavy oaken doors opening pulled all eyes away from Alverick. A little girl, no more than ten, dressed in a shimmering, translucent dress of pale yellow walked into the room. Her bushy auburn hair was unkempt and hung limply down her back. Her eyes were a brilliant green and her skin appeared to have an olive tinge, as though she fell into a vat of dye. She walked barefoot through the room and over to Alverick. Little patches of moss popped up behind her with each step. Alverick stopped his babbling and stared at the girl, wide-eyed.

"Little girl," Ronan began.

Thol shook his head and addressed the child. "My dear, what are you doing here? Where is your mother?"

The little girl shook her head. "I don't have a mother," her voice was surprisingly deep for such a small child. Pointing to herself, she said, "I am my own."

Thol gawked at the girl, nonplussed at her response. He opened his mouth to speak, but the girl walked right past him and continued her way to Alverick.

"So much pain for one so young," she said softly as she held his face in her tiny hands. His eyes stared into hers, lost in their brilliant depths. "I can help, but it will only be temporary. You're much too far gone for true healing." Her voice was heavy as she spoke.

Placing her hands on his temples, the girl stared through his eyes, her focus far away, as though searching for his soul. He did not blink as she stared back. His dark eyes shook, as though he wanted to break his gaze, but he held them constant. The girl began humming, her notes frantic and fevered as she maintained her intent focus. Alverick stopped shaking as he listened to her voice. His lids drooped as he relaxed into her hands.

Her eyes widened as she saw his memories. Sweat beaded on her brow. Her hair rustled slightly, as though there was a breeze. She abruptly stopped humming and let out a sharp gasp, her hands flying from the Avalanche's head. Alverick blinked slowly and looked around the room. His eyes focused on his surroundings and as he turned his head.

"How did I get here?" he mumbled.

Several shouts of "Al!" could be heard in the room as everyone rushed over to him. The little girl backed away and sank into a plush chair at the table. She cradled her head in her hands, shaking it almost imperceptibly.

"I'm so glad to see you," Brody said, clapping Alverick on the shoulder, wiping away a tear with his other hand. "You gave us quite a scare, brother."

"I, I'm sorry. I wish I remembered what I did," Alverick replied. His eyes locked onto Caitlyn and her red, puffy eyes. He stood up quickly, the chair scraping against the stone floor. "Cait..."

"Hi," she said weakly. The redhead smiled as tears ran down her cheeks.

"Hey!" Oldar exclaimed, his attention shifting towards the young child. "Are you all right?"

The little girl rocked in the chair, her hair dangling over her hands that still cradled her face. A faint moan escaped her. "The darkness returns," she muttered. Looking up from her hands, she looked at Alverick. "What did you do?" she whispered.

Alverick stared at the girl, his mouth opened slightly in shock.

A frenzied knock on the Great Hall door distracted the group. Cody made his way to the door and opened it up. Outside stood Praesh, King Jaste's personal servant. The man huffed and clutched a stitch at his side as he made his way into the hall. Cody remained at the entryway, holding the thick oaken doors.

"Your majesty," Praesh wheezed as he struggled to stand at proper attention. "We... Pharn... clans..."

"Praesh, take a moment and compose yourself," Cienna commanded. "We can't understand you if you can't breathe."

Praesh put his hands on his hips and worked to take deep breaths. As he managed to start catching his breath, Aeliana, her mother's hand maiden, stuck her head into the Great Hall. She made eye contact with the princess and ducked into the room as soon as Cienna motioned for her to enter.

"What is it, Aeliana?" Cienna asked.

"Milady, I come with good news. I've just received word from the healers that Queen Hera appears to have stabilized. They've put her into a deep sleep, but they said that she is not in imminent danger of dying. However, she's still close to death's door. With the gods' blessing, they think she'll make it though."

A sigh of relief escaped the young princess as her hand went to her chest. "Thank you, Aeliana. Please go and keep Mother company while she sleeps. See to her every need and keep me posted with any changes."

"Yes, ma'am," Aeliana said. She dipped into a curtsy before scurrying out of the Great Hall. The hurried sound of her feet could be heard down the hallway.

"I'm so relieved," Oldar told Cienna.

"Your majesty," Praesh said, his breathing finally back to normal. "I've received word from our allies, the Qu-ari, that their leader has been driven from the land. A rebellion is happening."

Cienna looked from Brody to Alverick before turning her gaze back to the servant.

The man looked perplexed as he addressed his master. "Do, do we have any allies in Xan, your majesty?"

"Brody," Alverick said, "ready our men. We need to leave for Xan as soon as possible."

"Ronan, Thol," Brody said as he turned to the two men, "we need every horse and soldier we can spare. I'm sorry, Princess, but we'll need to take almost all of Pharn's forces."

"I'm hesitant to do so," Cienna admitted. "With Mother in such a fragile condition, I would hate to leave her vulnerable."

"I can have some of my men stay behind to help keep up Pharn's defenses," Oldar said. "After all, you'll need Alocar's help in the matter."

"The darkness is upon us," the girl said. All heads turned towards her. "The silent can no longer just observe. It is time for action."

Without another word, the young girl strode out of the room. Behind her, her dress fluttered as she made a hurried exit. A trail of peat moss lay in her wake.

"Al," Brody said, ignoring the strangeness of what just happened. "Are you going to be okay for this?"

"I have to," he replied. "I fear that if I fail, the darkness will consume all of Corinth."

Brody clapped his friend on the shoulder. "Then, we will be the light." Turning to face the rest of the room, Brody called out, "We leave before the sun is past the horizon. We must make haste."

LIII

THE COOL AIR RUSTLED Brody's hair as he walked through the streets of Pharn. After the chaos of the last few hours, he was grateful to get a quiet moment to himself. He looked up to the heavens and exhaled deeply. The stars shone brightly, a myriad of pinpricks in the night sky. Despite the late hour, he somehow felt rejuvenated.

He didn't look to see where he was going. He let his feet guide him down the empty streets. As he wandered, Brody's mind raced. So much had happened in such a short period of time. He'd just gotten home, and now he needed to head out to Xan.

"Perhaps the end is nigh," he muttered. "Maybe Al is right."

The sound of a pebble bouncing off the cobblestones caught his attention. Brody's hand went to his hilt and his body tensed as he spun towards the sound.

"Who's there?" a voice called.

The light of the moon bathed the street in front of Brody with bright light. Using that to his advantage, he slipped into the shadow of a building. The figure staggered forward into the light. Brody felt his breath catch in his throat.

Alverick stood in the light, his eyes darting around as he tried to find Brody in the darkness. He looked haunted in the light; his cheeks gaunt. Alverick's eyes, though no longer wild from the Snapping, still hinted at the horrors he'd seen.

What's Al doing out here?

"I know you're out there," Alverick said. "Show yourself."

Brody walked out from the shadows into the moonlight. He felt a pang of sorrow as he watched his friend's eyes flash from wary to confused.

"Al," Brody said as he ran his hand through his hair. "It's good to see you out on your own."

"Why were you hiding?" Alverick asked.

"We've been through a lot, Al. Surely you can understand me being a little tense."

Alverick nodded, but Brody could see that sadness clouded his features. He scuffed his boot against the stones as he shifted his weight. Brody chewed the inside of his cheek. His exhaustion kept the knot in his stomach from getting tighter. Too much had happened in such a short period of time, it was just too much for him to process.

"What are you doing out here, Al? I thought you'd be resting."

"I needed to clear my head. I don't know what's real anymore."

"What do you mean?" Brody asked.

Alverick's brow wrinkled as he tried to answer the question. "I remember the gorge and Fyre. I remember the wyrm. The darkness. After that, it all feels like a nightmare." His eyes darkened. "... Things cut my body, draining me. I thought I was dying; I was so weak. I heard voices. And then there was a fire... two people talking. But you were there. And Cait and Vashe. And a... little girl? I don't know. Everything was fuzzy and when it all came into focus, there was that girl." The Avalanche wrung his hands, an uncharacteristic reaction for the normally composed man.

What in the hells did he go through? What did that girl see?

Clearing his throat, Brody pat his friend on the shoulder, trying to reassure him. "You're going to be fine. That girl, she healed your mind. We need to find her. I'm pretty sure she will play a critical role in whatever's coming."

"Is that what you were doing? Looking for her?" Alverick asked, his voice hopeful. Brody's contact appeared to be helping the man. His brow was no longer knit together and the tension in his face lessened.

Brody shook his head. "No," he admitted. "I needed some time for myself. To clear my head." He nodded to Alverick. "So much has happened. I just wanted a moment to absorb it all."

Alverick shifted his weight once more. The two stood awkwardly in the moonlight, the chirping of cicadas the only sound to be heard. An owl hooted in the distance; his call returned by another. Brody's exhaustion finally melted away as he watched his broken friend struggle.

"Come with me," Brody finally said. "I thought I'd grab a bite and maybe something to drink. Fren will be ecstatic to see you."

"I could go for a bowl of his stew," Alverick muttered, cracking a familiar smile for the first time since Brody'd seen him.

The two headed off in the darkness towards the Hoary Oak. Though they walked in relative silence, Brody noted the change in atmosphere. The tension that had hung in the air earlier melted away, and the two moved in sync like they had in the old days. Sneaking a glance at his friend, Brody saw that, indeed, his expression had lightened. Alverick's eyes no longer displayed his uncertainty. Brody felt a smile tug at his lips as the door to the tavern came into view. Grabbing the knob, the two entered the Hoary Oak together, just like they had countless times before.

<hr />

Glossary

Anchor: A form of mental discipline that helps Sparks and Tempests prevent or delay Snapping. In order to Anchor properly, the mage must focus on a specific mental image or idea until their mind is clear once again.

Apophmet: One of the two Ancients. Known as Apophos by those in the Northern realms.

Aramaine: An alternate realm inhabited by dragons, wyrms, and other evil creatures. Also known as the Abyss.

Avalanche: Practitioners of Earth magic. Their tattoos are thick and bulky, like the trunks of trees. Avalanches can trace the movement of others through the earth's vibrations. Strong Avalanches can cause earthquakes.

Draughting: The process of transferring the blood of one mage to another as a means to increase one's magical power and potentially acquire a new style.

Enlil: Ancient home of the gods. The land was believed to be deserted by all after the great collapse, but it was protected and preserved by the deep magic.

The Faceless: Thought to be old wives' tales, they are the demons of Enlil and part of Apophmet's army of darkness.

Flame: Practitioners of fire magic. Their tattoos twist into mesmerizing patterns and appear to dance on the mage's body like the flame of a candle. Their personalities can be erratic, but they do not suffer from the mental instabilities like a Spark or Tempest would.

Flicker: A derogatory term for a Flame.

Ghost: Practitioners of night magic. Their tattoos are slim and a metallic black color. They can manipulate shadows. Night magi are used in Scrymme as assassins. They are found only in Scrymme.

Jyarl: A term for Ghosts in the land of Scrymme.

Halls of the Fallen: Thought to be the final resting ground for kings and great warriors. It is a neutral place where the gods meet to discuss the events regarding Corinth.

Konugrr: The title for the ruler of Grimmrheimr.

Liche: Practitioners of necro magic. Their tattoos are thick and sluggish-looking shadows. Liches can manipulate the dead either through animation of corpses or scrying through the dead. They are found only in Scrymme.

Naran: The title used in Scrymme for one's master.

Nannohav: A Scrymmen request for judgement by the king and Host of Scrymme.

Plague: Practitioners of biological magic. Their tattoos are a combination of fine lines and delicate swirls. They can use healing magics and bring about plagues.

Re'nukhtet: One of the original Ancients. Known as Re'nukh by the Northern realms.

Shadow: Practitioners of shadow magic. Their tattoos are hazy. Strong Shadows can open dimensional gates and summon creatures to bring to their world.

Snap: The moment when a Tempest or Spark loses control of their mental faculties and succumbs to the erratic nature of their magic. Snapping usually occurs when a mage is fatigued or has recently draughted. In the case of Tempests, Snapping occurs when they lose their Anchor.

Spark: Practitioners of electrical magic. Their tattoos are sharp and jagged, like bolts of lightning. Those who use this style of magic are susceptible to mental destabilization but can control these side effects with great concentration and effort.

Stream: Practitioners of water magic. Their tattoos are graceful and flowing with rounded edges. Many practitioners of this style have calm demeanors and usually an interest in the healing arts.

Tainted: Those who tried to acquire blood magic, but failed. They are cursed with insanity.

Tempest: Practitioners of wind magic. Their tattoos are thin and branching with a hint of twisting or swirling. A practiced Tempest's mind is as fluid as the wind and constantly changing. This causes them to be highly mentally unstable.

Twinning: Taking two objects and linking them together with a mage's blood.

Other Works by K.N. Nguyen

The Easter Egg Hunt

King's Blood

Anthologies

New Beginnings: Science Fiction/Fantasy Anthology by DragonScript

New Adventures: Science Fiction/Fantasy Anthology by DragonScript

Coffins & Dragons by Dragon Soul Press

The Once and Future Kingdom by Irish Horse Productions

Towards the Sun by DragonScript

First Stain by Inked in Gray

Lightning Source UK Ltd.
Milton Keynes UK
UKHW021837200720
366872UK00009B/269/J